FREEDOM'S RANSOM

AN ACE/PUTNAM BOOK

Published by G. P. Putnam's Sons

a member of Penguin Putnam Inc. / New York

Freedom's
Ransom

Anne
McCaffrey

An Ace/Putnam Book
Published by
G. P. Putnam's Sons
Publishers Since 1838
a member of
Penguin Putnam Inc.
New York, NY 10014

ISBN 0-399-14889-2

Printed in the United States of America

BOOK DESIGN BY JENNIFER ANN DADDIO

ACKNOWLEDGMENTS

In putting together the details required for a book, the author is sometimes thrown out of his/her depth and seeks the help of experts in particular fields for advice and information.

In this fourth of the Catteni/Freedom series, I required more knowledge of dentistry than my experience or memory could give me. Dr. Les Latner, DMS, Los Angeles, and A. M. Price, DMD, were generous with their help in answering my somewhat rambling requests for information.

Thanks to my loyal friend, Lea Day, I was put in touch with Tony Diorio of Dariene Coffee, Babylon, New York, who gave me information about the transport of coffee beans from their various locations and how it is handled. Wendy Gilbert (aka Hishin) surfed the Web and friends and found out more about coffee plantations in Kenya, for which I am indebted.

Bobbie Parker (aka Short Wave, aka Jake) improved my understanding of satellites beyond the information I found on the Net at various locations. He put me wise to certain minor space difficulties and even designed the KDM ships that transported my heroic crew on their space adventures. It's not so much gaining information as interpreting it correctly for my needs that is my major problem. Therefore, all mistakes are mine!

My son, Todd J. McCaffrey, a licensed private pilot, was once again on the spot with accurate landing-type protocols.

I also wish to let it be known that I am grateful for the encouragement and help I received from chat line participants on my Web site. They were wonderfully generous with their time, thoughts, and encouragements. They even let me use some of their real names and not just their on-line nicknames. As I have met very few of them, I hope I did not offend in my portrayals from just a name and chats on-line.

My collaborator, Margaret Ball, found me more information about the Masai and their tribal system.

And finally, my thanks to my daughter, Georgeanne Kennedy, for her careful editing and comments. My deepest gratitude to Susan Allison at Putnam Berkley for her continued encouragement and especially for her patience.

This book is respectfully dedicated to the people I've met on my chat line: herewith listed in their on-line nicknames. I apologize in advance if I have forgotten anyone, and this list is current even to newbies as of June 19, 2001.

Many of you gave me your time, encouragement, and often explicit help throughout this book. I am pleased to have met all of you listed below. Ciao.

Alettah
Ambrosius
An
Anareth
Angele
Anneli
A'ron
Aviendha
Barbie
BD
Beck/Coelura
Belarion
Betsy
Birgit
Bonnbon
Bowser
Brina
Cami
Cheryl
Chris
Cindy
Clueless

Corsaith
C'ris
Dark Steps
Debbiedamoodymom
Dianna
Draig
Elfinfriend
Elrhan
Emma
Freev
Gail
Gill
Gizmo nine
Grainne
Grey Bear
Gynna
Habit 2
Happy Butterfly
Heideth
Hishin
Ivo
Jax

Jeffrywith1e

Jenna, Trivia Lady

John

Jojo

Jor

Jorine

Khricket

Kismet

K'Nan

Koolness

Kris raven

Kyky

Lady Cygnet

Laurel

Leia

Little Bit

Loiosh

L'rry

Mallory

Marie

MasterHarper 57

Mavron

Melissa

Michael

Miranda

Moomin

Mousertx

Mpatane

Natalie

NCC2235

Nemkitty

Nemlee

Nirgal

Peanuts

Princess Jennifer

Quixotic

Ranen

Rapunzel

Raz

Rimmer

Rogue Wolf

Rosli

Rube

Simon

Sparkies

S'ran/Sokar

SW

Tail Kink2Enniem

Tankiawee

Thalarob

Thunderchild

Tsarina

Wendy

Wolf Shadow

York Harper

FREEDOM'S RANSOM

"We dropped, we stay!"

SLOGAN OF THE BOTANY COLONISTS

PREFACE

When the Catteni, mercenaries for an alien race called the Eosi, invaded Earth, they used their standard tactic of domination by landing in fifty cities across the planet and removing entire urban populations. These they distributed throughout the Catteni worlds and sold as slaves along with other conquered species.

A group rounded up from the prisons on the planet Barevi, a hub of the Catteni empire, was dumped on an M-type planet of unknown quality, given rations and tools, and left to deal with the conditions of the planet. Chuck Mitford, former marine sergeant, took charge of the mixed group, which included sullen, pugnacious Turs, spiderlike Deski, hairy Rugarians, vague Ilginish, and gaunt Morphins, with Humans in the majority. Astonishingly enough, there was one Catteni, Emassi Zainal, who had been shanghaied onto the prison ship. Though there were those who wanted to kill him immediately, Kris Bjornsen, latterly of Denver, suggested that he might have valuable information about the planet on which they were stranded. Zainal's knowledge of the planet's predators, scant as it was, saved their lives.

Installed in a rocky site, with cliffs and caves to give them protection, Mitford quickly organized a camp, using the specific abilities of each species and assigning tasks to everyone in this unusual community. However, the planet was soon discovered to be inhabited—by machines, the Mechs, which automatically tended extensive croplands and the six-legged bovine animals. The colonists quickly learned how to dismantle the machines and design the sort of equipment they needed.

In a confrontation with yet another slave ship, dropping off more prisoners, the colonists got hold of aerial maps of the planet. Among the features of the maps was what appeared to be a big artificial installation, presumably constructed by the original owners of the planet. A member of the discovery team launched a homing device—more for curiosity than intent. Both the Eosi overlords looking for Zainal and the genuine owners of the planet noted the release of the device. An Eosi search crew sent to bring Zainal back to face his familial duty to be an Eosian host failed. The owners of the planet, whom the colonists named the "Farmers," came and were revealed as peaceful life forms with no connection to the Eosi. The Farmers made it clear that the colonists were welcome to stay, and even acted to protect them from the Eosi.

As they explored the new world together, Kris learned that Zainal had a three-phase plan—one that he hoped would end the domination of his people by the Eosi and, incidentally, would include the liberation of Earth. Zainal explained to Mitford and to other naval, airforce, and army personnel how he meant to proceed—initially by capturing the next Catteni ship to drop slaves on Botany.

The successful execution of Zainal's plan netted the colonists not one but two usable spaceships. Even with the capability of leaving Botany, Zainal was often heard to say, "I dropped, I stay," a defiant attitude, and a phrase that became a rallying cry for the Botany colonists.

While the Eosi surveillance satellites were on the other side of the Botany world, the two ships now available to the colony were able to successfully infiltrate Barevi and acquire much-needed fuel and supplies. Kris, who had already learned enough Catteni to deal with merchants, and other Catteni-speakers disguised themselves to accompany Zainal on this mission. While there, they rescued a number of Humans whose minds had been wiped by the Eosi. While on Barevi, Zainal also made contact with dissident Emassi, Catteni leaders also pledged to end Eosian domination.

With Zainal's first efforts so successful and Botany safe, the colonists were more than ready to follow his leadership. To continue his efforts to free not only his own people but also Earth's, a special mission was sent to Earth, where an active underground movement was already eroding Catteni occupation.

In *Freedom's Challenge,* Zainal risks his life in a bid to destroy the Eosi with the help of the dissident Catteni hierarchy and wins freedom for Botany and other enforced colony worlds inhabited by Humans. But that was the first phase of his plan. Kris knows Zainal well enough to understand that he still intends to make contact with the Farmers and discover their home world. But that wish is yet again interrupted when the colonists discover that most of the technical materials they need have been looted from Earth and are now stored on Barevi. As the Barevian merchants insist on being paid to surrender the loot, Zainal and Kris must again face the necessity of leaving Botany and finding a way to ransom the materials they desperately need to help both Earth and Botany.

1

Kamiton's messenger came in a Baby-type fast scout, and Jerry Short, the duty officer in the hangar, immediately informed Zainal of its imminent arrival and request to land. Zainal, in turn, called Kris, Peter Easley, and Dorothy Dwardie, as members of the Botany Management Board, to join him. He had good relations with Kamiton and wanted to keep everything "above-board," Kris's often-used idiom for openness. He recognized the call sign of the scout as one that Kamiton frequently used so he was somewhat prepared for bad news but did not warn the others, preferring that they take whatever news came with this messenger without any predisposition. It might not be bad news. But why else would Kamiton be sending a messenger, which suggested something he did not wish broadcast on the Botany comm lines?

Kamiton had chosen a nephew of Zainal's, firstborn son of Zainal's favorite sister, which confirmed Zainal's premonition that the news was bad. As Kris often did, she compared the new arrival to her beloved Zainal. She did not expect any familial resemblance, although she noticed as the young man—probably in his mid-twenties—approached that he was slightly shorter than Zainal but still tall for a Catteni. He had the heavy build of the true Catteni, born and adapted to Catten's heavier gravity. His grayish skin and yellow eyes were expectable. Zainal's Botany tan had altered his skin tone to a more vibrant shade of taupe and made Paxel seem drabber by comparison. But it was in the features that the main difference was plainly visible. She had always liked Zainal's nose, which was not as fleshy as most Catteni. Certainly, Zainal's mouth was better shaped, not as thick as Paxel's and far more flexible, often giving her hints as to his mood. It was severe enough right now, though; she noted the little flattening of his lips, indicating that he found this situation disagreeable and wanted to get it over with as soon as possible. She suspected then that he was anticipating a problem.

So, in his capacity as one of the governors of Botany, Zainal greeted his nephew Paxel affably and offered him coffee—a great new favorite of Catteni. Paxel grinned, showing three gold caps, a sight that caused Kris to have to hide an astonished grin. Zainal covered her astonishment by introducing Paxel, name and rank, first to Dwardie.

"This is a sister's firstborn, Emassi Paxel. I make you known to Eminent Dwardie, and my mate, Excellent Lady Emassi Kris, and Peter Easley." He reached for the message, which Paxel somewhat reluctantly handed over.

It bore Kamiton's name, plus the characters that confirmed that other Catteni officials were aware that a message had been sent to him. That did not bode well. He waved Paxel to a chair at the table in the hangar office. Then he broke the seal and could not suppress a grunt of dismay. When he had digested its import, he tossed the letter across the table to Kris, who could read some Catteni, though probably not all the diplomatic terms and courtesies. The gist of the message stood out as if written in red: "Barevi merchants will not surrender any Terran goods retrieved by the Eosi or Catteni captains."

Paxel's eyes had mirrored astonishment when Zainal gave the message first to Kris, rather than to Peter. Very few Catteni women were ever consulted on matters of significance.

"You mean, they need a bribe to give us back anything?" she demanded, outraged. "And sent your sister's firstborn with the news so you wouldn't kill him out of hand?"

Zainal managed not to grin at her quick understanding of the ploy. She flicked the message across the smooth table toward Peter.

"What?" Dorothy Dwardie was equally incensed. She read the note over Peter's shoulder.

"They're very acquisitive, the merchants of Barevi," Kris said, having dealt with them during her enslavement on the trade planet and more recently during her clandestine visit disguised as a Catteni officer.

"They don't mind dealing in stolen goods?" Dorothy asked, frowning at the message that Peter peered at in a total lack of comprehension, for it was in Catteni script.

"Most if not all of what they sell has been 'acquired,' one way or another," Kris said, watching Paxel's reaction.

"Business is at a standstill now that there is no new material coming in from Eosian"—Paxel cleared his throat—"development."

"Development?" Peter echoed, glaring at the young man.

"Polite terminology for forced acquisition," Kris translated composedly. "However, knowing how Barevi operates, this doesn't surprise me," she said, indicating the message. "I didn't think we'd get anything back without a quid pro quo."

"A what?" Zainal frowned at words he didn't understand.

"Old Latin saying. Something for something," she told him in a low voice.

"But we *must* have the loot returned to us," Peter said, "since the production lines for many essential parts are no longer functioning. The spare parts that the Catteni 'acquired' could rectify a great many useless vehicles."

"Agreed, to the necessity to repossess the parts, especially those communication elements," Kris said.

"Business on Barevi is at a standstill, and the merchants refuse to surrender trading goods," Paxel repeated, as if that was the most important consideration.

"Even if we used the same technologies . . ." Peter began, irate.

Kris held up her hand. "It's a fine sample of Catteni psychology," she said, smiling at Paxel. Being a firstborn was some protection for Paxel as far as *his* treatment as the messenger was concerned, but Kris did not intend to mince words or exchange false courtesies. "It drops, it stays—until it's paid for—one way or another," she went on, using the slogan facetiously in an effort to relieve the tension in the office.

"We were promised restitution of materials forcibly removed from Earth's manufacturing facilities," Peter said. She gave him a long, cool look.

"The merchants require compensation."

"That's piracy," Dorothy said, equally annoyed.

"That's business," Kris said. "I know the merchants. They love haggling. It's a way of life. Besides which, we've already made use of many pirated commodities that the first Barevi expedition brought back." She gave Dorothy a quelling look. Dorothy probably hadn't considered those goods as "loot" since they had been paid for, at least at the Barevi market. Now Kris could wonder if the merchants had been paid for the tab run up against a bogus ship's account. Oh well, that was for the Catteni accountants to resolve.

"But Kamiton—" Peter began.

"Supreme Emassi Kamiton," Paxel said, "promised in good faith what regretfully he cannot now deliver. He is trying to resolve a delicate situation for all concerned." His bow to Zainal was full of respect.

Zainal was impressed by Paxel's poise and tried to hide his disappointment at finding many of his own, perhaps too ambitious, plans now being thwarted by Barevian high-handedness. Establishing easy communication links between Botany and Earth was vital as the present connection was fragile and subject to more delays than mere distance. The "spurt" technique of communications, developed for contact with the Martian colony, was ideal for shooting wads of messages from Earth to Botany and reduced, somewhat, the time lag, but he had hoped to install similar links to the other forced colony worlds that would strengthen Botany in the new balance of power in this part of the galaxy—at least in having easy communication with like-minded, Terran-populated worlds.

The restoration of some basic commodity manufactories in the food industry, flour mills and food preservation, was essential not only to revive local economies and open the infrastructure of the damaged urban areas, but also to provide trade goods to the now hungry markets of Barevi. The setback of having to ransom what the Barevian merchants had lying about useless in their stalls was a further insult. Of primary importance was the repair and recommissioning of power sources that had fallen in the initial Catteni onslaught, or later when the Resistance forces were trying to force the Catteni conquerors off Terra. The restoration of easy communications was vital to the reconstruction effort. It was imperative to know where relief supplies were most critically needed as well as how to help relieve local emergencies. Priorities had to be assessed by appropriate experts and on-site information was needed to do so. He would like to see comm sats above the other nine Catteni worlds and links to Catten and Barevi. He grinned at Paxel: messages would then be easier to send and less dangerous to give. He wondered idly if Kamiton had quite anticipated the problems he was facing as the new leader of the Catteni. Certainly, when the man blithely promised the return of looted material—and Zainal had specifically mentioned what had been transported to Barevi, since he already knew how many captured goods were on display in that marketplace—Zainal had been dubious, even then, about the possibility of an easy repossession. Kamiton was obviously not enjoying as much support as he had anticipated or Zainal had hoped for. So Kamiton had dumped the problem back in Zainal's lap.

Zainal could bluster and threaten but, as he had no retaliatory power or armed forces, his threats were empty. Zainal had no effective way to force Kamiton to comply. His priority had been to secure Botany's autonomy and that of the other Terran forced-colony worlds. The martial arm of Catteni was still intact even if the Eosi had been destroyed, and Botany was in no position to succeed against the formidable Catteni fleet—especially now that the Farmers' remarkable and impervious bubble had been removed from the space around Botany. Kamiton would not have permitted an armed and defensible Botany nor had Zainal suggested it. He had aimed instead for restoring all the forced immigrants to their home world—if they wished to go—and independence from Catteni interference if they elected to stay. Botany was the most tenable and developed of the enforced colonies, so this had been quite a concession on Kamiton's part. Possibly it had come under review and criticism from the conservative Catteni, who were now in charge of their home world.

"But we have nothing more than food stores to ransom the goods we need," Dorothy said, adding, "that is, if I have properly understood what you said. A quid pro quo. Something for something."

"'Ransom' is the right word, Dorothy," Zainal replied, nodding graciously at her.

"And we can't in conscience use the Farmers' stores," Kris replied. She and Zainal had been leading opposition to that. "At least not for such a purpose. Feeding the hungry on our own world is one thing."

"Feeding the greedy on Barevi is not," Peter said firmly. "Have we nothing else with which to barter?" Peter was fascinated by Paxel's dental work, Kris noticed. He caught Kris's eye. "See what Mike Miller has in."

She nodded, understanding what he meant.

"An ounce for what quantity of goods?" Zainal asked in quick comprehension. "Kris, if you would be good enough to contact

Mike?" He jerked his head toward the main communications bank in the hangar. "First we have to know what we have. And perhaps, Paxel, you would be good enough to suggest commodities."

Kris smiled at Paxel and rose gracefully. "Be right back." She couldn't help lapsing into a provocative stroll since Paxel was obviously watching her. She was by no means vain about her tall, lithe figure or her long, blond, attractively arranged hair. She didn't consider herself beautiful even if Zainal often told her that he thought she was but she knew that she wasn't unattractive.

She made her way into the main hangar where Jerry Short was sitting, looking extremely nervous.

"It's all right, Jerry, we aren't killing the messenger," she said with a grin.

"I heard tell the Eosi did allatime," he replied, not completely reassured.

"The Catteni is a nephew of Zainal's."

"I don't think that would have bothered the Eosi."

"Neither do I, but Zainal is not Eosian. Would you please see if you can get Mike on the comm?"

"Mike Miller?"

Kris took what looked to be the most comfortable of the three battered chairs facing the comm unit.

"The very one."

"Why? Do we need more gold for teeth?" Jerry asked over his shoulder as he looked up Miller's comm-unit number and tapped it in.

"Now, you know, that's a very good notion, Jerry," she said, smiling at him. One of her private priorities was going to be new chairs for this place so no one would have back and coccyx problems from long hours on duty. "I wonder how many spare-part packages we could get for an ounce of dust?"

"How much dust does it take to build a gold cap? And do we have any dentists on our roster?"

On another board, Jerry tapped in a sequence. "I'll find out." Just then Mike's gravelly voice answered the prime call.

"Miller here. What can I do you for?"

Mike was in a good mood, Kris thought at his jocose greeting, and she hated to spoil it.

"Kris here, and it's what I can do you out of again, Mike. I'm begging. Have you mined anything valuable enough to use for ransoming our equipment back from the merchants on Barevi?"

"What?" The force of that simple word reminded Kris that Mike had a reputation as a brawler: a big energetic man who had done hard physical labor all his life and would have been a match in a brawl even with a Catteni. Maybe they should take him with them to Barevi. By the same token, maybe she should not. While Zainal had not yet mentioned a large mission, Kris knew that it would be necessary and would require every other Catteni-speaker. "As I heard it, all they've got is goods they looted from Earth. Thought they were supposed to give it over to us."

"That was the general idea, but it evidently doesn't work for the Barevian merchants."

"Thought Zainal had figured out how to make them," Mike said and started cursing under his breath.

"They've got crates of stuff they can't use, which they won't release until something is paid over. So we just have to cut bait and ransom what is most needed, Mike. I don't like it any better than you do, and Zainal is apoplectic." Which was hyperbole but she knew that Zainal was not at all pleased by the situation. Terrans had had to swallow considerable amounts of pride since the day the Catteni invaded Earth, and most people had had to do worse.

"You're in luck, Kris. We've been mining that diamond pipe Sergei found. Beautiful stones. Collectors would pay a premium rate for them," he added, with an upward inflection that suggested immense curiosity. "Uncut, of course, but it's the 'water' of the original carats that's important. Let someone else have the stress of cutting the stone to make the most out of it. Didn't think they'd be useful so we've been screening for industrials. The big stones are not something anyone here would want to spend colony credits on."

"Why? Could you put your hands on more?"

"Why? It was the Eosi who collected gemstones in the Catteni economy. I heard they were all gone."

"I wonder who'd want gemstones if now they're all gone."

"Good question, Kris. Anyone got answers?"

"There were a few who hadn't come to the big Council and are still alive and free, somewhere in the galaxy. But I doubt they'd know where the others kept their proceeds."

"Would they put in an appearance where they could be caught?" Mike asked, surprised.

"Not likely. All I care about now is that the Barevian merchants will take what we have to offer in exchange for what we need. We'll sort out the ethics later."

"Well, caveat emptor, then."

Kris chuckled to hear Latin for the second time that morning.

"Yes, indeed. Have you much gold?"

"Actually, we do. Bart Crispin was keen-eyed enough to spot some nuggets and flakes in one of the streams up here and we've had the devil's own time keeping everyone at work in the mine shafts. I let them go prospecting in the evening. Ain't much else exciting to do up here."

"D'you speak any Catteni, Mike? Does anyone else up there? We might need to muster you for the aid of the party."

"New faces would be nice, even if they are Catteni bastards. In fact, you can put me on record as saying that if I could suss out what they are selling, I might be able to suggest other likely items to secure what we need."

"I'll tell Zainal of your willingness to be in the ransom party," she said, knowing that Mike would not be a prime candidate, though she might be doing him a disservice. He managed difficult miners handily enough. If he could keep his temper, he might be an asset.

There was also the minor problem that she didn't think Barevi merchants would deal with a woman, beyond selling her food or fabric. She'd managed before only because she was in a Catteni uniform, disguised and bearing proof of her captain's authorization. She didn't care to be in disguise again unless it was absolutely vital.

"How much gold is available?"

"Its value depends on the rate of exchange, but I've over thirty pounds of dust, a bagful of forty-five nuggets of various sizes, and a couple of bars where we melted down the little stuff so we wouldn't lose the flakes." She quickly jotted down a note about the variety of raw materials. "About a hundred pounds each of tin, copper, and zinc. I'm told the Catteni are in chronic need of raw materials."

"Thanks, Mike. I'll get back to you," she said, signing off the line. She gathered up her notes, thanked Jerry with a nod, and went back to the office, where she passed Zainal the note without comment. When he pointed to her scribble of "gold," she tapped a front tooth.

"The main point is, Paxel, if we bring goods, will the merchants trade?"

The young Catteni leaned forward, opening his hands wide in entreaty. "Any business will be welcome right now, I think." He gave Zainal a knowing smile. "With the Eosi gone, and no new development available, they are feeling a pinch they haven't known in decades."

If Kris said "too bad" to herself, she smiled winningly at Paxel.

"Can Kamiton guarantee their 'cooperation'?"

Paxel shrugged diffidently. "He expected their cooperation before now, especially since your people have provided so many unusual items for Barevi markets and Barevi wants to continue the influx.

Barevi has a reputation to maintain." He grinned. "So the need is always to have many new items to intrigue and entertain customers."

"I wouldn't have taken the Catteni culture as consumer-oriented," Peter remarked.

"Never mind that they can't use half the stuff they have in storage," Zainal said, leaning back in his chair and smiling. "They always did display a wide variety of goods."

Paxel grinned back. "There are always Emassi to supply. Our scout ships, as you should know, Zainal, often use trade items when encountering a native species."

"Ah, yes," Zainal murmured.

"I always wondered," Dorothy remarked with an acid-sweet smile, "what they first offered Terrans in trade. Beads?"

"Those records are sealed," Paxel replied, but his eyes sparkled.

"Do you think someone sold you out to the Catteni?" Zainal asked, giving her a sharp look.

"'Take me to your leader' was never a headline prior to the invasion fleet," she said noncommittally. "But that didn't mean there weren't private deals made."

"Nor that it was a very equable trade," Peter remarked, "whatever was offered."

"Beads probably, or was it tomahawks and firearms?" Dorothy said with a very bright smile.

Paxel's reference to scouts and ships reminded Zainal of a very important fact. All scouting-mission reports as well as booty were processed through Central Barevi Air Traffic records, as well as where slave ships had taken their cargoes, so all the records they needed to repatriate Terrans were on file at Barevi—somewhere. Now that he had a legitimate reason to go to Barevi, he could possibly accomplish a lot more than just reclaiming loot. A gold nugget in the appropriate hand and he might be able to review those records. The Resistance movement had lists identifying which ships had landed in which major population centers on Earth, and now he could find out where the various ships had deposited their cargoes. So he'd be able to repatriate specialists vitally needed back on their home worlds. Zainal had no idea how he might accomplish such an exchange.

Lives were wasted on the mining planets. More workers had always been available to the Eosi "development" program. New supplies of workers had been one of the primary aims of Eosi searches. The other had been finding planets with the raw materials necessary to supply the ever-increasing requirements of the Eosi. The Turs had been the first reasonably intelligent species the Eosi had found and were almost as difficult to deal with as Catteni. The Rugarians had been slightly more cooperative, but the Deski had been physically unsuited to the hard labor required of captives. The Terrans were physically more suited to such arduous work. It was likely to prove difficult to exchange the current laborers at those facilities.

This Barevi trip might provide him with more information than Kamiton wanted him to have, but since the opportunity had been dropped into Zainal's lap, he would "stay" with it. It was also a chance for him to take his sons into a Catteni world where, he hoped, they would absorb more of the training they would need to function as adults. The Masai on Botany, where he had sent the boys to study a warrior culture, had done well with them, but they needed more than that to cope successfully in the Catteni culture. He would find a tutor for them at the hiring hall in Barevi. He was pleased that they had learned English—albeit with a Masai cadence—but they needed to acquire an adult Catteni vocabulary and adult Catteni skills. Kris always wanted to see more of his sons, and this would be a good opportunity. They had toughened and she would no longer feel "sorry" for them and treat them with the softness so often exhibited by Terran mothers. Not that he doubted Kris's sincere desire to do well by her mate's offspring. He had a lot to get under way now that he knew what the situation on Barevi was and how Botany could mitigate the problem. He would wind up this conference with Paxel and send him back—unharmed—to Kamiton, he hoped not much the wiser of how things were progressing on Botany: save that there were Catteni-style cargo ships, KDLs, lying idle outside the landing field.

"Well, Paxel, delighted to see you and do give my greetings to your mother, my favorite sister, and your sire. And to Kamiton, of course. I expect there will be no trouble if I arrive in one of the cargo ships?"

"No, none at all. Kamiton asked me to encourage you."

"To solve the problem, no doubt."

"I believe he hopes you can," and Paxel leaned in a little on the final word, and then realized that might have been less than diplomatic but had the sense not to try to retrieve the error.

"I'm sure he does," Zainal replied amiably, smiling. "Expect us within five days."

"Or perhaps a little later," Kris said. They'd particularly need Chuck Mitford's assistance and possibly that of some of the others who had returned to help rebuild Earth. "There's a lot to organize, especially as some of our more fluent Catteni-speakers are currently on Earth and will need to be recalled."

"That is all too true, Paxel."

Paxel nodded. "It is up to Zainal, and you, to set the time of return, Excellent Lady Emassi," he said, giving her a polite but stiff nod of his head. Plainly he was surprised that a woman would enter into a conversation with a male, especially one of Zainal's status. But, even on Catteni, certain mates did have special privileges, and doubtless he knew her reputation since he had addressed her with her honorary Catteni title.

"Then we shall collect the members of our delegation," Zainal said, straightening up and looking Paxel in the eye, "and inform Kamiton that we shall presently arrive on Barevi and settle this onerous problem once and for all. I need the security codes presently in effect at Barevi."

If Paxel's eyes widened at Zainal's demand, he placed one hand on his chest and bowed again.

"I return with all speed, Emassi."

Retrieving the message he had delivered, Paxel jotted down a few words and figures and passed the notation to Zainal. "That code will continue for the next five weeks."

Kris thought that Zainal had impressed his young nephew and hoped there would be no repercussions when Paxel delivered the response. Zainal shot her an amused glance as if he suspected her thoughts before he turned back to the other Botany colonists.

"We must first recall those Catteni-speakers who have gone to Terra. Does someone have the list?"

As there was no such list and Zainal must have known it, Kris made a move to the file cabinet and started flipping through documents. Peter urgently tapped a command on the nearest keyboard, and Dorothy was industriously writing notes.

"A safe journey, Paxel, and again, my regards to your mother and your father," Zainal said as Paxel made his way out of the hangar. A backward wave from Paxel acknowledged the civility even as Zainal turned to ask Kris, "Who is most drastically needed to return from Terra?"

"Without prejudice, I'd say Chuck would be invaluable," and Dorothy nodded from where she sat, grinning broadly.

"Maybe he even thought to make a list of the most urgently needed items. Won't we need to know which cartons to ransom?" Peter asked. "Wouldn't want to buy a pig's ear for a purse."

"Would it be quicker to take Baby and go to Terra and collect the people we need?" Kris asked.

"Might be in the long run," Zainal agreed. "We do have destinations for most of them. Like the Doyle brothers. I'll need Ninety, Gino, and Mack Dargle, and you, please, Kris. Can you leave your daughter?" He knew how she doted on six-month-old Amy but she nodded a quick reassurance. This mission had a priority she couldn't ignore to play Mommy. Besides, in her absence both Amy and Zane would be well taken care of at the crèche.

"What about our military?" Peter asked, referring to various admirals and generals who had been dropped on Botany and were now busy with the reconstruction of Earth's facilities.

"Hmmm." Zainal considered this. "I'd certainly like their thinking on this ransom business. Especially Ray Scott and John Beverly."

"Yes, Scott has a reputation as a strategist but he has no Catteni."

"No, but I'd value his opinion. I'll take any help I can get on this one."

"Good idea," Dorothy and Peter said simultaneously. Peter was plucking at his lower lip, a trait that most recognized as "Peter thinking."

"It's also a problem in public relations," Peter said. "We can get there with ransomables, but how do we know the merchants will then be willing to trade?"

"Kamiton said they would."

"Ha!" Peter sat forward with his hands clasped in front of him. "He didn't read the signs right when he thought he could get them to make restitution. I think we need a little more to make sure they'll exchange."

"How would you suggest we do that, Peter?" Kris asked.

"I'm thinking about it," he said with a grin.

"No better man."

"Wish your people had advertising or a public-service radio channel. Get word about."

Zainal grinned. "Actually, a few rumors wouldn't be hard to start."

"That's what we need. How?"

"By the very people we want to trade with us."

"The merchants?"

"They tend to trade gossip, too," Zainal said with a cunning smile. "And spread news."

"And?" Peter prompted him.

"And we can prime them, as it were."

"So they'll be lusting after our goods," Peter said, rubbing his hands in anticipation.

"We can hope," Zainal remarked, slightly skeptical.

"If we put out the right lures, they'll come. Especially if they are becoming consumer-oriented."

"We could also bring Botanical specialties," Kris said. "Like rock squats. Remember how our refugees liked them?"

"No, but I'll take your word for it," Zainal said with a grin, as he had been absent from Botany during the period when the colony had been a sanctuary for the families of Emassi who wanted them safe prior to the attack on the dread Eosi leaders.

"Even managed to get the boys to hunt with us," Peter said, amused by the recollection.

"Well, we should arrange a hunting party, then."

"And perhaps gather some of the tubers. I suspect that food is in short supply on Earth. Invasions do wreak havoc on crops."

"So, what needs to be done first?" Dorothy asked just as Peter reached the printer that had several sheets in its tray.

"Got a list here of Catteni-speakers who are away," he said and handed it to Zainal.

"And I have the list of possible barter goods," Kris said, pointing to her scribbled note listing what Mike Miller had told her.

"We do have a dentist," Jerry Short said, stopping in the doorway. "Name of Eric Sachs. Used to practice in New York. He's been on call at the hospital but doesn't have much equipment here. I've asked him to join us as soon as he can."

"Thanks, Jerry." Zainal made a check on his own notes and then paused. "How do you spell 'dentist'?" he asked.

Everyone told him at once but he got the word down on his pad, grinning as he wrote. "Thanks. I think these 'dentists' will be very useful. And we can get the equipment. What is generally needed?"

"I've never needed much dentistry except to have my wisdom teeth pulled," Kris said, looking around.

"Well, I have—you know the Colgate-bright smile," Peter said and exposed his white, even teeth. "A good smile is essential in public relations. However, to preserve the image I wanted to present, I did get my front teeth"—he tapped them—"capped as a business expense. Good teeth are a lifelong investment."

"What about gold ones?" Kris asked.

"That's not part of my culture," he said. "But a sign of importance or affluence in others. In present context, if it works, it'd be wonderful." He paused, raising his hand for silence. "To be Johnny-on-the-spot, we can also possibly provide the essential professional."

"Essential professional?" Zainal was totally confused.

"We bring our resident dentist with us—and he makes crowns on the spot?" Kris asked. Peter's wide smile answered her. "But a dentist needs a lot of equipment and supplies we don't have."

"Aren't we planning a trip to Earth anyway? We can pick up what we need, and sell the Catteni those gold teeth they're so fond of."

Kris snapped her fingers. "Just like that!"

"Why not? Who'd be stealing dental equipment?"

"Point," Kris conceded. As if on cue, there was a tap at the door and it swung open.

"I'm Eric Sachs," the man said, peering around the door. "Back on old Earth, I used to be a dentist. I was informed that I was wanted in here."

"Ah, good of you to come so quickly," Peter said, jumping to his feet and gesturing for the man to enter.

Aware of the scrutiny of everyone in the room, Eric Sachs moved with athletic ease toward the chair that Peter waved him to. He was of medium height, stocky build, dark hair cut close to his skull, as was the current trend on Botany, pleasant features, and brown eyes that sparkled with amused intelligence. He took the seat, facing Zainal, stretched out his legs, and folded his hands across his waist. Kris could see that the nail on his right thumb was distorted. He caught her glance and smiled at her.

"It wasn't my patients biting me," he said, "though some of them have. But my silly habit of holding dental X rays in exactly the position I want. Bad case of health and safety in the workplace but useful in obtaining clearer films. I'll probably lose more than the nail but . . ." He shrugged, philosophical over the price he would have to pay for that lack of attention to proper X-ray procedure.

"Thank you, Dr. Sachs," Zainal said. "Let me ask you a few questions about some procedures which may have more than ordinary significance for us right now."

"Such as?"

"Do dentists use pure gold for gold caps or tooth replacement?"

"We use seventy-five percent or eighteen-carat gold, which expands and contracts almost identically with tooth enamel, so gold is the best material. In some of the newer procedures the range is thirty percent gold supplemented by platinum and mostly silver—nine to forty percent."

Zainal looked askance at Kris and she nodded, after checking that platinum was one of the metals that Mike had on hand.

"What sort of equipment would you need to practice?" Peter asked. "Is it portable enough for you to set up your office where needed?"

"Well, as I have currently no equipment whatever, beyond a toothpick and specula, any office will suffice. There are portable dental units. Armies travel with them," Eric said with another easy smile. He obviously intended to enjoy this unusual interview.

"Would you know where to find the equipment you would need for a working 'office'?"

"Back on Earth, you mean?" Eric leaned forward eagerly.

"Yes, and no. Yes, to obtain the equipment you would need, and no, not to practice back on Earth."

"Where did you have in mind? Though we could use a facility here on Botany, with all these youngsters and oldsters needing effective dental care," Eric replied. "I used to specialize in orthodontics."

Zainal looked inquiringly at Kris.

"Orthodontics usually means repair work to crooked teeth and/or false ones."

"Dentures, please," Eric said with a friendly grin.

"False ones? Dentures?" Zainal didn't comprehend the distinction.

"For when people are required to entirely replace the ones they've lost to either age or caries."

"Caries?"

"Dental decay," Eric replied quickly, nodding an apology at Kris. She gave him a quick flip of her fingers to accept his reply.

"Dental decay?" Zainal looked surprised.

"Don't you Catteni ever have tooth problems? Apart from losing the front ones in your brawls?"

"The only ones we lose are in combat," Zainal replied. "What other way is there?"

"Bad bite, poor nutrition, lack of calcium, pregnancy, too much refined sugar . . ." Eric shrugged as he listed the main causes.

"If we could obtain equipment for you, would you be willing to dentify . . . Catteni teeth?"

"I have nothing against your species," Eric said. Then his expression turned eager and his eyes glinted. "Mind you, I would never use my professional expertise to cause unnecessary pain. Though, until I got here to Botany, I might have entertained a few vengeful ideas from time to time."

"At mercy in your chair?" Kris asked, grinning at the thought of a Catteni bully in helpless jeopardy in a dental chair. Sometimes, ethics went the way of other civilized behavior.

"I admit to some rather fanciful daydreams at a particular time; however, that's not only immature but also against all dental ethics. From what I've seen of your people, they aren't much in need of my skills."

"What about cosmetic work?" Kris suggested, pointing to the tooth in her head that was in the same place as Zainal's broken one.

"Ah, cosmetic work! That's something else again, and I fancy myself quite skilful in both orthodontia and cosmetic repair."

"What would you also need besides the basic dental drill?" Kris asked.

"It would be quite a list," Eric said tentatively, but with a dawning eagerness in his expression.

"But you'd know where such supplies could be found on Earth?" Kris asked.

"I'd know where there used to be suppliers in the Manhattan area, certainly. Whether they're still there or not, I couldn't, of course, be certain."

"Of course."

There was a pause that Eric broke. "Does this have anything to do with the rumor I heard that Catteni were investing in gold caps?"

Kris laughed, easing the tension that had been growing in her, partly because of the whole notion of having to ransom what was rightfully Earth's and partly because she was beginning to understand this bizarre element: providing a skill and treatment the Catteni certainly didn't have on their home world. Whatever worked!

"It does," Peter said.

Eric rubbed his hands on his thighs. "I am indeed your man, then,

Easley, Zainal. And I'd be happy to repair that incisor of yours, Zainal, for all you've done for us." He jerked his damaged thumb at his chest. "Then you could see firsthand how skilled I am."

"We don't doubt your abilities," Dorothy said, "especially since you made those marvelous repairs to Brenda Samuelson's dentures."

"The dentures were easy. All I needed was a decent adhesive." Eric twitched one shoulder. "So when do we go?"

"I suspect it is now necessary to figure out a flight plan," Zainal said, nodding to Kris, "to cover as much territory as we need to as quickly as possible. Please make a list of the items you would require. And where we'd need to go in this Manhattan . . ."

"Also known as New York."

Zainal shot him a look. "Is Manhattan the only place to acquire what you need?"

"No, but it's the one I know best. And, if they haven't been demolished in the Resistance, I could quite honestly retrieve the equipment I had in my office."

"Please give me the location," Zainal said, holding his pencil over his pad and looking intently at Dr. Sachs for his answer.

"My office was in the main city, on Fifty-ninth Street at Columbus Circle."

"Fifty-ninth Street?" Peter echoed. "I don't think it still exists, Dr. Sachs. Would you have any other ideas?"

"Well, quite a few dentists had offices in the general area."

"If you will agree to accompany us on this 'adventure,'" Zainal said with a little chuckle, "I'm sure we can locate what you need to take with you."

"With me?"

"Yes, to Barevi," and before Eric Sachs could rattle off the questions that must have flooded his mind, Peter told him what had to be done and how Eric was essential to spurring the merchants to action.

"By offering to those who want them immediate gold crowns?"

Eric asked, his eyes merry with appreciation of the scheme. "I must advise you that making a gold crown is not an 'immediate' proposition."

"The simple fact that you are there and an expert would allow us to charge them not only for the metal necessary to make their teeth, but for the expert to do the work, and would provide another reason to barter for the goods we desperately need which they are holding back!"

Eric was stunned by the explanation and then grinned broadly. "I like it. I like it. But as I said, it takes time to make proper crowns, and if I am to do the work, I insist on doing proper work."

"Of course, of course," Zainal and Peter agreed.

"I know there's gold available on Botany," Eric said, excitedly bouncing about on the chair, jotting down notes, "and platinum, too, I've heard." He rubbed his hands together enthusiastically before setting down more scrawls which probably only he could read. "What I need more than anything," he flushed and grinned sheepishly, "more than the equipment, is certain materials without which I cannot succeed. Such as an alginate to take good impressions and accessories like the carrying trays to secure the impressions. The gold caps would take time to prepare. One has to pound the gold into fold leaf. Rather fun to do, actually, and oh, well, you don't need a blow-by-blow description of the process right now. But I remember the dental supply house I used, and quite possibly no one bothered looting such items."

"Alginate?" Dorothy asked. "Seaweed. We have seaweed in quantity."

"I'd also need a mixing gun to deliver the alginate where I need it." Eric flapped his hands. "And a whole lot of stuff if I'm to do this properly."

"How did you hear about the gold and platinum?" Zainal asked.

"Same way I heard about gold crowns on Catteni teeth," Eric said. "Hey, could we get more than one set of office equipment? And find a few more dentists while we're about it?"

"And we will be about it!" Zainal said. He pushed back from the table and rose purposefully, gathering up his notes and the letter from Kamiton that he seemed to be rereading. "Kamiton will never know what hit Barevi." He grinned with total satisfaction at the prospect.

"Ahem, Zainal," Eric said, raising one finger to attract the Catteni's attention. "It would be useful if I had a trained dental assistant. Speed things up."

Zainal glanced at Peter. "Would you handle that detail, Peter? I'm going to draft the Catteni-speakers who are still here. We will have to go after some of the others who've gone to Terra. We can get what you need on that trip, too, Eric. Will you come with us?"

"Yes, and I think I'd better take some lessons in your language. I'll need to be able to give simple instructions to any patients you might wish me to attend."

"Like 'open,' 'spit,' 'close'?" Kris asked, her eyes sparkling with amusement.

"And some basic instructions about what I'll be doing. I'll also need analgesics like Novocain and procaine—"

"Oh, you won't need painkillers," Kris said, grinning broadly. "Catteni would disregard mere pain as beneath their notice."

"Not if I have to work close to nerves. Catteni do have those, I believe."

"Check with Leon Dane," Kris advised.

Eric wrote that down and then began to jot down more notes. "I'll need so much to even get started."

"A list of your requirements is a good start."

"There are talented scroungers on Terra," Peter remarked. "If it still exists, they'll find it for you."

Eric gave him a long, hard look. "I thought 'scroungers' were what put us in this position?"

"Oh, not those who will scrounge *for* us," Peter said with a grin. "I'll see if I can find you a dental assistant. And a technician. You'll need one of those, too, won't you?"

"If business is brisk, yes."

"Oh, it will be brisk," Zainal said emphatically. "No one ever developed tooth restoration under the Eosi."

"Did they have teeth?" Kris asked, shuddering as she remembered the awful grotesquerie of the one Eosi whom she had seen.

"Surely every species has teeth of some kind," Dorothy remarked.

"Eosi didn't eat as we do. They used some form of matter ingestion . . ."

"Osmosis?" Eric asked, startled.

Kris giggled and Dorothy smiled as she shrugged and replied, "Well, it's often been suggested as a possible means of nutrient absorption. But we don't have to worry about them anymore, do we?"

Zainal gave her a startled look and Kris frowned. "Not all the Eosi were . . . ah . . . terminated."

"They will be far too busy making certain they survive," Zainal said, "wherever they have taken refuge. And it won't be nearby."

"How many Catteni worlds are there, Zainal?" Peter asked.

"I know of nine. There may be new ones. That's one of the details I need to find in the files at Barevi, Peter. Scouts were constantly finding new worlds, for resources and colonization. I know many of them, but not all. And it is essential to have accurate information."

"Would the Eosi have taken refuge on a distant world?"

"Possibly. But they had strongholds on suitable moons as well as planets. I've no idea where the survivors might be. But it's wise to find out, if we can."

Peter nodded agreement with the sentiment. "I'll go find out if we have any other dentists or assistants or technicians on our roster."

"If you will gather what will be needed for my sons, Kris, I'll collect them first before things get busy."

"Let me come, too," Kris said. "It shouldn't take me long to set up two cots. But we should also, I think, bring some thank-you gifts to Chief Materu."

"As you will," was Zainal's reply. "And yes, presents are in order. Can you do that for me?"

Remembering the bright prints she had seen the Masai wearing, she thought there was at least one bolt of a tropical floral print that they might like in the cargo she had brought back from her last trip to Barevi. She supposed she should take something for Chief Materu, though she hadn't a clue what would be appropriate.

She borrowed the cots she needed from the day care center and told Sara McDouall that the boys were coming, and also told Zane that he would be seeing his two half-brothers while she gave her daughter a cuddle. Amy was a pretty baby but Kris could see no resemblance in the heart-shaped face to herself or to Chuck, apart from fair hair, blue eyes, and the long bones of her legs. Leon Dane, the chief medical officer, had commented that she would be tall. Kris borrowed a land cart, got the mattresses and the blankets down to the cottage, and set them up in the living room. If the boys wanted to sleep in the loft that had been built for that purpose, they could haul their beds up there to suit themselves tomorrow. She also put the bolt of wildly patterned dress material on the cart along with the leather belts, which Astrid had recommended as an appropriate gift for the chief.

2

ainal and Kris took the fast scout Baby to make the quickest possible run down the coast to where the Masai had chosen their new home. She hadn't been there in a while and was impressed by the neat huts within the kraal enclosure. Amazing that the Masai had found substitutes for their traditional materials. Their encampment, despite the night crawler–resistant flagstone flooring, looked like her memory of African settlements from *National Geographic* magazines. The tribe came filing out, men with their spears and long shields, arraying themselves in front of the curious women. The pre-adult children were ranged in their own age groupings in which they learned responsibilities and tasks suitable to their age-set. Camp dogs bristled and daringly ran at the ramp as Zainal and Kris walked down it. A shrill whistle called the dogs off but they sank to the dirt, still on their guard and not entirely happy to be called off the intruders.

Kris saw the bright gold hair of Floss among the women and realized with some remorse that she had only just then thought of the girl again. Floss and her band of abandoned and orphaned kids, calling themselves the Diplomatic Corps, had enjoyed the undisputed freedom of the Occupation and the leadership of a devoted band of young men and women. Sent to Botany to recover from their trauma and make a new home, they had been so undisciplined and rowdy that the Botanists were all for sending them back to fend for themselves on Earth. However, Dorothy Dwardie had suggested an alternative: place them with the disciplined Masai culture until they lost their wildness and were ready to "settle down." The Masai had agreed. Floss had been the most recalcitrant and reluctant to leave Retreat, but she was mostly to blame for being exiled. Across the distance separating them, Kris made eye contact. Turning back to the men, she noticed the unmistakable figure of Clune, solid among all the lithe, gaunt Masai, with his two former lieutenants, Ferris and Ditsy, standing beside him. Those Diplomatic Corps kids had survived the Catteni invasion and the roundup of Terran inhabitants. That was very clever of them. Idly she wondered if any of them had learned some Catteni. Such survivor-types might be useful.

Greetings and gift-giving aside, Peran and Bazil were called forward from their age-set by Chief Materu and sent to pack whatever they wished to take with them. Both boys had put on inches, vertically, and the deep tan that Botany's sun was giving everyone. Her glance strayed to Floss, who seemed to have improved. Chief Materu was examining the leather belts, noting the buckles and testing the straps with great interest.

Almost as if compelled, Kris wandered in Floss's direction and, when she was close enough, signaled for her to approach. Floss shot the older woman beside her a beseeching look while Kris made a formal gesture of asking for the girl to help her with the bolt. The head woman gave Floss a push in her direction. Floss corrected her balance and all but ran to assist Kris with the bolt.

"Hello, Floss. It's good to see you again. Do you happen to speak any Catteni?"

"Yes, Lady Emassi, I do. I had to learn enough to stay alive, you know. Just ask Peran or Bazil. I've learned a lot more words from them while they've been here. They aren't bad kids for boys!" The last word was spoken with the usual contempt of an older girl for a younger male. Then Floss hoisted the bolt onto her shoulder, balancing it with unexpected expertise, and walked with Kris back to the waiting women. There was no question that the fabric would not be put to immediate use.

"Do any of the others in your Diplomatic gang speak Catteni?"

"Besides Peran and Bazil? Sure, Clune did all our negotiating for us. Ditsy and Ferris knew enough to listen in to some int'rusting conversations. Saved our necks a coupla times." Then Floss cocked her head and looked at Kris with eyes far wiser than her years. "Why? Will it get me outa here?"

Kris held up a hand to indicate she did not wish to explain but she saw hope flare in Floss's deep blue eyes. "Please tell the head woman that this is a gift offering for her care of you." She ignored Floss's snort, then gestured her to follow her back to Zainal and Chief Materu, who were deep in conversation. Floss kept well behind Kris, trying to look invisible, Kris thought.

"Floss said she's been keeping up her Catteni with Peran and Bazil. Clune did their negotiating with Catteni. Back in DC they managed their own little trading enterprises. Could sell you your own teeth. Those two skinny boys standing with him also know the language."

"Really?" Zainal gave a snort that was half skepticism and half amusement. Just then Peran came racing back, a square of cloth held tightly in one fist with a spear while he had the framework of a Masai shield in the other. He came to a halt by his father, respectfully silent as Chief Materu was awaiting Zainal's pleasure.

"Does anyone here speak Catteni, Peran?" Zainal asked him.

"Yes, that one by Kris does and a couple of the other Terrans. We talk with them sometimes," Peran said with a diffident shrug.

"Their names are Clune, Ditsy, and Ferris," Kris murmured.

In Catteni, Zainal asked for volunteers who could speak the language. Clune, his expression astonished, made his way to the front of his age-set, as did Ferris, hauling the thinner, wiry Ditsy with his free hand. He had a finished shield and two fine spears in the other. Floss, taking no chance of being overlooked, held up her hand, waggling it at Zainal.

"Volunteers for what, Emassi Zainal?" Clune asked, glaring at Floss and urging his friends to catch up to him.

"A special mission to Barevi," Zainal replied.

"The trading planet?" Floss exclaimed and won points, Kris thought, by Zainal's response to her knowledge.

"What else do you know about Barevi?" he asked her.

She made a moue. "Not much except it was a place to avoid if you were captured by Catteni." She gave him an apologetic smile. "And it was low gravity. That's why the Catteni used it as an R-and-R place."

"It's where the Catteni took Terran slaves to be sold," Clune said, frowning. But he spoke in Catteni, his young baritone voice able to growl out the words with a good accent.

"They took a lot of stuff off Earth to Barevi," Ferris remarked.

"And we have to reclaim it," Zainal said.

"They're going to keep all the stuff they stole and be allowed to get away with it?" Ditsy muttered in a petulant tone.

"No, Ditsy. But he has the priorities right," Zainal murmured in an aside to Kris, and she grinned back at him. Now he stepped over to Chief Materu. "Chief, these young men and that woman speak my language and may be of use to us all. Will you allow them to accompany us?"

Judging by the fleeting expression that crossed the chief's face, Kris thought he would be glad to see the last of Floss, but he seemed more reluctant to part with Clune and the other lads.

His answer was a ripple of words that Kris didn't understand. Zainal looked at Peran for a translation.

"Father, he says that they are not yet in the age-set to be trained for a man's skills and responsibilities."

"Will you answer him for me, Peran, as I do not know his language, that they are trained in the skills I need for an important mission."

Peran did not smile as Kris thought a Terran boy might, pleased to be translating for his father. He rattled off phrases with a respectful air and waited for the chief to reply.

Materu shrugged but with a wave of his hand, agreed.

"Run, get your things," Peran said in Catteni to the three boys and, almost as an afterthought, included Floss. She angled her hips provocatively and stood closer to Kris.

"I won't need anything they gave me once I'm back in civilization," she muttered under her breath. But redeemed herself in Kris's good opinion by turning toward the group of women and making a broad gesture of farewell, giving the older woman a dignified nod. "Can I board the ship now?" she asked Kris.

"Can't wait to leave, can you?"

"You better believe it," Floss replied and sauntered, still swinging her hips in a sexy manner, which Kris thought was provocative; she disappeared up the ramp and into the ship. By the time Kris, following her, had made her way to the flight deck, she heard more feet on the ramp and the whine of machinery as the ramp was retracted. Zainal came forward to the pilot's seat. As if it were his prerogative, Peran took the secondary seat. Kris took the jump seat behind Zainal and motioned for the boys and Floss to strap in. As they took off and Zainal dipped Baby in a farewell salute over the Masai EnKang, Floss heaved a long sigh.

"Thank God you came. They were going to marry me off to a bag of bones and shriveled skin," Floss muttered to Kris.

Kris felt a pang of guilt for having forgotten Floss for so long and wondered how the girl had coped. There was little doubt in Kris's mind that Floss had filled out in a very womanly fashion, and she was glad they had rescued her from an ancient spouse. That would only have caused more problems and indubitably Floss would never have waited passively to enjoy marital bliss.

"So what's the caper?" she asked, leaning toward Zainal, her eyes glittering.

Zainal responded in his best Emassi manner but the only words Kris recognized were "know" and "time." Floss had no trouble understanding and leaned back in her seat, folding her arms across her breasts. Full breasts, Kris noticed, and hoped they could get the girl off-planet and to Barevi before she caused havoc among the unmarried males at the Botanists' main settlement at Retreat. The girl was much too young to settle down, although she seemed to have learned manners and deference among the Masai. Oh Lord, they only had spare beds enough for Zainal's sons. There were, however, bunks and cabins aboard the Baby, which must have been Zainal's thought because he landed in the clearing he had used before, not all that far from their cabin.

"Well, this is a step up," Floss said and winked at Clune.

"You boys can bunk on Baby tonight," Zainal said, gesturing down the companionway to the crew and officer quarters. "Floss, you'd better stay in the main house."

"Main house?" Floss echoed, glancing negligently at the cabin.

"Our home," Kris said with a quelling glare.

"Well, it beats a straw hut all hollow," Floss replied with more deference as Kris ushered her inside. "And I really do like the decor. Informal, rustic, but neat!"

"Thanks," Kris said. She sniffed, aware of an enticing aroma, and noticed the stew pan on the stove. "That was kindly," she said, picking up the spoon and stirring the mixture.

"I smell spices," Floss remarked, an anticipatory grin on her face. "Smells sort of like home and holiday." And her eyes suddenly filled with tears.

"We don't have many spices but this is one of Dorothy's pots, so we'll know who to thank. There are knives and forks in the second drawer in the chest, Floss, if you can remember how to set a table. I'll call the others," Kris gave Floss's shoulder a gentle squeeze.

Bread had also been left for them so they could make a good meal, which was devoured with much smacking of lips. Floss had forgotten which side forks go on but she had found glasses and poured water and put out plates. She was obviously accustomed to assisting, a definite improvement over her attitude before she was sent to the Masai camp.

Clune had asked where to wash his hands and the other boys followed his example, despite their obvious desire to eat. Kris dished out spartan servings since whoever had brought the food had not anticipated eight people dining on the pot's contents. She had some slightly stale cake to serve for "afters," which the boys and Floss consumed avidly.

"Sorry about the hard rations. But there's usually plenty to eat at the dining hall," Kris said. "We generally eat there and take our turns cleaning up."

"That was lovely," Floss said with a replete sigh. "Human cooking."

"We ate well enough with the Masai," Clune said, almost embarrassed by her remark.

"There was always enough," Ditsy blurted out, as if the quantity was far more important than the quality. Then he glanced at Clune as if he regretted having spoken.

"There were plenty of times we didn't have enough in DC, Floss," Clune said with quiet authority.

"Oh, we did well enough in the Washington kip," Floss said with an airy shrug. "You guys were good scroungers, and Jerry could make nothing taste like something!" She gave a sigh for "times past."

"I've always preferred to eat regular," Ferris added, speaking almost for the first time. He had a very husky voice and there was an old scar along his throat. Kris resolved to have Dane check all of them over before they were enlisted for this mission. They probably needed to be wormed: Kris squirmed at the thought.

" 'Scuse me, ma'am," Ferris went on, his brown eyes troubled, "but does anyone know who's left on Earth?"

"You had family there, Ferris?" Kris asked.

"Think they escaped the roundup but I don't know. Any way I can find out?"

"We've some survivor lists, Ferris, and a long one from the DC area. We can check for you later. What about you, Floss?"

She gave an indifferent shrug. "Knowing my father, they'd've survived in fine style. Somehow, somewhere."

Clune leveled a stern glance at her. "You used to worry about your mother and your sisters."

"Oh"—she twitched her right shoulder—"I did but I had to give that up as a lost job, didn't I?"

"You do know not to walk about at night, don't you?" Kris asked.

"Sure do. Never want that to happen to me," Floss said in a more subdued tone and grimaced at the notion. Night crawlers were indigenous creatures on Botany that would attack anything animal, or human, in the night and ingest them. "Thought there weren't as many night crawlers up north."

"You do know to stamp a lot at night if you are caught off the stone paths?" Zainal continued. And all six kids nodded solemnly.

"You boys can stay in the ship but I'm locking everything else down. I don't want anyone flying off on us."

"Emassi Zainal," Clune began formally, "what exactly did we volunteer for?"

"Translating Catteni into English and English into Catteni," Zainal replied. "And a little grunt work. The rest I'll explain when we get to Barevi and when you need to know."

"Oh, the old need-to-know routine," Clune said with a long-suffering sigh.

Zainal laughed and clapped him so firmly on the shoulder that, sturdy as he was, Clune rocked on the bench. "And now, boys, come with me," and he urged them all out the door and toward Baby.

Without being asked, Floss rose and started clearing off the table, taking the dirty plates and utensils to the sink. She turned on the faucet and crowed with delight. "Hot water!"

"Yes, we have all the comforts of home."

"Would you also have a shower? And maybe some shampoo?" Floss asked in a hushed voice, a look on her face of such keen anticipation that Kris felt all the more guilty for having forgotten the girl.

"Yes, but I think you'd better shower first and quickly. Zainal likes a wash in the evening, and we don't have quite enough water for two long showers and the dishes, too. Come with me." Kris paused only long enough to get a towel out of the cupboard and some shampoo—homemade though it was—from another cupboard before leading Floss to the shower room.

"Oh, if you knew how I've dreamed of this," Floss murmured, stripping off the wraparound garment.

"I'll have to get you some clothes tomorrow but for now I have only a clean, spare jumpsuit, Floss." Kris retrieved one from the closet as well as a spare leather belt, which the slender Floss might need around the much too ample waistband. "Nothing I own would fit you."

"Yes'm," Floss replied courteously and without a touch of sarcasm. Somehow, Floss contrived to give the utilitarian garment an air of style.

"You wouldn't have a scarf or anything," she asked as she reappeared in the main room. "It's kind of bare up here," and she touched her throat.

Kris had never cared much about fashion but she could see that a scarf of some sort of color would reduce the uniform look and also draw attention to Floss's bosom, which was certainly ample and pushing against the confines of the dull fabric. She wondered if there were any brassieres in the main commissary. With the ratio of four men to one woman, this nubile girl could be at risk. Maybe that was the real reason Floss had wanted to be released from the Masai encampment, where females were zealously guarded until a marriage had been arranged for them. Albeit Kris wouldn't have agreed to her being wed to an elderly man, she didn't want her to whore around Retreat either.

Zainal's appraisal of Floss, now clean with her blond hair gleaming in the last of the daylight coming in the window, only consolidated Kris's observation.

"Did the boys settle down?" Kris asked, opening a neutral topic.

Zainal grinned. "Being allowed to sleep in a scout?" He gave an indulgent laugh. "They are excited but Clune said he'd listen for them. He's more than able to handle them."

"Clune is respected among his age-set with the Masai," Floss said with a little smirk, as if she denied that status. "But he's worked a lot with both Peran and Bazil and they will obey him. This elder stuff works with impressionable boys." She shot Zainal an inquiring look.

"It is a Catteni attitude," Zainal said in his language, and she inclined her head to show that she understood him.

"I have put out an extra blanket for you, Floss," Kris said, wanting to be private with Zainal. "It is much colder up here than it is in the south."

The girl yawned and stretched, an action that showed off her lithe body in the jumpsuit.

"Oh, I'll survive," she remarked and sauntered, again with swaying hips, over to the cots. "It'll be such a relief to have a place to myself, with no one snoring or shouting in nightmares." She gave Kris a smile and picked up the spare blanket, to flip it deftly across the bed. "Even a mattress. A great luxury, I assure you."

Somehow she managed to make slipping into the cot a voluptuous action. Zainal grinned and turned his back on her, walking toward their bedroom. Kris waved a good night and followed him.

"We'll have trouble with that girl," she murmured when she closed the door behind her.

"Trouble's name is Clune," Zainal said. "He made it clear to me that he considers her, and her behavior, his business."

They were both tired, and although Zainal took a quick shower, muttering about lukewarm water, Kris wondered if Floss's presence in their living room had something to do with her own inhibitions, for she made no attempt to entice Zainal into her arms and he was equally reserved. Well, they needed the sleep.

A loud and eerie ululation woke them both the next morning. Zainal was on his way to the door before Kris stopped him, pointing to his naked body. He cursed but stopped long enough to don his trousers before he exited. She dressed more slowly and was relieved when Zainal poked his head into the room.

"It seems the Masai keep to daylight hours and it is daylight!"

She finished dressing and found that Floss and Zainal had put bread, cheese, and fruit on the table. Zainal called the boys in. Clune looked clean and neat and must have found the nearby stream for his hair was still wet. Peran and Bazil must have bathed also, for their faces were fresh and the fringes of their hair damp. Ferris needed to shave and Ditsy could have used a shower. There wouldn't be much hot water yet as the solar panels hadn't been recharged, but she wanted them all cleaned up before they went up to the main buildings.

Before they took off for Barevi, they would have to get some suitable clothing for Floss and the boys, who were wearing only the minimum required for Masai modesty. Breechclouts would not be acceptable on Barevi. If they wished to be seriously considered as negotiators, they had to look more presentable. This whole ransom business meant that Zainal would have to suspend his plan to seek out the Farmers' home world, or at least whatever depot they used to store the grain and the meat they farmed on Botany. She wasn't sure if she was relieved or disappointed that he would be denied that opportunity. However, it was only spring here and the Farmers' cargo containers did not come until after the fall harvest. He had some time to spare. And his plans for Botany, and the repatriation of Terran slaves, were certainly as important to him, she knew, as his somewhat grandiose and quite possibly dangerous scheme to track the Farmers' vehicle to its destination. She did wonder, as Zainal did, why the Farmers, with their advanced robotechnology, needed so much produce. She sighed. Every time she thought she understood a lot, she came smack up against something else unknown, tantalizing, unfamiliar, and, she sighed again, more than likely very dangerous.

Surely the Farmers would have had to have the means to supply themselves on any one of a number of Botany-type planets. Since the Eosi and Catteni had already explored neighboring space, surely they would have come across some vestige of the Farmers' culture. She wondered if indeed the Eosi had and merely kept the knowledge secret. Having secrets made people feel superior and secure. Or perhaps Human frailties were not part of Eosian characteristics. They certainly had extended their life spans by subsuming young hosts. For years, Humans had been investigating the possibility of cloning to sustain characteristics and supply body parts that would not be rejected in transplant. She shuddered. She could not, in conscience, go along with that. There was a reason for a life to have a span, predestined or not. How she would feel if she needed new organs to remain alive, she didn't know as she herself enjoyed vigorous health.

She caught the almost proprietary look on Clune's face as Floss swanned up to him, offering him more bread. Yes, she would have to speak to Dane about this young couple. She had no doubts at all, from the expression on Floss's face, that she cared very much for the young African-American man. It had been at Floss's instigation that her Diplomatic group had practiced birth control when they'd been running loose and free after the invasion. The same contingencies were not now in force but discretion was required until after the ransom negotiations were concluded. That is, if the youngsters proved as valuable as she thought they probably were, considering the success of the covert operations that had kept them free when most of the populace had been rounded up and carted off on Catteni slave ships. That might have been just luck but this mission needed that in quantity.

Everyone at Retreat pretended to be pleased to see Floss, approving the change in the girl from the intransigent, loud-mouthed brat of her first introduction to Botany. She was not overly enthusiastic about the garments produced for her to wear at the stores house. Most of the women had been making their own blouses and dresses out of the fabric and accessories that Kris had brought back from Barevi. Kris had to admit that utilitarian was not the style a girl Floss's age would appreciate, but she was offered fabric to make her own clothing, patterns, and even the use of the one sewing machine that Retreat owned.

"I learned how to sew skins together," Floss said with some contempt, "not how to cut and fit them. I wouldn't want to waste good material."

That won her some points with the stores keeper, who was a good seamstress, and Kris saw the two in conversation and hoped something would materialize. A girl in her teens as attractive as Floss would certainly want something pretty and well fitting to wear. Someone did produce a silk scarf for her and she spent time in front of a mirror deciding how to tie and drape it—her longing for pretty and becoming things quite obvious to others in the room.

Beth Isbell offered to trim her hair, which Floss instantly accepted. "You don't happen to have a conditioner, do you? I had to use a very strong soap at Masai camp and it's just ruined my hair."

"We do have an herbal rinse that will help," Beth said. "A local herb but much like rosemary—it brings out the sheen."

"Oh, that would be marvelous. I almost hate touching my hair, it's so brittle and dry."

"It works with mine," Beth said, fluffing out her blond hair, sun-streaked but shiny with health. "C'mon. The shower water should be hot. I'll shampoo and trim it, and it will be much improved."

"Oh, thank you very much," Floss said, showing a genuine warmth and enthusiasm.

"Why did you bring that renegade back?" Sally Stoffers asked in a discreetly low voice when they had left.

"She speaks Catteni and so do that gang of hers."

"She's a troublemaker, born and bred!"

Kris turned, almost defensively, to Sally, who also was a Catteni-speaker. "Zainal's option. Remember, those kids survived in the post-invasion turmoil, so they were either very lucky or very clever. Clune, the oldest boy, has negotiated and bartered with Catteni before and we will desperately need that type of experience. How are you at driving bargains?"

"She seems more biddable but she's a flirt, that one," Sally repeated, her tone and expression spiteful.

"Clune will watch out for her," Kris replied firmly and began folding the new clothing that would constitute Floss's improved underwear. She didn't think they would find any purloined clothing in the Barevi stores but perhaps there would be some. The Catteni had been magpies as to what they loaded on board their cargo ships. When she was nineteen, she had wanted to look well dressed at college so she appreciated Floss's lack of interest in long-wearing, sturdy work garments. The scarf would be treasured. She had noticed how Floss had run it through her work-hardened hands, savoring the feel of the silk. A sapphire blue would look very well on Floss, and Kris tried to recall the bolts she had seen, of silk and satin, the last time she was on Barevi. But then, she hadn't had Floss in mind when she'd bought fabric. Well, they'd have a look with Floss in mind while they were there this time. Who knows who would trade fabric for gold? She wished she knew what was most in demand at Barevi. Maybe Chuck could remember something. Gold teeth were simply not enough of an "inducement." What they needed was a real crowd-gatherer: something that even the most conservative of the Catteni would not ignore. Would kill to have!

Leaving Floss in Beth's hands and saying that she could be found in the mess hall, Kris went for a cup of coffee. The work roster, prominently located as one entered the mess hall, listed her as assigned to Zainal's mission with no concurrent duties. Their latest recruits had been listed at the bottom as being part of the Barevi team. She was glad that she didn't have to sign Floss up for mess hall duties—at least not immediately. Maybe by the time they returned from Barevi, Floss would be more willing to take her turn at the less glamorous duties. Even KP would be more appealing than marital duties to an old man.

As she entered the big room, she glanced around and saw Eric, hunched over printouts. She waved at him, indicating a wish to join him and he nodded vigorously. She got her one cup of the rationed coffee, some fresh rolls, inhaling the aroma of the drink and fresh bread. She also wondered how much longer this treat would be available and if they could possibly search out additional supplies, possibly as trade goods since the Catteni had come to appreciate the caffeine hit. How many coffee beans and/or cups of the brew would buy a carton of stolen goods? She wondered, not for the first time, if the merchants had set any value on the cartons of spare parts they were now trying to sell. She had seen such a diversity of goods on display on her last trip. Surely not all of them—toasters and electric frying pans—were viable on Barevi. Much less automotive parts and spark plugs. Well, you never knew what would capture another species' interest. Certainly not the Catteni, who now evidently prized coffee, chocolate, and gold caps. Did any of them realize how easily they had picked up Terran vices like coffee? She smiled at the notion of the conquerors corrupted.

She made her way to Eric's table and was cordially greeted, noticing that some of his paperwork included maps: maps that showed the destruction of vast areas of New York City.

"I think I might be lucky. The building remains standing," he began, tapping the map. "And there is relatively little damage below Fourteenth Street, where the dental supply house is. What'll we be able to use for barter back on Earth?"

"I think we'll be able to take some wheat with us. Possibly even the rock squats, as fresh food would be appreciated," Kris replied. "There are hunting parties out today to see what they can gather and, from the smell of the kitchen, some are being broiled even as we speak. And I smell fresh bread cooking."

"Now, all we need to figure out is how to hump heavy equipment down eighteen flights of stairs," Eric said with a despondent sigh.

"Oh"—she smiled at him—"you didn't know that the Catteni have 'lift' platforms that handle that sort of thing quite comfortably?"

"No, I didn't, but see me grinning," Eric replied, and he was, his eyes sparkling with relief and humor. "Glad I asked. Those units are very heavy and even with a lot of manpower, getting them down to where they can be loaded was worrying me."

She patted his hand. "Well, fret no more. That was actually the least of our problems."

"What's the most?"

Kris was thoughtful. "Being sure we have the right stuff to trade with the Barevi."

"Count on me, Kris! And, if we can find him, I know another dentist who does splendid work. Also in my building. He has the sort of personality that would deal well with the Catteni. Even as allies, they would be tricky, I suppose." He gave her a shrewd glance.

"Some more than others," she replied, grinning.

"Answer me a question, if it's not out of line," Eric went on, cocking his head to one side. "Why is Zainal seemingly working against his own people?"

"It might look that way, but it was the Eosi that he wanted to overthrow—"

"And did, I understand, with no small effort on his part." His manner was that of someone hoping to be told more than he had actually asked for.

"When he was dropped here as an unwilling colonist—with the rest of us"—her gesture included everyone in the dining room—"he wanted to free his people from Eosi domination."

"He did that," Eric agreed, wanting her to continue to explain a situation she really didn't have an explanation for.

"There were other like-minded Catteni Emassi, remember. He couldn't have pulled it off without their help."

"This Kamiton being one of them?"

"Yes."

"So?" Eric prompted, lifting both arms in a gesture of perplexity.

"I think the situation was not as simple on Catten itself and obviously not on Barevi. The Catteni are set in their ways, and Kamiton may have overestimated support from other Emassi. Zainal achieved freedom for Botany and the other enforced colony worlds. It wasn't just Botany that the Catteni dumped people on, you know."

"No, I didn't know," and Eric slightly stressed the last word.

"There are three other planets that the Eosi were colonizing the same way."

"Those planets that worked out were then taken over by the Eosi?" Kris nodded. "We were exceedingly fortunate, you know."

"To have someone like Chuck Mitford, you," and he pointed a finger at her, daring her to deny his role, "and Zainal."

"We were lucky," she amended, "to have the right mix of people to work with."

"I like your positive attitude, Kris Bjornsen."

"I dropped, I stay," she replied, with a broad grin, pleased that he was willing to accept Zainal and work with him.

"Is that Botany's motto? I hear it often enough," Eric said.

"It's been a rallying slogan as well as a promise, Eric."

Eric glanced around, from the duty roster to the glass doors opening outside. "I like the promise! If I could just practice my profession here, I'd stay."

"Don't you have family back on Earth?"

"Nephews; my wife, Molly, was in Florida when the Catteni invaded so I've no idea what happened to her. Her name hasn't appeared on any of the Florida lists of survivors."

Kris touched his hand sympathetically. "Not all the survivors are listed yet, Eric. We'll be picking up the updated lists when we touch down on Earth. One of the goals of this ransom trip is to widen the communication channels so we can find where survivors are—and get back those who were taken."

Eric's eyebrows rose high. "That's a large job to undertake."

"The Holocaust survivors managed to trace their relatives. And we have just as many dedicated folk!"

"Why don't you just relax and raise your kids?"

"I can't." She gave a self-deprecating grin. "Zainal feels responsible, in a bizarre way, and so do I."

"Responsible for entire worlds? Oh, c'mon now, girl. Be reasonable."

"I don't think 'reason' has much place in my feelings, Eric. People who are unreasonable sometimes achieve more than those who are totally rational!"

"Admittedly. Ah, here comes Zainal now."

Kris saw him entering, with his sons and Clune, Ferris, and Ditsy, obviously showing them around. The boys all wore new clothing, suitable to the cooler weather at Retreat, and had packs slung carelessly on their backs or over one shoulder.

She tried to keep Eric at the table but he rose, gave her a little bow from the waist, and, smiling at the approaching group, made his way out of the hall. Zainal waved for her to stay where she was as he took the boys to the serving tables and introduced them to the people on duty. With laden trays, they all converged on her. Zainal thoughtfully brought her an extra cup of coffee.

"The boys don't drink it yet," he said when he saw her expression of doubt. "You might as well enjoy a cup of their ration."

"We must get more coffee, even if instant is all we can scrounge," she said, turning the cup around to get the handle to the left for her to lift. "I see everyone is spruced up." She nodded to the boys as they took seats.

"Boy, this grub looks good," Ferris said, picking up his fork and digging it into a mound of mashed tubers. "Oh, it's not potatoes," he added, both surprised and outraged by the unexpected flavor.

"It's indigenous but not a bad substitute," Kris replied, grinning as he swallowed the big mouthful.

"Hey, it is pretty close! Will we be able to grow potatoes here?"

"I believe so, but we'd have to import seed potatoes, if we can find them. I believe it's high on the list of 'wish' items."

"You got rock squats up north here, too?" Clune asked, slathering a portion on his fork with his knife in the English manner.

"Principal source of protein," she said. "They were the main course in the first hot meal we had on Botany."

"Who named it Botany?" Ditsy asked, disgusted.

"We all did. After another colony of transported folk on Earth," she said.

"You mean, Australia?" Ferris asked, wrinkling his nose. "Not very inventive."

"What would you have named it?"

"I dunno," Ferris admitted, and then attended to the task of eating. "I'm not good at naming things."

"We put it up for a vote and everyone had a chance to put forward their names," Kris said, remembering the occasion very well. "Botany won, hands down. A good choice, I think, since it reminds us of a similar experiment that was successful."

"Yes, but that was ex-cons."

"What do you think we were considered?"

"Well, you weren't criminals."

"Most of the English and Irish who were transported to Australia weren't really criminals. There was great poverty at that point in history, and a person could be transported for stealing food to feed his family."

Kris wondered just how many of the present colonists had not finished secondary school or knew even highlights of world history. Maybe evening lectures could be instigated, just to disseminate vital information. Daytimes, there was so much work to be done only the crèche kids were being given lessons. She jotted down a little note to herself. Something else to be remembered and inaugurated!

She gave a little sigh. There was never enough time for everything, was there? When Zainal gave her a curious stare, she smiled
back at him and took a sip of her extra cup of coffee. She wondered
if she could make a habit of it . . . bring the boys with her for breakfast. But that was not the Botanic way: one didn't take advantage of a
flaw in a system. If she did, she lost her right to criticize others. Conscience was burdened enough as it was. If Council members didn't
toe the line, why should others have to? Transgressions could mount
to a woeful state, just as they had elsewhere. One had to show responsibility. Just as Zainal was. Though really, he could carry the burden a little too far! However, she could see that someone had to do it,
as far as reclaiming needful things was concerned.

Jerry Short paused in the main entrance to the hall, scanned the
diners until his eyes rested on her. He waved at her and, excusing herself, she went to see why he had singled her out.

"Just had a message from Chuck. He's on his way back and he's
very pleased with himself," Jerry said, grinning because he had good
news to tell.

"Chuck? Oh, that's great!" He'd gone to find out if his elderly
cousins, Rose and Cherry Mitford, were still alive. He'd also dropped
other Botanists where they could hunt out kith and kin as well as start
work repairing damaged infrastructures.

"Knew you'd want to know soon as possible," Jerry went on.
"And oh, he said to mention that he'd stopped on Barevi on his way
home to pick up a few things."

"Oh, goodness. What's his ETA?"

"Next hour."

"Do tell Dorothy Dwardie, Jerry. She'll want to know, too."

"I thought of her first, actually, and told her on my way here,"
Jerry said, grinning broadly.

"Thanks. Oh, Zainal will be so pleased. I wonder what Chuck

thought to bring back from Barevi," she muttered to herself as she made her way back to the table where the boys had finished eating.

"That will save us a lot of time," Zainal said, very pleased with her news. "Especially as he'll be able to give us a report on conditions on both planets. Wonder what he stopped off at Barevi for that would have been important enough for him to detour so far off the direct line to Botany. And how and with what did he pay for it?"

"We should know soon enough. Shall we go meet him?"

"Yes, and show him our newest translators. C'mon, lads." He signaled for the five boys to follow him.

3

C huck emerged from the spaceship accompanied by two women, and beside Kris, Dorothy inhaled sharply.

"Don't worry, Dorothy," Kris said quickly. "Look at their faces. They're Mitfords or I'll eat a night crawler!"

The family resemblance extended not only to the facial features but to the physical proportions of the two women: the same sturdy bodies and lanky stride, and a way of looking directly at people with an assessing look in the eye. The two women were equally weather-beaten, their eyes squinting from years of filtering out sun and wind.

"His cousins, I presume," Kris said, for Chuck was urging the pair to where Kris and Dorothy were standing.

"Dorothy, these are my cousins, Rose and Cherry, and I'd be much obliged if you'd welcome them. They've had a rough time lately, and I won't let them out of my sight until I know they've recovered completely." He gestured to the ground cart. "Dorothy, would you mind taking them to Dane for a physical? It was a bitter winter back in Texas."

"Of course. Rose, Cherry," and Dorothy gestured for them to

take seats in the cart. "I'd be happy to. And we'll have a lot to talk about, I'm sure."

"Dorothy Dwardie will see you're comfortable, Rose, Cherry," and he kissed each on the cheek. "But me and Zainal here have to have a conference. This is the guy I was telling you about. Who freed Earth and his own planet."

Rose extended her hand. "Charlie here bent our ears out of shape telling us all you did to save both the worlds." Cherry was a little more reserved but she shook Zainal's hand in as hearty a fashion as Rose had and murmured something about unforgettable heroism.

"We know you're busy, Chuck, and we're mighty glad to be here, Dorothy. We've heard so much about you, Kris. Will we see you later?"

"You will indeed, Rose, Cherry, and welcome to Botany."

"And who are these young men?" Rose asked, opening her hand in the direction of Peran and Bazil.

"They are my sons, Rose Mitford."

"I am pleased to meet you, too," she said, extending her hand.

Peran took it, giving her a rather stiff bow, which caused her to blink at the unexpected courtesy. Doubtless, Kris decided, the women hadn't ever encountered Catteni with good manners. Still, it proved that the Masai had trained the boys to respect age and females.

"May I introduce Clune, Ferris, and Ditsy, Misses Mitford?" Kris said to complete the introductions.

"Rose is a pharmacist," Chuck said, helping the older of the two up the first step. "And Cherry's a physiotherapist."

"You could have brought them if all they could do was knit," Kris said, dismissing Chuck's comment and smiling warmly at them.

"If you're of a mind to put your skills to use," Dorothy said, climbing into the driver's seat, "you'll be thrice welcome once Leon has cleared you. He's our chief medical officer." And she nodded goodbye to the reception committee.

As soon as the cart was off the field, Chuck turned purposefully to Zainal.

"I lucked out. Traded four tins of Nescafé instant coffee for some of those satellite parts we were trying to find on Earth. What we need is on Barevi, you know."

"We suspected that."

Chuck pulled a hand recorder out of his jacket. "Got a Jet Propulsion Lab director to give me a list of what we need. He said that there were some built most recently with switchable units. That would make it so easy to maintain those already in orbit. The ones the Catteni used for target practice. I did a quick survey of the loot on Barevi and they've got the replacements we need."

"We're organizing a ransom party," Zainal said.

"A ransom?" Chuck stared at him. "Yeah," and his shoulders slumped, "and I hope you got stuff they want."

"No coffee, but gold—"

"For their teeth?" Chuck's surprise was obvious. "How'd you hear about that?"

"Doesn't matter how but we did." Zainal gave an indolent shrug. "Though vanity has never been a Catteni problem. Still, no one ever thought lost teeth could be replaced. We also have a dentist."

Chuck's laugh was hearty as he gave Zainal's massive shoulder an appreciative buffet.

"I was wondering how I was going to break the news to you," he said, "about ransoming our own equipment back from those Barevi looters. And we gotta make tracks there, fast. Too much is being ground into the mud in the marketplace by those bozos working off steam." He shook his head. "When I think of all the hard work and the material we can't reproduce . . ." He stopped, took a breath, and then went on. "You wouldn't believe what they've achieved on Earth."

"Reconstructing?" Kris asked.

"More than just infrastructures. You'll be proud. Look, Zainal, can we call a meeting of the colonists?"

"One is set for this evening. We have to get permission to use the colony's assets as ransom, you know."

"Good. I'll grab a shower and change. Oh, and I got some crew with me." He looked over his shoulder at the open ramp of the KDL. "In-service training but boy, do they know their stuff. Of course, they should. Many of 'em are ex-NASA." Chuck's grin was broader. "Brought more than I needed for the KDs but we do have other ships." He gestured to the ones parked on the field. "They learn real quick and I had space available." He turned and called, "Olly-olly in free. Welcome to Botany, guys and gals."

Out filed a line of men and women looking very smart in flight gear. They made a double row in front of Chuck, who was still grinning from ear to ear.

"Sir, Excellent Emassi Zainal, Botany airforce recruits reporting for duty," said the man who took two steps forward toward Zainal and saluted smartly. "Sam Maddocks, with eight volunteers, all with flight and space hours. Not many of the latter but we stood shifts with Sergeant Mitford on the way here!"

"Delighted to have you on board, Colonel Maddocks." The colonel stiffened his spine still further as Zainal used his appropriate rank, having noticed the silver maple leaf on his collar.

How Zainal had learned to differentiate rank insignia and the service forms Kris didn't know, but it stood him in good stead now.

"What a beautiful planet you got dumped on, sir."

"Luck, Colonel, sheer luck! This is Kris Bjornsen, my mate, and these are my sons, Peran and Bazil. Clune, Ferris, and Ditsy, who will be accompanying us to Barevi on a shopping mission. We may need your services to accomplish the mission."

"Anything we can do, we will, sir."

"I am known as Zainal, Colonel, not sir. Now, if you will introduce me to the rest of your group, we'll take you back to the main settlement and find you quarters."

"We don't mind staying on board, Zainal, if there is any shortage of space. The sergeant said that things are pretty basic here."

"There are people you should meet, Colonel, and we will have a lot to discuss and plans to make."

"Yes, Zainal." With a perfect about-face, he marched to the first person in the line behind him, a woman.

"Captain Jacqueline Kiznet, sir, with twenty-five hours of flight time on F-122s. She was to be mission pilot on the Mars 10 Supply Rocket. Captain Kiznet has had training in the KDL series and stood five watches as duty officer on our inbound flight."

"Captain Kiznet, my pleasure," Zainal said, shaking her hand and returning her salute. She was medium tall, dark-haired, with a pleasant face and a twinkling eye.

"Captain Katherine Harvey also made herself familiar with the KDL and the KDM specs, did simulations on both in flight and was duty engineer." The captain was a tall redhead, with freckles on her nose and cheeks and a decidedly reserved manner about her.

"Lieutenant Gail Sullivan is a communications expert and has fluent Catteni." Sullivan had short blond hair, a stunned expression on her face, and was small beside the tall captain.

Zainal clasped the lieutenant's hand with vigor. "Welcome to Botany, Emassi, and are you familiar with docking and parking protocols?" he asked in Catteni.

"I listened to all the tapes on board the KDL, Zainal, and feel confident that I can park or dock the vessel at any space facility," Gail responded in Catteni, her alto voice managing to growl in a respectable accent.

"In fact," Maddocks interposed, "she has already done so at Barevi."

"Very good, very good indeed."

Perhaps it was only Kris who noticed the tension easing in Zainal's face and shoulders as he moved on to the next man, one who had the squint of someone accustomed to peering at small print or monitor screens. "Lieutenant Ed Douglas here can even read Catteni."

"You are able to read Catteni?" Zainal asked in the language.

"Slowly, sir, but I am also working on a Catteni-English glossary of technical terms, which I feel will be extremely useful."

"It will, it will. Welcome aboard, Lieutenant Douglas," Zainal said, pumping his hand with considerable vigor. Kris had to fight to keep her face straight.

"I'm apt to be slow with the really technical stuff, but ordinary messages are a snap." He emphasized this by snapping his fingers.

"Lieutenant Mullinax, astrogator, and Lieutenant Mpatane Cummings, also communications, sir, and both are fluent in Catteni. Last but not least, Major Alexander McColl, the most senior pilot."

"Where on earth did you find them, Chuck?" Zainal asked, though his delight was now apparent.

"There, on Earth, of course, sitting on their duffs, trying to decide if they could find some sort of a job. Airplane fuel is a low priority, you see, consequently most pilots are jobless. Gasoline/petrol is strictly rationed and goes mainly to ambulance or emergency vehicles. What airplane fuel is left in airport tanks goes to search-and-rescue copters, but I hate to see good resources like these sitting idle. You know me." Chuck gave one of his cryptic shrugs, implying any waste was intolerable. "And they wouldn't sit still long enough to be painted. Besides, I knew we had the birds but not the fliers. 'Course, they'll have to be checked out but they're right willing."

"Your timing is excellent, as usual, Sergeant."

"I also brought you two top flight mechanics, Dutch Liendgens and Dirk Fuhrman. They might not know much Catteni," he added, gesturing for the two men to come forward, "but they sure know their communications stuff and my 'friend' at JPL says they'd know inventory, too, for all the big manufacturers—like Teledyne and Motorola—and they also have some clues as to the very high-tech stuff JPL and NASA were experimenting with for the Mars Base. Mainly, they can help us service the KDs."

"Is the Mars Base still operational?"

"And manned." When someone behind him cleared her throat, Chuck added, "And womaned. Their gardens have been well wear-tested. Oxygen and food."

"That'll be good news to spread," Zainal said.

"The invaders were so smart they forgot to cut the Atlantic phone lines. And, as I'm told, most comm techs managed to hide the more important elements when they realized they were under attack from space. Those units are coming back into use as more power plants come on-line. Hell, in some places, like Kansas, they're using wind-mills to generate power. Hawaii and California are damned glad they have the wind farms.

"I got a lot more to tell you but maybe we better get the new crews organized, Zainal."

Zainal slapped Chuck across the back, displaying his delight in this surprise. "Welcome to Botany, ALL of you!" he added, throwing both arms open in the most expansive gesture, his mouth wide in a smile. "This way to Retreat."

"Retreat?"

"Don't worry," Chuck said, "it's not a fallback place. It's a come-to."

"Lead on . . . and our chariot awaits!" Zainal added as Jerry Short arrived, driving the commodious pickup sled.

"Hey, neat, Zainal," Sam Maddocks said. "Ground transport. Pile in."

"Pile" was nearly the right word, since all the newly accepted members of the Botany Space Force vaulted or jumped neatly onto the wide truck bed. Kris was hauled up by two of the lieutenants and decided that this bunch were all fit. She wondered if any of them had been trained in hand-to-hand combat. That would be handy, she thought, especially for the women. Maybe they could teach her some good self-defense moves. She was beginning to feel better about this ransom mission. The Council would have to agree—especially now they had reinforcements. She spotted Zainal talking amiably to the astrogator and the tall, willowy Mpatane comm lieutenant. Then he burst out laughing at something the woman said, which had everyone who overheard reacting with glee.

By the time Jerry reached the main building, someone had warned them because there was a crowd waiting, everyone wanting answers to their shouted questions.

Zainal stood and held up his hands "More reason to be sure you attend tonight's meeting, my friends. Right now, we have some tactics to plan. Okay?"

With some reluctance, the crowd was dispersing when Captain Kiznet cupped her hands to shout, "I have new lists of survivors and I will tack them up where you can see." Immediately people pointed to the duty roster board beside which there was a bulletin board for such notices. "Nineteen major cities in Europe and Asia, and some hometown news from forty-seven towns in the US of A," she added and was awarded another rousing cheer.

Kris slipped from the back of the load bed to guide the captain into the mess hall and help her put up the sheets with the tacks available. Then she maneuvered the captain out of the crowd that homed in on the new information. Would it ever be reduced to just one or two anxious seekers? Kris wondered. Zainal had given her a sign to bring the captain to the conference room, just off the main dining hall. Grabbing the captain's arm, Kris pushed her way through those thronging to check names into the relative quiet of the private room. She grinned when she saw Dorothy and Chuck hugging each other. There would be plenty of time to introduce him to their daughter, Amy. Right now, he looked as if he'd never let Dorothy go.

Zainal braced himself across the door of the conference room to be sure only the people he especially needed crowded in to see the new arrivals. He sent Peran, Bazil, and Ditsy to get coffee rations and whatever sandwiches might be available at this hour in the kitchen. When Kris was able to take his place after Zainal gave her a hurried list of those he wanted inside, he cleaned off the big blackboard and started slowly printing out headings for discussion. That done, he printed the list of his Catteni translation team. She was pleased to note she headed the list, which included Floss, Clune, Peran, Bazil, the Doyle brothers, Ferris and Ditsy, Chuck, Sally Stoffers, Gino and Mack Dargle, as well as Pete Snyder. He also chalked down the names of the nine new arrivals and she was delighted he had also grasped the spelling of the crew names.

"All right, folks, may I have some quiet?"

But just then, Chuck, holding Dorothy's hand, slipped into the room with the boys and laden trays right behind them.

"Get yourself your cup of coffee and some food first," Zainal invited, and Kris slipped over to the boys and snitched coffee and a sandwich, which she took to him. He lounged against the nearest table and ate almost ravenously. Then Beth Isbell approached to hand him a clipboard, which he perused while chewing his sandwich. She waited quietly at his side and then Peran brought her a cup of coffee from the tray. She was going to refuse but took it with quiet thanks. Beth was usually punctilious about having only her share though she had once confided to Kris that she was a caffeine addict and the worst problem with being "dropped" was the deprivation of coffee.

Zainal scrawled initials on the first page on the clipboard and extracted what must have been a copy, which he folded and slid into his shirt pocket, before handing it back to Beth. She started to leave but paused to chat with a group.

"Mike just brought in the planet's treasures, and they have them in safekeeping at the hospital," Zainal murmured to Kris, touching the paper he'd put in his pocket. "We're rich," he added with a mischievous wink. "Enjoy it while we can."

"Rich enough?" she asked in a whispered response.

He shrugged. "If we bargain closely enough."

"I'll shave the hair of anyone who cheats us."

"Glad I'm on your side, Kris love." The loving light in his yellow eyes stirred her deeply. She hoped the others would stay in the ship again that night.

Now he stopped lounging and held up his hands. Silence quickly fell on those in the room, abetted by a "shushing" noise.

"I have some better than good news, folks. We do have ransomable items, we do have the services and cooperation of Eric Sachs, DDS, to give all the Catteni gold crowns that wish them, and we do have extra flight personnel to man the other cargo vessels. What is your saying, 'we're loaded for bear'?" That got an appreciative chuckle. "We're mounting this expedition as fast as we can. Chuck Mitford, as ever resourceful, took a side trip to Barevi on his way back and checked warehouses there to see if they really do have the components we need. He seems to feel that they do. I must abide by the Council's decision in this but we'll know tonight whether or not we have the colony's permission to make off with its valuables to buy back what parts we most need to upgrade and repair our communications systems so we can remain in contact with other worlds. Meanwhile, I need the three KDMs space-worthy, so will those crew members please start the preflight checks NOW." He waited while various people made their way purposefully out of the conference room. "I'll need food. And any and all rock squats we can acquire between now and tomorrow morning at oh-nine hundred, when I hope we'll have the required permission to take off. As you can see, we have new faces, recent recruits to the Botany Space Force. Be sure to welcome them—later.

"Dick Aarens, I'll need you to converse with Lieutenants Mullinax,

Cummings, and Douglas and those of you here who have had experience with our satellites and communication units. I may be anticipating the Council's decision—"

"I doubt that," someone remarked, and another cheer resounded. Kris saw Zainal take a deep breath and smile in relief.

"I do thank you for your generous support," he said with a slight and dignified bow around the room. "I got us all into this spot, and I intend to get us out of it!"

"How the hell do you figure that, Zainal?" Leon Dane demanded as he entered the conference room on the end of that remark.

"Yeah, wasn't your fault the Eosi and Catteni invaded Earth," Peter Snyder said almost angrily.

"I should have known that the Barevian traders would throw a spanner in the works."

"You're not a mind-reader," Peter snapped back. "And you got most of what you wanted, didn't you? Botany and Terra free? And the other enforced colonies? And the end of the Eosi domination of your own people. Why should you continue to carry the burden?"

"I consider myself responsible!" Zainal said firmly.

"You got no reason to, Zainal," Leon Dane said, his voice carrying over other disclaimers.

"But I *do!*" Zainal replied. "And I can repair that oversight. I intend to."

"You've done more than anyone thought you would or could," Kris said defensively.

"Not as much as *I* think I should have or could have." He made a slicing movement of his hands to make that the end of the argument.

Kris made no further protest, knowing it would be futile, but there were others who were quite willing to deny him guilt. She knew him better, for she knew now that he was set in his path and nothing would distract or delay him from achieving what he considered his duty and responsibility. Catteni were relentless, if nothing else. She admired that in him, but she'd be glad when he felt he could relax. His sons looked adoringly at him but she knew he wasn't posing for their approval.

"Lieutenant Douglas, did you bring that glossary of technical terms with you? And could we make copies of it?"

"You have a copier?" the dark-haired officer asked in surprise.

"Any number of them who write a fair Catteni hand," Zainal said.

"In handwriting?" Douglas was dismayed.

"What's wrong with old-fashioned methods?" Zainal imitated someone writing with a pen.

"Nothing except that mistakes in copying are more than probable and some of those terms have to be precise."

"We have very good typists, Lieutenant," Kris said. "Not a problem. Beth?" She beckoned to the woman, glad she hadn't left yet. "How many typewriters do we have? And paper?"

"Depends on how much has to be transcribed and by what time."

"Takeoff tomorrow?" Kris asked, almost wistfully.

"If we can divert some power to the machines, I'll have typists work all night in shifts. Where's the copy?"

"I'll have to get my notes from the ship," Douglas said, a trifle rattled though he gave a shake as an animal might to settle ruffled fur. Kris thought wistfully of the family cat, which by now was either feral or eaten. "You move with awesome speed, Emassi Kris."

"We've had to, Lieutenant."

"Do you have computers here?" He was expecting a negative.

"The best I could find at Barevi the last time I was there," she said, wishing her tone hadn't been so defensive. He didn't look annoyed and grinned at her.

"Plenty of RAM and speed, Lieutenant. Kris got only the best and we do have printers," Beth went on proudly, "but not that much ink. Lordy, we've only just been able to find a source of pulp so our production of paper is still inadequate to the need. You'd think this planet ran on paper."

"I'd say you were speedy enough for an enforced colony, Miz Isbell."

"You ain't seen nothin' yet, Lieutenant. May I borrow a land cart to take the lieutenant back to his ship, Kris?"

"Of course."

"We may actually have enough paper in the stores on board. Ships publish a lot of paper, too, you know," Ed Douglas was saying as Beth Isbell gestured for him to leave the room with her. "What sort of printers did Kris liberate?"

"Hewlett-Packards, of course," Beth replied as they made their way out.

"Good for her!" was Douglas's approving reply, and then they were gone.

"I studied typing in high school," Clune murmured to her. "And I have a good speed and know Catteni so I wouldn't make mistakes."

"Thanks, Clune, but you may be needed for other priorities. Don't know what Zainal has in store for you and the other boys."

"Any damned thing he wants, Kris. Some guy!" Clune was clearly in awe. "Ditsy even says so and Ditsy don't waste words, you know."

"Did you boys have it rough with the Masai?"

"Not rough, Kris, but different. Masai have a much different culture than we do. Sure am glad you got Floss out of there when you did. You shoulda seen the old man they were going to tie her up to."

"I heard." Then she gave Clune a stern look. "You get Dane to give you some condoms, you hear me?"

"I hear you good, Emassi Kris." His face tightened suddenly. "But you don't mind it's me, do you?"

"Why should I? You have long-term loyalties I wouldn't think of challenging. And I appoint you Floss's undercover bodyguard."

"I've been that for six years, even before the Catteni landed. My father was a chief of his tribe." He tossed his head in a defensive if proud fashion. "Of all his sons, I was sent to the States to be educated."

"I should've guessed something like that," Kris said at her most approving. "You've an air about you, you know. You'll need that to deal with Barevian merchants. Floss said you've already done a lot of negotiating with Catteni?"

"Had to, Kris, though some thought we were trucking with the invaders, but we weren't. We were staying alive and out of the round-ups." His expression changed to one of intense concern. "Where did all those thousands of people get dropped, Kris?"

"We'll find out, Clune, we'll find out. Another thing to investigate on Barevi."

"They'll be sorry they ever invaded our system."

"The Eosi already are," Kris responded with an ironic laugh. "Barevi will be sorrier soon."

"I hope."

"Me too. Indeed I do," she said in a brightly positive tone, squelching once again that tiny fear of failure she refused to entertain. When she recalled all they had managed to do, she didn't think she was being too optimistic. Well, maybe a little. This expedition was going to be difficult even if all the breaks were on their side. What she really looked forward to was less adventure, dull as that might be after all that had happened to her in the last six years. But there was more, as Zainal had said so emphatically, that somehow had become her responsibility as well as his and Botany's. Well, that was Life, wasn't it? She hadn't even graduated from college yet and she had a lifetime career already!

The newcomers were mingling with the residents now, with questions of their own to be answered. Chuck's cousins were also in the room, looking bewildered. She was about to approach them when she saw Dorothy and Chuck gather them up. She also saw that Zainal's two boys seemed to be talking comfortably to a group of people, so she didn't have to worry about them. Even Ditsy was involved in a conversation, so she didn't see where exactly she might be needed. Then Chuck, Dorothy, and his cousins made a beeline for her.

"Do you have a minute, Kris?" Chuck asked, his face flushed. "I'd like to be introduced to my daughter."

"Oh, Lord, in all the fuss I forgot you haven't seen her. Let's go right away, before someone catches me for something absolutely essential right now."

Flustered, Kris started for the door, wondering how to explain her maternity when she had been introduced to the cousins as Zainal's mate.

She felt someone touch her elbow and realized that Chuck was striding right beside her. "Don't worry. Dorothy explained about the colony's decision to widen the gene pool."

Yes, thought Kris wildly to herself, but she didn't have to get drunk while stuck on that ship on Catten and all but seduce Chuck when he had been almost legless from drinking the local hooch with the airfield commandant.

Kris wasn't sure that explanation would sit well with two older-generation women who obviously adored their cousin.

"Don't fret, Kris. They're just so happy that I have a baby at all." He kept them a little distance ahead of Dorothy, Cherry, and Rose on their way to the crèche and continued his low-voiced explanations. "Leon says they'll improve here on Botany. Texas had a hard winter with more snow than usual and they hadn't any transport to get into the town when the community started. They didn't lack for much, but when they ran out of flour for bread, they put up a bonfire and attracted a rider who took Rose to town and then they were fine. Even had canned stuff to barter for flour." He looked extremely proud of his relatives. Then he swung his chin in Dorothy's direction. "They've always wanted me to marry, and they seem to like Dorothy."

"She's easy to like, Chuck. We don't know whom Amy looks like. Neither you nor me."

"She's pretty young to look like anyone but herself, ain't she?"

Kris was laughing then as she led them into the crèche. Amy was in a playpen, lying on her back and whirling her arms in response to the babble of sound around her.

"Great Lord above, she's the spit of your mother, our cousin Mary," Rose said, clasping her hands to her mouth in feminine shock. "Why, just look at her hair, and the darling shape of her face. I remember one of the photos in the family album . . . and that child is Mary Mitford to the life! Oh, may I cuddle her, Kris?"

"Certainly," Kris replied, delighted. Rose knew how, and Amy settled into her arms as if she'd always known them. Growing up as she had with many people attending her, she had never been shy. Few of the crèche kids were. Even Daisy, whom the medics had once thought might be muted by the traumas she had lived through, now babbled away without inhibitions.

Cherry began to sniffle and gulp back tears. "Oh, she's adorable, Chuck. How did you two ever manage to produce such a lovely girl child?" Then she, too, put hand to lips, widening her eyes in consternation at what she had blurted out.

"A happy match of compatible genes, I'd say," Dorothy replied quickly. "We've actually seen a lot of that since we started increasing Botany's indigenous population."

Zane, who seemed to have a special antenna for his mother's presence, came bouncing into the infant section of the crèche and pounced on her. So she introduced him to the Mitford cousins.

"This one looks so much like his dad," she said, ruffling Zane's hair, "that I'm relieved we've found how Amy got so pretty."

"You're pretty, Mom," Zane said loyally, daring anyone to defy him. "Who does Amy look like?"

"Very much like Chuck's mother, God rest her soul," said Rose, startled at the boy's question. "Oh, we do have a very old picture of Mary. One of the things you must rescue for us, Charles, the next time you're back on Earth."

"In the parlor?" Chuck asked, watching her cuddling his daughter.

"Of course. In the breakfront. Lower cabinet, first on the left. Where else?"

"I should have looked there first, without having to be reminded," Chuck said defensively. "Look, I gotta get crackin' on the mission. You two are in safe hands here, in case I don't get to see you before I go off."

"You be careful, Charles," his oldest cousin said, shaking her finger at him.

"Don't worry about Chuck," Kris replied, unable to restrain the urge. "I'll protect him."

"Yeah, you and who else?" Chuck demanded, halfway to the door, shooting her a droll look.

"You don't need more than my mom," Zane responded defiantly.

"That's all too true, lad, all too true," Chuck said with a final wave of his hand as he left.

"Would he be going into danger, Kris?" Rose asked timorously.

"No more than any of us," Kris replied. "Now, don't you fret, ladies. You are safe here and we're so glad that Chuck found you."

After listening to the two cousins cataloging his half-sister's graces, Zane returned to whatever game he had left when he'd heard his mother's voice.

"What a sturdy child he is," Rose said. "Oh, how can you leave such dear children?"

"Only because I have to," Kris said. "But knowing that you might look in on Amy will relieve me a great deal."

"Of course we will. You may be sure of that."

"Then, if you'll excuse me, I have some details to organize," Kris said and, with a little bow, left them. She had to organize some notes for the evening's meeting, but first she had to find out some details and so she made her way to the library.

"Yo, Betty? What stack are you hiding under?" she called as she came through the front door.

"Betty's not here," said Dr. Hessian. "What can I help you find?"

Since the doctor's recovery from being brain-scanned by the Eosi, he had taken on extra hours at the library, helping to catalog and shelve the rather bizarre collection of books they had liberated from Barevi.

"I need to know which countries on Terra produced coffee."

"Now, that is an odd one. As it happens, I once did a survey of the coffee-producing countries. Brazil, of course, was the major producer. Coffee beans take a tropical climate, you know."

Snatches of old television advertisements flashed through her mind.

"Which type? Arabica or robusta?"

"Coffee beans by any name."

"There are, or should I say *were,* twenty-eight coffee-producing countries. Asia, Africa, Indonesia, South America, the various islands in the Caribbean—"

"Twenty-eight?" Kris breathed a sigh of relief. "Thank goodness."

"Why?" asked the doctor, mildly curious by her relief.

"Because there will be coffee beans somewhere that haven't been seized by the Catteni. They're addicted to coffee, you see."

"Not quite, but I'm glad to know my errant memory could supply you with information. If you'll wait a moment, I'll just look it up in the encyclopedia."

"Not necessary right now, Doctor, but if you could bring the reference with you to the meeting tonight?"

"Yes, yes, of course."

"It's the roasting that does it, you know," he added in a helpful tone of voice. When she gave him a startled look, he expatiated. "Raw coffee beans have to be stripped of the exterior fruit pulp, which makes a good animal feed, the beans dried and roasted before grinding, you know. The coffee bean is a drupe."

She did remember about grinding, and the thought of freshly roasted and ground coffee made her inhale a deep breath, recalling just how good roasting beans smelled. Unforgettable as well as indescribable.

"Yes, yes, that isn't as important as knowing where to get more is."

"Get more?"

"Ransom, Doctor, ransom!" she said and left on the echo of that cryptic remark.

She fortified herself by chanting "twenty-eight" all the way back to the hangar, which was now as crammed full of busy folk as it had been empty earlier. She let herself into the office she usually shared with Zainal and plunked herself down at the first available station, flipping on the computer. She only needed to type a few lists. Like all twenty-eight countries and the major producers of finished coffee products.

What measure should they use in figuring worth? Would coffee beans be as valuable to the Catteni as gold? Hmmm. Imagine a scoop of freshly roasted beans being as valuable as a similar weight of gold? She chuckled to herself and began to type. "There are twenty-eight coffee-producing countries on Earth—in South America, Africa, Indonesia, Asia, and various Caribbean countries and they can't all have been ransacked by the Catteni."

The noise of happy laughter made her look up and peer out of the open hangar door just as an air sled, crammed with young people, every one of them festooned with the limp bodies of rock squats, lurched by.

And how much were rock squats worth by the pound? The ounce? The individual critter? Had anyone ever opened a shop with such diverse commodities?

"A carton a carcass?" The slogan slipped into her mind. Well, that would do until another crossed her mind.

Everyone turned out for the Council meeting. She had expected that much but she was delighted to see that even Mike Miller's miners and farmers from the northern reaches of the Retreat continent as well as Chief Materu from the south were present. As she hovered by the steps to the raised dais, she saw that Clune and Peran were escorting Chief Materu and introducing him to others. She couldn't see Floss but she did spot Bazil, Ditsy, and Ferris.

Chuck came in with Dorothy on his arm, his two cousins right behind him, looking excessively proud of him. They had more color in their faces this evening so she hoped they hadn't got too much sun, then reminded herself that they were from Texas and would know to be careful of too much sunning. Zainal arrived with Peter, Iri Bempechat, Yuri Palit, and Walter Duxie, the mining engineer. Sev Balenquah followed them, and uncharitably Kris hoped no one would include him on this mission since he had so nearly jeopardized them all the last time. But he was a qualified pilot and had flown the KDLs. Some people just brought bad luck with them and he was one of those. Like Pig Pen, you could almost see the aura of dirt and dust surrounding him.

Zainal escorted Judge Iri Bempechat up the steps and held out the middle chair for him. The ever courteous judge waited until Chuck had seated Dorothy and Chuck returned to his place by his cousins.

Immediately the chatter in the mess hall diminished. The new Botany Space Force additions filed in with Peter Easley, who gestured them to seats on the left before he came up to the dais. Kris took her usual end seat, nodding to the judge, who smiled sweetly back at her and took the gavel that he used for such meetings out of his pocket and put it conspicuously in front of him. Conversations went down yet another decibel and there was much scraping of chairs as people settled themselves. The last of the council members, Leon Dane, rushed in late as usual, as did Worrell, Beth Isbell, and Sarah McDouall.

The judge gave his gavel an authoritative smack on the wooden block and silence prevailed.

"Since all council members are clearly present, I shall ask Chuck Mitford to report on his recent trip to Earth. And a special welcome to the Misses Mitford. Glad to have you here."

The sisters twittered, somewhat embarrassed by the official greeting, then both smiled happily up at the judge.

Chuck took center stage.

"I got good news and I got bad news, folks. The bad is that most of the spare parts we need desperately to get other systems up and running on Earth are stuck as loot at Barevi.

"The good news is that there is a powerful swing to 'sharing' on our home world like nothing we've ever seen before. But then, we hadn't seen," and he swiveled to nod apologetically to Zainal, "Catteni either. Remember how the Red Cross and the other emergency units would go to disaster areas and sort things out? Well, of course you know we had disaster all over the world but that same sort of helpful, cooperative spirit got invoked.

"It started out with local communities banding together to help each other and discuss what was needed where. It's gone on to deciding where to spend effort and material to cause the greatest good for the greatest number of folk. I mean, guys and gals, it ain't like who should get more, but we all should get according to the need. The greatest help has been the Internet, mobile phones, and, as usual, ham radio folk. The first thing that was done was to reinstate the power supply, and that meant instant communication and also the ability to send drastically needed supplies where they needed to go. And we're solving as many problems as possible in the districts where it's critical. I've never seen anything like it, even with the worst of the earthquakes or hurricanes, or forest fire disasters. It's like we all turned over a new leaf. All national boundaries are down. I don't say they'll stay down, because people take pride in what they are and where they come from, but I'd say there's been a real forward step that looks good for world relations.

"Which is why we gotta make sure communications are established in all parts. We got this magnificent opportunity to sink a lot of petty little differences, and I'd say Earth is going to succeed. It's an ill wind that blows no good.

"Sorry to spout off at you like that," Chuck managed a self-indulgent grin, "but we did something like that here on Botany, and what we learned here we can now translate to old Earth and see it putting the right foot forward."

"But you need what the Barevis are sitting on, is that it, Chuck?" asked Mike Miller.

"Yeah, I did a recce, and it looks like the merchants are sitting on things they can't possibly use. As I'm sure everyone here knows," and he threw one arm out in an expansive gesture, "or should know, Zainal is mounting an expedition to Barevi to talk them out of stuff." He unfurled a rolled paper that fell to the floor of the dais. "This is Terra's shopping list." Then he let another, much shorter one, loose. "This is Botany's. Both are needed to make the necessary revival."

"Talk isn't what Barevis buy," someone yelled. "So, who pays them?"

"We'd like to, since we have things the Catteni want," Zainal said. "Earth is going to contribute some of what it still has left in storage—things that my fellow planetarians didn't realize was important to them, or us. But to start the ball rolling, as you say, we have some Botanical assets that are readily salable, but as they belong to all of us, I can't ask the Council to just give them to me. I need to have the consent of all of you."

"Just how will these communications help *us?*" Bob Taglione said.

"Not that I'm against anything you want to do, Zainal, but if we are doing everyone good, what good do communications do *us?*"

"Good question, Bob," Zainal said. "I know many of you have families you'd like to hear from regularly. I don't say the mail service will be fast but it will exist. The invasion forces knocked out most of the large number of satellites that relay signals from one part of the globe to another. We could not only replace that vital net, but we could install one above Botany so that no matter where you were here, you could communicate to any part of Earth."

There were appreciative catcalls, whistles, and stompings for that possibility. "You won't feel so isolated from family and friends anymore."

"I'll buy that!" Joe Marley yelled.

"Any chance of some of our families coming here?"

Zainal took a deep breath and, almost in unison, so did Kris. They'd discussed that imminent problem in Council. No firm decision had been made.

"There is a chance, certainly, Astrid." The asker was one of Zainal's own team. "It will depend on their needs and the availability of transport. But certainly some folks, like Chuck Mitford's cousins, would benefit by some months here on beautiful, scenic, do-it-yourself Botany, though I never thought we'd recommend this place as a holiday spot."

"Didn't think you Catteni ever took holidays," Leon Dane said facetiously.

"Living here is in its own way quite a change from what I'm accustomed to," Zainal said with a wry grin. "We will expect that any visitors are willing to put in hours for the general good of Botany or at their specialty if they have specific training we can use. And I can't think of anything we can't use here. Especially elbow grease?" He looked at Kris to see if he'd used the expression correctly, but his ingenuous remark provoked chuckles from many people.

To contain her pride in his response, she crossed her arms on her chest. Could he have been taking lessons from Peter Easley in public relations, or had he instinctively learned that much about how to mollify folks?

"Rose aims to help you, Bob, in cataloging our indigenous plants while she recovers from a winter in Texas." That got a laugh. "She's a pharmacist, too, and Cherry wants to help Ole recover from nearly ripping his arm off."

There were cheers and isolated instances of applause through-out the hall so that Cherry began to blush again and sink down in her chair.

"We've been making up a list of those specialties we could really use up here to balance our skills and technical pool, so we are open to suggestions, especially if you know where we can find such trained folk." He pointed to the bulletin board. "But to do all this, we need those satellites and bundles of mobile phones."

"Lord, spare us!" someone cried out in consternation, and that provoked another laugh.

"I also need a good excuse to visit Barevi, and dealing with the merchants is one way of stretching out my time as long as I need it," Zainal said in an ominous voice. "The records of where the other slave ships went are at Barevi, and I mean to uncover them."

"So this trip is also a cover operation?" Walter Duxie asked.

Zainal gave a brief nod. "But I can't go with empty pockets, and what edibles we can provide that might entice buyers would be useful."

"Just how much are you talking about in terms of Botany's assets, Zainal?"

"Mike Miller? Will you report on what you brought for us to barter with?"

"You mean 'ransom,' don't you, Zainal?" Dick Aarens asked bluntly.

"Yes, that is perhaps the more appropriate word, Dick," Zainal replied at his mildest, and there was restlessness from the audience.

Leave it to Dick, Kris thought, wishing the man were not so much his own worst enemy as Zainal's ardent opponent.

Mike had to be encouraged by Zainal to stand up. "I brought some of those gold nuggets we've been finding in the northern creeks—and don't any of you think you can come up and pan gold so easy. Ask any of my miners. Ask Duxie here. There ain't much of it at best, and, at worst, Botany ain't on a gold standard. We're on a work standard, which is much better for all concerned. I brought tin, lead, zinc, copper—but there's as much on deposit in what we are calling Fort Raps." Another laugh at that sally. "And a quantity of trace minerals. Nothing we don't have more of here and something we can certainly send to be used as barter. I don't know about you guys but I've friends back on Earth I'd sure like to send messages to now and then. That'd mean more to me than all the gold in Fort Knox."

"Hear, hear!" was the supporting cry from the audience.

"How do we know what standard Barevi is working on?" someone demanded.

"Fair question," Dick said.

"We're going to give them a little razzmatazz that they can't ignore," Peter said, flicking one hand in the air as if this weren't a problem.

"I hardly think roast or raw rock squat is what they're looking for," Aarens shot back.

"There's nothing on the list of what we have that can't be replaced with a little sweat and effort," Mike Miller replied, annoyed by Aarens's obvious attempt to disparage Zainal's efforts.

"I find it odd that a Catteni is trying to bargain for us with his own species. Strikes me as collusion," was Aarens's retort, and he included the miner in his angry glance.

"We'd still be under Catteni rule if Zainal hadn't intervened with that Kamiton," Yuri Palit said angrily.

"How do we know that? How do we know this business with the Barevi merchants isn't another way of robbing us and Botany of resources?" Aarens demanded, waggling an accusing finger at Palit.

"Considering what Zainal has already put on the line for us," Chuck said, his face flushed with anger, "your suggestion is impertinent."

"I'm always impertinent," Dick Aarens retorted, pleased.

"You are also out of order," Iri Bempechat said with a crack of his gavel.

"Let me straighten one thing out," Zainal said. "We have a Council," and he gestured to the dais, "to decide matters of planetary significance. Which this is, since it is Botany's assets that I hope to use to get the components we need to put more communication satellites in orbit around Botany and to restore the rest of the network around Earth. If that goal seems wrong to any of you, you have a chance to say so now, impertinent or pertinent. And I want Dick Aarens to come with us since he is an expert in circuitry."

"That's a safe enough offer," Dick Aarens said with a sneer. "You know I won't go out into space again."

Not everyone caught the second part of his comment because everyone wanted a turn to speak and the judge had to bang his gavel to restore order.

Zainal raised his hands high for silence, too, and when it was reinstated, he went on.

"We also have several spaceships which are currently not in use. I suggest that one of these could be profitably sold to cover costs."

There was a roar of disapproval at that suggestion. Botanists took great pride in their space capability.

"We can dig more gold and stuff, but we can't get another spaceship as easily!"

"We'll all get something useful out of that gold 'n' stuff. Go to it, Zainal."

"I'll dig for more. Just show me where!"

"Are you sure this'll work, Zainal?"

"I have been assured it will," Zainal said. "As sure as one can be. You all know my deal with Kamiton, but he didn't figure on the stubbornness of Barevi merchants. Therefore it's up to me to do a private deal with them personally. And I take that responsibility very much to heart. We wouldn't have the problem we have now if I hadn't forgotten how materialistic that group are."

"Not your fault, Zainal," Chuck said, bringing his fist down on the table with a bang that startled everyone sitting around him.

"Don't you blame yourself, Zainal," Dorothy Dwardie said, pointing her finger at him. "You made a deal with Kamiton, and it's not your fault that he welshed on it."

"'Welshed on it'?" Zainal asked, blinking at her.

"Couldn't deliver," Kris translated. "Make good on his word. Kamiton seems to have some internal difficulties in his new government." She grinned and then confided to the assembly, "We'll sort it out, I'm sure. And we'll bring some coffee back with us, too."

There was a cheer to that statement.

"They'll be sorry they started on a coffee addiction. We can make that work for us, you know. Demand for goods is always a good incentive to trade."

"What about the gold teeth?"

"It takes a lot longer to make teeth than it does to brew good coffee."

"Ah, coffee!"

"Hey, did they get a taste for chocolate, too?" a woman wanted to know.

"Hey, that can be just as addictive!" There was good-natured laughter at that.

"You will keep records of where the ransom goes, won't you, Zainal?"

"We certainly will," Chuck answered stoutly. "Every flake of gold, every ounce of copper, tin, and grain of minerals will be accounted for. Won't it, Sally?"

"Am I going, too?" Sally Stoffers asked, eyes wide with excitement.

"You were an accountant once, weren't you?" Chuck asked.

"Yes, but only on Earth."

"Accounting is accounting wherever it's done," Chuck said emphatically.

"I motion to put the matter of our colony's assets being turned over to Zainal for the purposes of obtaining technological parts to the vote," cried Walter Duxie.

"I second that motion," said Mike Miller.

"All in favor, please stand!" He signaled to Dorothy, as Council secretary, to count the vote.

It was not a unanimous vote but more than two-thirds of those attending the meeting approved and that was all, Judge Bempechat said, that was needed.

"Let's devoutly hope we succeed," Kris murmured to Peter, sitting next to her.

"That was almost too easy," he replied, "or have such diehards as Anne and Janet changed their tunes?"

Kris had not looked to see if those two conservative women who had such high and righteous morals and little compassion were in the audience. It took her a time to find them, sitting at the back. "They don't look happy, do they?" she said, for she had been certain they'd have a negative response from that pair.

"Well, they do have family back on Earth, as I'm sure you've heard them tell."

Kris nodded and then caught her breath as Janet got to her feet.

"I raise the question of relatives being allowed here on Botany. I know that some folk are in terrible physical condition and could benefit by being here, away from the scenes of stress and destruction."

Dorothy raised her hand to Iri to be heard.

"We have, indeed, been addressing that problem in the Council, Janet. As you will have heard, Chuck has brought his cousins back, and we will certainly entertain other applications for refuge. But, as you all know, Botany works because we all do. We can, of course, admit a quantity of folk whose mental and physical state would improve by a change of scenery, but we must weigh our resources and staffing levels. If you would like, Dr. Hessian and I will set up interviews with those wishing to offer space available to relatives. Would that be acceptable, Janet?"

"What about those valleys? And the one we fixed up for the Catteni families?"

"It has limited occupancy but it certainly figures in our plans to accommodate affected folk."

"Affected?" Janet retorted, incensed. "I'll have you know—"

"Discuss what you know with me in the interview," Dorothy said firmly, effectively cutting off Janet's spiel before she could get started. "See me after this meeting and we'll arrange a time, Janet."

Kris would have liked to throttle Janet—once again. Botany was a sanctuary and should be available to those suffering from trauma, but not on a wholesale basis. The recovery of those victims who had suffered from the effects of the mind-machine had proved that Botany's serene beauty could eradicate stress and injury. Certainly there were people here trained—and available—to help. One more reason to have better communications between the two planets: to forestall a mass exodus from Earth to Botany. This planet could sustain the people already here but not a mass immigration from Earth. She liked Botany as it currently existed, with a good balance of people and skills. If it were to be overbalanced in one direction—like becoming a vast hospital—it would founder under such weight. Still, it was the resilience of the community that had proved its strongest asset. Then she wondered about the feasibility of constantly running spaceships back and forth.

"Are there any more matters that need to come before the Council and the people?" Iri Bempechat asked, looking around the room.

"Hearyez, hearyez," Chuck said, using his parade-ground voice to cut through the babble to be sure Iri's message had been heard. "Any more business for the Council and the assembled?"

A long pause answered that query.

"We got schedules to keep then," Leon Dane said, rising to his feet.

The judge gave one more bang of his gavel then, getting to his feet—a little stiffer for having sat for so long in one position. Then he put his gavel back inside his official robe and walked off the dais.

The assembled broke up into small groups to discuss the meeting, and Janet was at the foot of the small flight of steps to intercept Dorothy Dwardie.

"Is this town-meeting approach how you've managed so much out of so little?" Captain Harvey asked Kris as she leaped down from the front of the dais.

"More or less," she said and grinned when she saw some of the male Botanists whom she knew were still single homing in on the attractive communications officer.

"Look, don't get yourself stuck with the shiftless coming in droves to live off the fat of the land here," Captain Harvey added, discreetly shielding what she said from the approaching males.

"What do you mean, shiftless?"

"There are always losers who assume the mantle of vulnerability to take the easy way out. What would you do with those who won't perform?"

"Don't know yet. We'll probably try to screen those who come and limit how long they can stay," Kris said. "But staying on Botany will definitely require showing they can contribute."

"That's what old Earth is discovering right now. Who can contribute? Not all in the same degree, but there are many ways of contributing to a common good, aren't there?"

"Yes, Captain, there are. Captain Harvey, may I introduce Bob Sterling, Ben Wately, and Ian Halstrip. You may have a lot in common since they man our communications."

"Thanks, Kris," Bob Sterling said in his unmistakable Aussie accent. "Appreciate the intro."

"Actually, we need the captain's advice if she wouldn't mind?"

"Not at all," the redhead replied, shaking hands in turn with each of them. "What have you in mind?"

"Well, if you'd like some refreshment," and Ben managed to take her arm in a courteous fashion as he gestured toward the drinks and desserts that were being served at the main counter, "we thought we might settle a few technical problems."

As the captain allowed herself to be led away, Kris grinned and looked around for Zainal. They still had a lot of details to sort out before the morning. To start with, where were they going first? Earth? The good Dr. Hessian, for all he could be a crashing bore, had turned up a tremendous amount of information on coffee, and if she couldn't find what she needed in Brazil or Venezuela, there were always Zaire and Ethiopia or Java. And she had had several tons of grain released to the expedition—less than a skimming of two silos, so she didn't feel she was plundering anything. It always paid to have more than one string to your bow, didn't it? And if the shine of nuggets wouldn't do it, maybe "black gold" would!

The KDM had its new ID painted on its bow and emblazoned along both sides: BASS-1, for Botany Airforce Spaceship 1. Or Baker Alpha Sugar Sugar 1.

Kris thought it looked pretty smart before she became involved in organizing the food supplies on board into the cargo space or the refrigerated unit. Flats and flats of broiled rock squat and loaves of bread were boarded as well as convenient twenty-five-pound sacks of wheat and a dozen of flour, enough for her to make bread on the journeys and at Barevi.

All the fluent Catteni-speakers were coming along as well as some specialists like Herb Bayes, an electrician who'd be needed on Barevi, plus Captain Kathy Harvey to complete her pilot training and Mpatane Cummings, who was a communications expert, Eric Sachs, Floss, Clune, Ferris, Ditsy, and Zainal's two boys, who were very excited about going. Kris wondered if Zainal had warned the boys that he would be getting them a tutor on Barevi. Well, she wasn't going to cloy their excitement with a detail that was, in some respects, not her business. Sally Stoffers was along as their bookkeeper and accountant. She was bunking with Floss, a situation neither woman liked but there was only so much cabin space on the KDM.

4

When they got close enough to Terra, looking much the same as Kris remembered it from NASA shuttle photos, they could also see some of the larger space junk.

"Let's just see what is still operational," Zainal said. "If it's only the spare parts that are needed, maybe we can supply those."

"We don't have them . . . yet," Kris reminded him.

Jacqueline Kiznet, who preferred to be called Jax, brought up a screen image of the satellite distribution.

"Earth looks like a porcupine with all that junk," she exclaimed.

"'Junk' is probably accurate," Kathy Harvey muttered. "As I heard it, the Catteni used the comm sats for target practice."

"Some are obviously still working since the communications network is functioning, even with occasional gaps," Mpatane remarked. "So not all are gone. Since I'm up here, I can get the working ones to respond to a code I happen to know."

Zainal drifted over to the nearest units, some with three long solar panels and some with only two, and eased close to one whose solar panels on the nearest port side were gone. The same damage was visible on the next four they passed. Mpatane kept a record of their IDs.

"They don't look damaged otherwise," she murmured. "Still have their ears."

"Ears?" Zainal asked, surprised.

"Those round objects are actually called 'ears,' and they catch the signals and bounce them on to their coded destinations."

"No power, no work," Gail Sullivan said, a sad tone to her voice.

"We shall need to get as many solar sails as we can find, then," Zainal said, as if that solved the whole problem.

Some did answer, feebly in a few cases, others more robustly, to Kathy's signals, each new response raising the hopes of the entire crew.

The suggestion of redistributing the operational ones was met with the remark that each satellite had a mission package that defined its parameters so that they were not interchangeable.

"And this next one," Jax Kiznet said from her pilot's chair, "is a loose cannon. See how it wobbles?"

"Looks to me as if it got its controls blasted," Harvey said, peering at the twisted protuberances that would have provided guidance. "Its solar wings don't seem to be damaged."

"This KDM has a tractor beam, doesn't it?" Mpatane asked Zainal, who nodded. "Could we capture it?"

"We could, but why?"

"Well, for one thing, it's small enough to be hauled on board so we could examine it at our leisure. Work experience for when we need to repair other units," she said.

Zainal enabled the tractor beam, which locked onto the spinning comm sat. The jerk of contact went through the scout ship, rocking several folks roughly about. But no one was injured.

Getting the comm sat on board was not as easy, although the cargo area could be sealed off from the rest of the ship so the outer hatch could be opened. Gravity on the KDM could also be turned off, to make maneuvering the unit easier. It was, Kathy Harvey remarked, rather like getting a whale onto a trawler.

"If we just had someone to give it a good push," McColl remarked, smoothing his white brush mustache as if that action generated useful thought. He was the oldest of the pilots Chuck had seconded.

"Do we have any cargo nets left on board the ship?" Zainal asked thoughtfully.

"Yes," Chuck Mitford replied. "Steel mesh, too. Are you going to do a cowboy act?"

Zainal merely widened his eyes at Chuck until Chuck gave a pantomime of a rope being thrown. Zainal snorted. "It is easier to match velocities and park in front of it."

"Snare it in the hatch?" McColl asked, astonished. He whistled. "That will take some piloting."

Zainal regarded him steadily. "I am accustomed to doing such things."

"Wasn't even suggesting you aren't a top-flight pilot, Zainal," McColl replied quickly. "But I do want to see you play catch." He grinned to mitigate any slur on his abilities.

"And so you shall," Zainal said. "Chuck, bring that net up to Number One Hatch." He settled himself down at the control panel to do the necessary placement and picked a comm sat that had had both "ears" blown off and much of its impressive span of solar panels cut off short. While he had said it was "merely" a job of matching velocities, it required very careful "puffs" of his thrusters to slow the KDM down and introduce a rate of closure with the satellite of about one-quarter to one-half meter per second.

"How are you going to intercept that much mass at that rate, Zainal?" Kathy asked.

"I do have to allow for momentum, velocity plus mass, but it shouldn't be too high for the mesh to handle if it's standard Catteni issue. As for the KDM, the winches are built much heavier than that. Chuck, have you got the net in the cargo hold?"

"Gimme a few, Zainal," Chuck said, obviously puffing from physical exertion. "Had to stuff it on a lift platform. Unhandy thing."

"Steel mesh?"

"Yup, standard Catteni issue."

"That's what we need," Zainal said, feeling more confident about all this. Kris gave him a look, implying that he was doing what she called "showing off" but what he called "proving" his skill as a pilot. "It'll also discharge the static on the comm sat in space instead of in the cargo hold."

"Zainal, got it in place against the hatch. We're getting back to the lock. Ah, now, we're all safe. Ready when you are. The net's rigged to go."

"Grab hold, crew. I've got to go weightless." He snapped off the ship's gravity, then opened the hatch and watched while first a bulge of the net cleared the starboard side of the KDM, and then the rest followed, ballooning into space but still tethered to the vessel. "Parking" the KDM in front of the object he wished to capture, he "puffed" the thrusters just enough to catch the rectangular comm sat in the mesh. There was an almighty flash as the steel mesh encountered the comm sat and discharged static.

Mpatane floated at a porthole, watching the mesh close around the satellite. Suddenly she was blinded by a burst of light, and she clenched her eyes shut.

"What was that? Looked almost like lightning," she exclaimed.

"What you saw was the voltage potential on the satellite equalizing. Visible here, too," Chuck explained. "Those things can build up quite a charge sitting there, what with all those solar storms and relativistic electron flux bombarding them all the time. It's a good thing we didn't send someone out on EVA! That would have been nasty."

Zainal grunted, as if dismissing the prospect of danger.

"Wow!" Kathy exclaimed, blinking against the sudden blue-white glare.

"Neat fireworks," Ferris said, awed.

Watching carefully on his starboard screens, Zainal saw the net tighten around its catch and slowly be reeled back to the ship. With a deft hand on his thrusters, he edged the ship so that the netted comm satellite entered the hatch.

"Mitford, make sure you get the satellite on the floor of the hold as closely as you can," Zainal said. "I don't want it smashing our deck plates when I turn the gravity back on."

"Will do. I'll need a minute or two. Got to repressurize the hold and whatnot."

"Take your time," Zainal replied, the model of Catteni patience.

After a few minutes of silence, Chuck said, "Zainal, this thing's heavy as hell. Can you push the ship up so it will drift toward the floor?"

"Get clear, and make sure there's nothing between it and the cargo flooring."

After two quick puffs of the thrusters, a dull and satisfying *thud* echoed through the ship.

"We've got it now, Zainal, thanks," was Chuck's enthusiastic reply. "Wait one while we get it braced with something . . . Okay . . . good to go now."

"The KDM," Zainal murmured to Kathy, "is a workhorse but you can get it to do more than just haul stuff from one planet to another."

"To be honest, Zai," Gino Marrucci said, and he'd already flown KDMs between Earth and Botany, "I didn't believe you could do that with this."

"Can we see what we snared?" Mpatane asked. "I've only seen pictures of the comm sats before they were launched. Never one on site, so to speak."

"Crew, gravity's coming on. Three, two, one." Zainal flicked the toggle to the "on" position. "Mitford, secure the hatch. Don't want that thing rolling out on us."

"Couldn't roll if it wanted to, Zainal. It's too heavy. And besides, it's square blocks stuck together, not a ball."

Those in the lock with Chuck were busy examining the catch before Zainal, Gino, and Kathy Harvey arrived.

"Hey, it's a Boeing 601. We can mount just about anything on this baby. Some of the parts for these things are on that wish list," Mpatane said with respectful delight.

"Can we service it then?"

"If we had the parts, we could," Mpatane said, circling the unit, putting her fingers through the holes some target practice had made in the "ear" and sighing at the blatant vandalism. "I wonder how many more fell to some Catteni's notion of fun. Ooops, sorry, Zainal."

"Not to worry, Mpatane. But it can be serviced?"

"If we can find the spare parts, sure. I don't notice any holes in the mission package or the control units, but you did keep a record of its orbit, didn't you, Zainal?"

"Yes, it's logged. So all we need to do is repair it and put it back in space."

"We'll have our work cut out for us," Mpatane said with a heavy sigh. "This one is one of many, you know. Do we get to do them all?" She cocked her head impudently at Zainal.

"As many as we have to to extend the working footprint needed to ensure worldwide communications. We'll need some sort of conference with someone down there to figure out how many satellites will be required to make a big enough footprint."

She exhaled over the enormity of the task.

"Well, it's a job," she said with such resignation that everyone chuckled in semi-agreement, semi-sympathy.

"Check the unit over, will you, Mpat, and see what else has been damaged. I'm hoping we can just unscrew, detach, and/or replace faulty parts."

"Plug in and go," Gino said, pushing a triumphant fist in the air.

"Now, crew, lash it down so when we enter Earth's atmosphere, it doesn't buck its way about the hatch," was Zainal's final remark as he turned to go back to the cockpit.

Part of the inbound journey was then occupied by a full examination of the comm sat by the communications experts, with an emphasis on how to replace damaged solar vanes and restore power to the damaged equipment. They kept a list of the deployment of those that they thought they could repair. *If* they had the spare parts.

"I never imagined we had so much orbiting the planet," Kris said that night in the mess hall as she served the assembled crew.

"Junk, a lot of it," Harvey said with understandable contempt. "Too far out to be burned up in the atmosphere . . ."

"Raining hot metal down on unsuspecting folk," Gail said. "It did happen, you know. Australia got quite irate over some instances."

"I thought Australia was sparsely populated outside of the major cities."

"There are people and sheep in the outback, as well as Aboriginals who didn't like their turf being pummeled by junk."

"Expensive junk," Jax added, "still makes trouble."

Chuck came into the cockpit then with a sheet of notes in his hand. "Look, guys, in the category of 'once bitten, twice shy,' we ought to get contacted soon. Those NORAD boys in the Cheyenne mountains are sharp. Catteni couldn't even budge them."

"You mean, they have a space station backup?" Kris said.

"Of course we do," Kathy said, almost contemptuously. "First world community project, called Watch Dog, with sensors at about forty-two kilometers from Earth. No one is ever going to catch Earth unawares again. Only, does anyone know what to say?"

"Of course I do," Chuck said, clicking his tongue. "I arranged a code before I came back to Botany. That's why I had a radio put on board. It's all set up. They ought to make contact about now. We are forty-three thousand klicks from Earth's surface, ain't we?"

It was one minute and forty-two seconds before the radio unit crackled, startling them all even if they were waiting for it.

"This is Watch Dog. What are you doing in our space?"

"Not very polite," Zainal murmured.

"To the point, however," Kathy said, pleased, and eyed Chuck Mitford sternly.

"Botany boys are back, Watch Dog."

"Oh, the Botany boys, huh?" was the laconic reply. "You are a green for go, Botany Boy. What's your destination?"

Chuck grinned fatuously around and winked at Kathy. "Newark Airport."

"What's your business?"

"Liaison with New Jersey Coord Dan Vitali."

"Roger that, Botany Boy. Is that Mitford talking?"

"Chuck Mitford, aboard the Botany spaceship Baker Alpha Sugar Sugar One.

"Roger that, Baker Alpha Sugar Sugar One. Who's your crew?"

"Emassi Zainal, pilot, and Captain Kathy Harvey, copilot; Gino Marrucci, radio officer; flight engineer is Lieutenant Mpatane Cummings. Twelve passengers."

"You are free to proceed. Will alert Newark Airport and Coord Vitali. Over and out."

"Over and out—and thanks, Watch Dog."

"Newark radio frequency is 118.3, Ground Control 121.8 MHz. Out."

"Roger."

"Clever Chuck," Kris said with a sigh of relief. "I didn't think about possibly getting shot out of the skies."

"A little late but we learned."

"Was the International Space Station blown out of the skies?"

"No, like its predecessor, it had a charmed life. It also had no armament when the Catteni came through and was hidden by the planet so it didn't come in for some target practice. Now it's armed and ready."

Chuck nodded approval.

"Botany boys!" Zainal said with a snort.

"Seemed easy to remember. Newark ain't much, but the airport's one of the few kept manned, and with the KDM being a vertical takeoff and landing ship, no problem to land there. Or anywhere. Newark's also closer to the coordinators we need to talk to."

"Wouldn't JFK be bigger and better?" Kris asked. She'd always been impressed by that huge airport.

"No, too far out in Queens, and we ain't got the right contacts there."

The KDM had reached the atmosphere, and even before Zainal called for a "safety-belt check, people," all were strapped down. Peran and Bazil occupied the jump seats and were fascinated by the approach to a planet they had heard about but never seen, even in pictures. The KDM nosed into the atmosphere and the bucking started in earnest. Then suddenly it smoothed out and the spaceship was running east with the patchwork of the midwestern states passing beneath them at incredible speed.

Gino warmed up the radio and got the Newark frequency, then nodded to Zainal. Gino's bright tenor sounded amiably bored as he requested permission for Baker Alpha Sugar Sugar 1 to use the runway.

"KDM, you're cleared into Newark," was the calm response. Gino blinked and even Chuck looked surprised at the insouciance of the acknowledgment. "We have you on radar at . . ." The voice suddenly was tinged with near panic. "Jeez! KDM, are you in trouble?"

"No," Zainal replied, "all systems are normal."

"Christ, KDM," Newark Approach responded, and noise of confusion filtered from the background. "You've dropped ten thousand feet in the last two seconds! You're going to be on top of the airport in—here, I'll patch you to the tower." In the background, very clearly, could be heard "Call out the crash trucks. This one's going to augur in!"

"KDM, this is Newark Tower. You are cleared for immediate landing on runway Twenty-two-R. Winds calm at two hundred ten degrees. Your altitude is—about three thousand. We have you on radar. Say your intentions."

"I intend to land, if I may. Main engines will engage in a hover at one hundred feet."

Newark Tower replied, "Hover? Roger, KDM, you're cleared to land." Since the operator clearly forgot to unkey his microphone, they could hear him. "He says he's going to hover that thing. Has anyone ever heard of the Cats hovering? Jeez, duck!"

Right on the mark, the KDM's main engines kicked in and brought the spaceship to a hover a neat one hundred feet from the runway. Zainal had Kathy bring the craft down to a mere ten feet before radioing the tower. "KDM requests parking instructions."

The tower operator was slow to reply. "Uh, roger, KDM, you are cleared to taxi to the West Park area. Take any convenient spot and any route you need."

"Yes, we are taking most direct path to West Park Area."

The tower contact cleared his throat suddenly. "Uh, KDM, what's your port of origin? For the record, I gotta clear you. Your port of origin and flight docket?"

"We are inbound from the planet Botany, wishing to make contact with Coordinator Dan Vitali. Do not have a flight docket, whatever that is these days."

"Inbound from *where*? Dan Vitali?" Everyone in the cabin could hear the barrage of questions from a number of startled voices in the tower with the operator.

"Ohmigod, get Vitali on the phone. Snap to it. We got I dunno how many tons of spaceship hovering above us."

"Hell, we ain't Bakersfield or the Space Center. What's he doing in our skies?"

"Trying to land, I think. Watch Dog cleared it with the boss about two hours ago. Code just came in. Have you got Vitali yet? This is— man, like, urgent. No messing."

Everyone in the cockpit, except the two Catteni boys, grinned at the panic they were causing.

"Baker Alpha Sugar Sugar One, have you a Chuck Mitford on board?" Tower asked a short minute later, this query considerably more courteous than his first reaction.

"Affirmative to that, Tower."

"Please await inspection and escort to the coord. They are on their way. Sorry, it's a bit of protocol."

"Inspection? Good Lord, and when I think of all the alien goods we have on board, we're in trouble," Kris said facetiously. "I wonder how much duty they'll charge for the electronics on board."

"I suspect they are more cautious now," Kathy Harvey said dryly, "than they used to be. And this is obviously a Catteni spaceship, even if you call yourselves the Botany Space Force. So we're not exactly aliens."

"Nor old-time, just long-lost friends," Gino added.

They were landing in the dusk of that day. Runway and perimeter lights came on. As Zainal lightly lowered the KDM to the paving in the Y that formed the international landing area, the view screen showed them the facade of the main facility. Someone wearing a striped luminescent jacket waggled lighted wands, directing them to turn into the appropriate bay, and Zainal obediently turned the nose of the KDM in that direction. As they approached, everyone in the cockpit could see that many people crammed the windows of the facility and the ground-level doors.

There was no way they could match with an airway but the KDM had an extrudable ramp so one was not needed for the spaceship. As the KDM came to a halt, Sally Stoffers, showing an unexpected humor, gave the usual flight attendant's warning about remaining seated until the seat belt sign went off and being careful about unloading overhead compartments. Her wit sent a ripple of laughter through the cockpit and the tension of landing eased.

"Well done, Zainal, well done," Kathy, Kris, and Gino said, and Chuck clapped Zainal on the shoulder to indicate his approval. Then there was the hollow sound of someone tapping on the hatch.

"Hey, in there. Open up. Don't keep Coord Vitali waiting." "Coord" had to be short for "coordinator," but they pronounced it as one syllable, "kward."

The announcement seemed to be blasted through the hull of the ship. The ground crew, which had originally been one man with the lighted hand paddles, had grown to a sizable crowd. Someone had a bullhorn, on which the "open up" message was being bawled.

"Let's go meet our hosts," Zainal said on the intercom.

"Can we spare some rock squats for the landing crew, Kris?" Chuck asked. "And some to present to Coord Vitali?"

"Bribery or landing fees?"

"I suppose a bit of both," Chuck said. "Good public relations. Latter-day Cattenis arrive bearing gifts. C'mon, kids." He cocked his finger at Peran and Bazil. They unstrapped their seat belts and obeyed. Kris followed, fretting over whether or not there was sufficient unfrozen rock squat to offer. She found Clune and had him bring up some wheat sacks.

"Don't know if these will be useful," she said when they had all congregated in the lock.

"Wheat?" Chuck grinned. "Always."

Zainal punched the open tab on the lock frame and the hatch slipped up while the ramp extended, forcing people to stand back from the port side.

"Hi, y'all," Kris said, wondering how her embarrassed greeting came out in a slightly southern drawl. She smiled broadly and then offered the tray of cold roasted rock squats to the man who had guided them in.

"These are cooked and taste a little like chicken," she said.

The tray was almost ripped out of her hands and passed around, everyone reaching for a section. The tray was empty in seconds.

"Call it a landing fee," she added. "And we have some wheat here, if that's any use."

"All supplies go to a licensed caterer," a stout woman said, charging forward and directing the disposal of the sacks. "Our thanks. And this is good," she added, waving the remains of her portion of the rock squat.

"Did she inhale it?" Kathy muttered to Kris, who shrugged.

Zainal led their mission down the ramp, Chuck close beside him, trying to find a familiar face in the dusky light.

"Yo, here, Chuck." A tall man wearing a baseball cap, a faded Levi's jacket, and oil-stained trousers with frayed cuffs over heavy leather boots stepped forward, waving both arms.

"Hi, Collin. Can we see the coord?"

"Yeah, sure, he's waiting inside."

"Kathy, grab another tray of rock squat, will you? And, Clune and Herb, hoist a coupla sacks of the wheat and flour," Kris ordered to those behind her.

"Can we come, too, Father?" Peran asked, bouncing behind Kris. She let him pass her to stand by Zainal.

"People who come in peace bring kids," she murmured.

By then, Collin was embracing Chuck with great masculine slaps on the back and, in between, broad gestures for the rest of them to come down the ramp. "Botany Boy gets back, huh? Coord Vitali should be here by now," Collin said nervously, resettling his cap on his bristle-cut hair as he motioned for everyone to proceed to the airport building. "He sure was surprised to get a note from Biff."

"Biff?" Zainal and Marrucci asked in surprise.

"Alias for Watch Dog," Collin said with a laugh.

Another man, also capped, strode out of the gaggle of observers to lead the way and hurry people along. Zainal nodded at Gino and Jax to stay behind, on guard, and followed the man, with Chuck and Collin joining the little procession.

They were led upstairs to what Kris identified as a once-elegant VIP lounge, though considerably the worse for wear now, judging by the stains on the upholstery and the general seedy appearance and stale air. Much at his ease in one of the armchairs was the man Kris thought must be this Coord Vitali. As his name suggested, he had an Italianate countenance, swarthy skin, black hair, and a beard barbered close to a strong jawline. He also looked to have been a much stouter person for his clothes, which were of good quality, hung loosely on him and his face was gaunt. But he flashed a genuinely welcoming smile and met Chuck with an outstretched hand, vigorously seizing Chuck's.

"Chuck Mitford, we have all heard of *you*," he said, his tone slightly awed.

"From your Texas colleague, I hope," Chuck said, ignoring, as he usually did, any reference to the legend of his efforts on Botany.

"From him as well. He said you might be paying this part of the Free World a visit."

"And let me introduce the rest of my motley crew," Chuck said, grinning. "Our Catteni friend is Zainal, his two boys, Peran and Bazil; Captain Kathy Harvey, copilot; Kris Bjornsen, Zainal's mate; Gino Marrucci, our radio officer; Lieutenant Mpatane Cummings, flight engineer; and Alexander McColl, one of our pilots; and Clune and Herb, with the wheat sacks on their shoulders. Dr. Eric Sachs, lately of Columbus Circle. Allow us to present a small gift from Botany," Chuck said, taking the tray of roasted rock squats from Kris and presenting it with due ceremony to Coord Vitali. He raised thick brows inquiringly.

"Rock squats, cooked and ready to eat," Chuck said. "We lived on these birds the first few months on Botany. Make good eating."

Between his offering and his words, those in the room who had stood back politely while the big men made their meeting looked eagerly at the tray.

"Don't mind if I do," Vitali said, picking up a half squat and taking a good bite with astonishingly white teeth. "Hmmm, very good. Pass it around," he mumbled as he chewed, his face lighting up with pleasure. "Hey, well, tasty. Nice to have something to sink one's teeth into. Chickens here are scarcer than their teeth."

The contents of this tray also disappeared very quickly, and then Clune and Herb carefully deposited the sacks they had hefted in.

"Some wheat and flour for your supplies," Chuck said. "Gift of the Farmers."

"Hey, don't look like no Trojan horse, do they?" Vitali quipped. "Accepted with thanks. Anyone seen Grace so we can turn the wheat over to Catering Supplies, legal-like?" There was a bustle in the room and someone had obviously made a hurried call because the same woman arrived, this time with her own helpers and, with another curt nod of thanks, gestured for the sacks to be taken off.

"Well, we got some business we need to take care of in Manhattan," Chuck said, perching on the edge of another armchair. "Can you get us there?"

"Ain't a nice place no more," Vitali said, his eyes flickering over the women and the two Catteni boys in the group.

"Being dropped on Botany wasn't any nicer," Kris said as Kathy came to stand by her shoulder, looking equally firm.

"No, I 'spect it wasn't. Please, sit." Dan Vitali gestured for them to seat themselves and pull their chairs closer to him.

"Dr. Sachs here," and Zainal gestured at the dentist, "would like to take possession of his dental chair and the equipment from his office."

"Oh?" Vitali blinked in astonishment. Then comprehension brought a knowing smile to Vitali's face. "Catteni like gold crowns, don't they? Hey, well, Doc, wish you luck. Where was your office in the good ol' days?"

"Columbus Circle."

"You're in luck. Big trading there with the Cardinal Coord in charge," he said, rubbing his jaw thoughtfully. "And we deal with him regular. Repossessing your equipment will be no problem."

Eric blinked, confused, until Dan Vitali gave him a reassuring look. "I can set up the repossession. No problem." Then he cocked a forefinger at Zainal before swinging it to Eric again. "Heard Catteni got into dentistry—replacing their front teeth. Hear tell they don't have dentists on their planet." Then Vitali tensed, his jaw dropped and he stared at Eric. "You going to Catten to set up your practice? Brave man." Then comprehension brought a sly gleam to Vitali's face.

"Well, actually," Eric stumbled and turned to Zainal again.

So Zainal, speaking in a low tone for Vitali's ears only, explained about Barevi and his assignment. As soon as he mentioned the comm satellites, Dan Vitali held up his hand.

"Wendell's the one you need to talk to about comm sats," he said, and waved a man forward. "John Wendell, Chuck Mitford and friends," he added, smiling at Kris, Kathy, and Zainal's sons. "John keeps my phone system working," he said by way of explanation. John acknowledged the introduction as he came forward, rock squat bones in his hand. He was a wiry man, in the Levi's that seemed almost a uniform. He also wore a broad belt from which depended pouches and on which were fixed special loops. Visible as a mound under his Levi's jacket was a mobile phone. He wore a baseball cap decorated with a Motorola M logo.

One of Vitali's cohorts passed around cups of coffee, thanking them quietly for the food. Instant coffee, Kris could tell the moment she had a mouthful, but it was welcome. She wondered if coffee figured in bartering at Columbus Circle. She remembered photos of that New York landmark with artists' sketches and paintings propped up against the Circle's balustrade.

"And you hope to trade dentistry, gold crowns, for spare parts?" Vitali asked.

"We have other things that may be tradable," Zainal said cautiously.

"You're going to need a lot if you're trying to ransom all the loot the Cats took . . . no offense, Zainal." The coord nodded courteously. "They got just about anything portable. We could restart some industries for the most urgent stuff but we haven't got ores. Mines are in production but it's slow, and we're just beginning to have coal for them. What you got handy 'sides wheat—which we appreciate, I assure you—that can pay for the gasoline and men to get you safely to Columbus Circle and back?"

Zainal was slightly taken aback by the query but, recovering, gave his broad shoulders a little twitch of acceptance. "Should have brought a lot more rock squats." He glanced apologetically at Kris. "We have some small quantities of ore. What had you in mind?" Zainal asked, his expression bland.

"We can use just about anything: copper, tin, lead, zinc, iron, right here in New Jersey, Zainal. Whatcha got?"

"Gold?"

"If that's all you got." Vitali's reluctance to accept the former standard was an interesting insight into the current economy.

"Could manage some copper and tin, I think," Zainal finally admitted. "How much?"

"Pure ore? Or recycled?"

"Some pure ingots mined on Botany."

"Well, in that case," and Vitali slapped his knees with flat hands, "I think we can do a trade."

"How much?" Zainal repeated. "We didn't think we'd need ores here."

"Here, there, and everywhere. We have some mines open, specially for coal," Vitali went on, "but it's transporting it to where it can be worked is the problem."

"They say they're going back to sail, Coord," one of his minions remarked with the smirk of a mechanically oriented man for such a primitive alternative.

"Don't knock sails, Binjy," Vitali said amiably. "It did Columbus okay."

"Yeah, Coord, yah. Guess it started the whole shebang."

"However they get it to Detroit and other places ain't our problem. Getting things started again is. We ain't got tires, batteries, spark plugs, windshield wipers. You know, the stuff we used to take for granted." Vitali waved one hand in frustration. "Some stuff doesn't require much ore but—"

"How much . . . in pounds, Vitali?"

"Pounds? Well, I'd say ten pounds would be the least I'd be able to accept for the loss of the irreplaceable supplies it'll take to get you all the way to Columbus Circle." He glanced down at the note on his pad.

"Eric has to go here, to get supplies," Zainal said, offering the exact address.

"Oooh," murmured Vitali but he didn't seem too put out.

"Subways don't run anymore?" Kathy asked sharply. "Thought they were working on mass transportation as a top priority."

Vitali flung his head up, regarding her with something close to pity. "D'you know how much it costs to run a subway, girl? Even if we had diesel fuel?"

"No, sir, I don't, but we've all been sort of out of touch with what's been happening recently on Earth."

"We do get electricity on at least part of every day, to do water pumps and lights in hospitals 'n' essential things like that. Ain't got no time for fripperies that we used to consider rightful."

"Five pounds each of copper and lead settle our account with you, Vitali?"

Vitali drew in a long breath, regarding Zainal and rubbing his hands on his worn Levi's. "Well, I think it might. Can probably trade them to someone for something. You're sure it's pure?"

"Smelted on Botany, never felt a pick or shovel before we came."

"Hmmm, pure stuff's worth a lot more."

"Indeed it should be," Zainal agreed amiably. "And that covers our expedition to Columbus Circle? And our second stop at West Thirteenth Street before we come back to the KDM? Deal?" Zainal held out his hand, hoping to conclude the bargain.

To his surprise, Vitali closed the deal with a shake. "This'll help more than you know. We're out of everything." He waved his hands around his head in frustration. "You bring us a load of tires back and you can name your price."

"I saw sheds full of tires and battery boxes," Chuck said. "All on Barevi."

"All looted from us, too," Vitali said, scowling. "I'll take anything off your hands you can get . . . for anything you ask for . . . that we might still have. It's raw materials we need right now, to get industry started."

"We'll keep your wish list in mind," Kris said with a courteous nod. "Our main objective is to get spare parts and repair the comm sats."

"Speaking of which, Mr. Wendell," Kathy began, and that man looked around him as if he didn't realize she could mean him. "Are you familiar with the Boeing arrays?"

"Sort of. Why?"

"We have one on board the KDM—"

"You what?" John Wendell's eyes went wide with astonishment.

"Zainal netted it, neat as you please. But I'd appreciate a professional survey of how best to repair it."

"Antennae and solar panels gone, I'll bet, sight unseen."

"Yes, exactly."

He motioned Kathy to one side and the pair engaged in a spirited conversation with many gestures on Wendell's part while Kathy listened, Kris thought, with far less reserve than she usually showed. Wendell was a personable-looking man and obviously well versed in his specialty. At least, Kathy looked impressed.

"Keeps us in contact real good," Vitali said approvingly. "Now, you guys want to go into Manhattan and grab the doc's stuff, right? It's essential to this operation of yours on Barevi, right? Aside from the issues of wear, tear, and personnel, what sort of a vehicle had you in mind?"

"Any sort of truck will do. Pickup, if you have one."

Vitali gave a little snort. "Even one with good tires. You're in luck. So that's the transport and you'll need a guide and some guards, unless you have weapons." He cast a wary glance at Zainal. "And I don't mean those nerve whips either, Catteni."

"We will need your guides, and your guards for we have no weapons, but we're not defenseless," Zainal replied, as he held up his big hand and made a sizable fist.

Vitali cleared his throat.

"We have more wheat, if that can be tossed in to sweeten the pot," Kris offered.

"That's a sure enough sweetener, little lady, being as it will feed everyone, and a full stomach makes people easier to live with. Okay, Zainal, you got a deal, a truck, guide, and guard and my safe conduct for you tomorrow. Night's not a good time for going through the tunnel anyway, to mention only one hazard."

"The Lincoln Tunnel?" Kris exclaimed.

"Yes, ma'am, that and the Holland are the only ways to get to the island. No fuel for ferries, though they may start commandeering pleasure boats soon," Vitali said in the greatest of good humor. "We'd be pleased for you to join us for a meal here."

"We wouldn't want to deprive you," Kris said, having seen the dismay on several faces when Vitali made his offer. "We have enough rations on board and we wouldn't want to tap more of your resources than absolutely necessary." Particularly, she thought to herself, if it takes more of our raw ores.

"You'll sleep on board then?" Vitali asked, beaming appreciatively.

"Yes, and be ready to move out whenever you have made the arrangements. We do need to replenish our water tanks."

"Water's still available—and guaranteed," Vitali said. "I'll have to check with the coords involved, as a matter of courtesy and for your security, but I can set up the transport personally," he said, so convincingly that Zainal nodded.

"If you've someone to take charge of the metal ingots, we can unload them tonight," Zainal said, showing goodwill.

"Our pleasure, I assure you," Vitali said. Then he gathered several of his officers around him and gave quick, low, confident orders. The men left to obey them.

Coffee and business finished, Zainal stood, ready to make delivery of the ingots, however much he may have wanted to hold such commodities back to trade on Barevi. Kathy asked to bring John Wendell on board to look at the comm sat, which Zainal thought a good idea.

"Fine-looking lads, Zainal. They yours?" Vitali asked, rising to his feet.

Zainal nodded and introduced his sons. Peran and Bazil made courteous bows and offered limp hands to the coord, who smiled benignly at them.

"Got one about the same age," Vitali said. "If you've got two on board for the trip, I've another I can lend you: my grandson. For the good of our relationship, of course."

"If we were returning directly to Botany, that would be a possibility, Coord Vitali, but we go on to Barevi, and that is not a place I would suggest a young Terran visit right now. My sons travel with us for tutoring there." Peran and Bazil regarded their father with such shock that Vitali grinned.

"I see." There was regret in Coord Vitali's voice but he concluded the visit with a firm handshake, and the two groups separated.

"A tutor, Father?" Peran began as they started back down the stairs to the ground level.

"A tutor, Peran," Zainal said so firmly that the boys bowed their heads in rueful acceptance.

"Oh, and Zainal, have no worries about your ship's safety while here on the ground," Vitali said, pausing in the doorway of the VIP suite. "We have an excellent perimeter security. Sleep well and soundly."

"We're obliged," Zainal said, winking at Chuck, who grinned back. There was no real chance that anyone could break into the KDM. She had good external security devices, too.

5

Once outside, a truck kept pace with them. As they neared the ship, Zainal opened the ship's comm unit to alert Gino of their return. The ramp was extended and Gino and the rest of the crew framed the open hatch as they watched the return of their crewmen. Kris noticed the pessimism on Zainal's face as he cycled the cargo holds to the one containing their metal ingots. He must have been wishing he hadn't said anything about having ores, but she felt paying for a convoy to safely acquire Eric's equipment was worth the swap. Botany did not produce much ore but the deposits were high quality. At least she thought the miners would object less to losing copper, zinc, tin, and lead even though in some instances those ores were far more useful than gold, silver, or platinum. Nevertheless, she could see how it pained Zainal to hand over the ingots and how eagerly Vitali's men received them.

Kris did not seek her bed yet. She was still absorbing the import of their interview with Vitali and other, less obvious information that she had gathered. Earth's victory was a hollow one, despite evidence of recovery. The rock squats had been worth their weight in any metal, and while they still had a few trays to spare, fresh bread might be useful to have on hand for goodwill and any unexpected "fees."

She hauled another sack of flour out of the supply locker and mixed up a triple batch of bread dough. It could rise overnight, have another quick rise as rolls, which would be easier to distribute than loaves, and be ready for their journey.

Kathy was still in heavy conference with John Wendell, who was almost drooling over the comm sat in the cargo hold. She was listening avidly to his remarks, jotting down notes and looking all too bright-eyed, Kris thought, and not the least bit reserved.

Kris was grateful to fall asleep once she hit her bunk, and answered Zainal's sleepily muttered "Who's there?" with a kiss, which sent him back to sleep with a smile on his face. She hated to be roused by the alarm the next morning but rose and flicked it off before the noise woke him. It was fair. He often let her have an extra half hour. In the galley, she started the big oven and punched down the dough, deftly separating it into convenient rolls before she made the morning's breakfast of boiled groats. She wondered if it would be hard to find cinnamon and maybe raisins somewhere in Manhattan. She had often longed for a Danish at breakfast.

It was the smell of baking bread that got folk out of their beds before the official Klaxon sounded.

Everyone was dressed and ready when the security sensors beeped a proximity alert. Chuck greeted those who arrived in a battered pickup truck. He eyed the load bed but it looked long enough to hold Eric's equipment. He also tossed in a coil of rope on top of the two lift platforms, which he and Clune carefully loaded, ignoring questions from the curious guards.

The truck had a wide front seat, which Zainal and Kris took. She was seated next to the driver, careful to keep her backpack full of rolls from being crushed against the battered dashboard. She was aware that the driver's pistol dug into her left hip and eased her buttocks slightly to the right. The smell of freshly baked bread vied with the smells of oil, diesel fuel, and unwashed bodies. As surreptitiously as possible, she held the pack closer to her nose. Then a final passenger wedging himself next to Zainal slammed her back into the driver's holster. The door was closed only because someone outside the truck gave it a good push.

"Sorry about the squeeze," the latecomer said, "but I'm Jelco, your official guide on this tour of New Manhattan." He nodded amiably at Zainal and Kris. "Driver's Murray. He don't talk much but he's a good driver. We were lucky to get him for this job. I believe he claims he knows every hole in every avenue and street in the city."

Courteously Kris nodded to her left and was startled by a toothless grin. She wondered if he knew he was driving a dentist to his old office. She also wondered if he could enjoy the nice crunchy bread they had in their backpacks. Murray hadn't so much as glanced at the backpack she held in her lap but he must have smelled the bread because his nostrils flared every now and then and he had to lick his lips frequently. Salivating, possibly. The smell of fresh bread had its own magic.

"Dover and Wylee are our guards, case you wanted to know. Good men."

Which was what Kris hoped they would prove to be. "We'll have Kejas and Potts through the tunnel. They're actually the Midtown Coords men this week. They wear red bands." He pointed to the kelly green one on his upper arm. "We do a week on, a week off tunnel duty."

Zainal nodded.

There were very few people around as Murray drove slowly out of Newark Airport, its vast parking lots empty, except for a few burned-out autos. Then Murray pulled out onto a three-lane highway. Along the weedy verge of the highway, damaged bushes and trees were showing growth with new sprouts, and the occasional forsythia had some blooms. Shortly they turned again, off the turnpike onto the approach to the Lincoln Tunnel. Signs had been torn down but the wide highway, though pocked with gravel-filled holes, was empty except for their pickup and a cart full of what looked like potato sacks to Kris, laboriously drawn by two raggedly dressed men. The wheels were not pneumatic but wooden, rimmed by metal, and the axle squealed for lack of lubrication. Three small boys, walking behind the cart, eyed the truck. From the dirt on their faces, Kris wondered if they had dug the potatoes that were in the cart.

The New Jersey entrance to the Lincoln Tunnel had never been a prime residential area in its heyday and certainly looked wartorn now, the high sidewalls full of pockmarks. Other types of debris, probably from fighting to protect the tunnel approach, had been pushed to one side, leaving two lanes of the once six-lane approach clear, one on either side of the dividing parapet.

"Heavy fighting?" she asked, unnerved by the desolation, and needing to talk.

Murray nodded. "Only good midtown access to the island, ma'am, and had to be defended."

To the last man? she wondered.

"Hmmm, well done," she said, noncommittally. And then the road on the left was free of the bombed buildings. This road had always provided a breathtaking view of New York City, as it swept around in a long right-hand curve to the tollbooths and the actual tunnel faces. But the view of New York was vastly changed from her recollection of it. It was as if all the buildings had somehow been blunted. Oh, the Chrysler and the Empire State buildings were still standing, but others, including the Radio City complex, looked as if they'd been sliced off. The once proud city had gaps in its fabled silhouette. They traveled down toward the huge entrance plaza, swinging past tollbooths that had been shattered into rubble. Pieces of burned-out vehicles had, as on the approach roads, been pushed to the sides but gave mute testimony to the fierceness of attack and defense.

"And to think I once griped about waiting in the lines," Jelco remarked. Then armed men appeared from a galvanized shed, tucked under the shadow of the eastbound tunnel entrance. Murray slowed to a stop and turned off the engine, reaching for a sheaf of papers that had been tucked behind the eyeshade. Jelco swung down from the truck's cab and strode to the approaching guards, whose weapons were slung over their shoulders. Jelco had a slip of paper in his hand that Kris thought was decorated with seals and kelly green ribbons. Jelco had an earnest conversation with a guard, showing him the paper, while a dour man who reeked of sweat was thumbing through Murray's papers. The breeze was, unfortunately, coming across him and into the truck cab. Evidently soap and deodorant were no longer available.

"Would you like some fresh rolls?" Kris asked nervously and held one up for the man to see. She thought for a moment that the rest of his squad would rush the truck but the man with Jelco issued a sharp order and they moderated to a swift walk. She handed Murray the rolls to pass around and noticed that he dropped one into his own lap, though how he would manage without teeth, she didn't know. He simply tore a piece off the roll and popped it into his mouth, his eyes widening with appreciation at the taste.

"Thanks, miss," said the first guard, tipping his fingers in a salute. He passed rolls out to the rest of his unit.

"Klaus?" he yelled, attracting his leader's attention, and lofted a roll, which Klaus neatly hooked out of the air. "Sorry, ma'am, but a search is required. Becky, front and center," he yelled over his shoulder, and a woman soldier quickly advanced.

Kris had never been frisked before but, considering what she had seen of the tunnel's environs, she had no intention of protesting such a security measure. Klaus gestured for Zainal to step out so he could be checked over, too.

"She's clean," Becky said after a fairly cursory feel of Kris's arms and legs, back and waist. Kris offered her a roll. "Thank you. Ain't had fresh-baked bread in ages." She bit into it with an almost savage gusto and chewed vigorously, nodding her approval. In all, a dozen rolls had been passed out before Kris was waved back into the truck. She was glad she'd made the offer, judging by the happy expressions on the tunnel guards' faces and the appreciative thumbs-up gestures as the truck was allowed to roll into the eastbound tube.

"I'm Wylee," said a small man who came back to the truck with Jelco. "Tunnel squad. Just wanted to reassure you that the fans have been circulating the bad air out. You got anyone in your group who's asthmatic or has respiratory problems?" He looked at Kris as he spoke, trying to ignore Zainal's solid Catteni form.

"None I know of."

"Well, the air in the middle of the tunnel ain't exactly one hundred percent unpolluted, ma'am. Anybody has any problem, call me, huh? We got respirators." He motioned to the backpack he was wearing. His expression suggested that he didn't want to use them unless he absolutely had to. Oxygen was still free, wasn't it? Kris thought, feeling almost rebellious. She did not really know what those left on Earth had had to face so she swallowed the smart rejoinder. She felt the tilt of the truck as those in the back hauled up Wylee.

As Murray was waved to proceed into the left-hand tunnel, she had more to concern her. She wasn't claustrophobic but she really didn't like the idea of all the water over her head, and looked at the cream-tiled walls of the tunnel to see any signs of lack of maintenance. She didn't know what to look for—but cracks or moisture staining the walls would be obvious signs. Yet if this was one of the only accesses to New York City from the mainland, it would behoove them to keep it in good repair.

She was somewhat surprised to see a huge Dumpster at the entrance and noticed that there were bits of cement and odd pieces of metal jutting from it. Then the truck swerved to the right and she saw the burned-out chassis of a car on the left. This was not the last wreck she was to see in the tunnel. Few had been burned out but all had been stripped down to the chassis.

"Recycling," Murray said around a mouthful of his roll.

"We'll get the junk out of the tunnel one of these years," Jelco said cheerfully. "And sometimes, when we have a group coming through, we get them to hump a chassis out for us."

When they were out of sight of the tunnel entrance she saw that the raised walkway along the inner side of the tunnel had been damaged, though most of the cement and tiles had been cleaned away from the break.

"That's as far in as the invaders got," Jelco said, pointing to where the damage ended with a hint of pride. "But then," and he cast a quick glance at Zainal, "Catteni don't like being underground, do they?"

There was a look on his face that suggested he'd hoped to see Zainal react.

"True enough," Zainal said with complete composure. "You did well to fight off Catteni soldiers. No other species has been able to."

"So I heard," Jelco replied amiably.

That exchange seemed to please both participants and the rest of the journey, past other cars stripped to the bare bones of their chassis, passed without remarks. Kris had to keep reminding herself that Wylee had said the air had been circulated so she must be imagining the stink, but the stench of gasoline, oil, and burned tires was heavy enough to keep her taking shallow breaths to keep her lungs as uncontaminated as possible by the stale air. Shipboard air got to smell stale, too, but this tunnel was rank with ancient odors.

"Nearly there, ma'am," Jelco murmured reassuringly. She was undeniably relieved to see more light on the tunnel tiles.

She smiled, turning her head in an almost regal nod in his direction. She would be glad to fill her lungs with clean air again. Then the truck drove up out of the tunnel. Debris from the old Port Authority Building was tumbled around the exit; she inhaled and wished she hadn't for there was a stench of rot and garbage that almost made the tunnel's air seem sweet. Two huge Dumpsters were on either side of the exit, filled almost to capacity with debris that had been cleared from the tunnel. Maybe they should have used the lifts and brought out more, like one of the car bodies. But Zainal had mentioned that the floats had only so much power in their batteries and he had no spares to replace them with.

Then they had to go through a second security check, and Kris passed out the rest of the rolls she had in her backpack. Again the identity papers were shown, and Wylee swung out of the truck and went to confer with the squad leaders, beaming as he passed out the rolls to grateful Manhattan recipients.

"Green for go," he said, coming to the window. "Roll away, Murray." He added a grandiose gesture for the driver. Murray grinned, crumbs of the roll he had eaten visible on his gums, and shifted into first gear, ignoring the complaints from the transmission. She hoped the truck would last to bring the heavy dental equipment back.

The truck rolled up the curved road at Forty-first and onto Tenth Avenue.

"I can detour up Broadway so you can see Times Square," Murray offered. "Won't take much gas."

"I think not, thank you, Murray," Kris responded. She had seen that landmark once when her family had come east for a wedding, and she vaguely remembered the place for the cigarette smoke billboard and the colored lights on in the middle of the day, but she didn't think she could stand seeing it in ruins. Likewise she didn't want Zainal to see it at less than its best either.

Tenth Avenue was really a minefield of potholes, through which Murray drove carefully. It had never been one of New York's finest neighborhoods and looked even grimmer now. Especially when she saw the remains of a huge spit that had been erected over one of the potholes, still black from the fire that had been laid in it. A pile of utterly unfamiliar, and large, bones occupied one corner. And the street sign pole sported a huge skull. She couldn't imagine from what animal it had come.

"Had us quite a party that night," Murray said, grinning at her. "Rhinoceros, wasn't it, Jelco?"

Jelco nodded, a slight smile of happy reminiscence on his face.

"Rhinoceros?" Kris couldn't help blurting out the word. "A rather large African beast. How on earth . . ." She looked across Zainal at Jelco for an explanation.

"Well, we couldn't feed the zoo animals," he said with a wry grin, "so they fed us."

"Oh!"

"Miss going to the zoo on a Sunday, though," Murray said. "But we had enough to eat for everyone. Tough to chew, even if you had teeth." He gave her another grin. "But we had soup for a week afterwards from the bones. One day, maybe, we can erect a monument on the spot. Sort of thanks for the best meal many of us had had in weeks."

"They were humanely put down, ma'am," Jelco added. "Better than all of us starving to death—and them, too."

"Yes, yes, I quite see the expediency," she murmured.

She was silent as she counted the streets on their way to Columbus. There were one or two street signs still in place—no more with skull adornment—and then the buildings turned from residences, if you could call the old shambles "residences," to the beginning of office-type buildings. By then she realized that very few, except upper stories, retained any glass panes in their windows. Many of the walls and entrances showed the pockmarks of bullets, and not a few entrances had no doors at all.

She hadn't seen many people about, but as they neared the Circle she saw folk hurrying in both directions, some carrying armloads or hauling the little wheeled carts as quickly as possible toward the Circle.

The Circle itself surprised her—no longer the place of artistic display but filled with carts and rudely made stalls, some with awnings to keep the sun and rain from whatever merchandise was on offer. She saw additional carts like the potato one.

"We got a bizarre every day now," Wylee said, and Kris blinked at his mispronunciation because the place was indeed bizarre. Not only were there ardent traders making bargains but also swarms of men armed with weapons slung to be brought to bear quickly. They wore brilliant red armbands and berets with some sort of an insignia on them.

"We're in the Cardinal Coord now," Jelco informed her, touching his own kelly green armband. "They keep the peace."

"Peace?" Kris blurted out, astounded.

"You've no idea how hot under the collar people can get when they lose a deal," Jelco said. "Newark runs its own bazaar Saturday and Sunday at the airport. No one really likes the duty but every now and then we get a chance at something fresh and tasty."

"Like the rolls?" Kris asked.

"Those were elegant, ma'am," he said earnestly. "D'you have more?" he asked hesitantly.

"It'll smooth our way here in the Cardinal Coord?" she asked.

"Yes indeedy, ma'am. You've no idea."

Possibly, she thought to herself, she didn't. But then, she'd had the reality of Barevi and Botany to open her eyes. Idly she thought of goru pears and how juicy they had tasted during her days of refuge in the forests of Barevi. And she thought she'd been deprived there! She wondered how much she could get trading fresh goru pears at this bazaar.

The truck was swinging around the Circle in the appropriate traffic pattern before Murray drove it up onto the wide concrete apron fronting Eric's office building, which dominated its arc of the Circle. Immediately Jelco swung out of the truck as guards from the entrance to the building came forward to protest illegal parking.

Jelco beckoned urgently at Kris, and she called for someone to bring out a fresh supply of rolls. It was Eric who hurried forward, the straps of his backpack looped over his forearm and a roll in his hand as evidence of the treat. The pack was quickly emptied and then Eric was fumbling in his pockets, producing his license and a business card, which were passed around to verify his bona fides. Several of the guards kept curious people moving along, and it was evident why Dan Vitali had said they'd need guards.

However, Eric was approved and he waved for Zainal, Kris, and the others to join him. If folks eyed Zainal warily, he was in the midst of armed men they patently trusted so they ignored a single Catteni.

"You're in luck," the head guard was saying as they approached, Dover and Wylee unloading the awkward-looking lift platforms. "We got electricity for another half hour."

"You mean the elevator's working?" Eric exclaimed, staring around at their party, his eyes bright with relief.

"Yup. The weekly dispensation. You guys got good timing," the guard said, taking another bite from his roll and urging them into the foyer.

This was evidently a prime location to judge by the sophisticated stalls set about. "Outta the way. Official business." He had cleared customers away from the stalls to the voluble complaints of the merchants. Then they were at the elevator banks and with a flourish the guard punched the button. The light in the cracked display above the door came on. The elevator had been called.

Kris was not so sure about the noise that was coming from the shaft but she had not thought about having to walk up eighteen flights of stairs, much less coming back down.

"Both ways?" Eric asked.

"Only if you ain't got no more weight than you took up," the guard informed him. "Thing's ancient and stubborn. Has a tendency to get cranky and stop between floors. Passengers get to wait hours."

Eric sighed. "It would have been a squeeze with my units," he said diffidently and was happy enough to step into the car, watching Jelco and Dover as they cautiously entered with the upright lift platforms.

The door creaked shut, and after Eric had punched the floor button with an air of importance, an alarming amount of chain rattling, hissing, and bucking ensued until the elevator began to ascend. Kris's eye caught on the inspection card that most elevators displayed. This was an Otis, which she knew to be a reliable make, and a hastily penned notation informed that it had last been inspected on July 2, 1992.

For the life of her, Kris couldn't remember what date this day should be. The weather had been warm but the forsythia bloom she had seen suggested early spring. Time seemed to have stopped . . . at least recordable time. It had been so for so long that she endured one day at a time and was thankful to live through each one, week after week as they added up to months and then years, but she couldn't have said what day, week, month, or year—Anno Domini—she was currently living in. Nor did she wish to embarrass herself by asking. Anyway, Botany time was different from Earth time.

The elevator lurched to a stop, terminating Kris's anxiety about getting stuck between floors. The elevator had not only ascended but also had stopped at the desired destination. There, as proof, on the wall opposite were the figures, gold, framed in black, that identified the eighteenth floor. Eric stepped out first, the others following quickly on his heels as he led the way to the right. Office doors on either side of the dark corridor were ajar, which lit their way, but also showed them that few offices had escaped pilfering. Mostly chairs had been taken though Kris rather thought some of the stalls in the foyer had once been tables in the upper levels. Torn curtains flapped in whatever breeze whined around the eighteenth floor.

Eric let out several startled exclamations. He did not need the keys he had brought with him, for his outer door, too, had been forced open. But as he charged forward into the inner office, he let out a cry of relief as he spotted his dental chair and the tower, which held the drill apparatus. Relief changed to mild expletives as he saw that the drawers of his accessory cupboards were pulled out.

"They only looked and saw nothing they could use," he cried after a closer examination.

"Now, where's your electrical supply? Like the man said, it's on and I don't want to electrocute anyone, especially me," Herb Bayes said, lumbering forward.

Eric showed him both the panels and then where he would have to disconnect the tower and the chair, which could be adjusted by the dentist as needed. Kris remembered such a unit, with its foot controls, from visits to her own dentist. They had to pull up the carpet and unloosen the bolts that held the two pieces to the floor.

"If you'd help me, Kris," Eric said, "I have more in my workroom." He pushed open the door to a small anteroom with worktops and drawers in wall cabinets, many of which had been opened. As he examined one cabinet, he exclaimed again in relief. "Enough jaw trays, I think, and some of them must fit Catteni-size maws," he was muttering to himself. He opened a wall cabinet and hauled out some paper shopping bags with the Saks Fifth Avenue logo on them as well as some bubble wrap. "Here, help me package these things, Kris. And I've more in the storeroom—I hope." He pulled out the drawers he wanted her to empty and then disappeared into a closet. "Good, good," he said, pulling some of the bubble wrap nearer so he could wrap mortars, pestles, and other items for which she had no names.

"Now, if only Eddie Spivak has anything left, we'll be in business even in benighted Barevi. You don't know how lucky I feel right now, Kris," Eric said, almost crowing with success.

"One for our side, Eric," she said encouragingly.

By the time they returned to the main office, the men had finished disconnecting the dental chair and had the lift tilted up to take its burden. Zainal was explaining the controls of the apparatus, embedded in one long side of the platform. They secured the chair with the rope that Jelco had tossed into the truck.

"Hey, don't use it all on this," Eric exclaimed. "The drill rig is more important than the chair."

"Whyn't you say so?" Bayes retorted huffily, tugging at a knot to be sure it was firm.

"See if you can find something else to tie it down with, Kris," Eric said, waving his hand toward the corridor.

Kris went out, as much to escape the tension in the room as to be useful. She hadn't a clue where to find more rope—someone would have found such a prize long before they arrived. But she did find some dusty draperies of a heavy fabric, and wondering that they had been left untouched, she hauled three pairs down. It must have been an attorney's office, to judge by the bindings on the books on the shelves. It was almost a travesty to have to use the draperies but once back in Eric's office, she asked him for something sharp to cut with and he provided her with a knife. She didn't ask what it was originally intended for, but with it she managed to tear the fabric into strips, which she then connected into a rope of sorts. She had yards of it, ready in time for the tower to be secured to its platform. Several of Eric's wrapped bundles were secured by adhesive tape (which he had also found a quantity of in his stores) to the empty spaces on the lift. They added a scatter of text- and reference books, nurses'uniforms, and some aprons. There were still more parcels for herself and Eric to carry. Zainal took several from those at her feet and then they felt ready to make the long descent.

The men, with Zainal showing them how to guide their cumbersome bundles, maneuvered into the corridor and toward the stairwell. Fortunately the powered units were easy to manipulate though the first landing on the way down took some angling, but once they found the trick to it, they proceeded at a fair pace down the stairs. Without the lifts they never would have managed. Even so, by the time they reached the last landing, everyone was sweating and winded, even Zainal. Kris leaned heavily into the final stair post, struggling to slow her heartbeat and pulse.

"Not as fit as I thought I was," Eric admitted, wiping his sweating forehead on his sleeve. "You guys have been splendid," he said, beaming at the team.

"Yeah, yeah," Dover said in a caustic tone.

"Free dentistry for your entire family?" Eric asked.

"If you got to start here, you'd never finish, Doc," Dover remarked, "but kind of you to offer." His tone was nearly sarcastic but he caught the look Jelco gave him and nodded his head.

Their reappearance, not to mention their odd cargo, caused a complete silence in the foyer as they reached the ground floor. A few nasty looks were cast in Zainal's direction, but he ignored them. The silence continued as everyone watched the levitated heavy equipment float to the front doors. These were glassless but Dover pushed the frames open, hauling the front of his lift with him.

"Hey, what'll you take for one of those things?" a bearded man asked, pulling at Eric's sleeve.

"No one has that much money," Eric replied.

"I wouldn't insult you by offering you money, man," was the retort.

"That's enough, Mac," the Cardinal head guard said, moving swiftly between the two men. Kris idly wondered what the man would have offered as she followed the others out of the foyer. The fresh breeze cooled her face and smelled of newly mown grass and other, less salubrious odors.

"What's in there?" the guard asked, pointing to the Saks carriers.

"Oh, there was a sale on," she said whimsically and deposited them in the truck bed on one side of the dental chair. Her wrists and arms ached from lugging the oddments down so many flights. If they hadn't had the floats, how would they have managed? With great relief, she hauled herself back into the front seat and reached for the bottle of water that she had seen earlier. She was parched. She handed it to Zainal when he slid in beside her. Murray pulled another container from the door pocket on his side and took a long swig before a whistle reminded him that a guard was clearing the sidewalk and street so they could depart.

"Where to now?" Murray asked.

"One-thirteen East Thirteenth Street," Jelco said, consulting his notepad. "Eddie Spivak's Dental Supplies."

"A snap," Murray said. "We can go right down Ninth, or would you prefer Broadway or even Fifth?"

"Most direct route, Murray. We gotta conserve gasoline, y'know," Jelco said repressively.

"Gotcher!"

"Murray, is Macy's still there?" Kris asked softly.

"Yeah, but it still don't talk to Gimbels, which ain't," and he bestowed another of his frightening toothless grins on her, reminiscent of Popeye.

"Oh!"

There was more traffic on the street now—most of it handcarts, many of them heaped with clothing and rolls of fabric. Kris remembered Floss and wondered what she had to trade for some blue cloth. As they passed a cart, she saw the blue had a huge stain down the middle of the bolt and she shrugged the incident aside.

They turned left on Fourteenth to Second Avenue and then turned right, and Kris noticed there seemed to be few vehicles. Maybe one-way streets were no longer required as traffic controls. She didn't remember this area at all, if she'd ever been in it. There were three- and four-story houses, all made into tenements to judge by the fire escapes, interspersed with concrete-block buildings that would house family-owned businesses of some sort. There were two cafes: she could see people at the counters eating whatever it was, and drinking. Coffee? She licked her lips. A cuppa would taste nice right now. Give her some energy. She was beginning to sag with fatigue. She wondered how the rolls were holding up and if there were enough to "do lunch" for everyone. They still had two trays of rock squats.

"One hunnert and t'oiteen," Murray said with some pride, pointing to a three-story building that had a storefront clearly marked EDDIE SPIVAK, DENTAL SUPPLIER.

Eric sighed with relief. Some of the ground-level stores on both sides of the street looked empty from looting. Eddie Spivak's windows boasted iron grills and there was a pull-up aluminum shutter across the front, a certain deterrent to pilfering. Murray pulled over to the side and instantly people's heads popped out of the upper-story windows.

"Neighbors!" he said with some disgust as he turned off the motor. "So?"

Eric had already vaulted out of the truck back and was running down the narrow walk between Eddie's and number 115. He pounded on the door.

"Eddie? Eddie Spivak? It's Eric, Eric Sachs. Are you there? Open up! Is he home?" Eric craned his neck up, looking through the iron slats of the fire escape at the observers. "I'm a dentist. An old customer of Eddie's. Where is he?"

"He's in. Leastwise," an old woman cried in answer, "ain't seen him or his missus today," she added warily.

"EDDIE!" Eric put his hands to his mouth to shout. "IT'S ERIC

SACHS!" He rattled the doorknob and then stopped, peering through the grill on the small window set in the door, trying to see inside.

Suddenly the door was pulled in and an old man stood in the doorway, staring at what to him was evidently an apparition. He had a scalpel in his raised hand that he immediately lowered after recognizing his visitor.

"Dr. Sachs!" The man came forward, embracing Eric enthusiastically. "I can't believe my eyes and ears. It's been years! Where did you go to?"

"Long story," Eric said, "but do you still have any supplies? I'm setting up my office in a new location and I need a few things . . . if you have them."

"Who'd rob a shop like mine?" Eddie said, shrugging. Then he saw the truck and its load. "You really are moving, aren't you? Sudden?"

"Sudden," Eric said, grinning as Kris and Jelco joined them, Zainal following more slowly. "These are my friends Kris Bjornsen and Jelco. And Zainal behind them is also."

"What's a Greenie doing on this side of the Hudson?" Eddie asked, suddenly half-closing the door as if he feared Jelco might barge into his premises.

"Escorting us. We had to work through coord channels, you might say," Eric said with a dismissive flick of his hand.

"Haven't done much business," Eddie said in a gloomy tone. "Who has time for dentistry when the world has gone to pot?"

"I do," Eric said. "How's Suzie? The grandkids?"

"Suzie's been ill, and I don't know where my son, the lazy wretch, has got to." Evidently the shortcomings of his son was an old topic of conversation between them, but Eddie stepped back and gestured politely for Eric to enter.

Kris, a spare pack with more than a dozen rolls in it looped over her arm, followed. There was an acrid smell in the air, similar to the one in Eric's small laboratory. Every profession has a special kind of odor attached to it, she thought.

However, nothing was wrong with Eddie's olfactory senses because he sniffed, probably catching the odor of the rolls.

"I need some porcelains. Some of the good Liechtenstein ones," Eric said. "The darker shades, if you still have any."

Eddie gave a shrug. "Darker shades aren't that much in demand. Come."

He beckoned them farther in and flipped at a wall switch. Lights came on.

"Well! Whaddya know. Lights. Lights, Suzie. She's been doing some knitting, you see. Someone supplies the wool, she supplies the hands," he said, again shrugging off such a necessity. "No one teaches girls housewifely arts anymore, you know."

The lights showed a small foyer with two stools and a countertop. Eddie lifted the edge of the section near the wall and walked back into an area where he stored his wares.

"Good to have light. You'll be able to see the Vitapan shade chart." He rooted under the counter for a moment and then handed Eric a piece of cardboard with what looked to Kris like teeth inserted around the edges. Eric immediately started examining it, glancing from time to time at Zainal. Then, as if recalling himself to the task at hand, Eric pulled a piece of paper out of his shirt pocket.

"I gotta list of other things I'll need. Jaw trays. Sizes one and two, mandibular—oh, twenty-one through twenty-four."

Eddie gave a little guffaw. "Whom are you doing dentures for? Neanderthal man? Don't know if I have any jaw trays *those* sizes. But maybe I have . . ." He walked straight to a row of cardboard boxes, neatly extracting one about halfway down with such a deft yank that none of the ones above it were disturbed. It clattered when he put it on the countertop.

"And some bonding gel. Several tubes of that, please."

"Hmm. Got that, and you're lucky," he added a moment later, four tubes flat on his hand. "Last I got and who knows when more will be made. Not that there's such a big demand for this either. Where are you setting up practice?"

"Botany," Eric said, then tapped the porcelain teeth. "I'll have all the colors from B-four through D-three."

"Done." Eddie was pulling out yet another drawer: they could hear the clicking of glass against glass, and then he started pulling individual vials out, setting them on a tray.

"Next? You don't know what a relief it is to be back at work," Eddie said with a huge sigh.

"Who's dere wid you, Eddie?" asked a querulous female voice from the small hall that led to the back of the building.

"Eric Sachs, Suzie."

"Eric? But I heard he got transported."

Eddie gave Eric a wide-eyed stare.

"I was, but I'm back, Suzie. Good to hear your voice," Eric said, raising his to be heard.

"Oy, Eric, you wouldn't believe what we've been through," Suzie said, and a very frail-looking woman came into the light of the foyer. Her hair was skinned back from her face and bundled into a neat chignon. She clutched an old plaid dressing gown around her and her face looked pinched with hunger and sorrow.

"I have a little idea, Suzie m'dear, and it must have been dreadful for you," Eric said sympathetically.

"Don't kvetch, Suzie. This is business," Eddie said, evidently to forestall a litany of disasters.

"How's Molly keeping?" she asked, willing to exchange information as well as kvetch.

"I don't really know," Eric said, darting a glance at Kris.

"We may be able to find out today," Kris said, hoping that Dan Vitali might have a connection to the Florida coords so Eric could check the registry lists of the area.

"So many friends dead, and gone who knows where?" Suzie said, her tone plaintive. "How are you finding clients these days, Eric?" She pointed with a worn and arthritically gnarled hand at the tray Eddie was filling.

"I find those I can," Eric replied. "It's good to contemplate being useful again." He shot a grin at Zainal, who was still in the shadows of the doorway.

"Useful is good," Suzie agreed and sat down abruptly on one of the stools. It rocked under her and Eric steadied her by the arm. She wasn't a big woman but awkward. She hauled a handkerchief out of her pocket and blew her nose. "Always a cold. Never am warm enough these days. I could have gone to visit Becky in Florida before *it* happened. At least I would have been warm."

"Stop with the kvetching, Suzie. Who's been warm this winter? No one." He evidently asked and answered many questions out loud, for she shrugged and inched herself to a comfortable position on the stool, hugging her thick dressing gown around her. Then she sniffed, looking around.

"I smell bread. Oh, God, I'm going out of my mind. I can smell bread." Then she looked at Kris. "I haven't smelled bread in months!"

"We have brought bread and some other food to trade for these items," Eric said. "We thought that was better than money."

"Never thought anything would be better than money," Suzie said, rubbing her fingers together in an age-old gesture.

Though neither Eddie nor Eric had mentioned paying for the items that were now displayed on the countertop, Kris opened the backpack and, indeed, the odor of fresh bread wafted out. Kris offered Suzie a roll.

"I baked them myself," she said, almost apologetically, and passed her a roll. The old woman tentatively reached out for the bread, glancing at her husband as if she didn't dare complete the gesture until he had agreed. He nodded.

"Take it," Kris said and extended her hand until the roll was nearly in the woman's fingers. They closed on the bread as if the woman was afraid Kris would snatch it away from her.

"Would you excuse me?" Suzie said, holding the roll protectively against her chest as she backed out of the room.

Kris placed the backpack on the counter and offered a roll to Eddie, who eyed it as Murray had, with longing.

"I've nothing to offer you to drink," Eddie said wistfully.

"We have all we need," Eric said soothingly.

Eddie took another deep breath. "You could charge for the smell of it, you know," he murmured. "What else?" he asked, hands on the edge of the counter.

Eric named a few more things, which Eddie scurried to find from his supplies.

"Now, I gotta tell you I can't charge it, Eric, though you were always one of the promptest to settle your account," Eddie said, eyeing the roll. "And two rolls ain't enough."

Kris peered into the backpack. "Fifteen, sixteen rolls."

"Well . . ."

"And some other food. Zainal, ask Dover to bring in a flat of the rock squats."

"Rock squats?" Eddie asked, surprised.

"A sort of avian from Botany that is very tasty. Game bird. It's been cooked."

"Kosher?" Eddie asked.

"You're asking kosher?" Eric said, surprised. He rested a hand on Eddie's and squeezed reassuringly. "I know God is everywhere and sees all, but you look like you need a few good meals. However, to reassure you, this is a kosher-type game bird and hunted, which is permissible, even if it is alien. Are you going to go kosher on me when I have good food to offer you in return for all this?"

"We do have gold," Zainal suggested.

"Gold, smold, what good is gold with shortages like we got?' Eddie demanded.

"You were never *that* orthodox, Eddie," Eric said so firmly that Eddie Spivak gave a little shrug.

"No, but I still got my ethnic pride."

Eric blew an exasperated breath out just as Dover came in with the rock squats. He had judiciously covered the tray with one of the clean bread towels. With a flourish, he flicked off the towel to show the browned halves of rock squat.

Despite long-held principles, Eddie peered at the display. Kris could see his lips moving, not so much from hunger as from counting. The flat held twenty-four portions. And, when he achieved the total, Eddie clasped his hands together, almost reverently.

"Enough food for days!" he said on a happy sigh. "And the bread, too?"

"Both. Enjoy and have good health," Eric said. " Is this enough for what I have purchased?"

"More than enough. Can we make soup out of it, too?" he asked Kris, pointing to the rock squats. "They look like chickens."

Kris laughed. "Chicken soup is good for colds. I don't know as we ever used it specifically for that on Botany, but it does make a good soup."

"You have saved us, then, Eric," Eddie said with great solemnity, clasping his hands together against his chest.

"The backpack isn't ours to trade," Kris said when she heard Jelco clear his throat. "And I could use the flat tray back, too, if you don't mind."

"A minute, please," Eddie said and, flipping up the counter leaf, stepped out. He started for the hall down which Suzie had disappeared and then whipped back, neatly picking up a rock-squat half before he was off again.

They could hear a shriek and then a gabble of excited comment before Eddie came back with a tray and a bread basket. He upended the backpack into the basket and carefully transferred the roasted meat to the tray, licking his fingers when he had finished the operation.

"Hmm, not bad." He grinned like a happy gnome.

Eric held out his hand. "Then we have a done deal?"

Eddie grasped it, shaking firmly. "Best deal I've been able to make in weeks."

Then Eric carefully packed away his supplies in the canvas carrier and pulled the loops over his arm.

"Will you be back again from this Botany place, Dr. Sachs?" Eddie asked as everyone shifted toward the door.

Eric gave a diffident shrug. "Who knows?"

They exchanged more good wishes as Eddie saw them to the door. Once in the alleyway, they could hear him closing bolts and turning keys.

Urchins had gathered around the truck, Murray trying to shoo them away while Wylee stood, legs spread, in the truck bed, trying to look fierce.

"Let's get this show on the road," Jelco said, motioning for Kris and Zainal to get back in the front seat. "Didja get everything you needed, Doc?" Jelco asked as Eric carefully handed the backpack up to Dover, advising him to place it carefully.

"Actually, more than I hoped I'd find," Eric said, swinging up onto the back of the truck. "Eddie Spivak always kept his inventory current. Nothing here is close to its use-by date."

Kris gave a chortle. "'Use-by' date has probably lost its significance. And I don't know about anyone else, but I'm hungry. We've enough rock squats for lunch, you know. And about two dozen more rolls."

"Let's do this down the road a bit," Jelco said, motioning to the kids who were now standing back from the truck. "I don't want to cause a minor riot, being seen to have food."

"Oh!" was all Kris could say. "Maybe we should . . ." she began, thinking of the wizened, hungry little faces.

"Charity begins at home," Jelco said so firmly that Kris put her usual compassion on hold. They really didn't have enough to share.

They pulled up farther down Thirteenth, where there was no audience looking out of upper stories. Murray almost gulped down his portion of rock squat, licking his fingers for any juice, before he pulled apart his ration of roll. No one asked for seconds. But there were still supplies left.

They proceeded back to the Lincoln Tunnel, Kris trying not to look at the pathetic little clusters of people at street corners, ragged and hungry-looking. They stopped only long enough for the Eastside guards to check them off as returning, though the cargo was eyed with curiosity.

Kris didn't even give a thought to the air she was breathing in this second pass under the Hudson River. She wouldn't die of a lungful of tainted air. She took a deep breath once they came out on the other side.

"Hey, New Jersey smells pretty good."

"Even Secaucus smells pretty good now there ain't no more pigs raised there," Murray said. "Mind you, I wouldn't mind the smell if it'd get me a roast of pork now and again."

They proceeded south on the turnpike until they saw the airport on the right. Also visible was the unmistakable bulk of the BASS-1, sitting on the runway just where they had left it.

6

Their return must have been observed because Jelco's phone buzzed. He answered it with an affirmative—evidently a response to a query about their mission's success. He listened silently for a moment, casting a sideways glance at Zainal before closing the phone.

"As soon as we unload the stuff, coord wants to have a chat with you. Nothing serious," he added when he noticed Kris was anxious. "Sort of kinda to get your impressions, I think. He's real proud of our sector and wants to be sure the other coords did right by you, too. Gotta keep discipline, y'know."

"You guys were marvelous," Kris said with genuine appreciation.

"Sometimes it works out that way, ma'am," Jelco admitted, saluting her with two fingers. "Glad we could oblige." He licked his lips, blushing when he realized what he had done. "Bread was super . . . and so was lunch. Those squats of yours are real tasty."

"Chickens all gone?" she asked, trying to put him at ease.

"Ages ago. Don't even think there are any eggs anywhere."

"Well, we've been farming rock squats awhile now so a supply of them is guaranteed."

"What's Botany like, huh?"

"Well, I suppose it's like this continent was before the White Man came. We got a coupla bad things—night crawlers." Even the thought of them made Kris's spine shiver. "And an avian beast about the size of a dive-bomber. But they've been quiet awhile. We got six-legged critters we call loo-cows, good eating, too, but they don't give milk. Say, anywhere we could trade for cinnamon or raisins?"

Jelco chuckled, raising his eyebrows like "you gotta be kidding?" before he shook his head. "Long gone. We could trade for spices if any were coming in. And if any were coming in, they'd be landed at New York." He gave a helpless little shrug. "We'd get some from the Waterfront Coord but we ain't had any. Raisins? Grapes come in the autumn, don't they? I remember my gran making grape jelly."

"A peanut-butter-and-jelly sandwich," Kris sighed with nostalgia.

"Now and then we get some peanuts up from the south, but we don't waste time making butter out of them."

She sighed again and then the truck pulled in front of the terminal and stopped.

Jelco got out and beckoned for Zainal and Kris to come with him, then issued a few low words to Murray to take the truck around to the BASS-1 to unload. Kris asked Eric for the last of the rock squats and any leftover rolls. Zainal hooked the straps of the depleted backpack over his arm while Kris took the last flat of rock squats.

"Would the coord have had lunch already?" she asked as she balanced the flat carefully. Wouldn't do to tip good food into the dirt and debris on the once well-swept sidewalk.

There was a bit of a delay while the door guards vetted them, and since the female assigned to frisk her pinched her, Kris was not of a mood to reward her clumsiness with a roll.

"You get to go in the front way this time," Jelco said and led them down a wide corridor.

She was surprised that most of the glass sides of the promenade were still intact, though several showed that the airport had not entirely escaped attack. There were a few bullet holes with cracks radiating out from the hit and some windows had been patched with duct tape. That was one item she had many requests for. How the world had run prior to its invention she didn't know. Not that she thought they should trade gold for it, but she might get an argument out of Herbie Bayes or Pete Snyder on that score. She smiled, and then they were swinging into the plush-carpeted executive area. This was well kept with even a few potted plants—of a high survival type—set about to give it a "decorated" look.

There was a busy inner office, with cell phones burping and buzzing, several PC stations and everyone busy. But not too busy to glance up and react to the sight of a Catteni being formally ushered in. Almost as if Zainal had taken a hint from her previous regal pose, he nodded to workers on either side of the walkway as they passed. A plaque on the door said VICE-PRESIDENT and below that a roughly printed sign read, DANIEL X. VITALI, COORDINATOR, NEWARK AIRPORT HQ. She took a firmer grip on the flat as Jelco tapped on the door. One of the secretaries, busy at her keyboard, looked up and jerked her head to indicate they should go right in.

The divine smell of coffee—real coffee, ground and dripped—assailed them as they entered. Dan Vitali, coordinator, looking no more rested than he had the previous evening, was pouring himself a cup. He greeted them genially, waving at the guests to help themselves at the coffee station.

"Real coffee," he said. "In your honor." He raised his cup in a toast.

"Real food to go with it," Kris said, knowing how to make a drama out of this fortuitous entrance. "And bread."

"More of the stuff you passed out last night?" The green coordinator smiled with considerable pleasure, seating himself at the big desk amid a stack of paperwork and clipboards. Kris served him first, Eric passed around the pack of rolls, and Vitali's expression was incredulous. "Real bread?"

"Fresh this morning," she said and served them to the half-dozen people in the room working at desks or waiting to present papers and letters to their commander.

"We eat, kids," Dan Vitali said, pushing his chair away from the desk and leaning back as he took his first bite of the roll, Kris was pleased to see him enjoy it.

"Oooh, that goes down easily, Kris Bjornsen, very easily. Jelco says everything went well?"

"He's right and we can't thank you enough for setting everything up for us," Chuck said, pulling up a stool and sitting down. He found a blank piece of paper, carefully folded it into quarters, then placed his coffee cup on a corner of the desk.

"I hope you take it black," Jelco was saying as he poured coffee into enough mugs to go around. "We ain't had creamer in ages."

"We take it black," Kris said. "Unless you have some sugar?"

"Packet?" Jelco said, holding up several of the packets that used to be served in restaurants.

"One'll do me fine."

When she caught his eye going to the sagging backpack, she gestured for him to take another roll. He did and once he had served everyone coffee, he leaned against a map-filled table at one side of Vitali's desk.

Vitali was busy with his impromptu snack. He, too, licked his fingers, drying them on a towel that he took from a lower desk drawer and wiping his mouth as well.

"That was an unexpected dividend," he said, burping once. He looked up and suddenly everyone in the room save Jelco found business that took them from the office. "Now," and he gestured to a sack on one end of his desk—a sack that bore the logo of a well-known pharmaceutical company, "I gotta deal pending I'm hoping you can help me with—since I know what humanitarians you are." His grin was devious. "You ain't got any restrictions on you about where you fly while you're in Earth's atmosphere, have you?"

"I don't believe so," Chuck said. "Though I might *need* a reason if I'm asked."

"Good! I didn't know if you had only an in-and-out license or not."

"I set it up to be able to get the stuff we need to trade with," Chuck said.

"Great! Now, that package is drugs, badly needed in Kenya."

Chuck *hmmm*ed diplomatically and glanced at Zainal to see if he understood. Zainal gave a quick nod.

"We don't have enough gasoline in any of our planes to make such a flight. How's your fuel situation?"

"Where do we have to go?"

"Like I said, Kenya. Outside Nairobi. If that ship of yours can do another short flight, it would help immensely if you could make a small detour to the west, to the Kiambu Ridge area—near the Great Rift Valley, to give you a landmark few could miss."

Kris's eyes went wide. Chuck knew what that place meant and he leaned forward, elbows on his knees, to listen more intently.

"It also happens to be one of the big coffee-producing areas of Africa. They do the robustas, if you know the difference. Kiambu Ridge coffees are the crème of the crème for full flavor. Use 'em to give more taste to lesser beans. I gotta deal going with the local coord that if I can get those medicines to him, he'll see I can fill my plane"—and now there was a decidedly wicked twinkle in the coord's eyes—"full of coffee beans. Roasted beans. Oh, we got a facility in Newark that roasts but they'd want their cut, too."

"Wow!" Kris said. Since Catteni had become addicted to coffee during their stay on Earth, to be able to trade roasted beans would mean they'd have a surefire commodity few Catteni would pass up. Maybe they could even set up a coffee bar to serve those dealing with Zainal and the others for more important items, like spare comm sat parts, tires, batteries, and what was the other thing so desperately needed? Spark plugs, she thought, but they wouldn't be at the top of the list.

"My deal is that if you take that . . . KDM did you call it? . . . you can keep ten percent of whatever you bring back to me."

"How do you know we'd come back with a KDM-load of coffee beans?" Chuck asked, grinning.

"You're the only one I'd trust to do so, Mitford," Dan Vitali said, looking straight into the sergeant's eyes. "Now I've met you, I believe everything I been told about you."

"Thank you," Chuck replied with a nod of his head, but the grin hadn't left his face.

"Of course, Jelco will come with you as he's dealing for me," the coord added with a sly grin of his own.

"Of course," Chuck agreed affably.

"Is ten percent much?" Zainal asked.

"That'd be one in every ten sacks of raw beans."

"Not raw, Chuck," the coord said firmly. "Roasted. And I don't want to split more than I have to. Each sack of beans weighs fifty pounds."

Kris sighed and Vitali laughed.

"We could do a lot with a KDM-sized load."

"They made a deal for a plane load," Chuck reminded him, "not a spaceship full."

"Jelco will handle that detail. The stuff we bring is more than they asked for but it will stop the epidemic of typhoid they got on their hands right now."

"Typhoid?" Kris said. "Is that back?"

"I don't think it ever went away in some parts of the world," Chuck said.

"There's broad-spectrum antibiotics in the package, polio, the latest cholera vaccine, on account of that's endemic where there's so little hygiene and lots of starvation, and some other stuff—ointments for the kind of sores that are rampant in Africa, which the laboratory said could be useful there. But Kenya is willing to trade for it. Especially as there won't be any ships going that way for a while. Not even by sea."

"Then we can be, as you said, philanthropists as well as haulers," Chuck said and looked at Kris and Zainal to see if they agreed.

"Coffee," Kris said with a sigh. "Wow!"

"There is an area down by the Masai encampment on Botany," Zainal mentioned idly, "hot enough and with sufficient rain on the mountains to grow coffee beans. It might be worth it to try cultivating our own coffee on Botany. If we were going straight back to Botany, I'd risk bringing some plants," Zainal said and shook his head in regret.

The coord leaned forward across the table. "How can someone get into Botany?"

"Like, immigrate?" Chuck asked. "We discussed that before we left, sir. We can only accept so many invalids before our economy is disrupted. We took in a shipload of those folks the Eosi tried to brainwash and they've integrated well into our population. We agreed to accept applications, preferably people who have some sort of skill that can help the commonweal," at which Vitali nodded sagely, "but we could use a discreet number of young folk to increase the gene pool for future generations."

"All sorts?" Vitali asked, his expression intense.

"All sorts," Chuck agreed. "We're pretty representative of races, creeds, and colors to begin with, on account of we had no choice in the first place getting dumped there."

"Hmm. So, what sort of occupations are you aiming for?"

"Anyone trained in biology, botany, medicine. Even another dentist."

"Will you be coming back here soon?"

"Oh, we'll be back when·we spring loose some of the stuff the Catteni heisted," Chuck said with a wave of his hand. "We can also send back more wheat, I think." He looked for approval at Zainal and Kris, who nodded solemnly. "Maybe some protein. We got these loo-cows. Got six feet and no milk, but they make good eating."

"Meat? Red meat?" Vitali asked in an almost wistful voice.

"I like the rock squats better myself," Chuck said amiably, "but any kind of steak goes down easily."

"Even rhinoceros, I hear tell," Kris murmured, overcome by whimsy. Vitali flashed her a startled look.

"Yes, well, I can see that this might be the beginning of a mutu-ally profitable association," Vitali said. He lifted the medicinal package toward them and some papers, including a map and airplane charts.

"Got these from one of the airlines in case they'd be any use to a spaceship," he said, handing them across to Chuck, who slipped them inside his shirt before shaking hands with the coord. "We don't, by the by, intend to hog all the coffee beans to ourselves, you know."

"Glad to hear it, Vitali," Chuck said, and then the man offered his hand to Kris and Zainal.

Jelco came forward and plucked the medicines from the desk and accepted his superior's handshake.

"Glad we could make a deal, Mitford."

As they left the coord's office he was calling his assistants back in, searching through clipboards to see which had the priority of his im-mediate attention.

"Coffee," Chuck said under his breath as Jelco led them down cor-ridors and steps and eventually back onto the deserted expanse of the airfield. "We can sure use ten percent of what the KDM can hold."

Kris was wondering about improving on a mere ten percent. She couldn't quite sort fifty pounds of beans into individual portions, nor how much weight the KDM could haul, but she did believe that they could probably sell any coffee they could bring to Barevi.

She wondered if the Kenyan coffee merchants might do a deal with them for tires, batteries, and spark plugs. She didn't want to be greedy but so much depended on their success. For both Earth and Botany.

She found herself rushing up the ramp of the KDM, grateful to hear voices, experiencing an unexpected nostalgia for the ship as a haven. Good Lord, what had gotten into her?

Then Kathy was there, giving her a big hug, Jax was beyond, grinning like a fool, and the boys rushed to greet their father, demanding his attention with glad cries at his return.

Kris and Zainal thanked Jelco and asked him to thank Wylee, Murray, and Dover for their assistance.

"Miss Kris," and for the first time she detected his southern accent, "it was a real pleasure. 'Sides, you bake a mean loaf of bread! I'll see you tomorrow. Until then, ciao."

And with another salute of two fingers to his eyebrow, he left them, lounging away toward the terminal building.

"We managed to trade for fresh food," Jax told Kris excitedly. "You should have seen Ferris and Ditsy. They just knew where stuff was growing." She waved a hand toward distant green fields. "And they brought back carrots! And potatoes! I haven't had them in years! We know you were successful with the dental stuff, and boy, did those guys covet the lifts."

"I don't know how we would have gotten those units down eighteen flights without them. And, Kathy, thanks for helping me with the rolls," Kris said, squeezing her arm gratefully, "because they opened doors everywhere."

"Those simple rolls?" Kathy was amazed.

"We'll do a full report at dinner, as we've a lot to discuss, but right now, is there enough hot water for me to have a shower? I feel sticky."

"You don't look sticky," Kathy said with mock horror and whooshed her down the corridor to her quarters. "We filled all the water tanks, and there should be plenty of hot by now."

The water was hot and Kris let it sluice down her body, soaping herself well, luxuriating in the warmth until Zainal tapped on the shower door. The amenity was not large enough for them to share the shower as they often did at home, but she gave herself one more rinse before she emerged and let him in.

While dressing, Zainal said that they would discuss the upcoming coffee-bean project with the entire crew. Considering the benefits of such an excursion for the commonweal, she doubted anyone would object to the detour.

Before they left, Kris had told Ferris to barter another sack of wheat for a good supply of carrots and potatoes. They did taste un-believably good. She wished they could take seedlings back to Botany but not with a long stopover at Barevi. There was a green salad as well with early lettuce (greenhouse lettuce, which Clune said was evi-dently a thriving business, delivering crates of fresh produce to be taken into the city) and spring onions, crunchy and sweet. She won-dered about dried beans. Well, besides coffee beans.

Jax Kiznet had had more air miles on Earth than anyone else, so Zainal had given her the charts to see what she thought of piloting for the trip.

"Well, I haven't flown over Africa," she demurred, looking at the flight charts, "but if we could land the KDM here, I don't see why we can't at Nairobi. The Jomo Kenyatta Airport's an international facil-ity—or was," she added. "There's a good one at Mombasa, too, plus the port. We aren't circumscribed to just this area, at least I didn't get that impression from our interrogation on the way in. I'll just check frequencies and weather reports."

"We need to go to the northeast of Nairobi to the coffee plantation area . . . and the Kiambu Ridge area." Kris found the place, which had been underlined on the detailed map.

"Oh, near the Rift Valley," she said, following Kris's pointing finger. "Well, that's hard to miss and so is Lake Rudolf."

"We don't need to go that far north."

"No, we don't," Jax said, staring down at the map. "I like the idea of getting coffee."

"I think we all do," Kris agreed. "Even Zainal's beginning to become addicted."

Jax grinned back. She was doing some figuring. "Look, if we can go orbital, we can do the great circle route at orbital velocity and it'll only take the KDM an hour and ten minutes to reach our destination. Wow! Hey, I like hypersonic!"

"Kenya's where Chief Materu comes from, isn't it?" Peran asked.

"Right you are," Zainal said, giving the boy a hug. "And we have another reason for being there. Alkoriti."

"Oh, hey, that's right," Kris said, remembering their earlier search for the acacia plant that had proved to be the unexpected weapon that had brought about the defeat of the Eosi, who had suffered respiratory failure from inhaling the dust.

She grinned at Zainal, spreading her hands in acceptance of the excuse. "As if bringing vaccines to Kenya isn't enough."

"Only how did you happen to get to be messenger?" Clune asked cynically.

"Evidently, individual coords will arrange things to suit themselves."

"We'll just hope that's a good enough excuse."

"Well, we know the Biffs are at two hundred and fifty kilometers and their sensors are fixed outward, not inward," Kathy pointed out. "So we're delivering medicines. Big deal."

Jax talked with the meteorology folk at Newark Tower, got the latest reports—no turbulence anticipated—and had her flight plan checked. There had been judicious gifts of rock squats to the tower staff, so they were disposed to be helpful . . . once they got over the shock of a vertical landing and takeoff craft.

"We coulda used a whole flock of the durned squats," Clune said as they finished the last of the supply.

"They're a game bird so they're also kosher," Kris said, and no one else quite appreciated why Eric guffawed.

The equipment that was now lodged in the cargo hold had fascinated Ferris. Later Zainal told Kris that Eric had explained to Ferris exactly what he had traded from Eddie Spivak and what it was used for. They decided that a number C-4 Vitapan shade matched the boy's tooth color, and Eric had pantomimed how he would use it, bonding it to a tooth in layers. Although Eric couldn't set up his equipment, he did check Ferris's teeth and found some cavities that ought to be taken care of as soon as possible. Ferris did not remember ever having been to a dentist and, because he knew Eric, did not have any anxieties about having his teeth fixed. During the evening, Eric checked over everyone on the ship, even Kris, and he shook his head over the state of her teeth. Zainal submitted and Eric said that he could probably fix the chip off one of Zainal's eyeteeth: in Zainal's case, not caused by a brawl but by a fall against something tougher than Catteni teeth. Peran and Bazil were pronounced to have excellent teeth with not a trace of decay, though Bazil's bite could stand a little correction.

The next morning, after Jelco boarded the KDM, they received clearance to leave Newark Airport, with many good wishes for a safe flight. New York Center was going to turn them over to Air Africa Control so certain protocols were taken care of. And now that they were aware of the surprise a vertical lift and takeoff vessel gave Tower

Control crews, they would handle their appearance at Jomo Kenyatta International Airport with more aplomb if they had to land there.

Kris decreed that, since the rolls had been so useful in New York, she didn't see why they wouldn't be in Kenya, where they might meet more people who would be delighted with freshly baked bread.

The notion of baking her way across the Atlantic and the Dark Continent left her grinning.

She did her baking with the help of Clune and Floss. The girl was still a restless type and had not liked being immured in the KDM the previous day when "everyone else" appeared to be out and about and having fun. She ignored the fact that Ferris and Clune had lugged heavy sacks of potatoes back to the ship, and that Bazil and Peran had carried in bundles of carrots and greens. *They* had been out and about *her* native planet. Kris recognized a certain merit in her argument and hoped she would be able to include Floss in some unusual activity at their current destination, even if she only helped with the rolls and bread they were going to use as goodwill offerings. She couldn't remember if Kenyans ate bread as a rule but it had once been a British colony and probably bread was known, no matter what other cereal grain was more popular. Jax remembered something about manioc but didn't know what it was. Kathy had suggested rice but Kris didn't think Kenya was rice country, which required irrigated fields. Kenya did have avocados, bananas, and other fresh fruits that might be available. They'd just have to wait and see. A banana, Kris thought whimsically, would taste very good. It had been so long since she had had one!

They were not challenged on the flight. The Atlantic Ocean was not that exciting from a high altitude. Even Africa was more a pattern of greens and beiges as they sped across it on the great circle route. Jax handled the controls well as they dropped out of hypersonic space, being high enough for a view of Lake Rudolph and the ripple of the

Rift Valley. Nairobi Tower welcomed them in their space and gave them directions to their destination.

Follow the big road northwest fifty miles: you can probably see it—it's the C-84 and keep the Karura forest on the port side. You're looking for a small town among ridges. About thirteen land kilometers from the airport. We understand that you are VTOL and there is sufficient parking in front of the warehouse to accommodate you."

"Over, Nairobi, and thank you. Out."

"They said they were from Botany," they heard the air controller say. "Where the hell's Botany?" Whatever response he got was lost as he shut off his microphone but those in the cockpit grinned at his confusion.

They found the site without too much trouble. The forest was unmistakable and the road twisted, visible to the starboard of the thick trees. Jax reduced airspeed. In fact, she laughed that it took almost more time to lose speed than it did to make the transatlantic segment.

It was easy to follow the road, visible through the lush forestry when the land swept upward to the very edge of the Rift Valley area.

As a final identification, the warehouse had KIAMBU RIDGE painted in big white letters on its roof.

"Hey, neat," Jax said with relief at having almost completed such a prestigious run. "Hope they don't freak out seeing a spaceship land."

"Open the hatch and let the smell of fresh bread waft out and entice them to our web, hehehehe," Kris said, doing her evil-witch imitation and rubbing her hands together. Chuck grinned but the display was lost on Zainal, though Floss, whom Kris had made sure had one of the jump seats to witness this landing, gave a contemptuous "Pshaw!"

Though the KDM was no longer supersonic, it made sufficient noise in landing to bring a number of people out of the warehouse.

The building had a galvanized roof, propped up by pillars of cinder blocks, but the facade was lined with local stone. As Jax cut the engines, Zainal and Jelco took places at the hatch until it was safe to open and extend the ramp. Several men, dressed in the long skirts used for cool comfort on this continent, came forward to greet them.

"Hi there, I am Jelco, representing Dan Vitali, Newark Airport Coordinator," Jelco said, holding the pharmaceutical package up so it was visible.

A very tall black man grinned, his teeth so white in his face that Bazil, standing by his father, was astonished and automatically came out with a Masai greeting.

Startled, the man halted midstride, staring first at Bazil and then at Zainal.

"Catteni?" he demanded, his nostrils flaring, smile disappearing.

Whatever Bazil said in response relieved the man, and he resumed his welcoming grin. He said something else and Bazil gave what was obviously a very courteous reply.

"He did not think our race could speak his language," Bazil said in a proud aside to his father. "He feels honored for his entire tribe."

"Good," Jelco murmured. "We have the medicines that were requested."

A second man, a stethoscope lying around his neck and sweat dripping down his shoulders, heaved a dramatic sigh of relief and stepped forward. "You cannot know how many lives you will be saving with this. Welcome, and thrice welcome. I'm Dr. Standish." He looked through the contents, sighing with relief as he identified the various packages. "Will you excuse me if I dash off?"

"Certainly," Jelco said. "We understand the need for haste."

"What I don't understand is how you got here so fast. My coordinator only got the radio message an hour ago."

"This ship is hypersonic, Doctor," Zainal said, "and we understood that time was critical."

"You have no idea," the doctor replied, somewhat distracted. "Father Simeon's prayers are the most efficacious I have ever encountered. Excuse me." He dashed off to a waiting jeep that bore a faded Red Cross insignia and some other emblems that neither Kris nor Chuck could identify.

"Please to come inside. Coffee is available for your pleasure," said the African. "I am Chief Sembu."

Bazil then suavely introduced the arrivals and included Floss, who was hovering, slightly out of sight. Sembu was once more astonished when Floss gave him a greeting in the Masai's Swahili dialect. Kris urgently gestured for her to accompany the party.

Jelco strode into the warehouse and into what was obviously a tasting room. The smell of rich, dark coffee was a fragrance everyone inhaled, and there was a small pot of brown sugar fragments to sweeten the fine brew. Underlying the coffee odor was something else, fruity, which she couldn't identify.

Jelco and Sembu sat opposite each other and began the dickering.

"A plane we could load easily," Sembu was saying, gesturing to the contents of the warehouse, glimpsed through the separating window. "That . . . aircraft looks as if it could take all we have bagged."

"And roasted?" Jelco asked.

"Well, not all are roasted," Sembu had to admit. "For one thing, we counted on an average-sized plane. Secondly, our buyers usually have their own roasters and prefer to have their people supervise such a delicate operation."

"Will Barevi appreciate 'careful' roasting?" Kris asked Zainal. She knew the process took time but did they have any to spare?

"How much is already roasted, Chief Sembu?" Jelco asked.

"We surmised that you would bring the largest aircraft you have," Sembu said with an understanding grin. "A 747, perhaps. We have sufficient to fill that size craft that have been roasted, as we agreed with Coord Vitali."

"And enough for a two-thousand-ton capacity?" Chuck asked.

"Hmm, but not all would be roasted."

"Beggars can't be choosers."

"Nor winners poor losers," Sembu said and extended his hand to Chuck. "I can provide you with a roaster and instructions, but roasting is a delicate business."

"We'll take the roaster, and the mistakes will be ours," Chuck said, taking the hand. "In all fairness to Jelco here and the green coord," he added, "they'd no idea we'd be dropping the KDM in their lap, so to speak."

The deal was struck and the chief gave orders to his workers to start loading. At which point Zainal called back to the ship to bring out the lifts. He suspected they'd be needed to load the roaster, though he'd no idea what size the thing would be.

That was providential because the large and bulky roaster could accommodate three sacks of beans at a time. It was loaded onto the KDM. Sembu was fascinated by the lift, even after Zainal warned him that its power pack was half-drained, but trading it bought them all the fresh produce they could store as well as four twenty-five-pound sacks of the rough brown sugar that Kris and Floss found in the local market. Kris also bought some lengths of a blue fabric displayed at the market so that Floss could finally have some new dresses. The girl was touched that Kris remembered such a detail amid all the others she was currently handling. Kris tried to find cinnamon and raisins but no one paid her much mind in the scurry to load the coffee beans. The entire warehouse of coffee bean sacks fit neatly into two of the three KDM cargo holds.

"Having all robustas is great," Kris said, "but we could use some of the milder arabicas, too." She had listened to enough of the spiel to have absorbed some details about the romance of coffee.

"They are grown elsewhere than Kenya," Sembu replied. "However, as ours are often used in combination with arabicas, and considering that trade is nonexistent, you might be able to exchange robustas for a few sacks of arabicas in, say, Santa Lucia in the Caribbean. If that's on your way, of course."

"That's an island," Kris said, trying to place it.

"In the Caribbean. There are many plantations on it. One, in fact, not far from the volcano."

"Volcano?" An acceptable landmark, certainly.

"Oh, it's not active. Or wasn't when I last had news, but you might do a deal with them. Their beans are very good—for arabicas," he said with a slightly deprecating smile for a lesser breed, "but excellent in its category."

Kris grinned.

"Asante sana," Bazil said politely, bowing slightly to the man.

"I never thought I'd hear a Catteni speaking Swahili. It is worth much to have you here," Sembu said, smiling benignly down at the sturdy boy.

"Would you know, sir, where we can get some Alkoriti?" Kris asked.

"But of course." Sembu was really surprised.

"We found some bushes the last time we were here," she said, "for the Masai tribe that now resides on Botany. They require the plant for a rite of passage."

"You have Masai on Botany?"

"Yes," and when the man frowned, Kris hurried on. "They have their own settlement on the southern peninsula and we brought them some acacia bushes, but there is always a need for more Alkoriti."

"The children grow well?" Sembu asked, interested. He had also beckoned a worker to his side and gave him a low command. The man raced down the hill at such speed Kris worried that he would do himself damage.

"Well and strong," Bazil said proudly, "so that my father wanted me with him on this trip."

Shortly, Zainal reappeared, having finished securing the cargo, and joined Peran.

"Sembu has offered to bring us Alkoriti," Kris said.

"Ah, very good. Our thanks, Sembu. We promised to find more for Chief Materu." He also winked at Kris, for now they could honestly answer queries—if there were any—as to why they had detoured to Kenya instead of departing spaceward from Newark. Jelco joined them while they waited for the return of the messenger, who came back panting somewhat from a quick round-trip, but carrying a pouch that he turned over to Sembu. Who, in his turn, passed it over to Kris.

"Please to say that we of Kenya are happy to provide this to your Masai chief."

"You must let the green coord know when you stand in need of medicines again, Sembu, and we will return."

"For more coffee beans, no doubt." The man's smile was understanding.

"I shall send along more power packs for the float, too," Zainal promised, before he bowed formally to Sembu and waved at the other workers who were unwilling to miss any of this pageant. Then Zainal led them all back into the KDM and pushed the button to retract the ramp.

Carefully, so that little dust lifted from the ground to discommode Sembu, Jax lifted the KDM away from the heights and eased the ship over the forestry before she increased power. Heading west, she turned the KDM's nose skyward and increased power until the ship could once again engage its hypersonic drives and take them back to Newark.

It was almost anticlimactic to be back in Newark air space barely two hours after they had taken off—a fact that the air tower personnel remarked on as they extended a warm welcome back, "so soon." They were assigned their previous landing spot, and by the time Jax had landed the KDM, there were all kinds of trucks waiting to offload the precious coffee beans.

Twenty sacks of robusta beans were left in the KDM's hold and a good half of the fresh fruit and vegetables they had acquired at Kiambu Ridge. On the way back they had all enjoyed various fruits they had acquired: bananas, oranges, passion fruit, cape gooseberries with their lanternlike husks, custard apples and guavas, avocados, coconuts, papayas, and pineapples. And there were even chicken eggs and milk. Kris made a huge custard for dessert and planned to treat everyone to pancakes for breakfast. The KDM had a freezer unit but not a refrigerator, so she could not keep milk fresh for long.

Rummaging in the galley cabinets, Kathy had found a grinder of sorts and managed to reduce some beans to the proper consistency to brew coffee, so everyone had enjoyed the spoils of their excursion.

She gave Murray half a dozen eggs and the same to Jelco as well as a carton of milk for his young child and a hand of bananas. She had a huge stalk to present to the caterer. And two green stalks to ripen on the way back to Barevi as well as several crates of oranges, limes, and lemons.

Then she got in touch with the tower controller and bribed him with some of their own coffee beans to give her aerial maps of Santa Lucia so they could plot a course and see if they couldn't exchange a quantity of robustas for arabicas. Nothing else they had, even the largesse from Nairobi, would be useful for trade, and they had only three sacks of wheat left with which to trade on Barevi.

There was no need to mention to anyone that they planned to stop off at Santa Lucia but they did spend the night at Newark. If this next stop was anything like the Kiambu Ridge one had been, Zainal thought they needed to be rested.

Kathy and Jax plotted the southern course, which they figured would take about twenty minutes, allowing another fifteen first to get to speed and then to slow down enough to land without damaging anything. The volcano, while not active, was currently sending a gray plume skyward so they had a fine guide to it on the northern tip of the island and a great look at the plateaus as well as the choice of several obvious landing sites. They saw several long, low, galvanized roofs that looked similar to the type used for bean storage in Kenya. Well, that made sense to Kris.

Somewhat to their dismay, they found that Catteni must have visited the plantation several years earlier for the KDM's type of ship was recognized and men armed with rifles and machetes were waiting as the ramp extruded. Chuck was their spokesperson and Zainal and his sons stayed tactfully out of sight. Kathy and Jax accompanied the sergeant, with the remaining float carrying a sack of robusta beans. The sight of the logo on the sack turned out to be the reassurance needed, and with a minimum of talk and an excess of pleasure, they managed to trade five robusta sacks and the remaining float for thirty arabicas, plus thirty more pounds of unrefined sugar. They got more green bananas and a case of local rum. Despite the fact that she was safe with Zainal, Kris did not join in the evening celebration once she had had a sniff of the liquor.

"That's stronger than Mayock's hooch," Kris remarked, after a smell of the rum and felt no desire at all to imbibe. She did reserve one bottle of the case for cooking. No one had cinnamon or raisins to trade. They were given more crates of citrus fruits, which would be novelties on Barevi. She wondered if she could manage to keep at least one stalk of the green bananas and a crate of oranges to bring back to Botany.

They stayed the night on the surface—at the owner's invitation— and evidently he had sent messages to his neighbors to come see what had landed on his parking lot. And they came in droves, on horseback. Peran was much taken with horses and was put in the saddle of one animal (very gentle, Kris was assured) for a walk around. Bazil, naturally, had to have a turn, too. It was a convivial evening and established their KDM as friendly, Catteni and all.

When Kris suggested that they would probably return, they were begged to do so, and she made a list of the items for which they would gladly trade. She was not astonished to note that tires, Toyota truck spark plugs, and twenty-volt batteries were the most important items.

"We could keep all our KDMs busy hauling stuff in and coffee beans out," she said to Zainal.

"Mmmm," was his response. "But these folks don't have what we desperately need."

7

The next morning, when the KDM lifted from Santa Lucia, everyone was refreshed and keen to get on with the next phase of their mission. They logged out of the system with the Watch Dog and were given a cheerful "farewell, come back again soon" from the Cheyenne Mountain NORAD facility. If Gino, who was pilot for the first leg of their flight to Barevi, cheerfully assured them that they would, there was no demur on their part.

"The Botany boys will be back," he crowed as he signed out of Terran space, and the powerful engines of the KDM sent them galactically north toward Barevi.

As they neared the trading planet, there was more chat on the comm lines between Catteni captains, and whenever possible the duty officer repeated Peter's carefully composed commercial about the new trader and goods coming soon to Barevi. The other key members of the ransom group now spent shifts listening to Catteni messages and practicing with Zainal's sons, who were delighted to be in the position of teachers instead of pupils. They also absorbed new vocabulary and phrases.

When not on duty, Bazil and Peran indulged in what Kris knew was simple sibling bickering, but she was unable to discipline the boys. They certainly resented any interference in their "discussions" or the way they teased Floss. Fortunately, Kris could distract Floss, and Jax and Kathy both helped the girl make a dress from the fabric Kris had unexpectedly found at the market in Kenya. Floss had gushed with appreciation for Kris's thoughtfulness. Of course, the boys teased Floss about that—when Zainal and Chuck were absent—but she was well able to make sharp retorts. There were a few incidents when they tried the same tactics on Ferris and Ditsy, but the two Terran boys were more than able to deal with the Catteni ones and earned their respect. Kris knew they resented her monopolizing their adored father's free time and were inclined to disregard any requests she made of them; she had expected that, even if she didn't know how to counter their impudence. But it was a long flight to Barevi. She would be very glad when there was a tutor assigned to keep them occupied.

When it came time for the BASS-1 to contact the Barevi space station that regulated all traffic in and out of the system, Captain Jax Kiznet was the pilot. This included her insistence that she did command the BASS-1, origin: Botany Free Planet. Zainal was sitting as copilot, letting her handle the contact and repeat the landing instructions. Barevi Tower was sarcastically upset over having a female answering their orders and evidently in command of a ship: a pilot of unknown ability flying in busy traffic space. Jax was quizzed on docking procedures by the space station commander, Ladade, who sounded surly until finally Zainal intervened and said that he, Zainal, had been her instructor and that she was competent to pilot, even in such a busy port.

"Hey, this Ladade backed down real quick when you said you were Zainal," Jax said admiringly.

"See that you prove my ability to teach you properly," was Zainal's reply.

She did, concentrating on the job. As they made their approach, Zainal kept checking the screen for any navigational anomaly. Although there were stiff penalties for abusing Barevian space, there were also hazards, which he hoped to help Jax avoid. The barges that carried inter-system traffic were known to deviate from their projected courses and provide obstacles. She had her eyes open for such problems and kept one eye on the screens.

"This is a very active spaceport?" she asked Zainal when he pointed out an erratic ship for her to avoid. "And I thought there was a lot of junk in Earth space!" She pointed to the mass in the upper starboard quadrant.

"Oh, that," Zainal replied, shrugging it off. "That's real space junk. Barevi port facility is equipped to do major overhauls and refits. That's where they put carcasses and damaged structural members. And ships that don't pay their docking charges."

"Oh? When they haven't a bean left?" she asked, flashing a quick grin at him.

She really was a good pilot, Zainal thought, wondering whom he should train next on their return to Botany. There were plenty of willing candidates. He had watched all of them on the simulator and they all had good reflexes and instincts. The Botany Space Force had enough cargo ships now that new pilots were always needed.

From space, Kris thought that Barevi Market really hadn't changed at all, except perhaps for its lack of eager customers filling the vast places. As they hovered above the docking facility seeking their assigned bay, Kris pointed out the overlapping squares of the market. She felt an almost—definitely almost—nostalgic relief at seeing it again. It was, after all, the site of the beginning of her amazing adventures. They'd already started the rumor mill with Peter's intentionally provocative commercial, and they had had to keep the comm unit manned on a twenty-four-hour basis with their best Catteni speakers. Even Peran and Bazil had taken short stints, enormously pleased to be allowed such a responsibility, and certainly Zainal was delighted that they handled their first official duty so capably.

The next morning, Zainal sought out the market's manager and paid over almost all the Catteni coin he had to lease appropriate space in the market. Over several hundred years, the facility had grown from its original square, each addition overlapping older ones. The corners provided enclosed shops that afforded some privacy. Zainal wanted one for Eric's "office." The first week's rental reduced his small store of Catteni coins to a handful of loose change.

"What commodities, Emassi?" Chief Kapash asked.

"Various. Food items from Botany and oddments. We expect to trade for items available only on Barevi."

"Yes, Supreme Emassi Kamiton told me"—the commander paused for Zainal to recognize the significance of his having had a personal interview with such a personage as the Supreme Emassi—"that you were coming and you must be accorded the respect and privileges of a trader. However, I will have no personal disputes set- tled in my market space."

"Will you also police the market to be sure we are allowed to trade freely?"

"I'll have you know we allow no brawling or bullying within the confines of the marketplace," Kapash said, straightening at the im- plied slur on his management. Zainal had known the man from his previous tour of duty on Barevi. Kapash was running more to fat than muscle for his extra flesh strained his uniform and destroyed the fit of it.

"My! How Barevi has changed," Zainal remarked and noticed the smug grin on Kapash's blunt-featured face as he accepted the keys to the enclosure he had just leased and left the office. He didn't fail to see Kapash give a sign to one of the huge Catteni in the outer room and knew that all his movements would now be reported back to the chief. Nothing new in that. May the fellow at least have the intelligence to understand what he saw. Zainal hadn't run Barevi's market for a full Catteni year without learning a few tricks and the counters to them.

His next task was to apply at the hiring hall for a tutor for Peran and Bazil. The two boys were running a little too wild for his liking. He knew they flagrantly disobeyed Kris and that they had gotten a little out of hand by the end of the long journey here. That must stop.

The hiring hall had the usual number of unemployed, some with the unmistakable look of "command" about them, but he required more than authority to control and shape his sons. He filled out the form, specifying a younger man, preferably one with pilot training, and definitely with a good educational background in the sciences. Considering the current situation with no new exploratory expeditions, there was surely some young man who would meet his requirements.

On his return to the ship, he passed by storage sheds with doors ajar, and men working among cartons displaying Terran manufacturers' logos. Yes, Chuck had been right. Most of what they urgently needed was here. To acquire tires and batteries and the spark plugs required to repair Terran ground vehicles might be less of a challenge than getting the comm sat components. He passed by a large locked unit that smelled aromatically of warm rubber, for the sun was hot enough to heat many of the inadequately vented warehouses.

He took one last look at his new premises, checking first on the electrical system and taking pictures with a small camera. Bayes had also supplied him with a unit that would test the circuits and power available. They did have some step-down transformers for Eric's equipment. The shop was equipped with a stout reinforced door, though only a broken chain and lock dangled from the latch. Well, there were many ways to lock a door. A faucet slightly askew on its pipe let out rusty water, which gradually cleared. When it did, Zainal filled a small bottle so they could analyze it in the ship's little medical station. Generally speaking, such resources were potable and the rust was only from long disuse. He was within his rights to insist on properly filtered water, and the last thing they needed was to distribute anything contaminated to their customers.

He also rented the largest lift platform that he spied in the street in front of Kapash's office, available from its owner, an old, one-armed ex-soldier whom he thought he remembered from his Barevian year as market manager. The man certainly recognized him. Veterans were allowed to work on the docks as compensation for their loss of limbs. A name came to mind—Natchi—and seemed to be accepted by the garrulous veteran. The poor devils all looked alike, distinguishable only by the parts they were missing.

"They'll all be watching you, Emassi Zainal," Natchi remarked out of the side of his mouth. "We have heard rumors of your return. And how you single-handedly accomplished the end of Eosi domination. This has not made you popular in all places. Do not lower your guard for a moment," the veteran muttered as he handed over the lift control hand unit. "You kept Barevi relatively calm the year you were here. May you prosper."

Zainal nodded in acceptance of the warning. "If you hear more, come to my shop. We shall always have a hot drink for you, Natchi, and a seat in the shop whenever you need to rest your old bones."

"Old they are, Emassi. Return the lift when you have no further need of it, and my gratitude that you remembered my name."

Zainal nodded and, guiding the lift in front of him, went back to the BASS-1's berth. He assumed his most aloof manner as he made his way, glad, after Natchi's warning, that he had already put Chuck on an alert status at their berth.

"They been around like flies," Chuck said, scurrying to join him when he spotted Zainal approaching. "I was improving Peran's and Bazil's targeting skills." He pointed to the dartboard hung from a convenient loading spike, and the number of green-fletched darts lodged in the King ring. "Bazil's got the keener eye, but what could be more typical than me teaching two kids an old game?"

"Nothing," said Zainal, though he suspected that Chuck had removed the boisterous youngsters to give Kris a break from their bickering. "Much interest?"

"Think most of the other ships in port sent someone to take a gander and had quite a few not-so-subtle inquiries. Merchants' reps, all of 'em, trying to figure out what we're going to sell."

"Make me a copy of these," Zainal said, tossing Chuck the keys. "And do we have digital locks with us?"

"I've got locks aplenty. I'll set up several, in fact, because I heard rumors that there are some who have bones to pick with Emassi Zainal." Zainal nodded for he knew many Catteni considered him a traitor, even if he had managed to end the restrictive Eosi domination. "Who's market manager? Vitters?"

"Kapash is market manager."

"Had dealings with him before?" Chuck asked. "Don't know him but Vitters was useless. Kept forgetting who took the biggest bribes from him. Wonder who killed him?"

"Not our problem, and we'll have more than our share, I suspect." Zainal gave a shrug. "I know of Kapash, let us say. He may not be an improvement over Vitters. And once we have goods on the premises, I'll want to be sure nothing is missing the next day. Natchi, a one-armed veteran, has also warned me. Natchi is to be given as much coffee as he wishes. He'll do more than cool his drink with his breath if he hears anything we should know. Is Clune the biggest man we've got? Or Ninety Doyle?"

"It'd be a toss-up, Emassi." Chuck grinned and, with a flourish, gestured for Zainal to precede him up the ramp and into the KDM. "Even the biggest Catteni would think twice before tangling with either of them unless they were totally nuts."

"Have I still got the spy on my tail?"

"Big ugly son, straggly beard, wearing dirty yellow pants and a blue vest?"

"You've seen him. The very one."

"Wouldn't like to upset that fellow!"

"I don't want anyone leaving this ship alone. Only in groups of two, preferably three. The women are definitely not to leave without a male escort."

"What would they leave for?" Chuck demanded. "All the comforts of home."

As Zainal reached the main corridor, he could smell the fragrance of fresh coffee and made his way quickly to the wardroom, where, as if she had known his exact moment of return, Kris had a cup ready to hand him when he entered.

"The boys saw you coming," she said, smiling. "I was roasting more coffee beans. Tell me what you think of this brew. Maybe I can get the right balance yet. Could you smell it on the dock?" He could hear the exhaust fan whirring but he hadn't smelled the aroma on the dock. Other things had been redolent—hot grease, oil, and stale ship fuel: the usual compound in this sort of area.

"They'll all know by tomorrow." Zainal shrugged with an indifference he didn't feel. In fact, he was seething with anticipation to witness the stir they would make in the unexpectedly torpid atmosphere of what had once been a hectic and active marketplace. He had also tread on parts stuck in the mud of the market aisles. The one he dug out was indeed a spark plug but too dirt-encrusted to be saved; another was a circuit board of some type. What Chuck had reported was correct: merchandise was being wantonly and casually destroyed. So much for Kapash's boast that he kept the facility in order.

Chuck came in then, hanging the dartboard back on the wall in its usual spot.

"Another cup, please, Kris, before I take a casual"—Chuck grinned that "casual" was not the most apt adjective—"stroll around the market."

"Take Clune and Ninety with you and show them Stall Ninety-two," Zainal said. "Northwest corner. There is a wooden floor to which we can attach Eric's equipment. We'll need new bolts and, of course, the locks."

"Is that far from what you Catteni euphemistically call a drinking spot?" Kris asked hopefully. She remembered all too clearly the brawl she had nearly been embroiled in the last time she'd been in Barevi.

"Yes, and not near the main intersections," Zainal added, satisfied. "On a good wide aisle."

"Did you catch the names of any merchants?"

Zainal handed Chuck the hand cam he had been using on his tour of the market areas. "Which one of our crew can develop film?" he asked, taking out the film he had used up on his return to the KDM. "Then we can see who our neighbors are."

"Gail," Kris said and, going to the wall unit, she depressed a toggle. "Lieutenant Sullivan to the wardroom, please."

"Coming," was the cheerful reply.

It didn't take her long to arrive, almost breathless, at the door. She raised her arm to salute, but changed the motion to pushing her hair back from her face. Zainal had long since requested that formality be reserved for those times when other Catteni were present, but service habits were hard to break.

"Can you please process these, Gail?"

"Certainly, sir. Are they urgent?"

"Reasonably. And no one is to leave the ship alone. Especially you women. Never leave without a man with you . . . preferably Clune or Ninety. Pass the word along."

"Yes, Zainal. I will." She widened her eyes briefly and then flicked her fingers at him in a salute and turned left down the passage. Kris took a new camera unit from a closet and handed it over. He pocketed it, patting the slim rectangle for a moment.

"Should we all carry one, just in case?"

"No reason why not. Photo proof might be necessary and some of what I shot might not develop because of shadow but . . ."

"We might be able to identify enough to help find the right ransomables."

Kris finished the thought. "We are adding tires, batteries, and spark plugs to the list, aren't we?"

He nodded a vigorous affirmative.

"The name of the market chief is Kapash. He would not want the world and Barevi to know that, at one time, he was storing illegal substances: flip, strew, and lily."

"Oh?" Kris said, her tone asking for elaboration.

"Flip destroys Catteni balance. It's a powder and, blown into the face, can cause vertigo. Often illegally used during fights. Too much can destroy balance completely. Strew clings to skin and has an obnoxious stink to it. It also clouds memory. Lily is the worst. It's toxic, especially to the Turs, and was often used to subdue them. In quantity it can be lethal to any of the known species. I don't think it was used on Earth, but it might have been."

"Lily is your word for a bad drug? I used to love stargazer lilies. They could scent up a room for weeks." She smiled nostalgically. "Why did you warn me about such substances?"

"I'm warning you about Kapash. You may threaten him with exposure if he makes any move on you or any of the crew. Dealing with any of those three drugs carries a mandatory sentence to one of the mining colonies. He'll know that."

"So he wouldn't want that bruited about."

"No, he would not. Your threat is—if you need to use it—that if you are not back by a specified time, such information will be delivered to the space commander, Ladade. He knows I know, but he can't touch me. Or hasn't tried to. As I told the lieutenant, no one is to leave the ship alone. I'd rather you," and he pointed his finger at her, "went out only with me or Clune."

"Isn't Alex McColl big enough, too?" Kris asked, grinning. She knew she shouldn't feel so cocky, but she had benefited from sessions with Mpatane Cummings in unarmed combat training, and was adept enough to have floored Clune and Chuck in exercise sessions. Mpatane might look delicate but she was dangerous with hand and foot. She'd had Kris doing some toughening exercises with the edge of her hand. Mpatane could split a hunk of wood with a blow. She'd also taught Kris how to send a man's nose into his brain with the heel of her hand. Not, Kris thought, that a Catteni nose would not be as fragile as the human equivalent, but a crack there would certainly smart enough for her to get out of a Catteni's clutch. Catteni used genital guards even when off-duty, so the classic ploy of a knee to the crotch would not be an option. Kris was glad to have other time-tried maneuvers, and got quite adept at flooring anyone who dared grab her: once you knew how, it was simple to use the force of a rush to the attacker's detriment. Most of the Catteni fighting she had observed had been flailing fists and butting heads. Not much finesse, more pure brute force. She now had countermeasures but would prefer not to have to use them.

"We could get in a few good licks in ten seconds," Kris said, noticing that the other women bristled a bit at the notion that they couldn't defend themselves. "But Catteni don't fight fair," she added.

"Just a safety precaution. Until you know the Barevi market area, you need to have a fail-safe," Zainal said, accepting their rebuff. When he gave Kris an admonishing glare, she gave him an impudent grin.

They spent the rest of the afternoon getting the bulky dental elements onto Natchi's big lift and checked to be sure they had everything else they needed. They had found a digitally locked strongbox for the smallest gold items. The metal ingots were a little easier to safekeep, being heavy and bulky in themselves and not something even a Catteni could slip into a pocket. They had more than enough of a crew to leave someone on board on comm watch at all times, and Bayes had rigged a perimeter alert in the berth against snoopers. The KDM, aka BASS-1, had integral shielding against electronic snoopers so one person on board should be sufficient. Possibly two or three. Herb Bayes knew some rudimentary Catteni.

One of the first things Zainal wanted to liberate was a carton of handheld comm units so that all members of his group could keep in touch no matter where they were on Barevi. He gave each of the women a tiny Mayday patch that would emit a ten-second yowl if they got cornered. The sound was one that was particularly irritating to Catteni ears and was guaranteed to let them escape while their would-be assailant was battered by the noise.

The water tested 99 percent pure without any unusual bacteria or noxious minerals. It was a bit high in iron but that would be temporary, as Zainal knew from his term as market manager that the piping was all properly done. The tap only needed to run a bit. Sometimes, just to be awkward, the market manager would do silly things, like health checks on a merchant. A water filter from the survivor kit would let them filter enough water for the first urnful of coffee—just to be on the safe side. Zainal hoped that the coffee could be made quickly enough so that he'd've collected some local credits before Kapash figured out a new way to derive income from their stall. Zainal surely hoped that Kapash would prove to be a caffeine addict. That would be useful. After reading the manual for the roaster, they had been able to dry several more sacks of beans on their flight to Barevi, and the results had brewed into a decent coffee. They'd do more once they found out how the beans were selling. Kris was keen to try some blending of the two bean types.

The next morning, when Zainal woke up early, he could already smell the onboard coffee. Dressing quickly, he went to the galley and found Kris pouring cups for those already gathered in by the delightful aroma. She had made pancakes, too, from the last of the flour, milk, and eggs on board. There were ripe bananas to start with and he was becoming quite fond of the fruit. They had several big stalks of bananas slowly ripening in the hold along with the oranges they had taken on board at Santa Lucia. They would see how things went before they offered the fruits in the market. But there was a three-week limit to the bananas and they might well have to trade them for what they could get, even if Kris had hopes of returning with some to Botany as a special treat. The oranges would keep and some of the other fruit had been bought green enough to make the trip back to Botany.

"I made another big pot of coffee," Kris was saying now, as Floss and the boys joined them in the galley, "so we could bring some to the stall just in case we have early customers," she told him, jerking her chin at the big padded thermal bottle.

"Good thinking."

"Do my best with the first cup of coffee," she replied. One of the things Zainal particularly liked about Kris was her ability to wake up in a good mood. It certainly started the day off well for those working with her. She had toasted the last of the baked bread she'd been able to make from the flour they had brought from Botany.

If Zainal remembered correctly, there had been a bakery in Barevi market, unless a fight had trashed it. The one he remembered had done good business, especially after some of the Terran breads had been offered for sale, when different types of flour became available following the mass looting of Earth. Coffee and bread from Terra were good things.

"We're ready when you are, Zainal," Bayes said. "All loaded on the lift."

Despite the heat of the coffee, Zainal managed to drink it down, felt it slosh in his belly and hoped it would have its usual stimulating effect on his system. Kris carefully handed him a nicely browned slice of bread, spread with some of the sweet stuff he liked. He smiled at her.

"Take the hottle," she said, nodding to the padded affair.

By its convenient handle, he swung it off the worktop and followed Herb Bayes, Chuck, Captain Harvey, Sally Stoffers, and the two Doyle brothers, who were on the first shift of the ransom team. His sons followed him, eager for their first glimpse of famed Barevi. Zainal hoped that someone would apply for the job of tutor. While experience in the market—as well as their command of both languages—would be useful, they badly needed training in other areas. They wouldn't like it, but then, he hadn't enjoyed his schooling either. Piloting was always good training to have.

Other merchants were beginning to open their stalls one by one, pausing in the process to talk to their neighbors and assure waiting customers that they would be ready presently. His team made short shrift of setting up, since they would be buying, not selling merchandise. Even the coffee wasn't for sale, offered only as a courtesy to those who came to show their goods.

"Filter the first water that comes out, Ninety," Zainal murmured to the heavyset Doyle brother.

"Smart, too," Ninety muttered back as the tap spat rusty water into the filter material, but there was soon enough to fill the big urn. Bayes nodded assurance that the power conduit was good and they wouldn't need a transformer to handle the electrical current, while Kathy Harvey set out cups, brown sugar, and the Botany sweetener and every spoon from the galley. Kathy had taken it upon herself to be sure the spoons did not go missing.

Zainal hadn't liked milk in his coffee when they'd had enough to use it, said it ruined the full coffee taste, which he preferred dark and sweet. Thinking about it made him pour a cup from the bottle. Second one was nearly as good as the first, and he could savor the taste. Then Natchi appeared at his elbow.

"Does that smell like I think it does?" the old man murmured, inhaling deeply. Oh, it does. It's coffee, isn't it?" He was salivating in anticipation.

"Coffee," being an alien word, sounded the same from Catteni lips as it did from Terran. Zainal had noticed that the Kenyans called it *kahawa*.

"I brought my own seat," Natchi said, holding up a battered crate as he reminded Zainal of the previous day's promise. Zainal poured him a cup.

"Put your seat where you will be comfortable, Natchi, behind the stall where you won't be trampled in the rush," Zainal suggested when he saw that sharp noses down the line were picking up the unmistakable aroma from his pouring.

"We have a list of items we are looking for," he said in a carrying tone, glancing down the row of stalls and catching the gaze of several other merchants, "and those who wish to peruse the lists might enjoy a warming cup."

By then, the others with the dental equipment lift had arrived, with Eric Sachs hovering at the tailgate, anxious that his precious equipment not be harmed. Only if it fell on someone else's toe, Zainal was sure, gesturing for Eric to use the cubicle they had rented for dental work. Ferris and Ditsy had offered to see if they could find men in the drink shops who might need Eric's skills and persuade them to come and see the wonders of tooth repair and restoration. As aids, Gail, who had a gift for printing and sketching, had done a flip chart depicting examples of the dental care Eric could provide, even putting a small diamond in one crown when she had heard that Mike had included some flat-cut stones in their barterables.

"You say you have a list?" asked a low voice at Zainal's side, and he saw a man, ostentatiously wearing a communications badge, standing beside him.

"Yes, we do, please step up," Zainal replied, remembering what Peter had told him of the ways of treating prospective sellers.

"Who speaks Catteni besides yourself, Emassi?" (Clune had mentioned during the journey here that no one would ever mistake Zainal for anything but Emassi class, no matter what he did or how he introduced himself.)

"All who are here, merchant. Captain Kiznet, I think list two," and he held out his hand to Clune for a copy of that list. They had printed up lists of units and numbers, as well as logos of the various manufacturers whose items they were eager to find. "And would you like a cup to sip?"

"The aroma attracted me first, Emassi," was the unusually candid reply, and Peran was quick to pour another cup from the hottle and present it with suitable dignity to the merchant. "I grew accustomed to this Terra drink, but it is hard to obtain in any quantity." Zainal chose to ignore the subtle request for more information about his sources.

"It may be stronger than the brew you drank on Terra, merchant, and you may wish to add sweetener."

The man took a sip and let it drain down his throat with an expression of delight and relief. "No, it is fine as it has been poured, Emassi."

Kathy was holding out a copy of the list to the prospective trader. She had also put out a little bowl, and totally without shame, she caught the merchant's eye and rubbed her thumb against her forefinger suggestively. "Have as many cups as you desire," she said very graciously. Zainal watched the man's face, but he showed no offense and, indeed, dug into his pocket and flipped a coin into the bowl, which already held some small change.

"We try to serve only the very best brew. This is called robusta, grown in the mountains of Kenya and considered the best of the best. It is, however, strong and you might prefer a milder brew."

The man cleared his throat and swallowed. "True, but exactly what is needed to start a chilly morning and a day's trading." He held out his hand to take the list from Kathy. "Ah, these all seem to be electronic parts from Terra."

"We are looking for spare parts to repair damaged machinery," Zainal said cautiously. "Do you know if you have any of these items in your stores?" According to the reconnaissance Chuck had done, this man did.

The man raised one hand over his shoulder, twiddling fingers, and suddenly two younger men were by his side.

"Check our stores and see if any of these items are in stock." He passed the list over. The clerks ran off but not without a longing sniff in the direction of the coffee.

"Return swiftly," Zainal added to their retreating backs, "and have a drink."

"Do not be so quick to offer enticements, Emassi," the merchant said, "or you will have all the raff and scaff of the market begging."

"The raff and scaff," Zainal said, gesturing toward Natchi, who was savoring each sip of his cup, "often know local gossip and fact. Natchi and I have known each other a long time and I find his talk is informed and genuine."

"I am Zerkay, Emassi," the merchant said, "and it is right that you should treat him with respect."

"As a veteran, he is due some preference." Zainal was not going to get into an argument about the treatment of ex-soldiers when he knew very little about the man to whom he was speaking.

Zerkay had finished his second cup, and when he would have added another coin, Zainal stayed the gesture and beckoned for Kathy to replenish his supply.

"Have a cup of the freshest brew, Merchant Zerkay, and from different beans and grind. Let me know which you prefer," she said in Catteni. She even had the right inflection of inferior to superior in words and cadence, and Zerkay raised his eyebrows in appreciation.

"Your Terrans speak good Catteni."

"They practice," Zainal replied, not without a touch of pride.

"Amazing," Zerkay said, lifting the freshly made coffee close enough to his nose to sniff appreciatively. "Hmmm. Yes, I can smell the difference. Lighter, milder."

"Arabica beans, grown on the highlands of Santa Lucia," Kathy replied.

"Highlands?" Zerkay asked.

"There are many sorts of coffee beans grown in Terra, Zerkay, and nearly as many ways of preparing the cup you drink."

"Are there? How interesting. I did not know. But then, I have had little chance to enjoy Earth." He inclined himself first toward Kathy and then toward Zainal, obviously quite eager to be indoctrinated.

"We can supply you with the beans you like best, Zerkay, that is, if we can agree on the items I require."

"Have you enough coffee to satisfy both your needs and my tastes?"

"That is what we must discover, Zerkay." Zainal held his cup up to Kathy for a refill.

"Ahhhh!" Zerkay raised his hand, signaled with his fingers for another of his young minions to attend him, and this one placed a stool by the table for his senior to use.

There was a bustle and reshuffle of people at the far end of the broad market corridor, and for a moment Zainal was afraid that the advancing pile of cartons would tumble off the lift that transported them. The cargo had not been tied to the lift bed and Zainal feared for the safety of all the so-irreplaceable items. Then the two young men appeared, one towing the lift, while the second made frequent adjustments to the piled cartons to prevent any from falling off.

Zainal caught Kathy Harvey's glance and the flick of white paper in her hand, doubtless a copy of the list. He made a flourish with one hand for her to check the items proffered. Most of the cartons were prominently embellished with the Terran Motorola logo, and some were indeed cell phones. Another carton seemed to hold switching mechanisms, vitally needed for the satellites. Zainal had memorized some of the relevant alphanumeric combinations of parts used by the various manufacturers of what he most needed, and these looked right: three letters and six or more numbers with a final letter.

Kathy Harvey was calling out the codes on the boxes to Bayes, who was checking them off.

"Pay dirt, boss," she said in English. "How about we give the nice man his own bean grinder as a special offer? Bayes hooked one up on an extension and we can give a demonstration. And let him smell the difference in the roasted beans. He has a big enough nose."

"Not that it'd work with all the stinks around here," Bayes remarked sotto voce.

"Coffee has its own indescribable smell. He may not catch the nuances, but would he admit that he doesn't when we give him the pitch?" Kathy replied.

"Which cup did you prefer, Zerkay?" she asked at her most deferential.

"The one I just had," the merchant replied, noting that Bayes had finished checking off the list and handed it with a bow to Zainal. Zainal nodded approval and settled himself on the edge of the stall top to see what was the most vital on this list to bid for.

"We must decide a fair exchange for this merchandise," he said. "Since you like coffee, are happy to find a supply, would you consider trading in coffee beans?"

"You have the beans themselves?" Zerkay was impressed.

"With great difficulty, but we have managed to obtain a small quantity," and Zainal thought of the full cargo hold of fragrant beans in their sacks, "which I will offer for the specific goods I have been sent to find."

"Sent by whom, might I be so bold as to inquire?"

"Why, by Botany, of course," Zainal replied. Which, at one level, was true enough.

"Ah yes, the planet that you have discovered."

"No, Zerkay, the planet on which I was dropped."

This information appeared to stagger Zerkay to the point where Zainal was afraid the man might tumble off his stool.

"You? An Emassi? Were dropped?" "Like a common criminal" was the unuttered qualifier.

"I was dropped, and I stay," Zainal replied firmly.

"Yes, I see," Zerkay said, and perhaps, Zainal thought, he really did. One day Zainal would discover who had made sure that a Catteni had been included in a disparate lot to be left to live or die on an unknown planet. However, Zerkay recalled himself to the business at hand, leaning an elbow casually on the stall, glancing at his half-empty cup and then at the list dangling in Zainal's fingers. "And how shall we judge the worth of each carton? For I think your friendly veteran will have already told you that trade has been very slow."

"Surely not slow for a man of your acumen." Zainal gestured toward Zerkay's obviously large and expensive stall, with its well-built amenities and outbuildings. "And trading finesse." Zainal indicated the fine fabric in which Zerkay clothed himself. So, Zainal thought, the initial courtesies were over. He had to play a very delicate balance now between desire and acquisition. His first encounter with a Barevi merchant was all-important . . . at least on what Kathy called their "coffee" standard.

"Is coffee another of those items no longer available on Earth?" Zerkay asked casually.

"What use could you possibly have for these parts?" Zainal countered, flicking his fingers toward the pile of cartons. "We Catteni are an inventive race, to be sure, but . . ." He let his tone drop off.

"But you would surely be searching them out to deliver the units into the hands of those who can assemble them effectively?" shrewd Zerkay replied.

"It is, of course, a tentative venture," Zainal said, lifting his hand in a diffident manner.

"There is uncertainty all through the system," Zerkay admitted. "But you have more command of particulars than a minor merchant on Barevi."

"Minor?" Zainal infused his tone with disbelief. "No merchant on Barevi has ever lacked up-to-date information."

Meanwhile, some of the younger people in the marketplace were sidling up to Eric's stall. One of them was bold enough to flip over the cards Gail had made. They giggled at the golden teeth. Instantly, Ferris stepped forward to give an explanation of dentistry and to forestall any attempt to make away with the cards in the spirit of mischief. For a little fellow, Ferris had learned from the Masai how to act with imposing authority.

Two pounds a carton was what Zerkay accepted to make the trade a deal. As well as samples of the other grinds, which Kathy packaged up before his eyes, making the measures generous. She marked the bags and advised him to keep track of those he preferred so they could supply him with his preference.

"And then I must produce more cartons for your inspection?" Zerkay was slightly amused. "This is not the way business is ordinarily conducted at Barevi."

"No?" Zainal asked politely, his eyebrows arched above an incredulous expression.

"Buyers do not set up stalls and woo the sellers to return items collected on another planet.

"Are you the man who brought about the end of the Eosi?"

"I am." Zainal dropped his voice to a somber tone of regret.

"You have already achieved much. I, as one of many, am in debt to you."

"Then do me the courtesy of telling other merchants that I deal honestly for the goods I require," Zainal said with great dignity.

"That will be my pleasure," Zerkay said, rising from his stool. It was retrieved by one of his escorts and neatly folded up. "Good trading, Emassi." He inclined his upper body respectfully and then, turning on one heel, walked back to his own stall.

As he was just out of sight, two of the young Catteni began to struggle over who had the right to look at the dentistry display. Eric came out and, by the simple expedient of removing it from contention and glowering at the miscreants, settled the problem. "If you should happen to know of someone with loose teeth, or who has lost teeth and wishes replacements, I am ready to supply the need," Eric said after them with a great deal of dignity. The younger Catteni withdrew before this unusual man took punitive measures.

"I could go to the drinking places. That's where most of the damage takes place, according to what Natchi says," Ferris suggested slyly to Eric. The dentist was somewhat taken aback by such a direct, if practical, method of finding customers. "I could speak to the owner and tell him where men who lose their teeth can come to have them repaired."

Discreet advertising was, of course, legitimate, so Ferris went off to see what he could discover.

While Ferris seemed fascinated by Eric, Ditsy seemed more interested in running errands and generally keeping his eyes open. It was he who remembered about the lift power packs and, somewhat diffidently, came to Zainal the next evening with an idea.

"We did pretty well swapping those lifts, didn't we, Zainal?" he began tentatively.

"We wouldn't have had as many coffee beans and the other good things we traded them for, that's certain," Zainal replied encouragingly.

"I know which merchant handles sales of new packs," Ditsy said.

"We shall need more, certainly, to take back with us," Zainal agreed.

"Couldn't we use more lifts?" Ditsy asked.

"We could."

"They don't recycle anything in Barevi. Did you know that?"

"Yes, I did," Zainal replied, thinking of the piles of waste gathered up by Rassi workers on a daily basis.

"Natchi said that's how he got his lift. He makes a living from it, even if he did get it from a stinking old garbage dump."

Said in Ditsy's crackly voice, "dump" sounded more final than ever.

"And you'd like to get one from the dump and see if you can fix it?"

"Well, they are useful items, and we don't have any now, do we, 'cause you traded the ones we had."

"That's right, I did. And I know that Jelco wanted one of ours very badly."

"Yeah, he was almost drooling over it," Ditsy said with a bit of malice in his smile. "Asking us stuff like its service longevity and capacity 'n' stuff that I didn't know. Natchi's been telling me about a lift's versatility and showing me how to make full use of one."

"Has he?" Come to think of it, Zainal had seen the two in deep conversation together. He wished that his own sons would find something honorable in the old soldier, rather than the usual contempt of the healthy for the infirm. But then, as Kris reminded him, his sons had had a very tough time for a few years and were probably still recovering from the "trauma." Certainly they were a little confused about where they belonged. A tutor would help them find their way.

"Yes. He says with the tools we got, he could fix any we could find and have them in first-class working condition. You see," and now Ditsy's demeanor changed, "no offense, but Catteni don't take care of their machinery at all well."

"I know that."

"Natchi said that there is normal wear and tear on any machinery, but a lot of that could be avoided with a simple servicing or minimal care. Mostly, in the case of the lifts, just not dumping the lift on its side in the dirt and muck around here." The boy had contempt for such irresponsibility. But then, he had lived through the terrible times of the occupation and his personal values came from that experience.

"So me and Natchi was—"

"Were," Zainal corrected without thinking.

"Were—thank you—wondering if we had your permission to bring a few things, like basically sound lifts, back to the BASS-One and fix 'em?"

"I think that's a very good idea."

Then Ditsy added forthrightly, "Between what I get in my hand for running errands now and then, which Kris said I don't have to throw into the coffee bowl, me and Natchi can get some bargains. We could use a coupla more lifts back home, couldn't we?"

"In Botany?"

"Either Botany or Terra," was Ditsy's response.

"That's a very good idea, Ditsy, and you have my permission, indeed my assistance, as well as my encouragement."

After that little chat, Ditsy was most often gone from the stall on pursuits of his own, and Ferris was looking for the toothless, to the point where running errands fell to Peran, Bazil, and Clune. Zainal was not so fond a father that he did not realize that it was his sons who complained about Ditsy and Ferris not doing their fair share.

It was not unusual to have to roust the boys from whatever discarded mechanical wonders they and Natchi were involved in to help bag beans for the next day's sales. And, to Zainal's momentary chagrin, Ditsy had to remind him about trading for new power packs. Ditsy said that, in point of fact, he needed several types.

"Natchi knows a great deal about machinery," Ditsy informed him, "and we got several things working real well but they need power packs. Are they like *our* old batteries?"

"The components are entirely different and the power more intensified."

Zainal was almost amused by Ditsy's careful separation of *our* as in Terran, and *yours,* as in Catteni. No harm in that since Ditsy was very careful about his manners in addressing any Barevian.

Two days after Ditsy and Natchi had successfully restored four lift panels, a young man appeared at BASS-1, asking to speak with Emassi Zainal. Natchi surveyed the man with shrewd eyes.

"Come from the hiring hall?" he asked.

"Yes, sir. A position for tutor is said to be still open."

Liking what he saw, for Natchi was a good judge of men, the old veteran gave him directions to Stall Ninety-two in the marketplace.

Not long afterward, Zainal saw a tall young man coming directly toward him, a tentative smile on his face. Could this fellow be a potential tutor? Observing him carefully as he approached, Zainal saw that he walked like a pilot, with a buoyancy, like someone not quite accustomed to a lighter gravity and yet with the balanced stride of an athletic person.

"Are you Emassi Zainal?" he asked, coming directly to Zainal. "I understand that you are looking for a tutor?"

"I am," Zainal replied, looking the young man over.

"My name is Brone." He offered Zainal a firm hand and shake. He stood squarely on his feet but out of the main flow of those using the aisle. Nor did he draw aside when several shabbily dressed Catteni passed by, as some of the other passersby did, as if not wishing to be infected by the lesser ranks. Zainal did not wish for his sons to be taught by a judgmental personality. They had endured enough of that sort of mental bias at the hands of their relatives.

"Tell me something about yourself, Brone," Zainal said and motioned for Kris to pour two cups of coffee. "And enjoy a cup of our coffee."

Brone reached into his belt pouch and withdrew several items: a sheet of paper, which turned out to be his educational background, neatly written, and an up-to-date license allowing the person (the ID picture was a slightly younger Brone) to pilot any inter-system craft.

"I see you passed in your first attempt," Zainal said, studying the card.

"I reviewed old test runs and studied hard," Brone replied, attempting to belittle what had been a sensible notion.

"Would you consider the position of tutoring my sons until such time as you might move on to captain your own ship?"

Brone smiled, an unusual response between two Catteni who had just met.

"I doubt, in today's economic situation, that I will have much chance to pilot a ship. Also, you must realize that I can only teach what I already know," Brone said.

"Your duties might include flying, for which you would get credit."

A look of hungry hope flashed on the young man's face and was quickly controlled.

"I want my sons to learn the basics and the protocols that every young Catteni must learn."

"That much I can teach, as well as navigational mathematics and port law," Brone said.

"You would not object to spending time on Botany?"

"I hear that it is a very beautiful planet, with a light gravity."

Zainal chuckled. Born on a heavy world and physically adapted to the problem, it was amazing how every native Catteni dreamed of living on a light-gravity planet. Of course, their gravity-bred muscles then gave them more advantages over the indigenous species. It was one of the main reasons they had been able to overcome soldiers pitted against them in the invasion.

"My sons should not lose any more of their heritage," Zainal said. "We are leaving shortly, Brone, to return to Botany. My sons are standing over there by the two Terran women. Would you be able to join us at such short notice?"

"They are well-grown lads," Brone said noncommittally.

"Peran is the elder and Bazil the younger."

Brone nodded. "I did not like my tutor."

"Nor did I," Zainal admitted.

"They wish to be pilots like their father? I heard that you were a scout."

"They have shown interest but they are too young to know their own minds."

"I didn't at their ages," Brone admitted candidly.

"I had no option," Zainal remarked.

"I heard that you were unable to answer your Eosi call."

That was a polite way of putting the matter, Zainal thought. And it also indicated that Brone had done some discreet questioning about him as a possible employer.

"I had been dropped on Botany at that point," Zainal replied with equal candor, holding the young man's steady gaze, though not telling the whole truth of the affair, which was no one's business. Zainal still had no clue as to who had included a Catteni in that hapless load of unwilling colonists.

"Which appears to have been felicitous," Brone replied diplomatically.

Zainal found that he liked the candidate's appearance, attitude, and answers. He saw Natchi coming in the back of the stall and nodding encouragingly. He saw Kris looking over at the close conversation they were having and decided on one last test of the candidate and beckoned her to join them.

"This is my mate, Kris Bjornsen, Emassi Brone," he said, and the young man acknowledged the introduction with a respectful bow.

"Lady Emassi Kris, it is my pleasure to meet you."

"Oh?" Kris drawled, slightly amused that he knew her by rank.

Brone bowed again. "I knew one of the families you sheltered on Botany. They spoke highly of you and were delighted with your rank award."

"Did they?" Kris replied, astonished, for the Catteni ladies had not been at all appreciative of her efforts during their stay on Botany.

"Come, Brone, I shall introduce you to my sons. Then, if you have no objection, we can quarter you on the BASS-1. They can help you bring your belongings."

"What text and study books do you have on the ship, Emassi?"

"Few, and no more than is usually carried on a KDM." Zainal scooped up what Catteni coins were in the coffee bowl and pressed them on Brone. "Find what you want to use from the secondhand bookstall. Spend as you see fit. You will be the one teaching. I shall reimburse you for any extra you spend. This evening we can discuss study subjects and hours at our leisure."

Brone agreed and went off with the boys.

"You know, Chuck, it's odd. There wasn't the usual brawl last night," Kris said as she watched the two boys walk away with their new tutor.

Chuck gave a snort. "No, because Natchi tells me Kapash really does keep order in the market. Of course, I wouldn't like to be caught."

"Oh?" Kris prompted.

"I don't approve of his methods."

"Which are? I wouldn't think Catteni would be impressed by his punishment triangle."

"'Tisn't that. He locks brawlers up and sells them to the next slaver in. Gotta keep those mines supplied, you know."

"Oh!" She almost tripped she was so surprised. "That would be quite a deterrent, wouldn't it?"

That was not as much reassurance as she thought a fight-free Barevi would be. However, there were customers awaiting their cups of coffee and queries about what could be traded for the beans. As Kris finished serving a new customer with the last cup of the current urn, Zainal decided it was time to close, and they packed up the things to be taken back to the BASS-1.

At dinner, Brone talked just enough to impress his new shipmates as well as his tutees with his basic understanding of current affairs on both Barevi and Catten. Natchi had the street gossip, but Brone had an overview. As Zainal had suspected, Kamiton had had trouble with his new government. No one had expected it to be easy. The Eosi were, as Kris might say, a hard act to follow since they had exerted such a strict, fear-based control over their underlings and total authority over their doings.

The loss of any new planets, rich with mineral assets, bit hard into the Catteni economy. Nothing ran as smoothly without the threat of Eosi disfavor. There were shortages at the existing mining planets and colonies. Catteni mines had not been producing their expected quotas since the Eosi, who had employed subtle ways of ensuring that quotas were met, were dispatched. No new products in the markets meant fewer buyers. Kapash's management of the market had indeed reduced the destruction caused by drunken spacemen, but they, in turn, found little to buy in the markets with their accumulated wages. Coffee, therefore, had an unusual popularity with those for whom it was a novelty and with those who had tasted it while occupying Earth.

While there was no place on this planet where coffee beans could be cultivated, there were jungle highlands on Botany. Kris had mentioned that this was a labor-intensive crop, since the beans had to be handpicked when ripe, but Zainal thought there would be plenty of hands to pick for assured supplies of the beverage. And if the Catteni addiction remained strong, they would have a solid market for export of Botany-grown beans. The very idea of exporting to the Catteni amused him. They could hold out for any price they cared to put on the commodity. "Black gold," Kris said they had once called coffee beans. Earth, of course, could export to Barevi, but first they needed cargo ships, which Botany happened to have several of for cargo runs. But first things first: like the spare parts that were needed. It might be decades before Earth could gear up its production lines.

The next morning started very well indeed, with an impatient clutch of people waiting for them to start serving the coffee. There were even some wanting to trade, and Zainal managed to obtain a carton of Nokia cell phones, a real prize.

"And most of them will do anything to secure a supply of the drink," Zainal replied, pointing to the ever-increasing diversity of cartons that were piling up as fruits of his labors to trade coffee for spare parts. "Gold and dentistry are doing well enough but take time." He waved to Eric's stall and the *rat-tat-tat* of his hammer on the gold he was pounding into the proper thickness for the crowns that had already been ordered: half payment on signing the contract and half on completion.

"Ah, another customer," Zainal said as a tall uniformed Catteni walked up to Eric's office, looking about for whoever manned it. He gestured to Clune to tell Eric that he had an interested party. There was a brief silence from the hammer, then Eric emerged and evidently Clune took over the flattening, though his blows weren't spaced as evenly as Eric's were and the rhythm of the *rat-tat-tat* was uneven.

"May I be of service?" Eric asked with the deference of a professional to any uniform.

"I have heard of your services and wish to avail myself of them."

As the man spoke, Zainal could see the empty spaces in his teeth—the four central ones. That seemed to characterize the usual applicant for Eric's skills. Three out of four, or so Eric had once remarked, adding, "Don't your people ever duck?"

"Now, sir, what may I do for you?"

"I am Emassi Ladade."

"I am Emassi Doctor Sachs," Eric responded, courteously proud. "If you would step this way where I may conduct a quick private examination." Eric ushered him into his "office." Much better for potential patients.

Ferris was proving extremely useful in sussing out genuine leads and had already saved Zainal from spending time with sellers who had nothing he wanted and were only there for the free coffee. But Zainal recalled an earlier conversation he'd had with Kris.

"We must watch him, Zainal," she had said, her anxiety getting the better of common sense.

"Why?"

"He's a magpie. A klepto," she said, trying to burrow into his shoulder.

"A what?"

"A magpie is a Terran bird who will grab anything that sparkles and take it off to its nest to play with."

"And the other word? Klepto?"

Zainal had excellent aural memory so she wasn't surprised that he queried an unfamiliar word. "That is a human who keeps taking things that do not belong to him or her, for a variety of reasons: sometimes it's merely envy of someone else possessing a pretty or valuable thing; other times it's just a psychological compulsion, the acquisition of the object as a one-sided game, played against the legitimate owners of the item. Or a denial of other people's rights to possession. It is considered a minor crime but a genuine obsession. The kleptomaniac often steals for the fun, not the need of the object stolen. Ferris is the second type, stealing for the fun of it and to win pleasure by giving it to someone."

"And he does not understand that stealing is wrong?"

"He understands that, but doesn't stop doing it. He became very deft, and I fear he was encouraged by his circumstances during the invasion to acquire things without paying the legitimate owners."

"The Catteni?" Zainal asked with remarkable charity.

"Not just the Catteni. He really is a Human sort of magpie, thieving because he likes the look of something or to outwit the owner."

"And you worry that he might start using his craft here?"

"I don't think Commander Kapash would turn a blind eye if Ferris were caught in the act."

"Is he often caught?"

"Now, only by those who know he has acquired without payment. Ferris has a grave character flaw. He really cannot understand buying and selling when he likes something or knows it's needed."

"Knowing it's needed might cause us more harm than good. I am glad you advised me about Ferris."

Even with that earlier conversation in mind, Zainal couldn't help thinking that the boy had been extremely useful on this mission. Ferris had supplied the numbers and names of store shed holders with whom Zainal could most profitably invest time and effort. However, Zainal dealt from a stronger position if the sellers came to him first. If he made known too publicly what he wanted, prices would be driven up. To date, Barevi merchants had found buyers thin on the ground so many had scrutinized him.

He had dealt as shrewdly as he could with those who had approached him, with beans and more carefully with what materials they had brought with them.

The morning when Eric started up his dental unit for the first time a new whirring sound broke through the usual noise of the marketplace. Zainal swiveled around, toward the sound made by Eric Sachs's equipment, and saw a huge Catteni sitting in the dental chair, his mouth wide open and the broken stubs of his upper teeth visible. There were also more merchants waiting to receive a cup of coffee and more coins in the little dish Kathy had put out.

There were three other very burly Catteni, guards from the look of their gear and clothing, watching as Eric attended to the man in his chair. The man did not dare flinch or squirm, and shortly Eric told him he could sit up. Then he began to tell him his options, with pictures he had provided himself for just such demonstrations, while Ninety Doyle did what translations he could with the technical terms involved.

"I can provide you with new gold teeth," Eric said. "It will take several days as well as quite a few visits to me to prepare and fit the crowns. And the work is not cheap."

"I have plenty of money," the Catteni said with a shrug, fascinated by the photographs of the step-by-step process he was about to undertake. From the textbooks he had removed from his office, Eric had, with Gail's help, organized some illustrative examples of treatment on yet another set of flip cards. "I am told you take cartons of things. I have cartons. I was a Catteni cargo captain. I took much from storehouses."

Eric snapped his fingers and Ferris, who had been hovering at his elbow, immediately produced copies of the lists. The man glanced down the columns of alphanumerically listed items and shook his head. Ditsy then produced the various logos for the companies that manufactured the spare parts wanted. The man tapped a finger on several, including, Zainal noticed, the NASA and Boeing logos.

"Have some cartons with these on them. You want?"

"First," Zainal said, stepping closer, "we will have to check the cartons to see if they are what we require."

The man grunted. "I am told you will buy anything."

"Not *anything*," Zainal said with a dignified contempt for such an assumption. "We have specific needs, and the services you require—as well as the gold for the teeth—will be expensive."

"I have gold," the man said with typical Catteni arrogance.

"It must be of a certain weight and purity," Zainal said, and Eric grinned at him—as much because Zainal had been relatively certain they would be required to supply the metal as because of his patient's attitude. Eric rummaged around in his supplies and brought up the gold-testing equipment.

"However, if you will show us your gold, we will see if it is of the quality that can be used for this unusual purpose."

"Gold is gold!" the Catteni protested.

"No, it is not," Eric replied, for he understood that much Catteni and the spirit of the remark. "For proper work, we need a certain quality of gold." He reached for his testing equipment, which their erstwhile customer recognized.

The man rose from the chair, signaled brusquely to one of his friends to stay and observe, then removed a nugget of gold from his pouch and handed it to Eric, as if certain of its intrinsic value and suitability.

"You come with me, then, and see what I have."

"Ditsy, if you will accompany me," Zainal said as he had no intention of wasting his time checking inventories.

"My pleasure, Emassi," Ditsy said with just the right touch of deference due a superior officer.

The man, who gave Zainal his name as Luxel, led them into the very depths of the marketplace, down rows of storage places, most with heavy metal doors and locks with complicated knobs and spikes.

"The kind you lose hands from trying to open," Zainal murmured in an aside to Ditsy, who then kept his hands close to his sides.

Luxel finally halted at an intersection of corridors.

"Stay, until I call," he said, pausing only long enough to be certain they stopped before he turned right.

They could clearly hear the snick of metal, a rasp of hinges, and then Luxel called to them to come.

Ditsy ran on a little ahead of Zainal, but when he stopped by Luxel's side he gave a whistle that Zainal had heard, expressing surprise or amazement.

"Opensezme," Ditsy murmured. "Ali Baba!" He was clearly impressed. And so was Zainal when he joined him.

Hughes and Lockheed logos dominated the mess of cartons in Luxel's little shed. Ditsy had his list out and was delving into its depths when Luxel suddenly yanked Zainal across the entry, himself assuming a blocking pose as three Catteni appeared in the alley. Zainal was quite willing to drape himself across the doorway, obscuring its contents from the passersby, who fortunately did no more than glance in their direction and quickly away, visibly picking up their pace to make speed past them. Luxel glared at Zainal as if he were to blame for their unexpected passage. Zainal returned his angry glance with an indifferent shrug. What did it matter if anyone saw what he had stored there? No one but Terrans could use it, much less buy it.

Clearly stenciled on the boxes were numbers and contents, and Ditsy had no trouble picking out items on the wish list. Solar Panel Array Assembled, HG-SP-88373-BO5, Expandable dish antenna: HG-MW-7712-d15-2-5. High on the list were circuit boards #A.05, but all Ditsy could find were A.01 and A.02. But that was a start.

"Jeez, Zainal, it's all the solar panel stuff," Ditsy said, shielding his jubilant remark from Luxel's hearing.

"Calm down, lad, calm down. Just check them all off as if they were quite ordinary."

"Oops, sorry, boss. Shouldn't have given myself away like that."

"No, you shouldn't have. Rule number one in bargaining: pretend you don't really want the items."

"I know, sir." Ditsy was most chagrined. "I'm sorry, Zainal, but most of the items are on here." He flicked the list as if it were annoying him. As they were speaking English, Luxel was unlikely to have understood. He then crammed the list in his pocket as if he were discarding it but could not presume to litter the slab floor with his trash. He went to the doorway and lounged negligently against the frame.

"There are some items here that might interest me," Zainal said, ignoring the disbelief in Luxel's expression. "But these are crates"— he mimicked their shape—"and the dentist man requires payment worthy of his skill, practice, and hard work, which is not as easily quantified as a mere crate."

"It is what the crate contains, Emassi," replied Luxel, still feeling he had the upper hand.

"You say you are a ship captain?"

Luxel nodded.

"How much are you paid by the day?"

"It cannot take a full day's captaincy to pay to replace a tooth—when I have provided the necessary gold metal," was his protest.

"And how long was it before you were allowed to dock a ship at Barevi port?"

"I had to serve only the minimum time before I got my full ticket," Luxel replied stoutly, expecting Zainal to be impressed.

"How long was that?" Zainal insisted.

"In my fourth year." He still felt Zainal should be impressed.

"It was in his seventh year in the practice of his profession that Eric Doctor was allowed to contrive gold crowns."

"Seven years?" Luxel was impressed. "It can't be that hard to do."

"Watch and see how cleverly he will shape the metal." Zainal ticked off points on his fingers. "Then, how carefully he prepares your tooth, which will take several days' work, how he makes a mold to fit exactly in your face." Zainal's expression suggested that this "face" was not worth so much effort. "And then fits the tooth. That is not as easy as parking a ship at Barevi port and takes much more skill and training." Zainal gave a nonchalant shrug and, jerking his chin at Ditsy to follow him, walked out into the alleyway, paying no further attention to Luxel. They did hear the click and snick as the captain secured his shed and his footsteps as he hurried after them. As much, Zainal thought, to be sure they were going to quit the sheds as to catch up with them.

On their return, Zainal was instantly disquieted when he saw the gaggle of folk, some in the tunics of the market police, clustered in front of their stall. Ferris had been anxiously awaiting their return for he darted toward Zainal, pointing out Kapash, who was speaking to Bazil and Peran with menace. "Questions, questions, and your sons have been answering in the negative. Which, of course, is only correct. You, Captain, must inform the merchants that you are the owner of that piece of gold and where you came by it." Ferris looked very worried and indeed, Zainal thought, had good reason to be.

The market security people were very careful to apprehend any thieves who might roam the market, and they were also on the lookout for suspicious quantities of any metals that might have been smuggled in without benefit of the percentage that by law the market should have on the sale of such commodities. Zainal had taken the precaution of making an inventory of all he had brought with him and the fact that it had been mined on Botany. He would not be subject to the tax if he used the gold in exchange for other items. But he knew the rules and he knew that Kapash was aware of that. Especially since Kapash had known of Zainal's time spent in command of Barevi. There were subtle differences between gold from disparate worlds, and the market had experts who could differentiate. Luxel's gold would obviously not be part of Zainal's inventory. Zainal just hoped that Luxel's sample had been appropriately declared by him.

As Zainal strode quickly to join his people and defend their innocence, he noticed that Eric had a very tight knot of young men around his place.

"Your father, all respect to him," Kapash was saying to a staunchly defensive Peran, "knows that gold must be taxed."

"Not in exchange for goods and services," Zainal said, charging right up to Kapash, making his squad break apart. He pulled Peran back to him, hands on the boy's stiff shoulders, tightening his fingers to show approval.

"Whatever," Kapash retorted angrily, aware that he had possibly overstepped his duties by bullying the son. "There is the matter of dispensing an unknown beverage that was not stipulated as the purpose for this stall."

"We are not dispensing a beverage for a price, but as a private refreshment while a bargain is being made," Zainal said crisply. He did not wish to antagonize Kapash but it was clear that the man wanted to cause trouble for him if he could.

"And the matter of that unusual equipment." Kapash gestured with a thumb over his shoulder at Eric's appliances. "They must be checked as possibly hazardous."

Zainal heard Eric's snort. "You obviously did not have a chance to visit Terra," Zainal retorted, "or you would know that this is dental equipment, to repair teeth."

"You there." Kathy Harvey pointed to a man in the forefront of the crowd that had now assembled to watch the scene. He had a grin on his face in anticipation of watching a fracas and it clearly showed his gold crowns. "You have gold teeth, so you can reassure Kapash that this equipment is useful."

"Me? How would I know that?"

"By the smile on your face. You have had similar work done on your teeth that Eric is beginning for the Catteni."

Kapash now gestured for the man to step forward. He did with great reluctance, jamming his upper lip down over his teeth. Eric stepped forward and met the man, putting his fingers on the man's chin.

"Open! Wider! Ah yes, good work," Eric said in Catteni, judiciously peering into the man's mouth. "And halitosis, too. Remarkable diet your folk have, Zainal. Whatever you paid for it, you got a bargain for that work," he added, amiably slapping the Catteni on the shoulder. "But," and now he waggled his finger at Luxel, "I do better work. Does he have the goods, Zainal? Because his gold is the proper quality. I would ordinarily cut it with platinum, but I think the piece will go far enough to provide him with the caps those tusks of his require. How do you grow teeth like that?" The last was said with admiration.

Eric shot Kapash a quick, measuring look and then resumed his place on his own dental chair and, folding his hands serenely across his chest, went back to observing the scene with amused detachment.

"You did not say that you were selling services, Zainal," Kapash accused him.

"You did not ask. We are selling services in exchange for goods, which is quite legal and requires no further licensing."

"But you are dispensing a beverage." He flicked dirty-nailed fingers at the cups on the table.

"We are, as I said, providing private refreshment for our customers as we discuss terms and prices."

"Would you care to discuss items with us, Market Commander Kapash?" Kathy Harvey said, with such a winning smile that Zainal hoped he'd remembered to tell her that the man was a known lecher. She offered him a cup she had just poured, and although he made a show of fighting with his principles, he took it quickly enough, savoring the smell of the coffee before he took a sip.

"That is splendid coffee. From Earth?"

"Yes indeed, a scarce commodity these days."

"And what are you trading it for? I need such facts for my report."

A report Zainal was certain would never be written, much less filed.

"As I mentioned before, we are looking for spare parts that were transported here during the recent occupation of Earth."

"Ah yes, Supreme Emassi Kamiton remarked to me that you might be seeking to purchase some bits and pieces."

"Yes, well, my success would mean that he"—Zainal lowered his voice and leaned toward Kapash—"would be able to improve his own communications network."

"How?"

"Ah." Zainal stepped back. "Now that would be telling, wouldn't it?" He gave a slight smile.

"What exactly do you wish to bargain for?" There was a little emphasis on the "bargain," and since Zainal knew that as market manager Kapash would know exactly who might have what, including items he might have secreted in case they became valuable, Zainal allowed his smile to broaden. Zainal thought rapidly of a diplomatic way of diverting Kapash, a man known for his greed.

"This and that," he said with a negligent flick of his fingers. "What have you to tempt us?"

"How do I know that when you do not tell me what you seek?"

Zainal thought quickly and noticed Ferris fondling his prized handset.

"Such items as this," he said, unclipping the unit from Ferris's belt and displaying the cell phone. "Invaluable communications unit. See, I am in contact with my ship at all times."

He depressed the panic button and instantly a voice, made tinny by the cheap handset, answered.

"Baker Alpha Sugar Sugar One."

"Zainal. Testing. Above board, out," he responded and closed the connection before offering Kapash the instrument to examine. They had devised a number of passwords for different situations. "Above board" was "Things are proceeding well," while "Mayday" meant "Emergency." "Marines are coming" would indicate immediate physical help would be appreciated.

Between finger and thumb, Kapash accepted the unit from Zainal and turned it over.

"Connects across miles of empty territory so even the fastest advance units may be in touch."

Kapash handed it back with an air of disdain. "I can do that with any unit on Barevi."

"Certainly. I would expect you to be so equipped. But Botany is not so well supplied. Nor could we find more in the few unlooted storehouses on Terra. Most of the type we need on Botany are probably," and Zainal paused to swing his glance around the market, "here. However, coffee, too, is in short supply on Terra." Which was basically the truth since there was no transport to bring the beans to foreign marketplaces.

"No more?" Kapash was startled and sipped eagerly at his cup.

"No. Much of Earth's agriculture was laid to waste. It takes time to grow proper coffee and it takes experts to harvest the crop and process it. There will be no more until the industry recovers from the occupation." Zainal didn't think the Catteni had looted all the items required for the production of coffee, but he was reasonably certain that he'd find some spare parts languishing here on Barevi, apart from those needed to repair the plantations' vehicles.

"None?" Kapash seemed genuinely upset.

"We have the last of the roasted beans." Which was certainly true of the beans they had acquired from Kenya and Santa Lucia.

Kapash continued to look dismayed, but a flicker of thought behind his eyes told Zainal that, not only was the man fond of his coffee, but he would also wish to enjoy it without stint.

"What standard would you use to trade for more of the hand units?"

Zainal hefted his. "Equal weight of beans for the unit seems fair."

Kapash turned toward the stall, saw the scales, and peremptorily gestured for Zainal to bring the unit over. He did and Kapash put it on one side of the scales. Zainal gave Kathy the sign to pour beans in the other side. She was scrupulous in making up the weight, even to the last bean, which edged on the side of generosity. Then she spread both hands out to indicate it was up to Kapash.

He looked at the beans, picked up a handful, and sniffed them.

"They make a rich cooked coffee," Kathy said winningly. She used "cooked" for "roasted" since there was no equivalent Catteni word to describe the exact process.

"How many cups of coffee would that lot make?"

"If you grind properly, this should make four large pots of good, strong, black, rich cooked coffee. You probably have a nut grinder at home." She showed him the one she had brought from the BASS-1.

"Is that what those are used for?" Kapash remarked, lifting his eyebrows.

Zainal wasn't sure which he meant but it had been a wise precaution to bring along grinders and what was left of the glass drip-filter cafetiers. They even had a carton of the glass insets on board the BASS-1.

"A special brew requires perfect equipment, as I'm sure you have discovered, Manager Kapash," Zainal said suavely. Peran was beginning to jiggle in front of his father, restless now that the adults were so obviously absorbed, but Zainal tightened his hand on the boy's shoulder to remind him of the respect due Catteni adults.

Kapash's coffee was now cool enough for him to take a bigger swallow, which he seemed to be rinsing around in his mouth, savoring. "This is different from other brews I have sampled."

"You are currently enjoying a mild roast of arabicas," Kathy Harvey said and reached for another pot she had recently made and a clean cup. "Now this is from robusta beans, which give a much stronger taste."

Kapash's eyes widened with appreciation as he smelled the steam and, blowing on the liquid, attempted a sip of the new coffee. "Mmmm, much stronger and far more to my taste."

"There are many different types of beans, and combinations of them, Manager Kapash, for those subtle and sophisticated enough to appreciate the finer flavors," Zainal said. "What else have we brewed, Captain?"

Kapash actually seemed to have sophisticated taste buds because he was able to distinguish the milder roasts that Kris had made from the stronger robusta. He summoned a minion and sent him off to collect the proposed merchandise. Of course, the handsets on Botany would be of no use unless they could put up the satellites, but Zainal was encouraged by the possibility. Leave it to the market manager to have set aside choice trading items.

Meanwhile, Eric was already at work on Luxel, pouring a substance into those wide jaw trays he had insisted he must have, and making Luxel open his mouth so wide it looked as if he might lock his jaw hinge. Then Luxel had to sit, those things in his mouth, while Eric consulted his wristwatch and fingered a little blob of the green substance he had placed in Luxel's mouth.

What a bizarre way to regain possession of the spoils of invasion! Zainal wondered exactly what deal Eric had fashioned with Luxel. Four teeth to be replaced? How could they get Luxel to give them items from eight cartons, instead of only four? How many had Eric bargained for? And then there were the larger necessities: the framework on which the individual units would be hung as well as the thermal protective material. That didn't come in a carton but was as necessary for the satellites as the major units that powered, controlled, and directed them in orbit. There were moments when the magnitude of the task he had committed himself and the others to complete overwhelmed him. Sometimes, he thought, very privately so he couldn't hear it himself, that his success as executioner of the malignant Eosi was leading him to think he was invincible. He could be vincible on another mission, but *not* this one! So much depended on his success here on Barevi. It would certainly set a precedent.

"There." Zainal pushed the six bags of coffee beans toward Kapash. "You will deliver the hand units tomorrow?" Kapash blinked, and at first Zainal thought the man considered the beans a bribe. "We shall be looking forward to your messenger." He had completed a subtle bribe with Kapash, giving him the coffee beans before taking ownership of the hand units that had been the object of the trading. They could also expect more business from Kapash: he was definitely a coffee addict. There were more sacks of coffee beans in the capacious hold of BASS-1, and they knew where to get more. Then he saw Captain Harvey trying to get his attention and he strolled over to her.

"We'll need more beans, Zainal." Her eyes sparkled with this evidence of success. "While you were gone, we had a coffee fiend who has delivered us five Motorola crates of orbiting controllers. We definitely need more beans."

"Do we have any coins to pay for a hire lift?"

Harvey thrust a hand into a pocket and emptied the contents into his hand: small coins, to be sure, but sufficient in number to pay Natchi's modest charge. He signaled the veteran from his box and then looked around for Peran.

The boy materialized beside him. "Return to the ship and ask Floss to come back with ten sacks of assorted beans. Here are tokens for Natchi's lift."

The veteran was almost as prompt in attending Zainal as Peran had been. "May we hire your lift again? Peran, my son, requires it for an errand."

"Such a sturdy lad, Emassi. Surely he will captain ships when he has finished his training."

Peran was agreeable to having such a future assigned him, and he straightened his frame to make himself appear taller, more worthy of such rank.

"Indeed, when his tutor approves his lessons," Zainal said, and Peran's face fell. "Now he must go about his father's errands." Zainal slipped Peran the tokens, which when he had offered them to Natchi, the old one-armed man had cheerfully waved aside.

"I owe you service for the many fine cups of coffee I have received, Emassi. I also need to walk. I will accompany your son."

"My thanks, Natchi, for your courtesy."

Natchi performed a maneuver more salute than bow. Then, with smartness reminiscent of other days, he turned and followed Peran to where he had stored his lift.

8

By the time they reached their stall the next day, a goodly crowd was waiting. So they scurried to get the next urn of coffee started and poured out what was in the hottle for the impatient customers. Among them were interested sellers, and Zainal and Chuck began again checking their lists against the proffered items. Much coffee was consumed: Zainal was beginning to think that he was getting all Barevians addicted to the beverage. Well, there was nothing wrong with supplying a desired substance.

About mid-morning, when Zainal was winding up a good deal with someone who had twenty-volt truck batteries to trade, Bazil appeared, a very anxious expression on his face. Unwilling to interrupt Zainal at what was obviously a crucial time, Bazil approached Kris, pulling her sleeve urgently.

"My father must help. It's Ferris. He's being hauled to Kapash's office as a thief," Bazil said.

For a moment, sheer funk robbed Kris of any strength.

"Where is he? What did he take? Do you know, Bazil?"

"He's been visiting all the drinking places, talking to the servers. Like he told Zainal he would do, to advertise Eric's services. Then a big guy arrived this morning, swearing Ferris had robbed him. He didn't say what, but Ferris ran, and one of the market guards caught him. They're hauling him off to Kapash's office. Oh, Kris, if he's put in that triangle, he'll be killed." Bazil was almost sobbing with fear.

Kris was really torn about interrupting Zainal. Maybe she could handle this. She beckoned to Chuck. Clune, having heard what Bazil had said, stepped forward.

"I'll come, too," he said, pumping up his biceps.

Chuck also saw how deeply involved Zainal was in the business of trading and he took Kris's arm.

"What could he have stolen? And yes, I know his history, Kris, but we'll get him out of it. I know Kapash has just been waiting for the chance." Chuck scooped up something from the digitally locked box before he slammed it shut and passed it over to Sally Stoffers, telling her to guard it. She knew it contained gold flakes and the smaller nuggets. "We'll just see if we can deal with this." Kris saw the marked hesitation on Bazil's face.

"I am Lady Emassi, Bazil. I can deal with a mere market manager. Tell Zainal we've gone to the manager's office, Sally, but *only* when he's finished dealing. It's this way, isn't it, Bazil?" Kris said, striding down the long side of their square.

Bazil still looked scared and dubious but he ran to catch up with her, worried about Ferris. While she knew that Bazil might be feeling cheated of his father's support, she also knew that Zainal would be annoyed with his son for interrupting him.

There was an interested crowd around the manager's office but Kris, with Chuck and Clune beside her, formed a wedge and pushed her way through, alarmed to hear Ferris sobbing.

"I stole nothing. It was on the floor. The man said I could have it," he was saying.

"Who are you?" the man demanded, and she saw the gap in the front of his teeth.

"I am Lady Emassi, a rank conferred on me by Supreme Emassi

Kamiton," she announced, squaring her shoulders and trying to control her panting, for they'd rushed to get there. "Ferris is one of our young people. What do you allege he has stolen from you?" She knew she was imitating Dame Edith Evans at her most regal and repressive, but perhaps it would work.

The man pointed at the gap in his teeth. "My toof."

Kris managed not to grin at his lisp. "How could a slender lad like Ferris steal your tooth?" she asked, managing to retain her Evansian pose.

"It was on the floor," Ferris said, as if that conferred legitimacy on his action.

"And that's where you found it?"

"Yes. On Sicrim's floor. This morning."

"But the toof is mine," the fellow insisted, becoming more agitated.

"I was just taking it to Dr. Sachs," Ferris said, looking penitent and put-upon.

"But it is mine!"

"If it was left on the floor since last night, sir, it may be presumed that you had abandoned it," Kris pointed out. "Therefore, the lad has not knowingly *stolen* from you as an act of bad faith. He was, in fact, bringing it to the one man on this planet who can replace it in your jaw."

"He can?" the man exclaimed.

Now Ferris shoved his hand in his pocket and displayed a tusk neatly bagged in one of the little plastic envelopes that Eric had brought with him.

"That's mine!" The fellow lunged to repossess it.

"A lot of good it does you in the bag," Ferris said contemptuously, recovering some of his usual impudence, and he folded thin arms across his chest. "I cleaned it off, which Eric says is necessary, and put it in the bag for safekeeping. I did not know who it belonged to."

Ceremoniously, a look of creditable innocence on his face, Ferris handed it over.

"It belongs to me." The man slipped the item into his pocket, leaving one hand protectively over his tooth, as if Ferris might somehow regain it.

Kris swiveled squarely to face Kapash, who had been listening and watching the proceedings with an odd expression on his face.

"How could Ferris have known the owner, Manager Kapash?" Kris asked earnestly. "Now that he does, he has returned it. No theft has occurred. There has been honorable restitution of a missing object."

"But he took what does not belong to him," Kapash said, his face severe and threatening. "He is a thief. Nor did he properly attempt to find out who owned the tooth."

"But Sicrim said I could have any teeth I could find," Ferris said plaintively. "I wasn't doing anything wrong. Ask Sicrim."

"Is this Sicrim present?" Kapash asked after briefly mulling that over.

He is trying to be reasonable, Kris thought, in these ludicrous circumstances, but Sicrim was not among those who crowded around the office.

"He is a thief!" the tooth owner said unforgivingly, pointing down at Ferris with a dirty, broken finger.

"He is a boy," Kris said, giving the plaintiff a long and sour look for his bullying attitude. "And the sooner you get to the dentist to replace that tooth, the better. The longer you wait for treatment, the less chance you have of getting it back into your jaw, you know."

"Aha!" Kapash said, pointing at Kris. "So this is how you get business for that expert of yours?"

"What? I'm not the one knocking teeth out, Kapash. He has to get that done for himself," she said, jerking her thumb at the plaintiff. There was a ripple of amusement from those so avidly listening to the discussion. She wished she'd thought to bring some packets of beans, although dropping some on Kapash's desk would have been too obvious a bribe. But, to judge by the onlookers' attitude, she also sensed that she had made a good argument.

"Let it be, Kapash," someone from the crowd said.

The faint wail of a siren was audible after that remark. "Besides, there's the riot alarm. That's your business, Kapash."

Kapash held up his hand to silence those in the office. Plainly heard were aggressive shouts and calls as well as the bray of the siren.

Clearly Kapash had to investigate, and with a glare at Kris, he rose and stalked out of his office, gesturing to his guards to fall in behind him as he went in search of more culpable and lucrative targets. Most of those gathered followed him to see what amusement the new diversion would provide.

Kris held out her hand to Ferris and led him out of the office.

"I did have Sicrim's permission, Kris, I did. I know you won't believe me."

"But I do, Ferris. You have more sense than to get us into any trouble with your taking ways. Especially after this," she said as they walked as quickly as possible out of the square.

Whistles, more sirens, and startled, hurt cries could be heard, and served to hurry them out of the vicinity.

They met Zainal, hurrying in their direction, in the main corridor of the next square.

"What happened? What's happening?" He pointed in the direction of the audible disturbance.

Kris gave him a quick summary while Ferris hung his head in shame for having caused the emergency and bringing trouble to his friends.

"I think Kapash would have loved to press charges, but . . ." Chuck added.

"It was a good notion, Ferris, but you see how careful we have to be here, do you not?" Zainal said, one hand jiggling the thin shoulder, making the boy meet his eyes.

"Yes, Emassi, I do. I will not cause you more trouble."

"Good lad. Now, we will not mention this to Eric," Zainal began when a stranger intruded on their circle. Ferris quickly took refuge behind Zainal because it was the toothless man who had barged into them.

"You!" He pointed severely at Ferris. "You will take me to this man who can put my toof back in my jaw!"

"Of course," Zainal answered pleasantly and gestured in the proper direction.

"I heard of this fellow," the man said amiably, as if he hadn't nearly caused Ferris considerable bodily harm. "But first I needed my toof."

The word still came out with a lisp but no one dared grin.

"The procedure takes a little time, does it not, Ferris?" Zainal said, since he knew very little about such matters whereas Ferris had been in constant contact with Eric, absorbing everything the genial dentist said.

"It does," and there was a little gleam in Ferris's eye that suggested to Kris that it was not all pleasant either. "But I washed it as Eric told me to do, and kept it safe in that little bag." He pointed to the man's pocket, where he had seen him deposit his errant tooth.

"I am indebted to you, young man," the fellow said, "and I apologize for the market manager's zeal."

"It has been well resolved," Kris said.

"I am Mischik," the Catteni said, and the others were required by courtesy to name themselves. "You are the Botany folk."

"We are," Zainal said proudly.

"And you are truly a Lady Emassi?" Mischik said, lisping more than ever on the double sibilants.

"I am."

"Remarkable," he said.

"I know," she replied equably.

By then they had reached their own aisle and Ferris ran ahead to tell Eric of a new customer. Zainal and Kris hastened to the stall since there seemed to be quite an influx of clients wanting to sample the coffee. More likely, Kris thought, to see if the Botany lad had survived the confrontation with Kapash.

"Nothing like a mild emergency to spread the word," Kris murmured to Zainal as they served coffee as quickly as they could pour it.

Word indeed had spread—though the riot Kapash had gone to suppress had not—and Eric had many inquiries about his services. He had ministered to Mischik and arranged for him to come back the next day and see if the tooth was settling in. Eric was forthright in saying that the sooner he could restore a tooth the better the chances of success, but Mischik was happy enough to be able to speak without the annoying lisp. Eric assured him that failing the natural reestablishment of the tooth, he could make a bridge to close the gap.

Everyone was tired when Zainal announced that they had better close and, after today's episode with Kapash, everyone was determined not to arouse any further attention from the market commander.

9

Among the many goals Zainal had set for himself, gaining entrance to the port commander's office—and the port commander's files—to access the information on the destinations of the slave-carrying ships was topmost on his list. He needed only to get into the facility and find an empty office with a control board to access the information. Another ransom to be executed. It was his responsibility to right that massive wrong done to Kris's people, even if she felt he was carrying responsibility too far. These Terrans should have been allies, not slaves, to the Catteni. There was the unassailable fact that unless he did something, he doubted those enslaved would ever return home, and with all those captives exiled from their home world, would Humans ever be on good terms with the Catteni?

He was glad that Kris had managed to save Ferris. The boy had been invaluable for discreet reconnaissance and had already saved Zainal from spending time with sellers who had nothing he wanted. Any excuse to waste time and have the chance to drink the fine coffee obviously motivated some of their visitors.

Trading continued briskly all morning and well into the afternoon, when the more prosperous merchants retired for the noonday meal, leaving their goods and stalls in the charge of their seconds. A few came to buy a cup of coffee when their masters had safely disappeared. Zainal hoped it would escape Kapash's notice that coffee was now for sale. He thought privately that it would take many busy days for what they earned for the beverage to make a substantial profit.

He had to discard that opinion later, after Floss, with Clune very close to her, took over from Kathy Harvey at the coffee bar. Kris had breezily told him that's what they had invented: the first Barevi coffee bar. There were also rumors that complaints had been issued to the market manager that people were obstructing the way to and from other stalls by gathering thickly in front of the "coffee bar." By late afternoon, however, they had enough money to rent another stall, which came equipped—for a price—with tables, chairs, and a proper catering area. Floss, safely ensconced behind the "bar," dealt capably with the flow of customers and ignored the laughs and remarks from the idlers gathered at Eric's office.

By early evening, Zainal began to watch for signs of the usual rampage of guards and spacemen who would have spent most of the day drinking. When he felt the time would soon be upon them, and he noticed that other merchants were beginning to close their stalls, he called a halt to the day's work. Ferris chattered away to Eric as he and Bazil helped pack away the dental office, adding the coffee urn and cups from the main stall. Zainal had seen to it that all the goods they had bartered for had been taken to the BASS-1 as soon as the deals were completed. So it was a relatively simple matter to pack up and return to the KDM.

Everyone was hungry and exhilarated by the success of the day, and full of ideas about how they could accomplish more the next.

Even Eric was in good form, having acquired several clients, besides Luxel, for gold crowns. Ditsy had said he should hire the man with the golden smile who had so fortuitously been there when needed.

"If word gets around, Zainal," Eric said, waiting until Kris could fill his plate again, "I will need an assistant. My clients do not strike me as patient men."

"Gino and I aren't doing anything much," Ninety Doyle said. "If it's just muscle work you need . . ." He made a pantomime of tapping a hammer.

"Well, not exactly muscle work, but it does take time to pound even the softest gold into a malleable foil." Then Eric perked up. "Old Natchi, what a talker. I understand about three words out of a dozen. I could fit him with a set of dentures that would do him better service than what he has left in his mouth."

"Most of the time in the drinking places, when people get their teeth knocked out, it's after market hours," Ferris said. "For emergency treatment, do I give them this berth number?"

Zainal did not like that idea, for he wished to be as private as possible on BASS-1, but he countered with a suggestion. "You can present yourself, and your qualifications, to the local medical men. Then, if they think your services are necessary, they can make an appointment for the patient to see you. Preferably at the market. As soon as we can, I will try to find a better place in which you can work, Eric."

"That would save us from being a raree-show, certainly," Eric said, accepting Zainal's offer.

"Does Floss have to go back?" Clune asked plaintively. The pair of them were holding hands under the table.

"I don't mind, dear," she said, soothing him with a hand on his much bigger one. "At least they can't pinch me when I have the coffee bar in front of me."

"Do not take any overt action, Clune," Zainal felt obliged to warn him.

Clune snorted. "I'm not crazy, Zainal. Every one of them there today outweighed me, and a lot would have had the reach on me. Stupid I ain't. Taking on one of those guys would put me out of action. I gotta stay on duty, pet."

"You could lick 'em one-handed," Ditsy said with misplaced loyalty. "You got skill! And Chief Materu taught you some dandy moves."

"There will be no competitions with Catteni brawlers," Zainal said, eyeing Clune, who nodded willingly enough, and Ditsy, who finally settled as far back in his seat as he could, as if trying to make himself less visible.

"I know it was a wearing day," Kris said, "but we have to pack more coffee beans for tomorrow. Having them on hand is very useful." She nodded toward Kathy Harvey, who had put forth the suggestion. Everyone groaned but even Ferris and Zainal's sons roused themselves from the table to attend to the chore, packing the beans in bags they had taken from a deserted Terran Starbucks cafe.

"We're running out of the sacks we brought with us," Ferris remarked. "They ought to pay us for universal advertising rights."

"Can we find anything as useful here as these bags, Zainal?"

"Quite possibly. You boys, see what you can find tomorrow morning once we've set up the stalls. And look around for something that will suit Eric's requirements. Usually private stalls are at the head of the blocks."

"You mean we can prowl?"

"Just keep order, Dits," Zainal said.

"We can look, too, Father," Peran volunteered eagerly.

"Perhaps, after your lessons with Brone, you may take a walk." He nodded at Brone, who accepted the suggestion with a nod.

Zainal was loath to let his sons loose since, as Catteni boys, they would come under the scrutiny of all male adults, but with Brone in attendance, he could be sure that their natural high spirits would not lead them into trouble.

"We will think Masai and ask ourselves if the chief would permit his band to do whatever it is we think of doing."

"Chief Materu was very strict but fair," Bazil said helpfully, "but by the Gods, he could scowl something fierce and that always meant extra duty." He wrinkled his nose in dismayed remembrance of such disciplinary frowns. "A question, Father?" he added, raising a tentative index finger. When Zainal nodded, he went on. "In most African tribal lands, if things get stolen, they get stolen back right fast. I mean, we all know the market's full of things stolen from Earth. Couldn't we just steal them back without all this bartering?"

Zainal cleared his throat. In some of the very primitive societies he had seen as a scout, the stealthy reclamation of stolen goods was considered part of training. The idea being to get in, get the purloined things, and return unseen. The Turs had made that into an art, and many had died following that tradition elsewhere.

"We abide by the laws of the planet we're on, Bazil. And, however tempting, theft is brutally punished on this planet, and Kapash would relish a chance to apply the full measure of the law against any one of us."

"Oh!" Ditsy and Ferris echoed Bazil's stunned response faintly.

"But if they didn't know it was us?" Bazil persisted, jabbing his thumb in his chest.

"Who else would they suspect, Bazil?" Chuck asked, frowning darkly as he leant weight to Zainal's comment.

"However, you may wander but just within the market area," Zainal replied. "And check in hourly with me or Kris," he added, pointing to their comm units.

"I got offered gold coin for mine," Bazil replied.

"Accept nothing less than forty," was Ferris's fast response until he noticed Zainal's frown.

"Do not suggest they are for sale," he said firmly.

"I saw where we can get more," Ditsy said, hauling a scrap of paper out of his pocket. Zainal leaned forward eagerly. "Iridium hand units, Stall Seventy-two-K. At least I think it's a K." Ditsy passed Zainal the scrap, a dirty finger pointing to the logo.

"Right. Good for you, Dits," Zainal said. "I wonder if Kapash will tell me who rents the stall."

"If he doesn't, Natchi will," Ferris said. "He knows everything there is to know about the market."

At that, Kathy wrinkled her nose. "I don't know about the male facilities, but the ones for us are deplorable. Really, what does stall rental go for if not cleaning up the toilets?"

"Repairing the damage the drunks do," Ferris replied with contempt.

Zainal gave Kathy a little nod. Such negligence could be a useful talking point in his next discussion with the market manager. But then, Kapash might have little interest in amenities for women. Zainal was certain Kapash held the traditional Catteni views on women: they should be grateful for what they get.

"I volunteer to do some cleaning there tomorrow," Floss offered. "I can't stand the stench, and who knows what I'd pick up from it."

Zainal wasn't sure why Kris looked so pleased by Floss's offer, but she clearly approved of the girl's willingness.

"Let's fill those sacks—"

"Tote dat barge, lift dat bale," Clune sang in a deep, rich bass that startled everyone.

"Git a little drunk and you lands in," Ferris sang in a cracked tenor voice and pointed to Clune to finish the song.

"Jay . . . ill . . ." was his response, dropping into the deepest part of his lush voice. A burst of applause ensued, which he hushed with his hand. "Ol' Man River, he just keeps rollin' along." He finished the impromptu recital with a flourish and a bow and was accorded another round of applause before he waved his friends to continue with their chore of packing beans.

Zainal did not know much of singing, but the work did go more swiftly as others asked Clune to sing their favorite songs. By the time Kris called a halt, they had worked their way through twenty-five pounds of dark-roasted robusta beans, and the same of the milder, washed arabicas, sufficient to meet unexpectedly high sales the next day. Sally finished adding up their income from the day's work and Eric reported on how many appointments he had made for dental work. He had insisted on being paid half of the cost of the work in advance—a fact that kept them solvent for local purchases—and half on completion. The dentistry was going to be a profitable asset of this tour. Zainal went through what he had done with the day's income and what he needed to do with tomorrow's.

"Then, we can take some profit," he figured.

"With any luck," Kris amended, and then covered her lips in apology for the negative comment. "However, I get the feeling that they are all holding back."

"I do, too," Kathy said.

"As if they were testing us, somehow? Or perhaps simply not willing to trade?" Chuck asked.

"But from what Natchi and that footless friend of his, Erbri, said, they have had no buyers for what's in their storage rooms, so why are they not willing to come forward and make what profit they can from us who are willing to buy?" Zainal remarked. "In fact, Natchi's bringing in two more mechanics besides Erbri to help fix the lifts and other reparable things left to rust. We've a good business going in repair and mechanics as a side venture."

"Could Kapash be inhibiting the merchants for all he pretends to help?" Kris asked.

"He's not been helping," Zainal said. "He's determined to thwart us. Be wary of him, all of you."

"Why does he have it in for you, Zainal?" Chuck asked, expression bland.

"I knew him when he dealt in illegal drugs, and he knows I know it."

"So he's the one made sure you were on that colony transport?" Kris asked.

Zainal let out a long breath. "I don't *know* that but I have been asking some discreet questions through Natchi, Erbri, and their coterie. Remember to give any disabled vet at least one cup of coffee, team." Everyone nodded.

"What better way to get rid of a possible informer than to put him where he might die from indigenous causes or, with any luck, be executed by angry slaves?" Kris remarked irritably.

Clune spoke up with great dignity. "Chief Materu said that you make your own luck."

"Chief Materu is a great leader," Zainal said. "Then let us make our own luck!"

"Right!" Chuck seconded firmly, and there was agreement in the circle of tired bean packers before they rose stiffly to their feet and scattered to their on-ship quarters.

"Is this truly a good beginning?" Kris murmured to Zainal when they were abed.

"You can't exactly say they beat a path to our door," he replied, smoothing her hair down, once again reveling in the silk of it, before he cuddled her close to him.

"Where'd you get that expression?"

"Ferris, of course," Zainal said, giving her a little hug.

He closed his eyes to get on with the business of falling asleep.

It was a long while, despite her appreciation of his proximity, before she could follow his example. And the morning came far too quickly.

veryone was awake on the call and came out quickly to eat their
first meal of the day. Then Peran went to see if Natchi had arrived
with his lift as he had agreed the previous evening. Peran had sneaked
a piece of good Botany bread, well lathered with honey, to give to
Natchi. They had struck up quite a friendship. Natchi was there and
grateful for the bread, which he said he had never tasted the like of.
Peran had accessed a recipe for the stuff from the ship's library but
didn't know where some of the ingredients might be had. He didn't
know what "butter" was, or "flour" or "yeast."

However, Natchi knew a great many things and would work on
the problem. At least they had the method to make bread and knew
its ingredients. You couldn't know if you could make things until you
knew what they were. Which was why Peran's father
was here on Barevi—to find the component parts needed for the
comm satellites and other such highly technical things, which were
supposed to make a vast number of things "better." Peran already
thought "life" was different and "better" when he recalled—which
he did not often do—that time of his life spent without his father and
being punished by his aunt and uncle for things that, for the most part,
Peran didn't even know he'd done wrong. He'd warned Bazil and thus
prevented his brother from receiving like measures of "corrective"
discipline. Now that his father was here, it was always "better." He
would have liked being with his father sooner, but life in the Masai
camp had been very interesting, too, and Chief Materu fair in his
judgments. He never had understood what his father, who acted in all
ways honorably, had done to deserve being an outcast from his family.

Peran, with Bazil's assistance, transferred the cartons of packed
beans to the lift. By then everyone was ready to go, Clune carrying
the hottle of coffee left over from breakfast. He had poured a cup for

Natchi, who was quite willing to drink it down with the bread Peran had given him.

"The last of the bread is in today's sandwiches," Kris announced as she deposited the basket—a hand-woven one from Botany—on the lift bed.

"Is it hard to make bread, Kris?" Peran asked, winking at Natchi.

"No, but you need certain things one can't find here on Barevi."

"I thought Barevi had everything," Bazil replied, eyes wide in surprise.

"Not quite *everything*," Zainal said, laughing and ruffling his son's hair.

"What, for instance?" Peran asked.

"Milk . . ."

"That white stuff you made us drink. The cow's milk? From Kenya?"

"Very nutritious," Kris said firmly.

"Doesn't it come in cans, too?" Ferris asked.

"It does, but I haven't seen any here in the food stalls," Kris replied.

"What else?"

"Flour, usually fine ground from wheat or corn."

"And?" Ferris prompted since Kris's intonation suggested flour was not the final missing ingredient.

"Yeast. Which I haven't ever seen here. Yeast is a leavening, which causes the bread flour to rise in the baking. Similar, I think, to your meal cakes."

"Meal cakes. Phooey," Bazil said, having eaten too many under- and overdone meal cakes as a child.

"But you like bread," Kris countered.

"Botany bread, yes," Bazil agreed amiably, qualifying his taste.

"Surely we can find a substitute for yeast, and maybe cans of milk," Ferris said.

"Quite likely," Zainal replied, noticing Ferris's speculative expression. "But these are not things easily found or . . . acquired."

Kris rolled her eyes because Ferris was not above proving doubters wrong, and Zainal had probably just piqued him professionally. She devoutly hoped that Ferris would take the hint, and he must have, because he shot her a hurt, accusing look. She wondered whether she should warn Floss and Clune to reinforce her warning to curb his acquisitive tendencies. On the way to their stalls, she made sure to point out the triangle, where minor market offenses were punished with lashes of a particularly nasty whip. There were no such things as trials or sentences in Barevi. Corporal punishment for infractions of the market laws, like thieving, was swift and did not allow for appeals. While Ferris looked sturdier than Ditsy, his undernourished bones were fragile. She didn't want to think of him under the whip.

10

The next morning started very well indeed, with an impatient clutch of people waiting for them to start serving the coffee. There were even some wanting to trade, and Zainal managed to obtain a palette of truck batteries, a real prize.

Captain Harvey was attempting to repair the damage to the iridium comm sat they had scooped out of the skies above Earth. In her talks with John Wendell, she had learned that many of the satellites the Catteni had damaged could be repaired in situ. The one they had in the BASS-1 needed only the necessary LNB, low-noise blockdown converter. They now had the solar replacement vanes that would power the comm sat once it was back in space. They had found two antenna "ears" that had been sliced off, but needed two connecting boards so the individual units of the satellite could exchange information. The controlling mechanism, which Harvey called the mission package, had survived and was operational.

"That's the most delicate of the stuff on board," Captain Harvey told him. "It'll keep the comm sat in the orbit where we place it." She cleared her throat. "Replace it, actually, because it's already programmed to stay in its proper orbit . . . except when Catteni use it for target practice. But then, they have to practice on something, don't they, to keep their edge?"

Harvey could surprise him with some of her wry comments and Zainal tilted an amused expression up to her. He hoped they could find more relatively undamaged comm sats on their return. They also needed to build some from the spare parts in the lower cargo level.

"What're the part numbers for these needful connector boards, Captain?" he asked her, wondering yet again at the greed that had occasioned looters to take such unusable items back to Barevi. The merchants could *not* sell everything: there had to be buyers who wanted the items. Of course, they now had them in Zainal's mission.

She yanked a scrap of paper out of her top pocket and handed it to him. "Got them from the schematics last night." She aimed the small tool in her hand at a bunch of twisted plastic on the floor. "That's what was left of them, so's you got an idea what you're looking for. Spiders, only you don't have spiders, arachnids, a multi-legged creature, on Barevi, do you? Once I have those to hook the system up, we can test to see if all parts are running. You can see the part numbers, loud and clear."

"I can?" Zainal cupped his ear, though he suspected she was using one of those maddening vernacular phrases Terrans so enjoyed.

"You're some kidder, Emassi," she replied with a grin and a waggle of her elbow.

The Terrans had so many of these little sayings, cryptic comments that confused him. It was as well that his sons were being exposed to such verbal wordplay. They would be able to speak Terran very well. So far he was quite pleased with Brone. The young pilot had proved firm with them and had gained their respect. Zainal brought himself sternly back to the work at hand: he must list the numbers for Ferris, in hopes the boy could discover who owned the relevant storage shed. Zainal had also told Clune and Ditsy to be on the lookout for anyone holding parts with the HCA logo on them and briefed both Natchi and his sidekick, Erbri, a footless man whom Natchi presented as thoroughly trustworthy and who knew every alley in the market. Why didn't the Terrans assign just one worker to the completion of a project, and then one would only need to find the worker and know from which "industry"—the word came to him—he had acquired the original parts? Of course, a single man could not construct an entire spaceship by himself but a comm sat, once the components were collected, would be within a good workman's compass.

So Zainal mused as he passed on the numbers for the connector units, explaining how important they were to Ferris before he resumed his bargaining position. His next client was a burly man named Kierse, a Drassi who had left space for the more secure port life. He had brought with him a list of the items he wished to sell, and Zainal felt a thrill of anticipation as he saw so many HCA listings.

"I do not know what good these Terran bits and pieces will do you, but I have developed a taste for this coffee, and you are apparently in possession of many sacks of the cooked beans. They are ready, I understand, to be ground and filtered."

"You understand correctly."

From a pouch Kierse wore on one shoulder, he took out a handful of what Zainal now easily recognized as vacuum-packed plastic sleeves, each containing a bouquet of wires of different colors with tips of different shapes, including several bars of tiny holes on a black plastic strip. As little as Zainal knew about comm sat innards, these looked like the blackened discards that Captain Harvey had pointed to on the floor of the cargo hold. Zainal covered his excitement by asking Floss to fill a cup for Emassi Kierse.

"I am not Emassi," Kierse said with a twitch of irritation to his lips. "I am but Drassi."

"You have the manner, however, and should be treated accordingly," Zainal said graciously, knowing that many Drassi were of the Emassi class but had failed some part of their training and thus were unable to use their birth-rank.

"These are useful to you?" Kierse asked, neatly dealing the packets of parts into a line across the table so the identifying part label was clearly visible.

Zainal quickly scanned his eye down the labels, having committed to memory the numbers of the ones he sought.

"Possibly," he murmured discreetly.

"They have the numbers I am told you are seeking," Kierse replied, settling into his chair to haggle.

Zainal wondered who had given that information to the market. Clune and Ditsy were notably close-mouthed. What had Kris been warning him about? Ah yes, Ferris stole. Or were Natchi and Erbri as trustworthy as advertised? No, Zainal reassured himself, Natchi definitely was and he had vouched for Erbri. And here were the connectors Captain Harvey required.

"What good did you think these leggy things would do you when you bought them?"

"Wait for someone who needed just such oddities," Kierse replied, then refreshed himself with a sip of the mountain mild that was currently on offer. As Zainal considered his next gambit—the sounds of the marketplace closed around them—the *rat-tat-tat* of Eric's eternal hammering, the scurry of feet on the dry aisles between stalls, the occasional raised voices as people pounded out a suitable bargain.

Zainal hefted one of the packets experimentally. "Not very heavy. Since you like coffee, perhaps beans would be acceptable." He leaned forward. "We have been trading weight of beans for weight of the packets. Is that satisfactory to you?"

"You may weigh them and we will see what the total comes to—in beans and then in the gold I understand you are using for barter."

"Coffee beans have been referred to as 'black gold,' Drassi Kierse."

"I thought that was the thick stuff they put into barrels. Oil." Kierse, who was much sharper than he looked—certainly for one of Drassi rank—pronounced the word in two syllables: Oy-yill.

"I have heard the term 'black gold' used for both," Zainal said blithely, "though I believe the barreled stuff is undrinkable."

Kierse chuckled and Zainal worried about the bargaining abilities of this client. Beans he had in plenty, but the gold was in much shorter supply. Still, that standard would be in keeping with the value—to him—of these particular parts and he wanted to conclude a deal with Kierse.

It didn't take long to put the packets into the weighing pod and the scales swung past and then settled on 50 grams. Zainal did not wish to part with that much gold no matter how essential the parts were to repair the connectors. It would take most of the dust they had in the little safe. And since the man had specified gold, he would probably not consider the lesser ores that Zainal still had available.

"If we deal with the beans, I am willing to throw in a grinder. The filtered bean gives a finer taste and goes further." Zainal hoped this would tip Kierse in his favor.

"I know how one makes this brew," Kierse said, dismissing Zainal's suggestion. "But, in truth, I do not have a grinder. Let me see it working. I prefer the filtered drink to the boiled grounds."

Floss, who had been listening to the exchange, immediately stepped forward with sacks of several varieties of bean.

"Which would you prefer, the milder roast or the hearty robusta bean?"

Floss, skilled now at tipping a handful of beans into one of the little saucers, filled two packets, one with the mild mountain and the other with the richer roast and offered each in turn to Kierse. Zainal made a little bet with himself and won. Kierse preferred the stronger brew.

"There are, as I am sure you know, Kierse, several methods of obtaining coffee. The percolator provides a stronger flavor. Grind the beans," Zainal began but Kierse waved off a discussion of the process and the percolator pot, which Floss displayed for him.

"Filtered. And that darker bean."

Floss withdrew the dismissed ones from consideration and reached under the table for the appropriate packages. These she placed in the other scale, casually adding a trickle of beans until a balance was achieved between the product and its payment. Zainal held his breath. Kierse looked longingly at the casket of gold, which Zainal had left on the table. Then he took another sip of the coffee in his cup.

"I have more packages. We will deal with the gold then," Kierse said and extended his hand to Zainal, accepting the barter.

Quickly Floss transferred the bags of beans to a carrier, wrapped the grinder and placed it on top, handing the convenient package to the new owner.

Zainal rose and gave the obligatory courtesy bow, which Kierse mirrored, though there was a smile in the man's eyes that Zainal read as anticipating a return with more valuable stock. As Kierse left, Zainal signaled for Ferris to follow him. He might merely go to his home with such a package, but he might also return to his stall to gloat over what valuable merchandise he still wished to sell to the bean man. Perhaps Ferris could discover exactly what else might be of value to them.

The tone of voices abruptly changed. There was some sort of a fuss coming down the aisle, much shouting and warnings. Zainal was instantly alert but relaxed when he saw what was becoming a daily occurrence, someone with a bloody mouth coming to see the tooth man. The victim had a bloody rag over his face as friends escorted him to Eric's booth. Zainal called out Eric's name for he was busy *rat-tat-tatting.*

Eric quickly emerged and, taking in the scene in one glance, ushered the Catteni into his stall, twitching the curtain across it.

"Good fight?" Zainal inquired, as Catteni courtesy permitted.

"I won," replied a burly man with the ship insignia of a minor duty officer. "Oh, this is where the coffee is. I could certainly use a cup."

Zainal gave him a wave toward Floss, who smiled engagingly up at the fellow and put the cup in his hand and indicated the coin pot.

"What's it worth?" he asked Floss.

"What you care to put in," Floss replied flirtatiously.

Floss might have learned vocabulary from Peran and Bazil at the Masai camp, but she had certainly not learned how to flirt from them. Clune stepped forward from where he was drying cups and lingered just beyond her. The officer did not mistake the warning in the young man's manner and moved judiciously toward Eric's office space, just as a bellow and a kicking foot stirred the curtain.

"It would not have lasted past the first thing you chewed," Eric shouted. His command of dental Catteni was now comprehensive enough for such remarks.

In her role as part-time dental assistant, Sally arrived with a glass of water and a bowl for the man to spit into. She disliked that part of her job but was becoming inured to it. She did like appearing in the form-fitting white uniform that Eric had said went with the duties. The uniform had been one of the things Eric had stuffed in at the last moment at his office, and fortuitously it fit Sally very well indeed.

Zainal then noticed a slight figure who had been parading up and down the aisle most of the morning.

"May I help you?" he inquired politely, as he tapped the man on the shoulder.

The gray-skinned fellow, rather scrawny even for a Catteni, jumped and whirled, his hands up in a defensive position. "This is where the man who does teeth works?" he asked, slightly breathless.

"Yes."

"I wish to learn how to repair teeth. It would be a very good business for me to get into," he added. And indeed, Zainal noticed that his upper teeth protruded in such a way that he looked like a burrowing animal the Terrans called a rabbit. Catten had a similar burrowing vegetarian creature, named a sukey. Then the man fumbled in a pouch and held out for Zainal's inspection some odd objects—squarish at one end and broken off at the other.

"Teeth?" Zainal asked in surprise, remembering Ferris's recent brush with Kapash.

"Yes, I saw him," and he looked about, evidently for Ferris, who was away from the stall on his errand for Zainal. "He was here earlier, but I've seen him collecting broken teeth after a brawl in a drinking place. So I followed him. I have a friend who has loose teeth."

Ferris was still collecting teeth in the drinking pits? At least this fellow was anxious to avail himself of the service, rather than attack Ferris, and had found the right place.

"Training to be a dentist demands many years of studying and can only be learned on Terra."

"But he practices here," the man objected. "I am Tavis," he added by way of introduction. "I would do anything to learn such a profession. And if he does, he teaches."

There was indeed a Catteni assumption that he who could *do,* could teach.

"I do not believe that the medical school where he learned is still functioning, and it is an expensive undertaking."

"But if he does, I could watch and learn."

"Do you read Terran?"

"I do," said the man, and Zainal saw that, for all he was young in face, he was not a boy. "And I have studied much." There was a sudden slump to his shoulders as he admitted, "Learning is all I can do."

"Learning is itself something that can be practiced. Have you ever considered being a tutor?"

The man shook his head. "Emassi and even Drassi find my appearance laughable." He pointed to his teeth. "I heard that the tooth man is able to alter the shape of teeth while still in the mouth."

While Zainal had heard from Eric that orthodontics was possible, it required long hours of work and much money.

"He can, but it is a long process," Zainal said noncommittally, only now aware of how much he had absorbed of Eric's evening dental lectures.

"But it is possible?" The man's hand traveled halfway to his mouth before he restrained the movement, dropping it self-consciously.

"I believe so, but you had best discuss this with the doctor. And how was your friend injured?"

"Took a fist right in the mouth. His teeth feel loose, he told me, and I thought of the tooth man."

"I am sure that Dr. Sachs," and Zainal paused to let that name sink in, "will be able to save his teeth. But sometimes the nerve in the tooth itself has been damaged and it is wiser to remove it before it can fester in the jaw."

Tavis blinked, as if that possibility had never occurred to him. Indeed, it would have been news to Zainal if he hadn't had a crewman once whose two front teeth, loosened in a marketplace brawl, had turned dark, with the gum above swelling from some unseen injury within the jaw. Zainal himself had had to yank the teeth before the man got some respite from the fierce pain in his mouth. There had been little nodes attached to the root of the teeth that smelled vile. So had the crewman's breath.

"First, bring your friend here." From Tavis's expression, this was not a suggestion that appealed to him. "Well, he will have to bring his teeth himself if they are still in his head," Zainal said a little impatiently.

Tavis nodded but was still lacking in confidence.

"Tell him Emassi Zainal requests his presence."

"Emassi Zainal requests his presence." Tavis considered this for a few moments and then drew himself up in resolve.

"You are doing your friend a favor. Fear not."

"I am not afraid of him," Tavis replied stoutly, as if convincing himself of that.

"Nor need to be, since you are doing him a favor."

"Yes, I am." With that, Tavis dashed off, leaving Zainal abruptly. Zainal shrugged and turned to other matters.

The day before, Chuck had exchanged a lump of their copper for a carton of Toyota brake linings and two cartons of spark plugs for truck transmissions. "We did promise Vitali we'd get such things," he had informed Zainal.

"I know. And we must prove reliable to the coord."

Indeed they must. And thanks to Ditsy's enterprise, they also had both a supply of power packs and more of the coveted lifts to bring back. Erbri had been useful in this sideline, as well, bringing in damaged equipment that he also helped repair. So Erbri could be useful on Botany as well as Natchi, and Zainal had half decided that he'd bring the two veterans back to Retreat rather than leave them to live out their hand-to-mouth lives. In fact, Zainal thought he had done better, in many ways, for the Terrans than for the folk on Botany. He had thought they would have had more buyers for the metals, which Zainal knew were in short supply on Barevi, but considering the green coord's trade with him, they could use the remaining metals to better advantage on Earth.

Zainal enjoyed a moment of peaceful reflection, wondering how much advantage he might wring from such insights. Barevi's main function had always been as a trading planet and only secondarily as a place for long-haul spacemen to vent excess energy and for sporting Catteni to hunt live creatures. However, one of Kris's cryptic phrases came to mind: something about a mountain coming to a man.

"What is that you say about the mountain and a man?"

She blinked for a moment, shook her head, and then her expression brightened. "If Mohammed won't come to the mountain, let the mountain come to Mohammed. Is that the one you mean?"

"The very one," and he smiled at her, just as a man stepped up to the stall.

"Excuse me, Zainal," she said and offered a cup to the Catteni.

The man had a noticeable squint and an unpleasant expression on his face but, watching him for a moment as Kris explained how to prepare the bean properly, she seemed to have soothed him. He sipped the coffee and turned to survey those passing by. Kris gave an exasperated look at Zainal but smiled pleasantly at the Catteni. Then he said he wanted to purchase a bag of beans and evidently could not make up his mind between the arabica and the robusta. Kris offered to give him a quantity of both so he could savor them in his own house. They meant to stop selling the beans as a separate commodity since they were better used as barter but, as in the case of this pompous person, it was easier to comply than deny. And they acquired sufficient Catteni coins to defray other costs.

"But that is more than a bottle of the best wine would cost," the man complained when Kris quoted him the price.

"Ah, there are some who maintain that good coffee is better than wine," was Kris's smiling reply. "It is the beginning of the day you should ensure, rather than the end."

He grunted as he deposited the half-bags in the pockets of his loose jerkin before he stalked away, still annoyed at the cost.

"Be sure to grind them properly, as we showed you," Kris called cheerfully after him. Then to Zainal she said, "Serving coffee has become de rigueur. All the *best* homes serve it." Then she grinned.

"What's so amusing? He was not," Zainal said, for the squint-eyed man was an arrogant type of Catteni and possibly had not even liked being served by a Terran woman.

"No, and what do you want to bet he doesn't explain to his wife that she has to grind them, much less that the water must be boiled to make a proper brew."

"I wouldn't bet," Zainal said. He knew how careful the women were to explain the correct process. Maybe next time they could bring proper pots and more grinders.

He was astonished that he was thinking in terms of "next time." But he was beginning to think of a fairly complex business possibility. He needed to turn it over in his mind before he voiced it to the members of his current crew, to say nothing of the Botany colonists, who were expecting so much from this venture.

Later that morning, Zainal saw Tavis accompanying a Catteni, stalwart even among their species, to Eric's office. The sort of man, Zainal thought, who was in the middle of brawls. Though it seemed true that the threat of transportation to a slave colony had remarkably reduced the number of brawls. Evidently Kapash had made good on that threat. The most recent fracas had involved two Catteni crews who had just landed on Barevi and had started by picking quarrels with each other even as they walked from the dock to the settlement. Ditsy had heard that half the crew had already been arrested and thrown into prison. Whether or not their captains would be able to bail them out of Kapash's reach remained to be seen. In the meantime, if the slave ship arrived, they would be transported unless their captain ransomed them. Either way, Zainal thought, Kapash won. He wished fleetingly that, when he had been market manager, he had had that option. But in that year, there had been plenty of captive species to send to the work camps. Idly he wondered how long Catteni survived in those conditions. Not all the quarrelsome crew members had been rounded up, so Zainal called a halt to their business early, in case the remaining men were still in the market before they went off to hunt or do whatever form of enterprise they considered suitable for relaxation.

They all got back to the BASS-1 with no problem and ate their evening meal—Gino enjoyed cooking and had put together some un-usually tasty meals. Eric was very pleased with his new patients and said he could easily support himself with dentistry on Barevi.

"What about that young fellow Tavis?" Zainal asked.

"The one who wants to apprentice himself to me as a dental as-sistant?" Eric asked with a smile. "Nice, earnest young man."

"I think he fancies that you can teach him how to *be* a dentist, too," Zainal said by way of cautioning.

"Hmmm. Fancies indeed. Not"—Eric paused to raise his hand—"that he isn't intelligent enough. I shall happily train him in the skills I need in an assistant, and Sally can go back to bookkeeping."

The next morning, Zainal was to meet with a merchant named Nilink, whom Ferris had brought to his notice as the owner of a large storage complex full of tires with the Goodyear and Michelin logos on their paper wrappings. Zainal was extremely eager to do business with the man but knew better by now than to appear keen. So he de-layed his departure, using the time to memorize the weights and sizes of the tires on the list he had compiled on Terra. It was always wise to know exactly what he was seeking.

As he moved through the morning crowds to their location, he was surprised to hear a commotion. Then Ferris came dodging through the crowds and all but ran into him.

"Zainal! Zainal!" The boy's face was terror-stricken. "Kapash's men have taken Kris and Kathy! Taken them," he gasped.

"Why?" Zainal grabbed the boy by the shoulders, holding him upright.

"'Misrepresenting goods' is all I heard. Chuck was arguing with them and so were Peran and Bazil. Brone tried to help, too. But they were taken away!" He had something more to say and not enough breath to spew it out.

"Steady, lad, steady! We can fix it."

"But they have Emassi Kris," the boy said. "And Natchi says there's a slave ship in. He says they load fast and leave."

"Go back, Ferris. Tell Chuck I have gone to attend to Kapash," he said before he started running through the crowd toward Kapash's office, pushing people out of his way when they were not fast enough for the pace he set himself. Kris! Not Kris! Not on a slave ship again. And Kathy. She, too, would be frightened, but it was Kris he could not do without.

11

Kris had more sense than to struggle as she and Kathy were hauled away, Floss and Jax weeping, while Chuck had to restrain Clune and the boys from giving the bullies accompanying Kapash any excuse to knock them about with the heavy cudgels they carried: part weapon, part symbol of their function. The last thing she saw was Ferris, disappearing from view, undoubtedly running to find Zainal. And Ferris would, wherever her mate was.

"Misrepresentation of products, indeed!" she muttered to Kathy.

"You know how careful we are to explain exactly how to grind beans and brew coffee," Kathy was saying, sniffling with fear and wringing her hands.

Chuck disliked hand-wringing women almost as much as weeping ones, but he felt like weeping in fear himself. Natchi had warned him that morning that a slaver had made port early and would leave as soon as it was filled. Frankly, he wouldn't put it past Kapash to ensure that Kris and Kathy were on it, a nasty result of the specious charge leveled against them.

Where was Zainal? Oh, and here was the merchant he was to see today! Speaking more calmly than he felt, Chuck greeted the man and asked him which coffee he preferred.

"The stronger bean," Nilink said with an easy smile. "I shall need my wits today, bargaining with Emassi Zainal. It is amazing to find coffee on Barevi. I should have filled my hold with the beans and I'd've done well with such spoils."

"You are a spaceship captain, Emassi?" Chuck asked politely.

The man's clothing gave away little about him, though it was well cut and of good, durable fabric. He also had the air of someone accustomed to giving orders and having them obeyed. Rather like Zainal, in fact, Chuck thought, wondering where the big Catteni was.

"I was indeed a captain," Nilink replied, "as was Zainal, I understand."

Ferris came running back, almost careening into Nilink but halting just in time with an apologetic bow to the Emassi. "I caught Zainal. He has gone to Kapash. My pardon, good Emassi," he added.

Kris and Kathy, still professing innocence of whatever it was the head steward accused them of, were thrust into a dark, dank prison cell, already well filled to judge by the number of people they disturbed by their entry.

Oh Lord, not again! Kris thought, for the ambience put her forcefully in mind of the first time she had been in this situation, before she had been dropped on Botany—when she and Zainal had been gassed during the riot of Terrans. Only this morning Chuck had mentioned that a slave ship had docked, and the thought filled her with dread.

Beside her, Kathy was trying to rearrange her clothing after the rough handling they had received from Kapash's police.

"We didn't misrepresent anything. Was it that squint-eyed fellow from yesterday, d'you suppose?"

Inadvertently she trod on someone's arm and the man tried to knock her feet out from under her, cursing.

Kris steadied Kathy and motioned her to the wall, where they might find a safer place to wait.

"Zainal will come for us, won't he?" Kathy asked.

"Yes, of course he will, Kathy," Kris said positively. "Chuck will have sent Ferris running for him."

They found a place to sit but they were not far from the communal slop pots and the stench was overpowering, so they moved, carefully, through the other prisoners to find a less redolent place.

Most of the inmates were sprawled, getting what sleep they could. The air certainly stank of stale beer and whatever other alcohol had been consumed: the stench was incredible.

"He *will* come?" There was understandable anxiety in Kathy's voice.

"He will come!" Kris replied in an unarguable tone of voice and then, finding a space against the wall in the corner, pulled Kathy down to sit beside her.

"I'm thirsty," Kathy said.

"Don't think about it, Kathy."

Kris did not think Kathy's courage would improve by being told that prisoners in Barevi prisons were rarely fed or watered: at least not until prior to being forced onto a slave ship. She composed herself to remain calm and await Zainal's arrival. Ferris would have found him, no matter where Zainal had been.

But barely had they got themselves settled when the prison doors swung open and jailors, cracking nerve whips, roused the inmates with harsh commands to stand up and move out. She was startled when a door in the side of the prison was opened to reveal a ramp. She remembered that sort of ramp and tried to suppress a surge of fear. Kathy didn't realize what was happening and Kris wasn't going to tell her. The prisoners were being driven toward the ramp. Kris caught Kathy's arm, holding her back. "Zainal, where *are* you?" she murmured urgently.

They were among the last to be driven up the ramp, Kris looking over her shoulder at the main entrance, hoping against hope to see Zainal's large form in the doorway and hear his voice commanding the guards to leave her alone. Surely he would come to free them. The tip of the nerve whip caught her arm, though her clothing absorbed most of the painful strike, and despite her reluctance, she was driven up the ramp and into the hold of a KDM.

"We're on a ship," Kathy said, frightened.

"So we are," Kris remarked, amazed at how calm she managed to sound.

"What are we doing on a ship, Kris? Where is Zainal?"

"Trying to get us free, I'm sure," Kris replied, though the smell of the hold was no reassurance at all. This was a slave ship: it stank of fear and human excrement.

The ramp door swung shut and was dogged tight by a guard.

"Find a wall space, Kathy," Kris said, holding tight to Kathy's hand so they wouldn't be separated as the other prisoners milled about aimlessly.

"Find us, Zainal," Kris chanted to herself. "Find us. Free us."

A sudden movement of the ship as it undocked threw both women to their knees, and Kris barely managed to keep from crying out with fear and pain as her right knee connected painfully with a bolt on the steel floor. There would be no pleasant Botany at the end of this forced journey.

They both felt the surge as the ship took off, sending them sliding into other bodies and pushing them back against the far wall of the hold.

"I'm scared, Kris," Kathy said as the metal beneath them throbbed with the power of takeoff. Her voice was close to a wail and Kris threw an arm around her shoulders.

"Me too," Kris agreed. "Zainal will stop this farce. Just you wait."

The accusation is a farce, Kapash," Zainal was saying, having stormed into the market manager's office demanding an explanation.

"An aggrieved client has every right to file a charge against a merchant who has sold imperfect goods or misrepresented his stock."

"You know how we have been trading the coffee. You've tasted enough of it to know that our product is exactly as represented."

Kapash merely smiled up at Zainal, obviously delighting in his discomposure, tilting languidly back in his chair.

"Now, what fine will you levy so that I can pay it and release Kris and Kathy?"

Kapash steepled his fingers, ignoring Zainal's urgency. "Well now, the standard fee is forty Catteni bunts."

"Gone up since I was manager, hasn't it?"

Kapash's chair crashed to the floor and he stared hard at Zainal. Then both men heard the rumble of a ship taking off from the dock and Kapash smiled.

"If those women are on that ship, Kapash, you will be sorry for it. They have been falsely accused and you know it."

"I do?" Kapash pretended an innocence that only made Zainal more positive of his complicity.

"What will it take, Kapash, for you to sign a release form and stop that ship before it leaves Barevi orbit?"

"What will I take, Zainal?" Kapash asked, idly drumming his fingers on his desktop.

"Out with it. I want the ship stopped before it can leave this system. What is it you want?"

"The location of the Eosi treasures."

"The what?" Zainal stared, in dismay and contempt. "How would I know that?"

"You were once to be an Eosi host and you would have been informed of such things."

"No, I wasn't because I never became Pe's host. Do not underestimate the guile of the Eosi, Kapash. They made no one their confidants, especially not an unhosted Catteni."

"But someone knows," Kapash exclaimed. "They had so much treasure. So much coin for their rents and deals, and most of the valuables taken from Earth."

"I'm sure they did very well for themselves, but I have no idea where they stored their possessions. What will you take, Kapash?"

Kapash looked extremely uncomfortable.

"I'm sure you talked with their staff assistants, didn't you?" Zainal continued, not wanting to waste too much time talking.

"They knew nothing," Kapash said, flicking his fingers. "And we spoke to every one of them."

And not gently, either, Zainal thought, but he had no pity to spare for those traitors who had lived extremely well, serving their Eosi masters.

"Something I can give you, Kapash." Zainal did not dare rush the man and yet there was a need for urgency. Only Kapash could have the ascending ship halted at the space station before it left the system for whichever slave colony was its destination.

"Your coffee beans," Kapash said, coming to a decision.

"I don't have that many left," Zainal admitted. "They have sold well." He tried to think how many sacks remained on the BASS-1.

"You have a ship. You can go back to Terra for more. You will go back, and I shall have the concession here in the market for as long as I wish." He scribbled some words on a sheet of paper and passed it across the desk for Zainal to sign.

It was a release for all coffee beans on board the BASS-1.

"Sign the prisoner release first, Kapash," Zainal said, pointing to the various colored forms in the cabinet behind the man. "The blue one," he said, remembering that detail from his own term as market manager.

"Their names?" Kapash asked, holding his writer over the blue sheet.

"Lady Emassi Kris Bjornsen and Captain Emassi Katherine Harvey." He spelled the names, watching intently as Kapash wrote. When the form was completed, duly signed by Kapash, and stamped with his office's seal, Zainal signed the release of the beans.

"You will also no longer use coffee as a trade item," Kapash said. With that, he must have known that he effectively ended Zainal's mission on Barevi. He reached out for the release. Zainal held it out of reach.

Zainal pointed to the communications board to Kapash's right. "Only if you immediately phone Ladade and order him to keep that ship from leaving Barevi space."

Kapash seemed to hesitate. When Zainal raised a fist menacingly, remembering how much of a physical coward Kapash was, the man grabbed for the hand unit and made the call.

"Yes, do not give the ship clearance, Commander Ladade. Two of the prisoners have been cleared of the charges falsely registered against them and therefore must be off-loaded. . . . It is entirely necessary, Commander. . . . Yes, and I am on my way to ensure their release. I have the required form. . . . No, not murderers, Commander, but merchants who have been unjustly accused. . . . Yes, yes, most unusual." He paused a moment, listening to Ladade. There was a flicker in his eyes as if he were experiencing some trouble in convincing Ladade of this necessity. "And I agree, Ladade. Neither of us needs these troublesome little problems, but I must maintain my rep-

utation as a fair market manager. This matter touches on my honor. . . .
Yes, yes, we shall be on our way with the release form."

Kapash was on his feet, then, disconnecting the call and hastily keying in another command. "Have my gig ready to depart by the time I reach my dock," he said and returned the hand unit to its holster. "Come, give it over, Zainal." He all but snatched the signed release from Zainal's hand. Zainal reluctantly let it go but, if somehow Kapash reneged on the deal, he would have it back—and break Kapash's neck.

The throb of the ship's engines ceased and Kris began to hope again.

"Has he made them stop?" Kathy asked, trying to keep her voice steady.

"Something has," Kris said. "Wherever they are taking us, they haven't had time to go far." She struggled to recall station protocol.

"Don't they have to get an all-clear from the station?" Kathy asked.

"Yes, they do," Kris replied, in some relief. "To be sure all their debts have been paid and to announce their destination. At least that's what Zainal said. Oh, we haven't left this system."

"No, we can't have."

Ladade met Kapash and Zainal at the airlock, clearly annoyed at this interruption to his schedule, but he obviously recognized Zainal and that seemed to alter his attitude.

"Ah, Emassi Zainal, I had not looked to encounter you again," Ladade said almost genially, bringing his hand to his chest in a salute of respect.

Zainal duplicated the salute. "Nor I, Ladade."

"You know the two released prisoners?"

"My mate and one of my KDM captains," Zainal said.

"An officious and spurious complaint was laid against them," Kapash said, dismissing the matter with a flick of his fingers.

Zainal handed Ladade the release form.

"You know how abrupt such slave traders as Fartov are, lifting before he obtained my clearance for his cargo," Kapash said, trying to shift some of the onus to Ladade.

From Ladade's expression, Zainal surmised that Kapash was not high in the station commander's estimation or guilty of much fair dealing. Of course, Kapash would get a cut of whatever profit Fartov made on his slavery mission. He shifted his feet restlessly, wanting them to get on with the release of Kris and Kathy before they experienced too much trauma in the fetid hold of the slave carrier.

"Please," he said, trying not to sound too anxious. Zainal didn't know Ladade except as a very competent station manager. "Let us get to the business at hand."

"Of course," the commander said and gestured for them to return to the gig. "I have ordered Fartov to await clearance, which he will not receive until we have released the unfairly detained persons. I don't know how you and Kapash settled this most unusual last-minute rescue, but I do not like disrupting my schedule unnecessarily."

Zainal knew a request for a bribe when he heard one. He considered what valuables he had left and could think of nothing that might tempt the man. "Have you any suggestion, Ladade, as to how I might ease such disruption?"

"You were to host an Eosi called Pe?"

"You surely are not another person who thinks I know where Pe hid his treasures?" Zainal scoffed. "If his assistants had no idea, then why would I? I met him twice, I never hosted him."

Ladade looked unsure.

"Besides which, don't you two think it was odd that a Catteni

Emassi was left in the common prison to be transported so opportunely for someone?"

"But you were to be a host," Ladade said, his eyes bulging with disbelief. Kapash made no comment. In fact, he held himself extremely rigid, a fact that suggested to Zainal that Kapash had been involved in his abduction in some way. Paid to ignore a Catteni in a mixed group, no doubt, since Kapash was notorious for his greed.

"Someone," and Zainal looked from one to the other, "evidently saw a chance to get me out of the way permanently."

"Hadn't thought of that," Ladade said, rubbing his chin in a pensive manner as he regarded Zainal steadily.

"By the time I was called to be a host, I had already been dropped, and therefore I stayed."

Ladade regarded Zainal with veiled approval. Once again, Zainal wondered who had been on prison duty at that time. Possibly a vacillating member of the dissidents had betrayed him for whatever profit such information had reaped.

"I do have one idea, though, which you, Commander, are remarkably well situated to explore."

"Yes?"

"This station keeps track of all ships in and out of the system, as well as their destinations, does it not?" he asked Ladade.

"You know it does."

"Have you never considered tracking Eosi ships to see if they made frequent stops at some out-of-the-way or unlikely port?"

Ladade considered this, glancing at the personnel currently busy on routine duties. The three men had been speaking quietly and now both Ladade and Kapash glanced around to be sure that no one had been close to them when Zainal made his suggestion.

"I would happily discuss this with you once my friends have been released," Zainal said.

"As I would be happy to discuss such a strategy with you, Zainal,"

Ladade said. "Tell Captain Fartov that we are on our way to release two prisoners."

Then he peremptorily gestured for Zainal and Kapash to board Kapash's gig.

I t was awful waiting in the stinking dark, Kris thought, but she would not give up hope until—no, even *if*—the ship's engines started up again. Zainal was resourceful. He would not let them be sent to a slave colony. But the waiting was terrible. And as everyone else in the compartment realized that they were being transported beyond hope or help, their moans and weeping were pathetic as well as contagious, and Kris caught back a sob in her own throat. Zainal will come. It was both prayer and litany.

She felt a bump reverberate through the ship's hull. More of an echo than a real concussion. As if a ship had connected with the airlock.

Oh, Zainal! Zainal!

She felt hands on her ankle, rough hands actually caressing her foot. She kicked against the grip as hard as she could and felt her foot connect with something soft. Someone groaned and cursed but the grasp on her foot had been broken.

"Don't do that again," she muttered, her growl very determinedly Cattenish, as much from fright as lack of moisture in her mouth.

Almost stunned, she heard the door to their enclosure slide open, the door guide grating against its groove, and a hand light shining in, flickering across faces.

"Zainal?" she cried, hoping against hope that it was him and they were being rescued. Beside her, Kathy stirred and struggled to her feet.

"Kris? Kathy?" an unmistakable voice called.

It was Zainal! "To the right, Zainal," she said, needing light to find her way among the tangle of bodies covering the floor.

The hand light swept to shine on her and Kathy. Kathy, already on her feet, gave a little shriek of relief and fled to the doorway. Kris, her knees sore from the earlier fall, had more difficulty getting up. But Zainal closed the distance between them, clasping her tightly in his arms and lifting her out of the prison. The door clanged shut as soon as they were in the corridor. Zainal set her on her feet and gestured to the Catteni she did not know. Kapash she knew all too well, and she looked through him.

"Commander Ladade, this is my mate, Lady Emassi Kris Bjornsen, and this is Emassi Captain Kathy Harvey."

The commander waved a blue sheet of paper. "You are officially released as unfairly accused."

"I told you we didn't do anything, Kapash," Kathy said, her voice croaking from her dry throat. She hated that display of weakness in herself. She would rather have stood unmoved by Kapash's attempt to debase her.

"You are free, are you not?" Kapash replied with a nasty smile on his face.

Kris gave him a long, contemptuous glare. "We did not misrepresent our product and you know it, Kapash."

He gave a shrug, lifting both hands in a disarming gesture, suggesting that he had only been doing his duty.

"Commander Ladade," a voice crackled from the ship's communicators, "to the control room. Ship X11-233 requesting permission to depart?"

The commander gave a little smile. "If you will follow me." He turned to port. They did, with Kapash trailing behind them.

Zainal had Kris tightly by the hand, his thumb stroking her fingers. "Be easy, dear heart. I have wanted a chance to be in the control room. Humor me."

It took all her concentration to make her legs manage the pace Ladade set and she suspected that both she and Kathy were operating on an adrenaline high that she hoped would last long enough to get them off this wretched station and safely among friends. But they were out of that hideous prison ship. They were safe with Zainal.

Then they were in the control tower of the space station, looking out at the parking lights of ships. One set of lights was blinking, evidently to attract attention.

"X11-233, this is Commander Ladade. Your affairs are now in order and you may depart."

The usual gravelly Catteni voice, remarkably polite, graciously accepted the permission. Within moments, Kris could see the flare of inter-system thrusters igniting and the ship ponderously moving toward full space—without her and Kathy aboard. She leaned into Zainal, almost fainting with relief. Kathy had taken the nearest free chair, ignoring a dirty look from a subordinate for such impertinence.

"Where is it bound?" Zainal asked, as if he felt required to make some comment. She could feel the tension through his body and wondered what he was after. She realized that his gaze was fastened on the nearest screen.

Shrugging indifferently, Ladade directed someone to bring up the file. Only Kris knew how important that file was to Zainal. She could feel the small sigh he released.

"Zerion 28.4.32. One of the mining colonies," Ladade said. "A resource planet that I believe you yourself discovered for the Eosi."

"I believe you're right, Ladade," Zainal replied equably. "I did discover the planet. Too bad it had such rich metal lodes. It would have been suitable to colonize."

"Please." Now Ladade gestured for them all, Kapash included, to proceed to the portside door, which turned out to open into his private office, just off the command bridge.

"Perhaps you ladies would like some refreshment," Ladade said, all courteous.

"Water would be welcome," Kris said with great dignity, and he waved her to serve herself at the small catering unit. She poured two glasses of water from the pitcher and gave one to Kathy. She finished her glass, trying to sip slowly so as not to upset her stomach. Then, with a movement she hoped would be graceful, her sore knee barely supporting her, she sank into one of the chairs.

"Where would you put the parameters of Eosi Pe's possible stops, Zainal?"

Zainal pointed to the screen on Ladade's desktop. "If you will bring up his file," he said, moving to stand behind Ladade so he could see the screen. "Ah yes, well, if you notice, he makes quite a few trips to those coordinates." He tapped the screen with a finger.

"Yes, yes, but there's nothing there. Not even a moon," Ladade protested.

"I think you will probably have to achieve those coordinates and then see what might be in space nearby."

"But, in space?"

"Where else to secrete something when only you know the place you left it?"

"But . . . but . . ."

"I'm sure it will take some searching, but think of the rewards, Ladade."

"Where? Where?" Kapash came around the desk but before he could see the screen, Ladade altered the display, glaring at Kapash. Zainal straightened, but Kris, knowing him as well as she did, saw a gleam in his eyes. Whatever he had wanted to find, he had. She wondered what it was.

"What about Au? Where would he have hidden his treasure?" Eosi Au had once commanded both this station and the Barevi market.

Zainal shrugged. "You knew him better than I did, Kapash,

Ladade. Probably even his habits, if you will stop to think, instead of being blinded by greed, Kapash."

"You owe me." Kapash waggled a finger at Zainal, barely able to contain his aggravation.

"Then let us discharge that debt to you with all possible dispatch, Kapash," Zainal said in such an ominous tone that even Ladade, fascinated by Zainal's theory, looked up from his screen.

"Indeed, Kapash," Ladade said. "I will detain you on the station no further." He motioned toward the door, and Kapash had no option but to leave at such a curt dismissal. He did so reluctantly, despite Zainal's guidance.

"What did you give for our release?" Kris asked in Zainal's ear as they strode along the corridor to the airlock where Kapash's gig was docked.

"The coffee," he muttered.

Kris was both appalled and pleased to hear that her life had been ransomed by coffee beans. She really did mean a lot to him. But did he mean *all* the coffee? For someone who had given away one of their most important commodities, he looked oddly pleased. She hoped whatever he had found here was what he had wanted to discover.

She found that she had barely enough strength in her legs to get inside Kapash's gig. Kathy looked frightfully pale and sank instantly into the nearest seat. Pride kept Kris erect on her feet.

"Zainal, is there anything to eat on board? And I'm still thirsty."

"I'll see. " He rummaged in the small alcove, finding only some Catteni dry rations. He gave one packet to her and another to Kathy and then brought them water. Kathy found a small packet of coffee beans in her tunic pocket and handed them to Zainal.

"Do you have a grinder on board, Kapash?" Zainal asked.

"Why ever would I?" Kapash replied in a surly voice.

"We have some beans."

"They are all mine, Zainal. Remember that!" He snatched the packet from her fingers. "And we go immediately to your ship so I may see that no more of my beans are distributed on Barevi."

"Oh?" Kathy looked up at Zainal, her eyes wide with alarm.

"It's all right, Kathy."

But on Kathy's face was the dismay he was going to see from everyone else involved in their Barevi mission. Not that he felt any would rebuke him for bartering the beans for the lives of the two women. Zainal winked at Kathy, who was so astonished that she dropped her eyes and continued to chew the hard Catteni rations.

Kris managed to eat enough to let her stomach work on something useful and then leaned back in a seat and thought of the long shower she would take to get rid of the stench of the prison.

Natchi and Erbri appeared at the gangway of Kapash's gig as they disembarked. Ferris was with them, and so relieved was he to see the women being escorted by Zainal that he let out a ululation that startled everyone on the dock. Then he raced away to find transportation.

It was Natchi who helped Kathy onto the small motorized cart that arrived, and it was actually Natchi who paid for the hire when they reached the KDM. Jax and Floss wept with relief when they saw their friends gliding past the berths. Then Clune and the Doyle brothers appeared. Ninety all but carried Kathy on board, seeing that she was by now so weak with shock.

Chuck arrived with Gino and Sally Stoffers, having been summoned back from the marketplace by Ferris. Eric came, too, looking as concerned as everyone else, though he went back to his current patient, whom he had left in the chair with Tavis in attendance.

There was freshly made coffee and Floss sliced bananas, deciding that the last of the ripe fruit would be easy to digest as well as good for them.

Kris and Kathy both finished the snack, grateful for Floss's care and solicitude. Then they decided they would feel better after a shower and clean clothes and excused themselves.

"Well?" Chuck asked Zainal, cocking a bushy eyebrow. "Kapash, your people took off with the rest of the coffee." Then leaning close to Zainal, he asked in a lower tone, "Was that the price of their freedom?"

"It was," Zainal admitted.

"Well, they're worth it. They don't look as if they suffered any great harm."

"Fortunately, no," Zainal said with such an edge to his voice that Chuck grinned. "Do you care to inspect our holds, Kapash, to be sure the bargain has been kept?"

Kapash flicked away such a consideration. "You are an honorable man, Zainal."

"There were only two full bags left," Chuck said, "and what bagged beans we brought back from the market while we awaited your return." Heavy in Chuck's eyes was the suspicion that Kapash might have trumped up the charges just to get the beans.

"Shall I give you a refund on your stall rental, Zainal, now that you have no reason to remain?" Kapash asked with studious politeness.

"We still have tradable goods, Market Manager," Zainal said with equal courtesy and showed the man to the main exit.

"He did rig it, didn't he, Zainal?"

"It's a possibility," Zainal admitted, knowing how devious the market manager was. Greed was Kapash's main motive, which, of course, meant that he had seen how popular the coffee was. Zainal left the galley to go to the control room. Curious, Chuck followed and found him lighting up the main computer screens. Zainal entered four let-ters and sat back, watching the unit deal with the code.

When a menu appeared, Zainal typed in another series and sud-denly the screen scrolled down line after line of what Chuck thought were ship IDs.

"And what have you got here, Zainal lad?" Chuck asked, taking another seat.

"I met our beloved space station commander and he very kindly accessed some files for me, updating me—though I'm sure he didn't mean to." A smile wreathed Zainal's usually bland expression. "He gave me the chance to see two of his codes. One, this"—here he struck a save button and then an order to print the entire file—"is a list of all ship activity in and out of the station for . . . oh, probably ten years. That's as much as it's necessary to save."

"And what was the other code, Zainal?"

Zainal went back to the menu and tapped another code. "This one will take more time and effort," said Zainal. "But it might be worth it. It will give us the movements of all Eosi ships in and out of Barevi. I have also learned that the Eosi did not keep their share of earnings in any holding establishment, but secreted their treasures where only they could access them. If we examine their flights and destinations, we might discover where they stopped along the way."

"Well, a good day's work for all the anxiety. You got Kris and Kathy back, and also found what you've been looking for."

Paper was spewing out of the printer now. "Yes," said Zainal with satisfaction, "we'll know considerably more about the ins and outs of all shipments of slave labor following the Catteni invasion. I might even find out how much Ladade earned from his cut of the cap-tains' loot."

"I heard that Ladade is pretty honorable." The end of that sen-tence posed a question.

"Depends on your standards of honor," Zainal replied. He reached over and removed a wad of the hard copy from the basket, riffling through the pages. "We must get back to Botany and then return to Earth. Did you get any more automotive parts?"

"We got some truck tires from Nilink, the man you were supposed deal with earlier, and he was right annoyed when Kapash's men cut him off at the pass, as it were."

"Did he deliver to us or did you collect from his warehouse?"

"We collected but he has that place well secured."

"Full?"

"What you got is only a single column of the hoard he has. Whatever did he have in mind when he stocked up on tires? You can't use them on any Catteni vehicle, and there's nothing you can do with tire rubber. It's not something you could melt down like metals. By the way, he has batteries, too."

"You know, Chuck, I think we've gone about this the wrong way round."

"If you're thinking what I'm thinking, Zainal, indeed we have." He smiled and chuckled, rubbing his hands together. "And that'll show Kapash."

"Speaking of whom, let me just see . . ." And going back to the original menu, Zainal picked another file and opened it. "This is exactly what I need: the prison duty roster." He scrolled backward and stopped at a date. By now, Kapash's name was familiar to Chuck in Catteni script. Zainal finally highlighted the name "Kapash" and a date.

"Now that wouldn't just happen to be the date we got launched to Botany, would it? With Kapash on duty?"

"Perceptive of you, Chuck. That's exactly what it is." Now it was Zainal who rubbed his hands together.

"Wish I had access to Kapash's office files," he muttered, though he was well enough pleased to discover that Kapash had, indeed, connived in his being dropped. For he now had proof that Kapash had been on duty the day he and Kris and the others were sent off to

Botany on a slave ship. Kapash's "duty" should have included the rescue of an obvious Catteni from such a shipment. "And now I have proof and cause." An odd smile played on Zainal's lips but, with a shake of his head, he changed to his customary bland expression.

"Speaking of greed . . ." Zainal paused, jiggling his fingers on the worktop. "Where would one least expect to find treasure?"

"Right out in the open?" Chuck suggested.

"Quite likely. Pe was an odd personality, even for an Eosi." Zainal chuckled softly. "It's worth a look on our way out."

"Our way out?"

"We would be less noticeable then and we can always come back. Meanwhile, I intend to reduce Kapash's greed. A thief should not be allowed to enjoy it."

"But you gave him the beans for the women's safety."

Zainal gave Chuck an odd smile. "As market manager, Kapash is not only allowed to punish thieves, but he also has to indemnify the merchants for any losses they may incur while their products are under his protection."

Chuck's jaw dropped open. "Zainal?"

"He owes me a debt, as one Catteni to another, for unlawful imprisonment, and I shall take no more than is legal to acquit that debt and the several insults to my women."

For the evening meal, celebrating the safe return of the women, Natchi, Erbri, and Tavis were included among the guests. Erbri had brought in a roast of a beef-like animal that was hunted in the forests of Barevi. As the hunters were usually Catteni enjoying shore leave, they often sold their kills to local merchants, though occasionally they had the beasts butchered and took the best cuts back to their ship for better food than their captain would supply. The roast was tender and juicy, and everyone had second servings.

"I have one more task to complete," Zainal said when everyone, even Ferris, said they had eaten enough. He glanced at Peran and Bazil. "Then we will lift for Botany."

"Oh no, I can't do that," Eric said, looking astonished. "I have too many clients waiting for crowns and bridges to leave right now."

"Oh, we'll be back, I assure you," Zainal said.

"Look, Dr. Eric," Tavis said, "you can stay here. My family will be glad to have you as a guest, and I have so much to learn from you."

"And I will stay, too. Can't I, Dr. Eric? You know how helpful I can be. Please, Zainal, please?" Ferris begged.

"I'll think about that, Ferris. You could be vulnerable."

"No," Tavis said with suddenly unexpected dignity. "If he was in the employ of Dr. Eric, of course he must stay. And my family will protect him, too."

"You have learned much already, Tavis," Eric said kindly. "Zainal, I really can't leave or all the groundwork that has been laid for dentistry on Barevi will go for nothing."

"I have no objections to your staying, Eric. In fact, I would prefer it, though it does leave you exposed. Professionally, you are not involved," Zainal said cryptically. "However," and now he stared at Tavis, "can you keep Eric safe within your family compound?"

"We would pledge his safety if that is necessary, Zainal," Tavis said with an upward jerk of his chin to show his willingness and determination. "Emassi Doctor Eric has many, many influential and wealthy patrons. No harm would come to him."

"Good. We shan't be gone long, but there may be some repercussions."

"Repercussions?" Eric asked. "Oh, because no one's going to like dealing with Kapash for their coffee."

"I did hear something that puzzles me," Natchi said, looking dour. The old veteran had really enjoyed his early-morning cup and a place to sit in the sun. "That Kapash would be dealing with coffee beans from now on?"

"His supply is limited to what he has," Zainal said.

"Then he doesn't have the single concession to sell beans?"

"He may *think* he does," Zainal said with a little smile, "but this market is free to all traders, and that is not a rule he can bend. As we shall make certain. Now, I have discovered sufficient evidence to prove to me that Kapash was the duty officer at the prison the day we were dispatched to Botany."

Wide-eyed looks and gasps echoed the surprise of those around the table.

"I knew it, I knew it," Natchi said, swearing oaths in such a jumble that no one quite caught their sense, which was just as well, Zainal thought. "Greedy swamp wart. May he drown in his own slime."

"He might—quite legitimately, if you are all willing to take some risks before we depart tomorrow."

"What? What do we have to do?" was the eager response to risk-taking.

Even Kathy looked determinedly eager to cooperate, judging by the vengeful light in her eyes.

Zainal propped his elbows on the table but gave first Natchi and then Erbri a long look.

"I had already intended to take you two back to Botany for your mechanical skills but it might be as well—if you agree to tonight's business—to take you with us for other reasons."

"Such as?" Natchi challenged.

"We are still missing considerable spare parts—"

"And we're going to steal them so Kapash has to pay insurance!" Ferris bounced up and down in his chair, believing he had perceived Zainal's plan.

"But, Father . . ." Bazil, his more conservative child, protested, glancing at Brone, who evidently had no qualms with what was being suggested.

"Yes, yes, it is wrong to steal, but it is very proper and Cattenish to respond to insult. And Kapash has insulted me and mine once too often. Especially now I have proof of his complicity in my transportation."

"What proof do you have?" Brone asked blandly.

"I have the duty roster for that particular day, and he was on it as prison warden. That means he was supposed to oversee who was shipped out. I know he had orders to include everyone caught up in the riot, but that did not include a Catteni."

"And Zainal was certainly not part of that riot," Kris said firmly, eyeing Bazil sternly. "Neither was I. But I was Terran and unconscious, so I had no chance to proclaim my innocence in the affair."

"So, what must we do to assist you, Emassi?" Erbri said.

"Since you and Natchi have repaired all those lift glides, can you also help load them?"

"Sure, but all the places you need to get into are secured," Natchi pointed out.

"Some are even guarded," Erbri added cautiously.

"Shorting out the security system is no big problem," Bayes said, as their electrical expert. "Most of it needs to be repaired. Plenty of faulty lines." He shrugged. "Could go anytime."

"You can always get in from the roofs, too," Ferris said, and Ditsy nodded emphatically.

"Oh, can you? To which storage sheds in particular, Ditsy?" Zainal asked, suspecting that Ditsy had checked out such matters when he was looking around all the storage places.

"Oh, like Nilink's and Luxel's. Cut a panel out of the ceiling and with a lift on the roof we could load it in next to no time."

"And leave all the front tiers of tires to make 'em think no one's tampered with their stuff," Ditsy added.

"Zerkay's merchandise can be handled the same way. Steal the back layers and he won't be much wiser."

"He was the nicest of the lot," Kris said with dismay on her face.

"He has no need of the things he looted, and we can't play favorites if we're planning a widespread heist."

"It's *not* theft," Peran said. "It's restitution of impounded materials that were stolen in the first place."

Zainal gave his son a quick look for that bit of sophistry. Brone shrugged as if to imply he had not put such words in the boy's mouth.

"We have to be careful to go for only the things we know we can use or we're cut of the same cloth," Zainal said. "Where are our lists?"

Sally Stoffers opened her account book and held out copies.

"Nilink definitely. Natchi, figure out how many lifts we'll need to take the back third of his stock. Kathy, figure out the weight and cargo space this'll take. Fortunately, lifts can be taken right into the ship from the shadows of the dockside. There oughtn't to be too many people up and about in the early dawn. We'll need some light to operate by."

"We could arrange for some diversions, Zainal," Erbri suggested. "Nothing violent, just distracting?" His suggestion, as well as his expression, was so eagerly helpful that Zainal saw the merit of it.

"We'll have to figure out exactly when, Erbri, but we would appreciate it and I'll repay any expenses when I can."

"Your word is good, Emassi," Erbri replied.

"Good. We mostly need to shift what Luxel's been sitting on—the satellite components—and Nilink's tires and batteries. They'll be bulky and heavy so we'll need six or seven lifts for those two sites alone."

"I'll volunteer for that," Bayes and Clune said simultaneously.

"Brone, you'll stay out of this," Zainal said when the young tutor held up his hand. "In fact, Tavis, if you can shift Eric's things, with Brone's help, to your family compound, it will give you both alibis."

"Indeed, Emassi," Tavis said, expressing strong relief. Brone nodded with dignity, an attitude that did him no harm in the eyes of his young charges.

Zainal reached for a writing wand. "How many lifts have you been able to repair, Natchi?"

"Ditzy helped me, Emassi, but we have twelve in top working order and all powered up."

"Twelve . . ." Zainal murmured and started calculating weights and the time it would take to make round-trips from the storage sheds to the ship.

"No one would question our leaving after today," Chuck said. "I can stay on board on comm watch."

"No, I can assume that duty," Brone said. "I can also get our port clearance organized. I don't think there'll be any questions about that."

"Good idea." Zainal nodded his thanks. "Now," and he began to issue specific orders as to how many lifts would go to which destination. "It won't take more than ten minutes by lift to make it to and from the most distant storage unit—Luxel's—so allowing half an hour for Ferris and Ditsy to load, Erbri, start your distraction at three forty-five. Clune, Chuck, the tires and batteries will be heavier to load at Nilink's, so if Erbri keeps a good watch, you should get in about the time the boys do. Ninety, you and your brother take another lift behind Clune and Chuck. It's tires and batteries—and windshield wipers—we can use the most. You've got time to get some rest. You," and he pointed to Gail, "have some special signs to make for us."

"My pleasure. Who will you be raiding, Zainal?"

"Kierse," he said.

"I'll come along for that," Kris said.

"Not in your condition. Floss comes with me. You and Kathy get a good night's sleep. You'll have to be all smiles and sociability when we close down our market stall tomorrow."

"But what if the thefts have been discovered?" Ferris asked, wide-eyed.

Zainal merely laughed. "All the more reason for us to be about the business of closing our stall and leaving in good order."

Very pleased with her assignment, Floss shooed Kris and Kathy to their quarters, saying loudly that Bazil and Peran would help her clear the galley. "And leave it spotless!"

Zainal would have preferred to keep his sons innocent of the larceny, but since he had announced the reasons behind his actions, he felt they would understand that he didn't behave this way without cause. Revenge for an insult was a proper Catteni ritual under any circumstances, and insult had been done not only to Zainal, but also to Kris and Kathy.

He awakened after a few hours' sleep and went to the galley, thinking that this morning, of all he had recently enjoyed, there would be no hot coffee to savor. He was amazed to find Floss ready to pour him a fresh cup.

"Kapash's men thought they were so smart, Zainal—they thought coffee was just bags of beans," she said with a laugh as he inhaled the fragrant steam, "But I had just poured three sacks of raw beans into the roaster when they arrived. They never looked there. Kris will be very pleased, too."

The rest of the men and boys who followed him were equally pleased, none more than Natchi and Erbri, who had kipped down in the hold for what rest they would have before the dawn's action. So, tugging the lines of lifts out of the main hatch as soon as Natchi declared the docking bay free from casual traffic, they spread out to their various assignments.

Floating above the marketplace so late at night proved an eerie voyage as there were few around, most of them hired guards who would not necessarily think to look above their heads for transgressors, especially since Zainal kept to the deepest shadows, well able to avoid them as they did their rounds to check door locks.

Just as Zainal was hovering over Kierse's storage space, he saw the blue flash that meant Herb had effected a short in the power system. Such shorts happened so frequently that the guards would not be suspicious. Zainal had had a chance to note that there were sentries near Kierse's shed, so he dismounted the lift and went to the dark alley between Kierse's and his neighbor's units. Wrapping the lead line of the lift around his wrist, he carefully eased himself off to the now unsecured entrance. He was in, lift and all, in moments. With a tiny hand light, he found the materials he wanted from Kierse, in revenge for bearing false witness against Kathy and Kris. He peeked out before he ventured into the side lane and then, lying uncomfortably on his purloined goods, eased the lift up and began his way back to the BASS-1, sticking to shadows whenever possible—which meant he cruised just above the roofs of the sheds.

He heard the noise of the distraction Erbri had promised, though he hadn't a clue what it was. But, as he entered the docking area, there was no one running up and down the corridors, and keeping to the shadows cast by ground lights, he made it back to the BASS-1 and into the open cargo hold without detection. It took only moments for him to find the nets he had assigned for the goods he would retrieve and tip the lift to send its burden slipping into the shrouds. Then he put the lift into its storage brackets. A sudden shadow caused him a moment's panic but when he saw slender legs dangling over the side of a lift, he realized it had to be one of the boys. The lift was very heavy and sank slowly. He made his way over and opened the netting so that the contents could be slid into place.

"We could go back for another dip," Ditsy said, clearly elated with success. "We fixed the security lock so it won't come back on again."

"We must not be too greedy ourselves," Zainal said, but he

thought of what use the tires would be at their destination and how the rubber was slowly perishing in its current site. "Let's make sure everyone else is in safe and sound," he added as the black prow of another lift appeared in the cargo entrance.

He did send Ditsy, Clune, and Ninety back for another load of tires and batteries but after that he called a halt to the operation. Brone returned to the ship to report that he and Tavis had settled Eric and his equipment safely in the compound and would see them in the morning. Brone gave the appearance of not noticing the cargo bay's new contents.

Zainal would have preferred lifting as soon as possible now but he had good reasons for wanting possible clients to know that he was leaving. Even appearing at his former site the morning after mass pilferage might deflect blame from him. Gail's signs had already been put up at the stall, announcing its closure. Those who had enjoyed early coffee were milling around, as if hoping to continue their coffee habit against all visible evidence to the contrary. It was also a relief to know that so far the previous night's burglaries had not yet been discovered. Kapash would know soon enough but he would not immediately suspect Zainal. He was surprised to see Kierse among those viewing the emptied premises.

"Where are you going? How will I sell what I have left of that unsalable stuff from Terra?"

"I will tell you when I know," Zainal answered and started to pass Kierse. The man grabbed his tunic. Ninety Doyle took a step forward but Zainal stopped him with a swift glance.

"But I have to sell it," Kierse said. "You've been my first buyer in months."

"I was willing to buy but you wanted more than I had to pay."

"I have to return a profit to my investors, you know."

"That is your problem, not mine." Zainal chopped at the restraining hand and Kierse did not persist, though his expression remained defeated. There were any number of inflammatory remarks Zainal could have made about greed and the irrationality of stealing things without knowing of available marketplaces—though Zainal now had a novel idea about that little problem.

"And what about more coffee?" Kierse asked plaintively.

"You have enough beans to last awhile," Zainal said with no sympathy.

"And then?"

"Kapash has the rest of my beans," he suggested helpfully, and waved farewell to the man, standing in the middle of the aisle in front of their stall, looking bereft, as he hurried off on his next vital errand of the day before someone else detained him.

When Zainal got to the market manager's office to pay Eric's rental on a better stall situation in the first square of the market, Kapash's haughty assistant announced that Manager Kapash was too busy to see to any minor details, but he was quite willing to write out the lease for the space Zainal wanted and give a receipt for it and Eric's "office." Zainal was relieved not to see Kapash again but he would have liked to have been an insect on the wall when Kapash discovered that he would be responsible for reimbursing the merchants (perhaps with the coffee beans he now owned) for their losses from the burglaries of their supposedly safe lockups. Since Eric had so many prominent clients, including Ladade, who had no use for Kapash, he felt the aggressive dentist would have no trouble, and probably take pleasure in, contending with Kapash if the man was stupid enough to contest a lease signed by his own assistant. Eric was smart enough to make use of Ladade's patronage if needed. Ferris wanted to stay, and Zainal was half-tempted to let him, except that Ferris's light-fingered ways might also make things awkward for Eric.

Bazil and Peran had learned valuable lessons here, but not the ones young Catteni—especially Emassis—should acquire. Brone now had them well in hand and actually liking their lessons. Perhaps, Zainal thought, this venture had primed the pump for a return even if this first visit had not been such an overwhelming success in itself. Although, in some respects, they had achieved more than they had had any right to expect: he had the all-important information that would be of benefit to Botany and his goals. There were other options now for how to proceed.

And he had another idea that might solve all their problems soon, if not immediately. He wished he could think of a reason to go forward with the plan right now to give the Botany group the resources to buy up everything they had come for, but acting too quickly might cause more problems than it solved. As wise to give the diffident merchants a little time to regret missing the chance to empty their warehouses of useless products. Do them no harm.

Besides which, he thought with humor, they had to leave soon or the bananas would be overripe. Kris had her heart set on producing them at Botany. She had been much relieved to know that, although Kapash's men had taken all the remaining bean sacks in the hold, they had overlooked the beans in the roaster. Kris was glad for anything that diminished the benefit to Kapash of her trumped-up "ransom." There would be some beans for Botany as well as bananas.

"We shall get coffee plants the next time we're on Earth," Zainal told her, to cheer her up. "I think I remember that someone on one of the plantations told me that the plants would travel well and could adapt to new environments as long as the temperature and the rain were correct."

"We are going back to Earth, are we?"

"I've got data for folks to figure out which slave ship went where, and who among the missing might still be located wherever they were sold," he assured her.

She gave a little shudder at how close she had come to being another name on those lists. "And we've loads of merchandise to ease the current shortages."

"And we did get the most updated register from Vitali, along with the air charts," Zainal said, nodding toward the worktop where he kept such things. Then he leaned back in his chair, locking his fingers behind his head.

"Why are you grinning, Zainal?" Kris asked, suspicious of such good humor.

"I think I have justified a short detour I want to make on our departure."

"Detour?" Kris repeated, mystified.

His grin widened. "As Chuck said, the best place to hide something is right out in the open."

"What?"

"I won't say because I could be wrong . . ."

"Who are you trying to impress now?"

"I want to show Botany more results than we've had."

"I don't think we've done that badly," Kris said encouragingly. "Sally said we got the most profit on the coffee beans—"

"Since they cost us nothing—"

"Apart from two lift platforms . . . and we do have a range of comm sat parts, the tires, the batteries and spark plugs—though they're for Earth, aren't they?"

Zainal nodded.

"So you intend to go back to Earth, just for coffee beans and the plants?"

"And possibly to find someone with enough experience to manage a Botany coffee plantation and bean warehouse."

"And the roasting," Kris said firmly. "I don't think I quite got the hang of it."

"But Floss saved the beans for us."

She flushed but managed a tentative smile for him. "Yes, but it isn't something I planned to do. I still have a score to settle with that smirking Kapash."

"Oh, last night was a good way to settle that score, dear heart," he said, pushing himself up out of the chair. On his way out of their "office," he gave her a warm kiss. "I wonder if Brone ever had to visit the junkyard."

She stared after him.

They received permission to clear Barevi port the next morning, with Kathy, a willing but slightly nervous pilot, handling the disengagement of the docking clamps, easing the KDM into the traffic heading out for the space station. When they had passed the space station with an "all clear" to proceed, Zainal motioned Kathy out of her seat.

"But I did it right, didn't I?"

"Yes, indeed you did, Captain, but we're making a short detour," Zainal said and altered the settings so that the BASS-1 veered toward the jumble of waste material in the junkyard. Almost immediately a comm unit buzzed and Zainal answered it.

"You have changed course, BASS-1. Is there a problem?"

"No, I cleared this with your operations yesterday, Captain. We need to see if the junkyard has any spare KDM water tanks. We need one."

There was an obviously hasty conference at the space station.

"All clear, BASS-One." Zainal didn't recognize the voice. "You may proceed. Good luck."

"I hope that wasn't Ladade," Kris muttered, more to herself than to anyone else.

"No, it was not," Zainal said. "Only the duty officer knew that my flight plan included the side trip."

"I didn't know we needed a spare tank," Kathy said.

"I want to see what else is there, in case we *do* need it, Kathy," Zainal said, slowing the forward motion of the BASS-1 as they approached the jumbled elements of the junkyard.

"How are you going to find one in all that?" Kathy asked.

"Oh, one of us may spot what we're looking for. See if you can find anything that looks out of place in its company."

"Say again?" Kathy asked, confused.

"Brone, come to the control room, on the double," Zainal said on the interior com.

"Yes, Emassi," was the immediate response. Brone came with Peran and Bazil, who wedged their boyish bodies into the jump seat next to Kris and strapped in, as they were now in free fall. Kathy had vacated the second officer's position for Brone at Zainal's request but she hung on to the safety rail, not wishing to miss whatever was going to happen.

The loosely spinning objects, some of them sides of battered hulls, twisted structural members, some of them fused together, continued on their intrinsic orbit far from Barevi. Zainal matched velocity and, deftly using his thrusters, inserted himself into the moving mass, adjusting his speed as he edged farther into the swarm.

"Watch the passing parade, crew, and point out anything that looks like it shouldn't be here."

Peran gave a snort. "How would we know what shouldn't be here?" he asked.

"You mean, like that large loaf of bread?" Kathy asked, pointing to a tumbling object whose matte-black angles reflected a gleam from one of the perimeter warning lights.

"Which one?" Zainal asked.

"Oh, I'd put it at eleven o'clock," Kathy replied, pointing.

"The scan says the contents are metallic," Brone said, reading the screen's assessment.

"Looks like an immense loaf of bread to me," Kathy repeated. "Wrapped with heavy chain, too, so whatever is in it won't fall out."

Zainal inched the KDM closer.

"There's another one just like it at four o'clock," Kris said.

"Also full of metal," Brone said, having checked it out on the screen.

"Now, why isn't the metal just emptied in with all the other stuff?" Kathy asked—because, not only were the ship's proximity warnings shrieking, but there were pings as much smaller objects bounced against the hull of the BASS-1.

"Very good point, Kathy," Zainal said with an air of satisfaction. He switched on the intercom. "Chuck, stand by the airlock. We're going to try to collect some space garbage. Can you defuse the charge as we did with the comm sat?"

"Sure, Zainal," Chuck said. "In a few. I've been checking manifests."

They were closing in on the loaf when he announced his presence at the airlock, with a handy chain to take the static charge away from the BASS-1.

"Open airlock and be prepared to lose gravity," Zainal said and deftly hit the altitude thrusters so the broad side of the ship was presented to the intended captive. Then, with a blast on the warning hooter, he flipped off the gravity. Once again, the object sparked as the defusing chain hit it and not long after found itself eased into the airlock and the hatch closed on its prize. "Stand by, Chuck. We have a possible second."

On the open link, they could hear Chuck wondering out loud why they needed garbage from an effing junkyard.

"Because they are right out in the open where anyone could see them," Zainal replied cryptically.

"Oh!" Chuck's response indicated enlightenment. As soon as the second bread loaf was in the airlock, Zainal ordered it closed, the maneuver over, and internal gravity was restored.

"Now, we're out of here," he said, turning the nose of the ship to starboard and easing it, by means of cautious spurts of the forward thrusters, out of the junkyard and safely into open space. "Captain Harvey, if you would resume piloting, we can proceed, full speed, to Botany."

"Aye, sir," she replied, still mystified by the diversion.

"Hey, there's another bread loaf," Peran said, pointing at three o'clock.

"Why, so there is, Peran. Good eyes on you," Zainal said cheerfully, tousling his son's hair—something he knew Peran disliked, but it distracted the boy. "It'll be interesting to see if it's still there on our return. Meanwhile, let's go see what we snared."

Peran and Bazil were both pleased at that invitation.

"Coming, Kris?" Peran asked.

"For the sake of my insatiable curiosity," Kris said. Peran and Bazil had both been much nicer to her lately, though she didn't think it had much to do with Brone's influence. The change had started just after she had so staunchly rescued Ferris from Kapash's vengeance. She would miss the boy's cheerfulness, but he'd be fine with Eric and Tavis, and she was glad Zainal had relented and let him stay behind.

"Okay, Zainal," Chuck said when those from the control room had made it to the lock. "I never thought I'd be rescuing junk from the deep six."

"Because they were there, Chuck," Zainal said. "Have we got any metal cutters for those chains?" he added as he took full note of the garlands of chain looping the objects.

Ditsy said he had some and went off to the hold where he and Natchi had stashed the tools they used to repair what they found at the Barevian junkyards. The boy didn't have quite enough strength to make the tool bite through the chains, but Brone did. The chains fell away and Zainal opened the first lid and looked in. He gave a long whistle and then pushed the chest over to scatter its contents before the wondering eyes of the onlookers.

"Jackpot!" Ditsy said, kneeling down to scoop up handfuls of the coins that spilled out, and the larger oddments that had been disclosed. "Hey, look! A crown!" He picked up the huge, jewel-encrusted affair and put it on his head. Its rim fell to his shoulders, being much too wide to sit on his narrow skull.

Kris held up another golden band, and then pulled out from the coins a long rod with a globe on one end.

"This looks like the English scepter of state," she said, trying to look queenly. "Just like the Eosi to enter the Tower of London and steal the crown jewels!"

Zainal held up a beautiful drinking bowl in gold, its jeweled rim sparkling in the hold's overhead lights.

"And that's a Cellini bowl," she said, pointing to it. "I've seen pictures of something like it from a museum. The Eosi obviously were in line for the best of the best. What are the coins?"

Zainal sighed. "We could have used these." He let some trickle through his fingers. "Catteni gold bunts, large coin as well as halves and quarters . . . probably mined from one of the Eosi's holdings or the rents they were paid as landlords. These were minted in Barevi though. See the *B* stamped on it." He showed it around the admiring circle.

Fascinated by the heavy coins, Bazil began to stack them in piles before casually scattering them back on the floor of the hatch.

"Didn't know there could be so much coin," Bazil said, awed. "We'd've got everything we wanted for just this much. " He scooped up a double handful and then let it fall back, tinkling. He chased a piece that rolled away to the edge of the deck, catching it just before it disappeared into a slot by a girder. He carefully replaced it. "If we went back to Barevi, we could get just about everything else we needed."

"We probably could, Bazil, but not today, I think. I don't want to arouse suspicions," Zainal said. "Our sudden wealth would make Kapash as well as Ladade very suspicious."

"Won't they be suspicious because we made that detour?"

"Possibly, but while they are greedy men, the KDM is faster than any of their ships and I did explain why we went there. Not unusual for a ship to search through a station's junkyard. They would also have to have been watching very carefully to see what we took."

"But I saw more loaves," Bazil said.

"And we have other duties to perform right now."

"They'll keep," Kathy said.

"I'd love to put their noses further out of joint," Chuck said, setting his jaw as he remembered all the slights and delays they had suffered at the hands of the merchants. "D'you think this was a wise idea, Zainal?"

"If we went back now, it would be a stupid move. I asked for a water tank. This is about the right size and conformation to anyone who might have been watching us from the station. They've yet to discover last night's work. I certainly wouldn't want to be back on Barevi when they do. Let's organize the contents. And what's in the other one?"

That chest proved to contain very carefully rolled-up paintings, some of which Kris recognized.

"The Eosi really knew what to loot," she murmured, carefully rerolling one painting.

"They would," Zainal said. "And you spotted another loaf, didn't you, Peran?"

"Yes, Father, I did."

"Well, we won't go back for it now. We know what we're looking for and Ladade and Kapash will not. We shall hope that the Eosi's deception lasts until our return, when we will search for any other unlikely objects in that junkyard."

"And they do look like bread loaves!" Kris said, regarding the rounded lids and the rectangular ends, with a shade of respect for such subterfuge. "Whoever would have thunk it."

Brone reappeared in the lock with writing materials and started an inventory list. Floss tried on the crown, which fit her better than it had Ditsy, although she declared that it was very heavy. "Uneasy is the head . . ." she said in a "quoting" tone but did not explain further. Then she spotted a diamond-and-ruby bracelet, which she fastened on her arm. Pleased with that, she started sorting through the coins for other jewelry. The boys found more and shortly had filled both her arms and found rings for all her fingers.

"Never thought I'd see this much ice! Nor so many kinds of rocks," Floss crowed, striding gawkily around the hatch, her arms held out to display her finery in the manner of a fashion mannequin. "What would you like, Kris? Diamonds, emeralds, rubies, or sapphires? Dress-up time."

Kris was attracted by the translucent glamour of pearls and wound several long strands around her neck, imitating Floss's catwalk posture.

"Way cool!" Floss said when Kris stalked about.

"We have to return the crown jewels," Kris said, almost regretfully, as such items were not much use to them. Only beautiful! She unwound the pearls and put them carefully in Brone's lap. "C'mon, Floss, we'd better find something more appropriate to wrap those things in. I think I have some coffee bean bags left and enough labels."

"Beans for the baubles, huh?" Floss said blithely, but she spent the afternoon with Jax, Gail, and Kathy playing with the jewelry as they packed and Brone inventoried it.

"Won't buy much in a bazaar on Earth though," she said once, scornfully. "Who'd trade this sort of stuff for a loaf of bread?"

"Would you believe a country?" Kris said, remembering her history lessons as she carefully padded the crown in a worn old rag of a towel. "At that, I think the towel is worth more on the open market. *Sic transit gloria mundi.*" She gave the crown a final pat.

"Sick transit Gloria . . . Who's she?" Floss asked, curious.

"It's Latin and refers to the transitory nature of human vanities."

"Hey, look at me, Gloria. I ain't sick," was Floss's giggling rejoinder.

"Well, look where all this," and Kris motioned at the still large pile of jewelry awaiting packing, "ended up. As junk, orbiting hundreds of miles from civilization."

"That is, if you can call Barevi civilized," Floss said contemptuously.

12

No one was happier to see Botany's sphere grow larger in the forward screen than Zainal. Kris was delighted, too, because there were still five good-sized hands of bananas that were ripe but not yet overripe. They'd have to be eaten immediately on arrival. The two bushels of oranges had lasted fine, but the guavas and papayas were only sweet memories.

The last day everyone was busy cleaning up and smartening their downside clothing. Sally Stoffers had worked on a report for a formal presentation to the Council. Zainal issued orders that the BASS-1 be in readiness for a quick turnaround. Kris rather thought that, even if he admitted to wholesale robbery to the Council, they wouldn't take as much offense if it would be received with rapturous gratitude on Earth.

The challenge to their presence came right on the dot of their entry into the sensor satellite's range.

"This is BASS-1, returning to base. We are all well and accounted for," Zainal said, formally replying to "Who goes there?"

"Hurrah! It's Zainal back. Did you get everything we needed?" Zainal recognized the duty officer's voice as Worry's.

"More than we expected, Worry, less than we wanted, but there are distinct alternatives that must be examined," Zainal replied, wanting to be honest if not explicit. "Can you call a general meeting for tonight?"

"Can and will. Welcome home, Zainal. All's well here."

From the size of the crowd that had gathered to welcome the wayfarers at the landing field, Zainal thought that anyone who was off work was there. And lots of the kids, so perhaps they could just hand out the bananas and oranges right there and then. It was afternoon on Botany, a cool, sweet-scented day. And midsummer of the local seasons. That meant he would have time to make another trip to Terra, and if that proceeded with dispatch, he'd still have time to catch the autumnal visit of the Farmers, collecting the harvest from their side of the planet. If the wheat looked to be a good crop, he could, in all good conscience, ask for more to take back to Earth.

Zane and Amy were there, Zane's hand held by Rose Mitford, while Cherry was bouncing Amy to keep her happy. The bustle around her had startled her. Zainal happily counted the KDMs and KDLs settled on one side of the field and mentally assigned them crews and captains for their upcoming missions. That is, if he managed to talk the Council into going ahead with this venture. Maybe the bananas should go to the judge and the older folk, who would remember them from happier times.

It was good to be back on Botany, Zainal thought, as, hand in hand, he and Kris led the crew down the ramp. They had loaded the lifts with the bean sacks and fruits and these came into sight to cheers. Most of the cargo, however, was to remain in place. Sally had done an inventory, as well as the mission accounting.

There were cheers and happy reunions, and during all the fuss, Zainal introduced Brone to Worry, the judge, and Dorothy Dwardie— when he could get her out of Chuck's arms. He was pleased, and

Brone was astounded, by how courteously he was received. Zainal decided that perhaps his wildest imaginings might be feasible. Space was big and there were so few intelligent species. Why be enemies when being allies was far more practical?

There were so many queries fired at him that Zainal moved to the top of the ramp and held up his arms for silence.

"We're very glad to be back, and it's wonderful to see you all. You know that I've called a general meeting for this evening, and we'll give you a complete account of our travels, and our adventures. We didn't bring back all we went for," and he anticipated the groan, "but we brought back a lot we didn't expect to get." He pointed to the bananas. "We can get more where they came from, but I think the kids ought to have bananas and oranges with their suppers. We do have a hundred and fifty pounds of coffee beans!"

A really enthusiastic cheer greeted that announcement. "And I think we can probably grow our own beans down on the peninsula." He pointed to the south and west. There was a wilder and happier response to that suggestion. "We've more things to talk about and decisions to make because we need to consolidate our position, both on Earth and on Barevi. So save your questions for tonight. Only don't make up any I can't answer." Good-natured responses to that followed him as he saw Judge Iri Bempechat arriving late on the landing site and beckoned him to wait around for a little private chat.

Kris had gone to hug her children and talk to Cherry and Rose. Amy had "made strange" with her mother, and Kris was trying to coax a smile from her. Gradually people began to drift to their homes and toward the main buildings of Retreat.

"Yes, Zainal," Iri said, stumping forward on his cane. "Your trip was eminently successful, but I perceive from your expression it brought up more questions than it answered."

"So it did," Zainal replied, relieved that the judge was so shrewd a man.

"Run them past me." The judge beckoned for Zainal to accompany him as he stepped into his little motor cart. "Are you going home?"

"No, I must be sure those ceramic caskets are put in safekeeping. Ninety's in charge of them but I want you to see what they contain."

"Oh?"

"Eosi treasure—most of which I have no difficulty putting to the colony's use, but some of the items should be returned to their original owners."

"You found Eosi treasure?" The judge was fascinated. "What would they have considered 'treasure'? And where did you find it?"

"In space, so technically, I think it can be considered the property of whoever finds it."

"Hmmm . . . yes, traditionally, flotsam and jetsam are usually the property of the finder," the judge suggested.

"I'm glad that is your opinion, too, but there are some very beautiful jewels and whole casks of what Kris said are old-masters' paintings. Probably looted from museums. Apart from not knowing what to do with them, they are no use to us."

"Not even as trade items?" Iri asked.

"Coffee beans and metals are good trade commodities. Fancy jewels, which in any case would look silly on a Catteni, are not. The Eosi had a huge appetite for acquisition just for acquisition's sake. I think we can find out which museum owned the paintings. We also found that Earth isn't interested in the nonedible or noncommercial at the moment. There is, however, a considerable treasure in Catteni coin, which I would like to put to use acquiring the rest of the items Botany and Earth need."

"You are concerned for Earth?"

"Yes, the planet was raped by the Eosi, for the sheer pleasure of acquisition, it would now seem. My plan is to return there as soon as we can resupply BASS-1 and restore to them some of the loot we reacquired. I also have a plan, which I must take up with the Terran coordinators, about establishing commerce with them. And bazaars." Zainal couldn't help but grin. "The Catteni captains took anything that wasn't nailed down, as Ninety phrased it, Earth has gone back to bartering. I think that if we can get them to allow Catteni, or at least the Botany-registered Catteni ships back in their space to land at their trading points, everyone could find what they need and manage to barter viable objects for Catteni consumption. The market is very slow there and it needs new products. Mostly, it needs to dump unusable merchandise. Earth needs what's sitting in warehouses uselessly. Barevi commerce would improve if we cross-traded, but I'm not sure if Botany, much less Earth, would be willing."

"We come in peace. Take us to your bazaars?" Iri saw the irony.

"Why should Botany make all the effort to establish a rapport?" was Zainal's next question.

"A good point. Is there a new stable government on Earth, as Chuck said?" Iri asked with hope.

"Yes, a coordination of efforts and resources," Zainal said, approving what he had seen. "For instance, we traded medicines from one coordinator's sphere of influence to another's in Africa, and we got coffee beans, which turned out to make a remarkably tradable item on Barevi."

"Catteni like coffee?" Iri asked Zainal in his dry way.

"You should have seen what a few pounds of beans could buy us. And you will. I plan," and Zainal could feel enthusiasm return, "to obtain coffee bean plants on our next visit to Earth and try them in the southwest, near the Masai lands."

"I do like a cup of coffee or three in the morning," Iri said. "You didn't bring back an espresso machine, did you?"

"No, but I'm sure I can trade for one on Earth. Whatever it is."

Iri sighed again and put a veined hand with swollen knuckles on Zainal's arm. "You get to my age and you find that food is about the only thing that tempts you."

"We have coffee, from the Kenyan mountains, and the milder bean from Santa Lucia."

"You spanned continents with no problems?"

Zainal nodded. "Surprise was our main advantage. We were, however, met with courtesy. I'm not so sure how other Catteni groups would be received."

"Doubtless with suspicion?"

"Possibly, until we clear their peaceful arrival with the Watch Dog security force. I don't know how they would now rebuff a hostile force, but they would know before it reached Earth. Kris said, 'once bitten, twice shy.' There is also the matter of resources. Catteni enterprise has been cut back considerably since the controlling force is inactive."

"Kamiton and the others are having more trouble with the transition from the Eosi."

Zainal nodded and the judge went on. "History supports the supposition that it's one thing to have a revolution and another to recover from it. Earth is doing the better job. This time," the judge remarked succinctly. "And if they have, it will be the first time in the long struggle of humanity. May I live to see it!" He gave a long sigh. "What else do you plan, Zainal?"

"I plan to use our ships to run between Earth and Barevi, and to start an orderly collection of the products of Catteni mining worlds."

"What about the rest of our missing folk?"

"That will take far more organizing—and exchanges—than I can currently contemplate, but I was able to secure lists of which slave ship went where. Exchanging workers may be more difficult, if not downright impossible. Your species is admirably suited to the work required to keep such planets and facilities operating. Earth needs the mineral resources as much as Catten does. A little competition might be beneficial. What I envision is cooperation, too, between Catteni and Terrans."

"Politics has always made strange bedfellows," Iri remarked.

Zainal did not quite understand his reference as it might apply to their two species, especially as he saw nothing strange about having Kris as his bedfellow.

"Coordinators run Earth, you say?"

Zainal nodded.

"I must think how coordination can best be extended." He patted Zainal's arm again as they came to the main settlement of Retreat. "You have done well. You are thinking. It is thinking men we need right now."

"There is much our two races can exchange to the benefit of both."

"Then we need more coordination and cooperation." The judge dismounted from his motor and looked inquiringly at Zainal. "You called a meeting for this evening?"

Zainal nodded.

"We will then coordinate efforts." The judge strode away, nodding right and left at those who greeted him.

Zainal went to the main dining room, aware that he was hungry, and hungry for Botanic food. A nice juicy broiled rock squat would taste fine right now, and some tubers. Seed potatoes were another item that he must try to return with. And other Earth vegetables that might do well. Hadn't Kris said one of their drivers had farmed nearby? There was still so much to do and plan. Would he ever be able to drop back to Botany and stay put? Why must duty keep calling him away to attempt the impossible?

Because that was what he had undertaken to do and felt responsible for completing. He wondered if that was what had driven the Eosi. But he was not Eosi: he was a Botanist—no longer a Catteni, but of, and for, this world. And of and for this world, he would do everything possible so that it would continue with all its promise and plenty.

A hand caressed his shoulder and he looked around to see Kris beside him in line waiting to be served.

"Rock squat, please," he said, pointing to the browned segment he liked. "You'll never believe how important those rock squats were to us in our travels," he told the server.

"Really?" The woman was surprised. "Nice to see you back, Zainal, Kris. And thanks for the coffee beans—even if we still have to ration them."

"Not for much longer," Zainal said with the airy confidence that suddenly enveloped him.

Kris also chose rock squat and as they picked other selections from the salad bowls, she paused to point out Bazil and Peran, sitting with Brone and looking very pleased with themselves.

"I think the teacher is being taught," she murmured, since Brone's head was turning this way and that, constantly observing those in the hall.

As they looked around for a table, they saw other members of their crew dining with friends and relatives. Floss, Clune, and Ditsy were, however, alone at a big table to which Kris and Zainal made their way.

"Good to be home, isn't it?" she said conversationally.

"Well, it's nice not to have to be . . ." Floss shrugged.

"Apprehensive?" Clune asked, reaching for her hand and smiling down at her.

"Yeah, that's the word. Everyone likes my dress," Floss added, stroking the fabric down the front over one hip. "No one has one like it."

"Nor are they likely to," Kris said.

"Aren't we going back to Africa?" Floss asked. Clearly she wanted to get more brightly colored material. It did suit her.

"That's up for discussion," Zainal said in a tone that suggested an end to that subject.

"We'll have to," Clune said, lifting his cup of coffee to his lips. "I'm as addicted to this stuff as everyone else." He took a sip. "We'd get clearance just by promising to ensure a supply of coffee."

"There's more to be done than that," Ditsy said with some scorn.

"D'you miss Ferris?" Kris asked.

"Yeah," Ditsy said in a bleak tone, slumping in his chair and laying an arm on the table to prop his head on, in a totally disconsolate mood. "Never thought he'd desert me for a dentist!"

"Speaking of that, we never did get one of his dentist friends to come work here on Botany," Kris said in mild self-reproach.

"There are a lot of things we didn't get to do," Zainal said, "this time!" He gave a sharp nod of his head to indicate that he intended to perform at a higher level soon.

"Think of the things we did do, Zainal! Not too shabby," Kris replied. Lord, was everyone down in the dumps? Post-something-or-other depression? Kathy Harvey very much wanted to achieve more miracles of repair on satellites, especially with that nice young fellow at the green coords—Wendell? Wasn't that his name? Yes, John Wendell. Kathy had been mopey now and then. It was Jax who had clued Kris in to her interest in the attractive young communications expert who was worlds away from them right now. Oh, well.

Many people came up to have a few words with them and the general drift of the comments suggested to Kris that the majority of Botanists were impressed with the visible results of this first mission, even if it had not been as successful as Zainal had anticipated. He had returned the remaining gold nuggets and flakes to Mike Miller, who had been extremely surprised to receive them. He'd also asked about what other metals were available in good supply: not that anything wouldn't be welcome on ore-starved Earth.

"Shucks. You coulda used it all, Zainal. We don't need it here."

"I couldn't use it all, Mike, as most countries are no longer on a gold standard. Coffee beans were more acceptable. And the copper, tin, lead, and zinc."

"Who'da thought it?" Mike said, slack-jawed with surprise, but he carefully signed a receipt for the gold, and Zainal told him the combination of the digital lock on the safe box.

"Got more of those lesser metals if you need them."

Zainal did not remark on that, which implied that Mike, for one, approved of further expeditions. Kris smiled and thanked Mike.

"You know," she said, "I got the impression from the green coord that the problem might not just be that there is no transport for what resources Earth has left. They need more miners, too. I suspect he could use all who would come."

She could see that Zainal was turning things over in his mind. He'd been doing a lot of thinking lately, more silent than usual—even for him. Still, she had a few things to ponder herself.

This time she'd bring a lot more flour and rock squats. She began to itemize the other natural supplies of Botany's bounty in terms of how they would trade on Earth. They could share more until Earth recovered its own agriculture.

Leon Dane's appearance at their table seemed only natural to her, and she broached the subject of their mission to Kenya and the typhoid epidemic. She knew that Leon and his staff had been busy trying to catalog the therapeutic herbs and roots of Botany. They had done so to provide alternatives for the medicines they'd used on Earth. So far there had been no epidemics of anything except for measles. That had run its course—through the crèches, of course, but there had been no serious side effects for any of the children.

"Is it true that some pharmaceutical companies are still operating down on Earth?" Dane asked, sliding into an empty chair and sipping his coffee. "Best thing you could have brought back," he added with a grin. "Really good beans, too."

Kris sniffed. "You have some of the Kenyan robustas. My nose got better in Barevi."

"So I heard," Leon said with a broad grin. "So, can I possibly get some stuff on your next trip?"

"You assume there will be one?" Zainal asked, raising his brows in surprise.

"Hell's bells, man, I think that was just the start. You are going to bring back coffee plants, aren't you?"

"Where'd you hear that?" Zainal asked.

Leon scratched his head, contorting his face to aid his memory. "Dunno now. Probably Sarah McDouall or possibly Chuck. He reminded us about the equatorial peninsula. She thought it would be climatically appropriate for coffee beans and maybe even bananas and sugarcane. Say, that unrefined brown sugar you brought in is the best treat. I did scrounge an orange."

"Good for you, Leon."

"Bananas went down well in the pediatric ward. Not that the kids knew what they were. They just liked the taste."

"Wish we knew more about banana and coffee culture," Kris said, wistfully.

"Just give us a chance. Ol' trial and error is a great instructor," Leon said airily.

"Ain't it just," Kris replied, sneaking a glance at Zainal to see his reception of such ideas.

"We'd have to trade for what you need," Zainal was saying. "Maybe something you've been using here on Botany would work."

"I'll get Sarah to do up some botanical files and slides and see how we can send specimens for their investigation," Leon said, and slapped his hand on the table as he rose to his feet. "Gotta go. Just wanted to say thanks." He drained the last of his coffee and detoured on his way out the door to put his cup in the dirty-dishes basket.

"I wish we could do something spectacular for Earth," Floss said. "While you were off in Manhattan, we got to talking to some of the airport crews. None of them knew anything about Botany or the Catteni forced colonies. I think everyone wanted to smuggle on board the BASS-1 and come back here."

"Neither world is problem-free, Floss," Kris said.

"No, but we got a better deal going here than they do," Floss remarked. "C'mon, Clune, I'm due for my shift."

"And me for mine," Clune said, checking whether the other mugs on the table were empty before clearing them off, deftly slotting his fingers through the handles.

Zainal turned a surprised expression to Kris. "She's due for kitchen cleaning and she goes willingly? My, what is it you say about wonders?"

"May wonders never cease," Kris said. "I think she learned something from our travels."

"It would appear so. Now, my dear heart, we have some planning to do."

"I rather thought we might. You've been very thoughtful lately."

"More of my"—he raised his right arm in an expansive gesture—"wild imaginings." He leaned over and kissed her cheek. "I have time before the Farmers collect their harvest. And we have gathering of our own to do."

Just at that moment, Gino Marrucci entered the mess hall and came over to Zainal with a clipboard, on which a sheaf of papers fluttered from the speed of his entrance.

"Hi, glad I caught you, Zainal." He looked down at his notes. "Got supplies lined up for all of the KDMs and the KDLs. Did you plan to use Baby, too?"

"She should be ready to fly in case we need her. Did Peter and Aarens manage to figure out a long-distance homing device?"

"Not for the distances we'll have to travel."

"Well, we can use Baby to check out that old Eosi excavation on our moon."

"D'you think an Eosi actually hid stuff there, too?"

"It's a remote possibility," Zainal admitted.

"So were the bread-loaf chests in the junkyard," Kris reminded him. He gave a diffident shrug.

He went over the supply sheets with Gino and initialed the crews. "This is all contingent, you know," he reminded Gino.

"Every kid, including your own, is out hunting rock squats and the kitchen is prepared to roast and toast until they're all done."

"Hope someone finds some nests and eggs. We can get an incubator for the trip out and present them with rock squat chicks," Kris remarked. "Personally, I don't like rock squat eggs but they're better than nothing." She had a vision of rock squat farms taking over from the piggeries on the Secaucus meadows, and Murray as a squat farmer. She giggled and waved off Zainal's look of inquiry. There was of course the problem of bringing alien life forms to Earth. The first incursion had not been a success.

Zainal got touchier and touchier during the afternoon and she worried about him. He had done so much already. What did he expect of himself? Certainly far more than others expected of him.

Sally Stoffers called in briefly to deliver a note.

"There never was a quotation on the stock market for the value of Catteni bunts against American dollars or English sterling. But Mike suggested we use the gold rate as a standard: those coins are twenty-carat gold, just enough impurity to keep them from being too soft for use or clipped." She handed him her note. "That gives the equivalent, and it's far more than we borrowed from Mike Miller. That doesn't even include the jewelry, just the coin. The stones in some of those necklaces and rings and stuff would buy what's left of Manhattan. If it was still on the gold standard."

When Zainal finally decided it was time to go to the evening meeting, he looked more woebegone than ever and Kris couldn't think of anything to cheer him up.

"I didn't get everything I said I would get," he remarked as they reached the hall. Then he squared his shoulders and walked boldly into the meeting.

It was even better attended than the previous one, which encouraged Kris even if Zainal did not seem to notice. Brone sat in the front row with the two boys, who waved wildly to catch their father's attention before Brone murmured something to them. They both sat on their hands then and tried to contain such un-Catteni-like reactions. Ditsy, Clune, and Floss sat behind them, and Floss, her hair trimmed and neat around her face, wore the second of her two new dresses: the bright blue patterned one. Their shipmates had taken seats in the same row and were beaming at the entrance of Kris and Zainal, which caused a ripple of comment throughout the hall.

Dorothy Dwardie, Dr. Hessian, and the other members of the Botany Management Board, including Worry, took their places on the platform, so this time Judge Iri Bempechat was last in, raising his gavel, preparatory to starting the meeting. A respectful silence fell over the hall.

"As you know, Zainal and his exploratory crew have safely returned and our coffee mugs are full. He wishes to explain in detail what occurred and why. Please give him your complete attention."

Zainal did not go up on the platform but faced the audience on their level.

"We did well, but not as well as I led you to believe we would," he said and was surprised when someone booed.

"You got back, you brought us coffee and a whole raft of materials we can't get anywhere else, Zainal. What's your problem with that?" It was Worry who had spoken, and Kris was relieved that it had not been one of the more vocal detractors.

"Sally Stoffers has a record of what I traded the Botany resources for," Zainal said, pointing at Sally in the audience.

"He did real good, folks. We all did. Got quite handy with bargaining, even when those Barevian merchants were being damned stingy."

Zainal gave her a grateful nod for her comment.

"I didn't do as much as I promised you I would and could."

He was not apologizing, Kris realized, but explaining.

"Barevi's a different world now than the one I knew."

"Yeah, they lost the war."

"That isn't what I meant," Zainal replied, exasperated and possibly unable to explain what was prompting him to make this confession. "Though on balance, I think your planet has made the better adjustment."

"Good for Earth!" Someone hoisted a clenched fist skyward in an old gesture of supremacy.

"Botany is in an extraordinary situation," Zainal went on. "Both worlds are at a crossroads, I think. I know." Kris could see his chest rise as he took a deep breath. "I would like to think that we can do more . . . both for Earth, your planet, and for mine."

"Invade them?" someone called.

"The Eosi were manipulative and . . . and evil," Zainal said. "They perverted my world and subjugated many more. Many more."

"That's their problem."

"No, it is ours as well. We inhabit the same galaxy. There is more we can do to assist recovery on your own world. I would like to have the same discretion to help mine . . . and ours!" He hurried on lest someone interrupt him. "The Botany Space Force would be invaluable to both worlds, or I should say, all three, including Barevi."

He took another quick breath. "I would like you to consider using our ships—"

"The ones we stole from the Catteni in the first place?"

"Yes, those. To bring what's needed on Earth from Barevi. We were able to discover two chests of Eosi treasure with which we can probably buy out everything in all the storage rooms on Barevi and bring it back to Earth. They trade there, you know. If we make the Barevi merchants hire our ships, we can see that everything gets back to Earth!"

"Wow!"

"Hey, man, think *big*."

"We'd charge the Barevis for the shipping, wouldn't we?"

"What about the captives, Zainal?" a woman asked, nearly having to shriek to be heard over the comments from the audience.

"Well now, I've thought about that a lot, since some of you may know that Kris and Kathy nearly got sent to a slave colony. It's one of my plans. Look, if we start transporting Botany ores and metals to Earth, and to Barevi, we will hurt their markets, which, I must tell you, are already hurting. One"—he held up his hand as he ticked off his points—"Earth gets the ores it needs to start manufacturing again and, two, cuts off the market for the slave colonies' produce. If they don't need slaves to work, maybe we can buy their freedom. That's what we all want, isn't it? The slaves freed?"

"This civil war has to do with planetary rights," someone with a marked southern accent cried.

"D'you think it'd work?" a woman called.

"I'd like to give it a try," Zainal said. "Now, what I'm going to say may distress some of you, but I was talking to the judge," and Zainal swiveled his body so he could see the judge, who was nodding encouragingly, "and, with all due respect, we—Catteni and Humans—are not that different."

"Yeah? Since when?" No one was quick enough to see who had asked that.

"Since I know that both our species want to explore space and both our populations need additional worlds on which to develop."

"A point well taken," the judge said with a little tap of his gavel.

"Are you suggesting we make partners of the Catteni?" Dick Aarens jumped to his feet.

"Why not? They couldn't dominate you, could they? Your tactics made them leave."

"But partner the Catteni?" Aarens objected.

"Beat them at their own game?" the judge suggested.

"It's better than fighting them," Dorothy Dwardie said firmly. "Where would Earth be if we had had Catteni technology?"

"Look, I don't know what the coordinators on Earth—the effective governors of Earth, I should point out—what they'll think about this notion, but I'd like to put it to them and bring them some essential supplies that we *know* they need. And bring back to Botany coffee plants and banana trees and other Terran plants that might adapt here, as well as people who can teach us how to grow them properly."

"We're all for the coffee," someone yelled.

"Tea bushes would do well here, too," a woman suggested. "They grow tea in Kenya, you know."

Zainal nodded and made a note on his clipboard.

"It wouldn't cost Botany anything," Zainal said, "now that we have how much, Sally?"

She stood. "I figured out that the Catteni gold coins equal about three quarters of a billion dollars on the last gold-exchange figures."

"That's enough to buy out everything the Barevis looted from us, if we get good prices," Zainal said. "I want to ask the coordinators in the metropolitan New York area if we can use Newark Airport for the swap meet of this century. We'll supply the coinage, which we got free anyhow, and your planet can ransom back all they need to reequip abandoned manufacturing. Why should we waste our time and fuel bargaining at Barevi when we can make money off them by carting it all to Earth and getting other folks to haggle?"

"Haggling's the fun of it," a female voice protested.

Worry got to his feet and waited until there was silence. "I think Zainal's suggestions have merit and provide positive advantages—to us, to Earth, and, however inadvertently, to Barevi. I was talking to Chuck and Kathy Harvey about their adventures on our home world. It'd be real fun to outsmart the Catteni, no offense meant, Zainal, but you're more Botanical than Catteni anymore. In any event, since you don't really need our approval, being a free citizen and the person who helped us acquire the ships that comprise our Space Force, I think you ought to have a say in how they are used. And if it takes some shenanigans to free the slaves, why, work away. No one else's doing anything to get them back, are they?"

While that straight talk ruffled some sensibilities and caused an outbreak of loud conversations and rebuttals, the judge permitted it to continue until he felt the need to curb some of the more vociferous arguments.

"Let us vote first on whether or not Zainal should go back to Earth with the goods he acquired for them by trading coffee beans on Barevi."

Chuck sprang to his feet. "I request that the assembled allow Zainal to return to Earth and deal with the authorities there on how best to relieve their shortages. I request that he be allowed to suggest to the Terran coordinators that the Botany Space Force can transport Barevian goods to Earth for the purposes of barter."

"I second both motions," Dorothy Dwardie said, jumping to her feet.

Others were as quick to support the motions, and they were very quickly passed. Zainal bowed his head at such support.

"I think this idea of forcing the slavers to give us back our people is a bit far-fetched, Zainal," Dick Aarens said, but he had stood in support of the first two measures.

"It probably is, Dick, but if you can think of another way, I'd be interested. I also intend to suggest it to the coords. I'm hoping to meet with more of them when we return." He held up his hand for silence again. "And I wonder if I can bring back a select number of folk from Earth. My crew will tell you that people were envious of what we have here and how often we were asked to make room on Botany for deserving cases."

"We don't need a population explosion on Botany, Zainal. Hell's bells," Leon said, "we just don't have the facilities."

"We can always build more homes," Dr. Hessian said, rising to his feet in his ponderous way. "We cannot be lost to compassionate assistance."

"I volunteer my services," Dorothy said, "to assist in winnowing out applicants, and since we now have a spaceship business, they can come for limited periods."

"Under proper contracts," Sarah McDouall suggested.

There were so many other comments fired back and forth in the hall that the judge had to make vigorous use of his gavel.

"If Dorothy is willing to volunteer her services," Zainal said, "could we bring back a limited number of folk? Limited, of course, to how much space we have on a KDM." He gave a wry smile.

"No one will come first-class," Kris said.

"The Newark coord, Dan Vitali, has an asthmatic grandson who would benefit from our clear Botanical air," Zainal said.

"And he asked if he could take applications. We need more trained botanists, Leon Dane tells me, and possibly more miners. Right,

Mike?" Kris said, pointing in the direction of the men. "Practical specialists like agrarians to see what Terran things, like potatoes, would do well here and what might be sent back to Earth to be propagated."

"And a dentist. With his equipment. Where is Eric Sachs?"

"Doing a very good business on Barevi. He didn't care to desert his patients at short notice."

"We'll pick him up on our next visit," Kris remarked, though she wondered if they would repatriate the ebullient Dr. Sachs.

"I'm sure we need time to discuss the details of these ideas," Judge Iri said, banging his gavel so he could be heard, "but let us be resolved, here and now, to do what we can to relieve Earth's problems as best we can and to try to establish harmonious relationships with the Catteni government and the Barevi merchants. What say you?"

There was a roar of approval, much stamping of feet, and loud applause.

"You're stuck with it, Zainal," the judge said, with a tap on Zainal's shoulder for the work that he had cut out for himself. "You asked for it. You got it."

Kris rushed forward, ahead of the crowd, to hug Zainal, who was now grinning widely with relief.

Maybe this exceptional man could indeed manage the feats he had promoted himself for. He returned her embrace, not embarrassed to be seen displaying such an un-Catteni demonstration of affection.

"I dropped, I stay."